Also by Aviva Bel'Harold

Chip

Safe

෬ ◆ ஓ

BLOOD MATTERS

AVIVA BEL'HAROLD

EDGE SCIENCE FICTION AND FANTASY PUBLISHING

AN IMPRINT OF HADES PUBLICATIONS, INC.

CALGARY

Edge Science Fiction and Fantasy Publishing
An Imprint of Hades Publications Inc.
P.O. Box 1714, Calgary, Alberta, T2P 2L7, Canada

Edited by Tracy Blaine
Further Editing by Allister Thompson
Copy Editing by Ella Beaumont
Interior design by Janice Blaine
Cover photo by Dave Harold

ISBN: 978-1-77053-073-7

EDGE Science Fiction and Fantasy Publishing and Hades Publications, Inc.
acknowledges the ongoing support of the Alberta Foundation for the Arts and
the Canada Council for the Arts for our publishing programme.

Canada Council   Conseil des arts
for the Arts   du Canada

Library and Archives Canada Cataloguing in Publication

Bel'Harold, Aviva, 1972-, author
      Blood matters / Aviva Bel'Harold.

ISBN: 978-1-77053-073-7
(e-Book ISBN: 978-1-77053-074-4)

I. Title.

PS8603.E443B56 2014   jC813'.6   C2014-905509-9   C2014-905510-2

FIRST EDITION
(F-20141212)
Printed in Canada
www.edgewebsite.com

DEDICATION

To Aubyn Bel'Harold

ONE

FOUND

BRITTANY GLARED AT her father. "If you hadn't ordered him out of the house I would have still been taking care of him. Now I have to walk through the snow to see him."

"Are you telling me that having to bundle up is the excuse your using for not caring for your pet like you should?"

Brittany wanted to retort that Ella was the reason she didn't get to see her bunny any more, but she bit her tongue. The longer her father had been dating the woman, the more protective he was of her.

Woman, she scoffed to herself as she trudged through the calf-deep snow, *more like overgrown girl. Ella* — even in her thoughts the name was said with a snide tone — *isn't even half my dad's age. She's closer to my age than his.*

Brittany's next step sunk her leg deeper into the cold snow. She cursed Ella even more profusely. *She doesn't even live in our house! She's not a part of our family! Mittens was here two years before she showed up.*

"It's not fair," Brittany said aloud as she made it to the door of her old fort.

Normally, after all the snow that had fallen the day before, Brittany would have to struggle to get the door open. It opened with ease. She failed to notice this.

She stepped in, still feeling the burning sensation of anger in her stomach ready to spout more insults. However, as her eyes focused on the scene in front of her, it all went away.

ᘓ ◆ ᘒ

1

"Brittany? Brittany?" The man who was standing in front of her was a police officer. At least he was wearing a police officer's uniform. There were several there— and not just police. "Brittany, is that where you found her?"

Brittany blinked. She wanted to answer but she couldn't seem to find her voice.

"She's in shock," someone said.

Brittany couldn't turn to see who was talking— every one of her muscles was locked in place.

The lights from several emergency vehicles flashed around her. They were dancing on the snow, making the ground glow red.

Red, Brittany thought. That's what had been missing— there had been no blood.

The moment she saw the body she'd known it was Emily, even though she couldn't see her face. She could see the hair. Emily had the most beautiful golden blond hair, and her short page cut made it unmistakable. Brittany also recognized the sweater she'd bought her best friend for her last birthday, and the sneakers from their latest trip to the mall.

What Brittany didn't recognize — what she didn't understand — was the odd-shaped object that stuck out of Emily's back. It looked like a crowbar. Brittany had bent down and touched it. It was as cold as ice. When she touched Emily, there was no contrast in temperature between Emily's skin and the hard metal spike that went right through her.

She'd heard people say that everyone reacts differently when they see a dead body. Some get ill. Some scream. Some sob. Brittany didn't remember doing any of those. She didn't remember doing anything at all. It was as if time had suddenly stopped, freezing her along with her cold, dead friend.

ଓ ◆ ଅ

"Brittany, when was the last time you saw Emily alive?" The person who asked was a woman. Brittany couldn't remember if she had heard the woman's voice before.

Brittany was still in her PJs. Still had a rough, grey blanket draped over her. But she was now in a brightly lit room. *The doctor's office?* She blinked a few times. *Hospital?* The woman who'd asked the question was wearing a police uniform. *The police station?*

"Brittany," the woman's voice rose, "the last time you saw Emily alive, did she say anything to you? Was she acting differently?"

"She..." Brittany stopped. Her voice had distracted her. It sounded raw, like she hadn't talked for days. *How long had it been?*

"Brittany?" The woman was waiting for the rest of her answer.

"She's been different ever since she got back from her family's farm."

"When was that?"

"At the end of summer."

Brittany thought back to that summer. *Had it really only been four months?*

"She looked different, I guess."

Brittany remembered the day Emily had returned. She was mad at her. She was mad because Emily had only called once all summer and even madder because of how happy she felt to see Emily again. She had figured Emily wouldn't be coming back.

"Different how?" the policewoman asked.

"She was... sad," Brittany said once she'd thought about it. "And she kinda looked smaller, like she'd shrunk. She was also quieter and... distracted."

The policewoman nodded and jotted down some notes. "Did you ever see Emily cutting herself?"

Brittany shook her head. Never had she seen Emily cutting— but she had seen the cuts. At first just a few but as time went on there were more and more. *Why would she do that*? Brittany wondered, angry that Emily hadn't trusted her enough to confide in her. *She should have told me. I was her best friend.*

"Did you ever see Emily eat?"

Brittany was brought up short by the question. Slowly she shook her head. "No." She was surprised at her own answer. *She had been mutilating herself and starving herself,* Brittany thought now, feeling guilty. *I should have told someone. Maybe I could have stopped Emily from… from…*

Brittany didn't hear the policewoman telling her that there was nothing she could have done. Instead she thought of Emily while she rubbed her hand over her dirty jeans. Her palm itched and the sensation of it sliding over her rough jeans tingled half in relief and half in an even itchier feeling.

She was still dazed and numb when she was released from the hospital nearly twenty-four hours later. Her father drove her home. They pulled up in front of their house to a wintery sunrise casting pink and red hues across the sky.

Red, Brittany thought, feeling the color burn the back of her eyes, *why wasn't there any blood*?

"I need to sleep." Her father's voice cut into her thoughts. She blinked.

"Ya," Brittany said, "I'm tired too."

TWO
REMEMBERED

THE DREAMS BRITTANY had were a mixture of memories about Emily; some were older, but the majority were more recent. Through the focussed eye of her unconscious, Brittany now perceived her time with Emily filled with subtle cries for help.

ର ◆ ଛ

They sat in the old tree fort, Mittens cuddled down on Emily's lap while she stroked his soft fur.

"Did your mother at least explain why she left your father?" Brittany asked, trying to understand Emily's parents' sudden breakup and her mother's abrupt return to her family's farm.

Abrupt didn't even come close to covering it.

Emily's mother had shown up the last day of school with the car packed. The only explanation Emily was given as she was ushered into the car was "Because I'm leaving your father." When Emily had called, the next day, she was still shocked and more than a little confused.

"She said he had changed overnight. That it was like he had become a monster."

"Is that true?"

Emily gave a non-committal shrug.

"Did you at least have fun on the farm?" Brittany thought about her parents. She was now appreciating the way they had handled their breakup. At least Brittany hadn't been carted halfway across the country because of it.

"I..." Emily's voice trailed off as she stared blankly at nothing for a moment. Then she pulled her hand away from Mittens with a strange expression on her face. The bunny hopped off her lap to lie next to his cage, where Brittany kept his treats.

"How's your Gran? Did she do tons of baking while you were there?" Brittany said, trying to sound excited.

Emily held her hand in a tight fist. When she didn't answer, Brittany noticed.

"Something wrong? Did you cut yourself?"

Brittany didn't ask if Mittens had bitten her. He wasn't a biter, but after being exiled to the tree fort, he had become testy from time to time. Still, she hadn't asked and Emily never said anything about that.

"I've... I've got to go home." Emily stood and left before Brittany could protest.

As Brittany lifted her bunny back into his cage, she couldn't help noticing how fast his heart was beating. Bunnies, by nature, have a faster heartbeat, but Brittany hadn't ever felt it racing like this.

ʒ ● ⁊

Emily had come to school the next day with a bandage across the palm of her hand. When asked about it, she said the knife had slipped as she was cutting a bagel. However, Emily seemed nervous about it, like she had something to hide.

"Did you at least show your dad?" Brittany asked, concerned. Emily's father was a vet, a very good one. He was pretty good with people too. He had doctored up Brittany's leg once when she fallen down outside their house.

"No, he'd already left for work."

"Still, you should have someone look at it."

"Why? There wasn't any blood— it's more like a paper cut."

Looking back at it, Brittany now realized that that was the first of many cuts Emily would have. She should have noticed.

Instead, Emily had changed the subject to clothes or something much more entertaining. And Brittany had gone along with the new topic, eagerly and willingly. Now she wished she'd asked better questions and paid closer attention to Emily's answers— even if she hadn't said anything at all.

ભ ♦ ૪૭

"Do you miss your mom?" Brittany had asked one day when Emily seemed extra quiet — introspective — like she was replaying memories of her own.

Unshed tears made Emily's eyes shine.

Trying to cheer up her friend, Brittany added, "So, I guess you'll be going to visit her over the winter vacation?"

"No. I won't." Emily sounded angry. "And I don't want to."

It was clear that the whole thing was affecting Emily in a deep way. She acted almost as if her heart had literally been broken. She kept pressing her palm against her chest as if to check her heart or to hold it in place.

Brittany didn't bring up the subject again.

The last time Brittany saw Emily was the last day of school before their winter vacation. They were walking home in silence. That seemed to be their routine now: they still did things together but they didn't talk. *When my parents were fighting and separated, Emily was the only person I wanted to talk to; the only one I trusted*, Brittany grumbled to herself. That Emily didn't reciprocate made her question how good their friendship really was.

"Is your dad taking you skating this year?" Brittany was trying to keep her conversations with Emily as upbeat as possible.

"Not this year." Emily wasn't making it easy.

"Why not?" Brittany couldn't remember a time when they didn't go.

"Because he's tired." Emily's voice was always flat and emotionless, so Brittany didn't notice it any more.

"He's been tired a lot lately, hasn't he?"

"Ya, well, he's... what's it called? Anaemic. The doctors have him taking iron pills. But if he doesn't start feeling better soon, they're going to admit him to the hospital for testing."

"That sounds serious." Brittany stopped walking because Emily had. She put her hand on her friend's shoulder in a show of concern and support. Emily pulled away like she'd been cut.

"I gotta go." She walked away, holding the spot where she'd been touched.

"Come visit me over the holidays?" Brittany called out hopefully.

"I can't..." Emily's voice faded away before she could give any explanation.

Now Brittany woke up feeling cold, like someone had forgotten to shut a window in the house. She rolled over, gave a shiver, and pulled her comforter tighter around herself— noting how very *not* comforted she felt.

The next three days were a blur. She remembered very little. The only thing that stuck in her head was the way the police tape surrounding her tree fort fluttered in the wind and how cold she felt inside. Of course it was winter, but this year Brittany felt colder than she ever had in her life— like it wasn't just cold outside, but it was cold inside her.

THREE

COUNSELLED

THE SCHOOL NURSE watched as Brittany ran the palm of her hand over her knee for the hundredth time. For Brittany, the sensation the rubbing produced was soothing relief. Her palm still itched and she wondered if it had been bitten by some something. Yet the more she rubbed it, the more relief she experienced, and the itchier it got. It was a catch-22.

"Do you think it was too soon to return to school?" the nurse inquired again. The question had hung in the air for longer than was conventionally acceptable.

Brittany gave a non-committal shrug. *My father did*, she thought. He had requested three weeks off. He'd also jumped at the offer to see a therapist.

For Brittany, one week had been plenty to be stuck at home with nothing to do, no one to talk to, and no distraction to take her mind off the one thing she didn't want to think about. She'd also declined the offer for her to see a therapist, because she didn't want to *talk* about it. Besides, talking about it required thinking about it. She was trying to avoid the subject altogether.

She scowled at the school nurse.

"Brittany, I'm only trying to help."

Brittany could think of a million replies, all of which would get her a strict reprimand. Most were some snide way to say that if the nurse really was good at her job, she would have kept Emily from killing herself and Brittany wouldn't have to be here in the first place.

Instead she locked her lips shut.

"You don't want to answer, that's fine." The nurse sounded anything but fine. "How about you tell me your thoughts on Emily Daminko's funeral."

"You were there," Brittany retorted.

"Yes, I was, but I'm wondering about *your* thoughts on it?"

Too many answers cluttered Brittany's head. Worst of all was the sting that her tears brought to her eyes. They didn't feel right. *Maybe I did return to school too soon*, Brittany thought. *If I had stayed home I would have avoided this*!

"Did you get a chance to see Emily's body before the burial?"

Brittany scowled at the memory. Her father had forced her to the pre-viewing thinking that his daughter needed a better last memory of her friend than the one where Emily had a crowbar stuck through her. So Brittany had gone and she had seen and she had felt... ANGRY. Angry that her so-called friend had been so pathetic and weak to die so senselessly.

Once those feelings started to overwhelm her, Brittany'd become numb to everything and everyone. Almost like she wasn't herself at all; like something or someone else was in control of her brain and she was merely a passenger... or at least that's what she wished would happen.

Again with the rubbing of the hand. Brittany ran her palm over her knee in increasingly quicker intervals.

"Have you had a chance to speak with Mr. Daminko at all since..."

Brittany's eyes flashed up to the nurse's face. She was feeling extra irritable now. "How? He wasn't at the funeral."

Mr. Daminko had been either too ill or under house arrest. The rumors were flying about why he hadn't made it to his only daughter's funeral.

The ex-Mrs. Daminko had been there, looking pale and sickly and fragile and empty. She'd stayed in her old house with Mr. Daminko the night before the funeral to collect some of Emily's things, but she hadn't stayed in town after. Once her daughter was in the ground, she'd left to who knows where. All anyone knew was that she wasn't returning to the family farm. There was no reason to— Mrs. Daminko's mother had passed away within weeks of her and Emily's arrival. At least, that's what Brittany had overheard.

Brittany was angry about this final insult her ex-best friend had been able to deal from beyond the grave. *Why didn't Emily tell me about that?* she wondered.

"You could call him and give your condolences. Or, even better, go over to his house. I bet he'd be happy to see you. He's all alone now. He needs people..." The nurse stopped as if thinking better of saying more. "I've been to see him a few times now. I've gotten to know him a little. He would be grateful to see you. You should visit him. It could bring you some closure."

Brittany shook her head. She'd seen Mr. Daminko on the news. He looked creepy, with huge black bags around his eyes, standing in the shadow of the doorway of his town home. He didn't come out anymore— at least not during the day when people could see him.

"Brittany," the nurse's voice was soft but not soothing, "you're going to have to talk about this sometime, with someone. Trust me, the sooner you do, the sooner you'll start to feel better. It's a pretty traumatic thing you've had to endure. But you aren't alone."

When Brittany didn't say anything the nurse continued in a harsher tone. "Brittany, Emily is dead and she's not coming back. Don't you want to say something about that?"

Brittany gave another shrug. She knew Emily was dead. She knew her friend wasn't coming back. That didn't stop the image of Emily huddled in a dark place from filling her head. She'd dreamed of this scene the first night after the funeral and every night since. Three nights now. Each time the image became clearer, as if smog was lifting from the scene. And last night Emily had said Brittany's name.

Brittany shuddered.

The nurse leaned forward in the hope that she was finally making progress. "Is there anything, anything at all, that you'd like to share? You can tell me."

"Nope." Brittany slumped back against the blanket-covered sofa. "Nothing. You are right. Emily is dead. It's time to move on." She stood quickly to go.

"Brittany Watts." The nurse stood, also extending a hand. "Come back and see me soon."

Brittany shook the nurse's hand with a hungry desire to leave and be done.

FOUR
VISITED

IT WAS DARK. It was dark and cold, and beyond that, Brittany was experiencing a general feeling of discomfort. She didn't dare open her eyes; she knew it was some time around three a.m. "The witching hour," her mother had called it. The last time Brittany had seen three a.m. was four years earlier, the night her father had left— or stormed out.

ⓒ ◆ ℩

Brittany had wakened to what sounded like the front door slamming. It was confirmed by the telltale giveaway of the screen door snapping shut. She'd hurried downstairs to see what was up. She chastised herself afterward because, in all honesty, she knew her parents had been fighting. Perhaps she knew, deep down inside, that she would find her mother crying at the kitchen table.

"Oh, hey Princess," her mother said once she noticed her. "What are you doing up at this witching hour?"

"Dad left?" Brittany nervously took a seat across from her mom.

"Ya. He left." Her mother tried to smile at her reassuringly. It was empty.

"He's not coming back?" Brittany spoke her greatest fear— she liked her father better. Given the choice of who to live with, she'd pick him.

Brittany's mom chuckled.

She wasn't laughing about the situation but about her daughter. She'd always said her daughter was all business: an earth-born Vulcan, she'd teased when Brittany was younger. Sometimes it was unbalancing how cut-to-the-bottom-of-things honest her daughter could be. Just like her father.

She reached out to her daughter, placing her hand over Brittany's as she explained. "No. He'll be back. He's not the one moving out. I am. He's just going away for a few days to give me time to collect my things."

"He's staying?" Brittany was now sure that three a.m. was the witching hour because it was the time of day when things made the least sense. "He gets the house?" she asked.

Her mother chuckled and gave a nod.

With a wrinkled brow, Brittany asked, "Who gets me?"

"He does," her mother replied with a catch in her throat. When her daughter didn't respond, she continued. "It's not that I don't want you, it's just that you are so much like your father, I thought you'd want to stay with him. He's always been all business. 'Just the facts, please,' he'd always tell me. In the beginning I found that refreshing. But in the end I just found it lonely. With your father, there's no room for emotions, no passion, no romance, no love. It's not his fault; it was me who got cold and had the affair. I hope one day you'll be able to forgive me."

"Okay," Brittany said, but she pulled her hand out from under her mother's. "I'm tired."

"Sure. We'll talk more in the morning."

As she climbed back into bed, she saw the digital clock displaying 3:33. Brittany had an intense dislike for threes ever since. Especially three three's in a row.

ભ ♦ ಸ

This morning was the ninth day of waking up at 3:33 a.m. She wouldn't dare check the clock to confirm.

"Still not talking to me?" a familiar voice said from a dark place in Brittany's mind.

"How can I talk to you, you died!" Brittany squeezed her eyes shut tighter. It didn't help. She still saw the image of Emily lying on the floor — impaled — cold. So clearly dead.

"Well," Emily sat up and pulled the crowbar out of her chest, "I guess I can wait. I've got *some* time."

"You're dead!" Brittany said, her voice shaking.

"More or less," her old friend answered casually. Dropping the crowbar she added, "I'm more alive than you think, and I am less alive than what that word means."

Brittany just rolled back to stare at her clock. Three thirty-seven. She shivered and pulled the blankets up to her chin, feeling cold, dark, and generally uncomfortable. She started to wonder if it wasn't the world that was out of sorts but her.

MISSED

"AND HOW DID that happen?" The teacher was reading from a book that Brittany couldn't for the life of her remember the name of. Normally she was a very astute student.

"Gradually, then suddenly." The teacher kept reading.

Gradually, then suddenly, Brittany scoffed. *Nothing happened gradually then suddenly! Unless it happened gradually, but you didn't notice the signs until it was too late— like the story of the frog in water: put a frog in cold water and gradually heat it up and it won't jump out, but if you put the frog in hot water it will jump immediately.*

Brittany doodled some more on the otherwise blank piece of paper in front of her. The bell rang, and she was so startled she actually jumped. She wondered what had happened to most of the hour. It felt like it had completely disappeared.

"Gradually, then suddenly." A familiar voice echoed in her head, but she continued to ignore it as she concentrated on packing up her notepaper. She realized that she hadn't written down one note— but she had created an elaborate patchwork of interlacing scribbles and scrawls. Miss Hem, her art teacher, would be impressed. Mrs. Rose, her English teacher, would not. That was the polar opposite of the way things usually went.

 C&R   ♦   ⅌

"You gonna finish that?" Coby asked. He sat across from Brittany in the cafeteria.

She looked down at her untouched pizza. "Na, go ahead. I'm not hungry."

Coby didn't question until he'd wolfed down the whole slice. "You haven't been that hungry since..." He didn't finish. He didn't need to. Before Emily's death the three of them had been the best of friends, always together.

Brittany shrugged. If she was completely honest, it was true— food had lost all its appeal ever since she found Emily.

Coby seemed to have moved away from the thought without any suspicion. Brittany, however, stayed stuck on it for the rest of the afternoon. She'd gotten stuck because she realized that over the last thirteen days she'd lost her appetite, gradually at first, then quite suddenly.

ଓ ◆ ଚ

The day after Emily's body was discovered, Brittany and her father had slept until that evening. He'd ordered a pizza, and even though she said she wasn't hungry, he insisted she have a slice. Her body had responded with gratitude, and it was then that she realized that she wasn't hungry because she was famished!

For the next thirty-six hours, she couldn't seem to feed herself enough. It was like she had a tapeworm; she was never quite satisfied, no matter how much she ate. After that, however, Brittany lost interest in food because whatever she tried never tasted quite right.

Brittany knew about cravings. When her mother had been pregnant with Jack Junior she'd demanded some really strange things, insisting that NOTHING else would "hit the spot."

So that's what this is, Brittany thought. She was craving *something*, but nothing she tried, or even thought of trying, would "hit the spot." Then, after a great deal of effort and time, and wasted food, Brittany conceded that the real truth was she missed Emily and wanted her back. There was no cure for that craving.

That night was the first night she dreamed of her dead friend— seeming very alive. The vision hadn't helped the cravings to cease; in fact, they'd intensified. That made sense because it wasn't her need being met in a REAL way. If anything, seeing Emily, but knowing that she was dead, only made Brittany miss her friend more.

NUMB

BRITTANY SHIVERED AS she walked home. Winter was cold, but it was always worse in the north as Valentine's Day drew closer. Today, however, Brittany couldn't feel her fingertips and toes as she walked.

She'd dressed warmly enough that morning, she'd thought. But twenty minutes into her first class she'd noticed that her toes and the tips of her fingers were so cold they were numb. As she continued to make doodles in English, having now missed six classes of notes, her pencil had slipped from her hand and she found it almost impossible to pick up.

With the pencil now on her desk, she tried to covertly shake her hand to get blood circulating down to her fingertips. At the moment, it felt like she'd slept funny and pinched a nerve. However, no amount of shaking helped, so before she drew too much attention to herself, she gave up.

After the bell rang, Coby arrived at the door of Brittany's classroom and waited for her to collect her things so he could walk with her to the lunchroom. Brittany was distracted; her dexterity wasn't improving, it was getting worse. Coby carried her things as she followed him. Her mind continued to wander aimlessly.

"Not eating again?" Coby asked as he finished his pudding and looked hopefully at Brittany's tray.

She slid it toward him, noting that her hands were so numb, she couldn't feel that simple action.

Coby had noticed that this was now the third lunch period where Brittany didn't eat. He assumed that she was eating at home. When he snuck yet another glance to appreciate her figure, he couldn't see any signs of starvation: her cheeks glowed, her eyes sparkled, her waist was appealingly curvy, her chest was — he swallowed hard — perfect.

"You up to a movie tonight?" he asked, his voice thick with hope.

"Sure." Brittany shrugged. It was Friday, after all. "Just us, or are you planning a group thing again?"

Coby continued to stare at her while she gazed around the cafeteria, distracted, as she had been increasingly since... she couldn't think it— that might invite one of those strange and highly unnerving visions of Emily.

Coby misinterpreted her distraction for lack of interest. He'd become infatuated with Brittany over the summer as their threesome was reduced by one. With the absence of Emily, Coby and Brittany had become a couple, if in number alone.

He cleared his throat, trying to find the right words. That drew Brittany's attention back.

"We could make it a group thing..." He had wanted this to be a date, but he was way too nervous to ask outright.

With her undivided attention on Coby, Brittany realized that she didn't want to be around a bunch of people. Looking into her long-time friend's face, she felt that strange *craving*. Her whole body stirred at this, with her heart beating faster, almost as if it wanted to burst through her chest and run to him.

"No. I don't want to go to a movie with anyone but you," she said, simply stating the truth.

Coby had taken kinder-gym when he was five and six. He was suddenly sure he could flip off his chair backwards and pole vault over every table, perhaps running right up the wall and across the ceiling. Instead, he gave a coy smile and reached out to put his hand on hers.

For Brittany, the physical contact felt exceptionally nice. His warm hand seemed to bring hers back to life. It tingled as it heated up under his.

"Whoa, you're cold." Coby took both Brittany's hands into his and rubbed them to create friction.

Brittany liked this. It was as if his touch was life-giving. The room brightened, her lungs expanded, her head cleared, and her heart banged a staccato beat in her chest. Ga-thump-ga-thump-ga-thump; it reminded her of something...

"Ok," Coby said trying to sound casual, "it's a date." He released Brittany's hands.

She almost tried to recapture his in hers and cling to them.

"I'll come by your house around six to pick you up?" He felt unsure as he interpreted the expression on Brittany's face as disappointment or regret.

"Ya, sounds good," Brittany said.

ɔ ♦ ʚ

She was looking forward to their *date* with an almost obsessive desire by the time school finished. She shivered and doubled her pace. She was cold and her fingers had gone back to being numb. Not even the instant replay of Coby's hands holding hers could bring that warm sensation back. That didn't stop her from replaying it incessantly.

Brittany didn't call out as she unlocked the front door. Her father had returned to work at the beginning of the week. She'd been relieved that he had— she actually liked coming home to a quiet, empty house. That was one reason she had declined moving in with her mom and stepdad (and half sister and brother), even though they lived in a mansion that was three times the size of Brittany's father's house.

ɔ ♦ ʚ

"But I worry about you being alone too much," her mother had complained during her last weekend visit. "You're barely fifteen."

"When you left Dad four years ago, you gave *me* the choice. I chose Dad, and I still do," Brittany retorted.

The conversation had ended with both Brittany and her mother upset. Even though she was due to visit again this weekend, Brittany debated skipping it. Her mother's house was overrun with a sixteen-month-old and a newborn. Someone was always crying.

ɔ ♦ ʚ

But there was a positive side about being around people, Brittany thought as a movement caught her eye.

"I'm hungry," a familiar voice grumbled.

At least when she was around other people, her visions of Emily happened less frequently.

SEVEN
REFUSED

"I SAID, I'M hungry." Emily had walked out of the kitchen looking all too real and very much alive.

Brittany sat down in one of her comfy chairs in the living room.

Emily crossed her arms and leaned into the doorframe. "You're not still ignoring me, are you? It's been over three weeks. How much longer can you keep this up?"

Brittany had fluctuated between telling the hallucination that Emily was dead and pretending she didn't see it at all. Today she was employing the latter.

"Come on, Brittany, I've waited as long as I can. We have important things to discuss."

Brittany centred herself facing the TV. She reached for the remote but couldn't seem to get her fingers to curl around it. She couldn't even press the buttons.

"No, Brit." Emily moved to stand between the coffee table and the TV. "I need to tell you something and you need to listen."

At the moment she didn't care what was playing, she just wanted the TV on. Brittany obstinately tried to use her wrist to punch the on button. This action caused her to wince and pull her hand back into her lap.

She'd first noticed the thin paper cut that ran across the bottom part of her thumb and over her wrist, while she was playing volleyball in gym class. Normally, Brittany was a pretty good player, but one hit on that tender area was enough for her not to want to repeat it. She'd tried to use her left hand; her team had lost.

She looked at the cut, noting how dry and cracked the edges had become. She was also highly aware that this wound looked chillingly familiar.

"I can explain that," Emily offered.

Brittany didn't even look in her direction. Instead, she went to the bathroom where her dad kept the medical supplies. It was a tough go with her numb, non-cooperative fingers, to put some anti-bacterial cream on and cover the cut with a bright pink bandage.

All the while, Emily was trying to engage her in conversation. "You don't have to suffer like this. If you'd just listen to me, I really can explain. I may be dead, but I'm still your friend."

After she was all doctored up, Brittany inspected her hand. She regretted convincing her father to buy the neon Band-Aids. She didn't want anyone to notice the strange and unpleasantly familiar abrasion— this Band-Aid would be like a huge spotlight. She worried that Coby would want to know what happened if he saw it. She didn't even know, so what could she tell him? Maybe she'd take the bandage off before he got there.

Now she stood in the kitchen with a not so healthy but usually considered quite delicious after-school snack. Her hands were so dysfunctional that she couldn't detect the cold from the ice cream as it seeped through the glass bowl and into her palms. Dishing it out had been no easy task but she was determined.

Emily's attempts to engage Brittany in conversation were becoming more relentless. "You won't be able to ignore me much longer! You'd better listen to me now before things get worse. I'm only trying to help you."

Brittany held the spoon like a small child and was methodically stirring the sundae into a big, gooey mess.

"Don't eat that," Emily said in the most commanding voice she had yet used.

Brittany looked down into the double chocolate, caramel, marshmallow-laced, maraschino cherry-doused ice cream concoction that had been her favorite for years. She was waiting for her mouth to water, or her stomach to growl. It was as if her stomach had gone silent and her mind echoed the sentiment. Yet she continued to stare at the rapidly melting mixture of all her favorites, hoping she'd feel something soon.

"You can't," Emily said, speaking more softly.

It was the kindness in her old friend's tone that made Brittany *want* to respond. It was the first time she'd heard Emily speak like that since before she'd gone to stay on the farm.

Still, Brittany resisted acknowledging the voice. What was that saying? *If you talk to yourself it's ok, but if you start to hear someone talking back, you've lost it*? Brittany was sure she'd already gone well past "lost it," but by not responding she was holding out a vestige of hope that she wasn't full-on insane.

She tipped the bowl over the sink, watching the swirling mess of melted ice cream drizzle out and down the drain.

Emily was right. She had been right for days now. And as much as the messy concoction was Brittany's favorite, she was completely uninterested in it. Uninterested and, quite frankly, repulsed by it, all the way to the last bit.

As a portion of the cherry juice had stayed separate from the rest, it spilled out at the end in an undiluted, bright red stream. Without thought Brittany caught the stream in her good hand and lapped.

"No! Don't!" Emily tried to warn her.

Even with the smell not quite right, nor the taste, Brittany got three mouthfuls down before a stronger, more urgent and much more unpleasant impulse took over.

Brittany began to vomit. Not just those three mouthfuls of maraschino cherry juice but a full bucket's worth, and not the light red stuff that had gone down. What came up was deep red, almost black-looking. As it passed through her lips it tasted good and smelled right.

Once the heaving was done, Brittany swooned and slid to the floor.

"You are the most stubborn person I've ever met!" Emily chastised as her form became more translucent, winking in and out of sight. "We NEED to talk! And you need to listen to me. We are running out of time!"

EIGHT
ARGUED

THE EVENING SUN streamed in through the window. It was bright and, with the glass keeping the winter cold out, it heated the room to a toasty warm.

Brittany shivered.

With the disappearance of Emily, Brittany had found the strength to stand up and rinse out her bowl (though not well). She stack it at the edge of the sink where she'd left the rest of the dishes she'd used to serve herself food she'd thrown away without eating.

That reality had started to sink in as Brittany washed away the ice cream mixed with her bloody puke. Despite it looking like the leftovers from a badly choreographed murder scene, Brittany couldn't ignore the fact that she was still drawn to it.

The smell pulled at her and gave her the first feeling of hunger that she'd had in days— no, weeks. Actually, this hunger was stronger than any other she'd experienced in her life. Normally, when she was hungry, the feeling was limited to her stomach and head. Now it was a full molecular experience. She was hungry in every cell of her body.

Yet, just like the ice cream wasn't right, Brittany knew that absolutely NOTHING eatable would do. There was only one thing Brittany was craving and she had washed it down the sink. She'd left the kitchen shaking from hunger and fear.

She'd crawled onto her bedspread, too overwhelmed to do anything more, and passed out only to wake all too quickly.

Before she could even hope it had all been a bad dream, the vision of Emily reappeared.

"We need to talk."

Brittany shook her head. Tears stung the corners of her eyes. This was it. She'd snapped — lost it — gone completely mental. She missed her dead friend so much that her mind had conjured up an image that was so lifelike and real. And now she just couldn't get rid of it. Soon she'd be institutionalized, locked up, and the key thrown away.

"Listen, I want to make this work, but I need your help here."

"You're dead!" Brittany moaned.

"Oh, come now. You aren't going to play that game again!" Emily sighed. "We are losing precious time here."

"I don't want to be crazy. I don't want to be insane." Brittany continued to moan.

Emily didn't reply.

Brittany removed her arm from over her eyes and turned towards where she'd seen Emily standing. There was nothing, and no one, there. A few more tears escaped before Brittany was able to pull herself together. She sat up, wiped away her tears and their salty tracks, checked her room one more time (she was still alone), and went to the bathroom to clean up.

It might be time to share my secret, Brittany thought as she washed her face. Her hands cooperated even though she still couldn't feel them. She debated about who she should tell. Clearly, it was time to talk to someone.

Maybe I should tell Coby when he comes to pick me up? She tried to imagine his reaction. Would he laugh at her? Or would he understand? Would he freak out and call the police? Maybe he'd take her to the emergency room and insist she be admitted to the hospital that very night? Perhaps it had gotten bad enough that she needed to talk to someone trained for this. The school nurse? Maybe someone more qualified like her dad's therapist.

It was rapidly nearing six, and Coby would be here soon. He was known for his punctuality.

"You can't tell him," an unfamiliar voice said from behind Brittany. When she turned she found no one there.

"Who... who's there?" she stuttered.

"You can't tell him, dear," the voice cackled.

"Why not?"

No one answered. Slowly Brittany turned back to her reflection. The voice had sounded old, worn, like whoever owned it would possess wrinkles and white hair.

Brittany wasn't sure if having a bodiless voice tell her not to talk to Coby made her want to tell him more or less. If voices in her head were advising her against seeking help, surely she needed it more than ever. Then again, admitting to seeing her dead friend and hearing her voice was one thing. Now she had two voices to admit to.

With no answer, Brittany went back to her bedroom. Mercifully, both voices left her alone while she changed. Once she was dressed, that was another story.

She was admiring her image in the mirror when she noticed that, although she looked less tanned than usual, as everyone did in the cooler months, her cheeks had a slight pink glow. Her lips were a deep burgundy and her wavy, chestnut-brown hair had a new gleam. But best of all was her abdomen. She'd always had a decent figure, but now it was flat and fabulous. She had smooth abs. The shirt she'd chosen clung to her, showing her figure nicely. Even her chest appeared perfectly shaped. She smiled at the reflection of herself, appreciation clear in her face.

"Ya," Emily's familiar voice said. She stepped out from behind the full-length mirror. "I liked that part too." Standing next to Brittany, she took in both their reflections.

"No, no. NO!" Brittany covered her ears and squeezed her eyes shut.

"Come on," Emily huffed. "We need to talk!"

Brittany felt Emily's hand on her shoulders. She instinctively pulled away from it and held her hands tighter to her ears. But the voice couldn't be blocked out, because it was in her head.

"Go away. Please go away! You're dead."

"Alive, dead, or something in between, you are stuck with me. I'm not going anywhere. I can't go anywhere. We need to talk."

Brittany sighed but didn't argue.

"Listen, you're changing."

"Changing like how?" Brittany slowly moved her hands off her ears.

"Changing like… I can't believe you haven't noticed. Can't you see that you are now experiencing slightly different needs?"

Brittany didn't want to think about earlier that afternoon. Thinking about the blood made her squirm. She was mostly disgusted but also a little excited. That was way too much to admit to.

"That's what I'm talking about," Emily replied like she'd heard Brittany's thoughts. "And if you don't do something about it soon, it's going to get worse."

"No!" Brittany's hands returned to her ears, but she didn't shut her eyes. She was still looking into the mirror, staring at the reflection of her dead friend.

"Brit, don't be stubborn," Emily said soothingly, her voice strong in Brittany's head. "We don't have any more time for your stubbornness."

Brittany shook her head and kept her hands planted over her ears, though she didn't know why.

The doorbell rang.

"Damn it!" Emily faded away but her voice stayed strong. "I needed more time!"

Brittany dropped to her knees. Her face twisted into a haggard expression as she clutched at her chest. Her heart throbbed, her head spun, her vision dimmed and then failed.

NINE

DISCOVERED

IT HAD TAKEN everything in Coby's power not to be early. He'd failed. As he stood before Brittany's door, fifteen minutes before six, he sighed. He stood and waited until he was at least a few minutes closer to the right time.

When no one answered the second ring of the doorbell, he reminded himself not to be impatient. Brittany wasn't as punctual as he was. She might still be in the middle of changing.

To distract himself from trying to imagine that, he thought about when she'd said yes this afternoon in the cafeteria. Funny, he'd felt so excited he had been sure he would have had enough energy for gym class. Yet halfway through, his energy was lagging. Maybe it was because her saying yes had been such a rush that he crashed afterward. Regardless, and just to be safe, he had two energy drinks before coming over.

He stepped back from the door wondering what might be taking so long. He could see Brittany's bedroom window. Her light was on. He rang the doorbell again. When no one answered, he contemplated walking around the house.

As he continued to ponder his next move he felt a sense of urgency, as if something were wrong and he needed to hurry. From those feelings alone he picked up the fake rock, with the key in it, and opened the front door. Without hesitating, he rushed in, leaving the door open. He ran through the house calling her name. When he didn't find her on the main floor, he ran upstairs, taking them two at a time.

When he got to Brittany's room he found her on the floor, face to the ground, completely passed out.

"No!" he exclaimed and ran to her. She was cold. She was unconscious. He knew his CPR training but was having trouble remembering it.

He gathered her into his arms, and his heart started to thud. It beat so fast it ached. She wasn't wounded in any way: no punctures, no crowbars (he'd been worried about that most of all). He put his hand on her wrist, noting that she had a bandage covering a small cut, but he was more worried about a pulse. He thought he detected a weak one.

Next: breathing.

He brought his ear to her lips— nothing. Without a thought he covered her lips with his own. This was not quite the way he wanted his first kiss to go.

Brittany hadn't lost consciousness but she was paralyzed, trapped in complete stillness by… by what?

She'd heard Coby ringing the bell again, and again, then him pounding on the door. Finally he'd stopped. She'd wanted to scream out that she was there, that he shouldn't leave. He needed to find her— to rescue her. Somehow she'd known that once he found her, she'd be ok.

It was true.

When Coby put his lips over Brittany's mouth, the reaction was instantaneous, like sleeping beauty coming to life. Brittany opened her mouth in response. Coby, recognizing that she was alright, relaxed. He was no longer trying to administer CPR, but he didn't remove his lips and Brittany didn't pull away.

They stayed lip-locked for what felt like an eternity. With each passing second Brittany felt more alert, healthier, happier, and more energetic than she had been in a long time. The feeling returned to her fingers first and eventually her toes in a warming sensation. Warm, warmer, hot even, and the craving felt satisfied.

For Coby this was very different than he'd thought his first kiss would feel. He had tingles, but they felt the opposite from the figurative kind he had been prepared for. His whole mouth felt like it was on fire, especially his tongue. His heart beat so fast it felt like it was being pulled from his chest, and eventually he couldn't catch his breath.

He pulled away, panting like he'd run a marathon. "Are… are you ok?" he asked once he was able speak over his lungs trying to fill. He stared down at Brittany, his eyes feeling dry.

She nodded.

"Ok," He continued to pant trying to catch his breath. "Good."

"Yes." Brittany pulled herself out of Coby's lap. "I'm ok. Are you?"

He had to think about that for a moment. He wanted to answer yes, he wanted to be good. He was with the only girl he'd ever loved, and he'd just kissed her. This was his dream come true, but his heart continued to race and his muscles started to feel fatigued like he really had run a marathon. He also wanted to answer yes because he didn't want to alarm Brittany, but he wasn't really ok at all.

"Just scared," he lied. "What happened?"

"I must have fainted." Brittany rubbed at her lips, which felt hot, and her tongue itched like it had when she'd eaten kiwi that first time before she'd discovered she was allergic to it. As she continued to sit and stare at Coby, she realized she was warm all over. Not just warm, hot, as the blood raced through her veins.

"Do you feel ok now?" Coby was watching her. Her eyes sparkled, her face was a beautiful flushed pink, and her lips looked even more appealing than before. He wanted to lean forward and kiss her again, but he resisted. He was suddenly so fatigued, he worried that if he closed his eyes he would fall asleep.

"Much better," she said, being completely honest. "Are you sure you are?"

"I'm fine." Coby went to hop to his feet. He'd intended to stand then help Brittany up. He only made it halfway out of his crouch before his limbs faltered. He grabbed the full-length mirror for support.

Now Brittany was really worried. "What's wrong?" She stood and helped Coby straighten.

He shrugged. "I was a little tired this afternoon," he admitted over a yawn. "I almost called you to postpone our date till tomorrow." In his exhaustion he couldn't chose his words well. "I guess I should have," he continued into another yawn, "I wouldn't have had to embarrass myself like this."

Brittany was practically carrying Coby to her bed. He was falling asleep on his feet.

"I should," his yawn cut him off, "I should go home."

"I don't think you'll make it." Brittany patted her friend's shoulder. "Just lie down here." She'd gotten him to her bed.

"I... I could... n..." He was asleep before he'd made it down.

Brittany caught him. She was feeling quite strong and very in control right now. She was also feeling guilty. She wasn't exactly sure how, but she knew that whatever was wrong with Coby was her fault.

"Are you ready to listen now?"

The appearance of Emily didn't shock or scare Brittany. In fact, she'd been hoping for it.

"Alright." She left the room, taking a last look at Coby as she shut the door. He lay passed out on her bed. She took a seat on the top step of the staircase and looked up at Emily, whoever or whatever Emily *was*. "What happened?"

"I was trying to warn you before it came to this," the image sniffed, "but you wouldn't listen to me."

Brittany was furious at this, whatever this Emily was. She knew it was *her* that had hurt Coby, and she was beginning to believe that whatever *it* was had also been responsible for the real Emily's death. Yet under her rage, Brittany couldn't deny that she felt good— no, great. She hadn't felt this good since before the funeral.

"I'm listening now."

The image of Emily slowly lowered herself to the hallway floor, crossing her legs like the real one would sit all the time. It, the hallucination, the thing, Emily seemed to be thinking about what to say. It appeared to be hesitant.

TEN
INFECTED

"WHAT DID YOU do to Coby?" Brittany demanded.

"We took what *we* needed," Emily responded with a snap.

We? This thought made Brittany feel ill. How had she been a part of it? Though if she were being completely honest, she had felt it happen. She wondered if there was any way she could have stopped it. But as much as she didn't like this, there were far more pressing things to figure out.

"What did *we* need that was so important? So necessary that *we* had to take it from Coby?"

Emily started cautiously. "I'll explain, but I want you to stay calm. It was his blood." Emily winced. "We needed blood. We've almost completely run out of yours. If we hadn't taken from him, we would have died."

Brittany nodded, her suspicions confirmed. It made sense, and it explained everything: her numb fingers, her dimmed eyesight. She had felt herself dying, and now she felt alive and strong. It was a strange sensation— that she felt good made her feel bad. She took a deep breath to calm herself before she asked, "Why Coby?"

"There wasn't time to find anyone else."

Brittany made a sour face. "Why do we need blood? Why did we need to take it?"

Emily turned away. "*We* need it because... just because."

Brittany wasn't ok with the vague answer she'd gotten, but she needed to know the answer to a more important question. "Will Coby be ok?"

"Sure," Emily answered too quickly.

"How much did we steal?" Brittany said *steal* like an accusation, because that's exactly what they'd done.

She remembered the feel of her tongue in Coby's mouth. There hadn't been any taste of blood. *Why hadn't she tasted it*? She almost wished she had— but she had felt something. Like a desert in a rainstorm, her whole body had stirred.

"How much can a person live without before they've lost too much?" Brittany wondered aloud as she continued to recall the feeling in her veins— sucking it in, buckets worth of it! She had felt it pulsing through her. She'd thought it was her own blood stirring, but now she realized it was his blood racing through her!

"We didn't take so much that he won't recover," Emily answered. "I was careful, but it was hard— we were starved. I stopped before I killed him." Emily said this like it was a huge accomplishment. "He'll be fine, he'll just need a few days to recover before we take from him again."

"You plan on taking from him again?" Brittany felt a surge of rage. "What kind of monster are you?"

"I'm not a monster!" Emily's voice rose. "I only did what I had to to survive. Are you humans not capable of much larger monstrosities? North Americans have forgotten how they became North Americans. All through history you have committed far worse massacres! How quickly mankind can forget his own transgressions! In the grand scheme of things, a few drops of stolen blood isn't really…"

Brittany stopped listening. She didn't care. She wanted answers, not arguments and accusations. She cut into its tirade. "How long have you been around?"

Emily's voice fell flat. "A long while."

"Of course, and I bet you've done this before." She was sure that *It* had done this at least once before. "You did this to Emily."

Brittany couldn't imagine Emily going through this. Emily, by nature, had always been more sensitive. Brittany could only guess at how upset and how frightened Emily would have been. But apart from that, she felt guilty because she was secretly relieved to finally understand what had been wrong with her friend.

The vision of Emily stayed silent as if watching Brittany put things together.

"How old are you?" Brittany wondered aloud. *This creature could be older than time,* she thought and wondered what that would mean. Brittany looked at the vision of Emily as if waiting for it to do or say something timeless.

All she saw was the corner of its mouth twitch like it was fighting a smile.

When it didn't answer Brittany asked another question. "What are you?"

It fidgeted — just like Emily would when she was nervous.

Brittany was sure that this *thing* had been responsible for Emily's death. It had infected her and when she'd died it had somehow infected Brittany. But where had it come from before Emily — or who? And how did it go from one person to the next?

"I know you aren't Emily — not really?" Hearing herself, Brittany realized how crazy that made her sound.

It shook its head. "But Emily is now a part of who I am."

Not knowing what to make of that, Brittany said, "You aren't Emily. You're not even her ghost. So what are you? A hallucination? A vision? Or are you just something my imagination cooked up."

"Well…" it looked irritated, "I am all those, but I'm none of those."

"This can't really be happening," Brittany said more to herself.

"I assure you it is," the creature replied.

"Ok," Brittany shook her head, "fine." She took a deep breath and exhaled slowly. "You said Emily is a part of you now. Am I now a part of you too?"

The creature spoke softly. "No, not yet. Right now *I* am a part of *you,* but when you are no more — a part of you will remain with me."

It sounded like some stupid riddle. Brittany hated riddles.

It cracked a mischievous-looking smile, and suddenly Brittany felt nervous. "Wait a sec, are you going to kill me?

You killed Emily, right? Is that what you do? Make people crazy and kill them?"

It shook its head. "No!" Anger flashed on its face then receded. "I didn't kill Emily and I have no intention of killing you."

Brittany didn't believe this thing. She said more for confirmation, "But I bet you could kill me if you wanted to."

"I could." It shrugged.

Brittany nodded. "Can I kill you?"

"Not without killing yourself in the process."

Brittany felt like something had clicked into place. *Was that what Emily had been trying to do? Kill herself to kill this thing?*

"And I'll just tell you now," it said sharply, "I am much more resilient than you are."

"So it would seem." Brittany folded her arms across her chest.

The creature shifted forward. "Brittany, I am on your side. I want the best for you. I am a part of you now— I need you. And you, in turn, are now dependent on me. It's a symbiotic relationship."

"But it was you that hurt Coby," Brittany said. "It was *you* that needed the blood."

ELEVEN
DISCUSSED

"LET'S GET ONE thing straight," the creature said. "Yes, I needed the blood. But you needed me to get what *I* needed. Because if I don't have blood, I can't feed you. And if you aren't fed, you will starve and die and I will be forced to move on to the next person. Understand?"

Brittany's nodded, satisfied that at least one of her questions had been answered.

When Brittany didn't say anything, it continued. "Brittany, I want to be your friend. I want to keep you healthy."

"Sure you do," she said. "Sure, and to do that you need blood. It's your food. You need it to live and you use it to keep me alive. But if you don't get enough, it's me that will suffer and eventually die— not you." To Brittany, the relationship didn't seem very symbiotic; it felt very one-sided, and she seemed to be on the losing side.

It nodded. When it spoke again its voice was softer. "I don't want you to die, Brittany."

"I know what you are," Brittany interrupted. "You are a vampire." Even though she said it, and she was sure it was true, it felt strange to be talking like such a creature could really exist.

"I wouldn't exactly call *myself* that."

"Then what exactly would you call yourself? You drink blood. You just said you needed it. That's why I had to get it for you."

"You didn't get it for me!" it snapped. "You can't do that! I'm the one who gets it. *I'm* the one who shares it with *you*."

This kind of reaction was reminiscent of the mood swings her friend (the real Emily) could have. "Oh, Em— don't be so melodramatic!" Brittany said without thinking.

The comment worked. The creature was instantly calmer. That didn't surprise Brittany— it would have worked on the real Emily too. Brittany always knew exactly what to say to defuse Emily.

What did surprise Brittany was that she'd said it and how cheated it made her feel. Cheated and mad. Though Brittany knew it was impossible to look at an exact image of her old friend and not be confused into thinking it was actually Emily, she was mad at herself for forgetting that it wasn't. Brittany was also mad at *the thing* that had stolen Emily's form. Brittany's eyes narrowed as she continued to stare at it.

"What?"

"You are nothing more than a crook. A horrid, monster of a thief."

"I told you, I am not a monster," It said through clenched teeth.

Brittany felt a pain in her heart that seemed to radiate through her veins. She arched her back, squeezing her eyes shut, and choked on it. "I'm sorry," she lied. "I won't call you that again, I promise."

"Fine." The pain stopped as instantly as it had started.

Even though the physical pain was gone it took Brittany several more moments before her voice would work. "What's your name?"

"My original name was lost a long time ago," It said.

"Fine then, if you don't like to be called a monster and you don't agree with vampire, what's left? What do people normally call you?"

The image of Emily cocked its head to one side, appearing almost perplexed at the question.

Brittany huffed. "What did Emily call you?"

"Gran."

"And what did Gran call you?"

"Henry."

"Why Henry? Henry is a boy's name."

"Yes." The image of Emily rolled its eyes. "Gran called me Henry because that's who I looked like to her."

"A boy? Why did you look like a boy?"

"Well, a man really. At least he was a man in the end." The creature seemed distracted for a moment then continued. "I am not limited to possessing only girls. I can be either gender."

"Ok. Fine. Whatever." Brittany ground her teeth in frustration. "What did Henry call you?"

"Soo Sung."

Brittany shook her head. "Hasn't anyone called you a vampire?"

"Not me specifically." It seemed to be debating saying more, but it didn't.

Brittany made a face. She disliked this thing. Vampire, or whatever, why was it making such a big deal out of a name? She watched as the vision of Emily fidgeted with its fingers like the real one would have when trying to avoid something.

"So, E.V., why do you need to eat blood?" Brittany said.

"E.V.?"

"Ya, Emily the Vampire— E.V."

The creature seemed to find the title endearing. "E.V." It smiled.

Brittany cleared her throat. She hadn't meant it to be endearing, but it was probably better that the thing liked it instead of understanding it as the insult it was meant to be.

It looked in her direction. "I eat blood because that is what I was created to eat. Why do you eat carrots, apples, or chicken?"

Brittany shook her head and rephrased the question. "But why do y... we need blood from other people. Don't I have enough?"

Now Brittany knew that E.V. was trying to avoid answering the question because it seemed to look everywhere but at her. Finally it said, "I'll tell you. But you have to stay calm. You don't have any blood left because I have already consumed it."

Brittany was impressed with herself; she didn't gasp or scream. She didn't swoon or throw up either, though she did feel herself turn green as she held her breath. "You've consumed all of my blood," she repeated. "I don't have any blood in me? But I'll make more, right?"

"Not much." E.V.'s voice was soft.

"Then... then how am I still able to..." She'd wanted to ask: talk, think, stand, breath, hear, see— everything. *How was she existing at all without blood?*

E.V. hated this part: the fear. The adrenalin that was created was meant to be pumped into Brittany's nerve system so it could circulated through her veins and be distributed to the muscular components that would need it to either fight or flee. But E.V. would feel the worst of it, and the only way to be rid of the intensely uncomfortable feeling was to aid the adrenalin in doing its job. However, that would mean Brittany would have to deal with it.

Feeling her muscles tense, Brittany balled her hands into fists. She wanted to run, but where to? She wanted to hit someone, but there was no one to hit. She wasn't sure what she should do, so she took a deep breath and focussed on only that. She felt her lungs fill, the expansion of her chest, she listened to the sound the air made as it was drawn in through her nose and then released.

Brittany's heart rate slowed. Along with it came the clearing of her thoughts. "You've taken my blood. Eaten it all up. But I'd be dead without blood. So, there is blood in me, right? But it isn't mine, it's Coby's." She didn't know how to feel about that. "And once his is used up, we will need more." Brittany didn't know how she knew it but she could sense that they'd need more soon.

E.V. nodded.

"What else did you do to me? You've obviously done something so I won't or can't make any more blood. What else have you changed?"

"During the past few weeks I have taken over your veins. They've become, well, for lack of a better explanation, my appendages. That's why I had to consume most of your blood— to grow into your veins."

Brittany was focussing on her breathing again. Once she'd calmed enough she asked, "You've taken over my veins?"

TWELVE

FED

BRITTANY SAT ON the top step, back against the wall, her head resting just under the banister. She held an arm up in front of her. Her veins showed through her skin as they always had: purple-blue under creamy white.

The vision of Emily sat a little ways down the hall—watching.

"You've taken over my veins," Brittany said. "Or, you are my veins? My veins are your appendages. Appendages are like limbs. So my veins are your arms and legs?"

The creature started off slowly. "My appendages are a little different than arms and legs, and certainly not as dexterous as hands and feet. They are much closer to tentacles really. The most important thing for you to know is that ninety-five percent of the time I work within the confines of your body's original design. Most of the time I don't do anything your veins wouldn't do."

Brittany couldn't take her eyes off her arm. She stared at it, expecting something to happen. Nothing did. "And the other five percent?"

"The other five shouldn't be a problem for you."

Somehow Brittany doubted that. "What are you doing that other five percent of the time?"

"It's like I said." E.V. watched as Brittany flexed her hand and released it a few times. "I get the blood."

Brittany's hand dropped into her lap.

"Your veins are my tentacles. Normally, I stay put and supply your organs with the sustenance you need, just like your veins would. However, when you touch someone, I can sense it. I sense the blood, and when that happens, I send my tentacles out to extract what *we* need."

Brittany held her hand to her mouth, feeling ill. "Every time *I* touch someone, *you*'ll be taking their blood?"

"It doesn't have to be every time," E.V. replied.

"It doesn't?" Brittany didn't believe it.

"No. If I am well fed — I mean if *we* are well fed — then I won't have to take every time. I'm not greedy, I only take what is needed for us."

Brittany crossed her arms. "How do you do it?"

"I am not a monster," It said.

Brittany felt herself tense. *Was she tensing or was E.V. flexing its tentacles*? She worried that the creature was going to hurt her again. "I didn't say you were."

E.V. gave a nod. "Oh, ok."

"Good." Brittany felt herself relax. "Now, how do you do it? How do you take the blood? What does it feel like? Does it… does it hurt them?" Her last words came out strangled as she thought about Coby.

"Brittany calm down!" E.V. said sternly. "I can't handle your feelings."

Brittany leaned her head back against the wall. Tears filled her eyes and flowed down her cheeks to slip silently off her chin as she forced herself to calm down. She brought her hand up to look again at her veins— now E.V.'s tentacles.

"It doesn't hurt anyone, not you, not them, not even me."

Brittany wondered if she could trust what It was telling her.

E.V. continued. "Today at lunch I took nearly three ounces from your friend while he put his hands on yours to warm them up."

Brittany ran through an instant replay of the event. "I didn't feel…"

"No, you wouldn't. Not if I'm good at my job— which I am. And I assure you he didn't feel it either. But you don't have to believe me. If it had hurt him he would have reacted, said something, pulled away. He didn't do any of those things."

Brittany nodded while thinking about it. She ran a finger over the bandage at the base of her thumb. "This was you?"

she murmured, only mildly aware that the cut wasn't there anymore.

"That was from me. Three ounces wasn't nearly enough to replenish what was needed, but it was something. I know that you noticed how much better you felt and without understanding what was going on, you wanted to do it again."

Brittany was picking at the bandage. She couldn't deny that she had felt better and had even liked it. Did that make her bad too?

"No," E.V. answered softly, "it doesn't make you bad."

Brittany's head snapped up. "Can you hear my thoughts?"

E.V. smiled. "I am impressed with you. You are impressive."

Brittany was aware that E.V. hadn't answered her, but allowed herself to be sidetracked by the compliment. "Why would you say that?"

"Well," the creature deliberated a moment, "you are unlike most other humans I've teamed up with."

"Is that so?" Brittany said. She had removed the bandage and was admiring the soft scar that had formed, almost as if it was a wound from months or years ago. It was a crescent shape, her skin slightly thicker where it had separated and reattached.

Brittany looked up and folded her hands into her lap. "And you are good at avoiding my questions. You are in my veins. Are you in my head too?"

THIRTEEN
UNDERSTOOD

BRITTANY WAS SURE that E.V. hadn't taken over her mind, because she still felt like herself. She also felt like she was still in control of herself. She was the one who ran her index finger over her new faint scar, she chose to take her next breath, she closed her eyes, and she was the one who opened them. But she couldn't stop her veins from snaking out of her and sucking up other people's blood.

"Yes, I am in your head. But I'm not really in your head," E.V. answered.

"What?"

"I am in your veins, or your veins are now mine. They are me and they are connected to your brain, so I use them to communicate with you."

"So you are in my head?" Somehow this felt like the worst violation. It was one thing to have something inside of you, taking over your veins, but in your head? "Are you taking over my brain too? Will my brain be yours soon? Will you able to control me too?" Brittany couldn't imagine what it would be like to slowly lose control of her mind. Would she become a puppet, reduced to watching as E.V. made her do more and more unspeakable things? Or would she just eventually cease to exist?

"Unfortunately, I will never be able to control your mind."

"Unfortunate for who?" Brittany said. She didn't trust this thing. If it were lying, if Brittany was doomed, would E.V. tell her? She wondered if suicide would be the more humane option and if she could be brave enough to go through with it. Suddenly she had a new respect for Emily.

E.V. saw Brittany's thoughts. "No! No, please believe me, I don't control you. Not now— not ever. No! Don't think like that." It didn't relax until it saw Brittany's thoughts change.

"How come I see you over there if you are in me?"

"Because the way I communicate with you is by projecting myself into your thoughts. Your mind places the image of me where it sees fit."

"So why do you look like Emily? Don't you know how hard it is to see her, an exact replica of my best friend who I know is dead?"

"Yes, I understand. But I also know that as upsetting as it is, you are also comforted by it. And it's the easiest image for you to accept. If I showed up as the form I had been before Emily, a person you never knew, you'd be less inclined to trust me." E.V. hesitated like it was regretting saying so much. "You need to trust me because we are a team."

"So you want me to believe that you are projecting an image of Emily into my brain to make it easier for me?"

Brittany could see E.V. squirming in front of her. She also thought she could detect a feeling coming from inside herself that made her skin crawl.

"Yes," the creature answered in a forced voice, "yes, for your comfort, but also because it's the easiest image. After all, I was just Emily so I can remember what that form felt like. However, I wasn't Emily for that long, so I can also recall the previous host's voice, but I'd have a hard time conjuring up her image— especially because you don't have any memory of her yourself."

It was hard for Brittany to take in everything E.V. was saying. She understood it all, but it was hard to grasp that this was really happening. "You control my veins; you communicate with my brain through visions of Emily and voices; you steal blood from anyone I touch. Is there anything else I need to know?" This sounded too much like some person's idea for a popular novel than real life.

"Not for now."

"Ya," Brittany scoffed. *Of course the vampire wouldn't volunteer information if it didn't have to*. But Brittany didn't get a chance to say anything more.

From her bedroom came a noise like something big and heavy falling to the floor. Coby's voice followed with an "Ouoof."

E.V. disappeared.

"Are you gone?" Brittany was hopeful.

"Nope. I'm right here, with you— in you. I just thought it would be better for you if I didn't distract you right now."

Coby pulled open the bedroom door. Leaning on it, he locked eyes with Brittany. "Who are you talking to?"

Brittany's gaze automatically focussed on the spot halfway along the wall where the vision of Emily had been only moments earlier. There was no one there.

"No one." Brittany tried to sound cheerful as she got to her feet. "Are you feeling better?"

Coby wanted to confront Brittany, but he wasn't really sure if she was lying. He felt light-headed. Maybe he'd imagined that he had been hearing Brittany having an intimate conversation.

"A little, maybe." Coby lowered himself to the floor just outside her bedroom door. Ok, he was more than a *little* light-headed.

Brittany moved to stand over him. She was worried. He didn't look well at all. His skin was pale and his eyes were sunken, with deep circles and bags under them. But she tried to reassure herself it was a good sign that he was awake.

Brittany continued to stare. Two emotions were warring within her. First and most powerful was remorse; she knew she'd hurt Coby. The second was… hunger— she now knew that that longing she'd been feeling for weeks was actually hunger.

"I think you need to go home," she said.

"You're probably right." Coby looked up at his long-time friend, his newly discovered love interest, and found himself desiring to reach out and touch her. Her face glowed, her eyes were bright, her cheeks rosy, and she seemed to be exuding warmth.

"Coby, go home," Brittany said, forcing herself to step over him to reach her room. It took all her strength, because her hunger was growing.

She shivered. Ideas she was ashamed of filled her thoughts. *Were they really hers or those of the creature that lived within?* With Coby so close, Brittany could sense his pulse and almost hear his heartbeat.

Would it kill him to take just a little more? she thought, and she was sure it was her thought, not E.V.'s.

"Yes, it would." The creature's voice rang clear in Brittany's ears.

But I'm SO hungry! Brittany said as she figured it out herself. She couldn't believe how hungry she was— as if she hadn't just eaten!

"You think I don't know that!" E.V. said. "I've been trying to get you to listen to me for weeks!"

Coby pulled himself to his feet, standing mere inches from Brittany. "You ok, Brit? You look like you're in pain." He reached out as if to touch her.

Brittany jerked back, and his hand dropped to his side— but not before Brittany noticed the huge bruise on his fist.

"What happened to your hand?"

Coby looked down and shrugged. "I'm not sure. Pretty nasty looking, isn't it? I noticed it in shop, after lunch. I must have hit it while I was working."

Brittany shrank back even further.

"You sure you're ok?" Again Coby was reaching out to her.

Brittany wasn't sure if E.V. could keep its tentacles to itself, and more so, she wasn't sure she wanted it to. It felt like her skin was crawling, reaching for him, even if her hands weren't. Before his hand made it to hers, she stepped solidly into her room and shut the door.

"I don't feel well," she said through the door. "I'm sick too. Go home, Coby!" She didn't hear him leave; she didn't wait to hear it. Instead she dove into her bed and pulled the covers over her head.

"Brit?"

As she shut her eyes, Emily appeared in her thoughts.

"Brit, it's going to be alright."

You! Brittany screamed in her mind. *You've turned* me *into a BLOODSUCKING MONSTER! I'm the vampire.*

E.V. stayed quiet, because Brittany had figured out the truth.

FOURTEEN

ALTERED

IT WAS E.V.'S silence that confirmed Brittany's revelation. "I'm the vampire. I'm the creature that is talked about in the stories— not you! It's me!"

Again E.V. had nothing to say. There was nothing *to* say— not really. Yes, Brittany was the vampire.

"Being a vampire isn't all bad," It said quietly, using the voice Emily would have to try and convince Brittany to do something she wasn't sure about. "It's not like the myths or the legends. They got everything wrong— well, a lot of things wrong."

Brittany hadn't gotten into the whole vampire obsession the way most the girls her age had. In fact, when it had come to the subject of vampires, Brittany had been looking forward to its popularity dying out. She felt cheated. Why couldn't E.V. have chosen someone who would be grateful for this curse?

Brittany could think of at least a dozen girls in her class who would have been thrilled at the idea of becoming a cold-blooded killer. Or, perhaps more to the truth, of meeting a boy who was one. Then she wondered if any were. *How common was this*? How many other people could have their own secret E.V., or something like her, inside them, changing them?

"Are there many more of your kind?" she asked. "Or, I guess, our kind?" she amended.

"No." E.V.'s voice was soft. "I am the only one."

Brittany went to say more but was cut off by her own yawn.

"You are tired," E.V. said using Gran's voice. "Despite what some stories say you still need your rest."

Brittany wrinkled her brow but didn't argue. She was too tired. She fell asleep as soon as she closed her eyes.

ભ ◆ ৯০

When Brittany woke she felt refreshed and restless. The time on her digital clock read 3:33 a.m. For a hopeful moment she was convinced everything had been a very bad dream.

To be sure, she whispered into the darkness, "Are you asleep?"

"Did your heart stop beating?" E.V. replied.

Brittany spoke past her disappointment. "Wouldn't I be dead if it did?... Wait, are you in control of my heart too?"

Emily's image shimmered into appearance next to Brittany's bed. It took a seat. "Your heart is the most important part of you and me."

Brittany sighed. The riddles were starting early. She changed the subject. "I feel better."

"Yes, we are doing very well now."

"Can you duplicate Coby's blood?" She wasn't sure how she knew, but she knew she had more blood in her than when she'd fallen asleep.

"No." E.V. answered cautiously.

"Can I?"

"No."

"Then why do I feel fuller? Was I able to make more blood?"

"No." E.V. picked at imaginary lint on its body. "No, you've stopped producing your own blood."

"How?... Why?... Less than seven hours ago you said I was still making a little blood." Brittany remembered about E.V. telling her to control her feelings. "Why?" she asked while forcing herself to stay calm.

"Because, Brittany, the human body — your body — isn't weak or stupid. Once it identified me it saw me as a threat. To protect itself it created antibodies against me. As I took over more areas of your body, those same antibodies were not able to distinguish the difference between what's me and what's not. Which, in the end, are all the same." It added hastily as Brittany's face crumpled. "But, don't worry, as I changed you I reversed the damage."

"Why did you infect me?"

E.V. paused, still watching Brittany for a moment before answering. "Because you were the first person to touch Emily after she died."

Now it was Brittany's turn to pause. "Fine," she said, though she didn't feel fine. "Because of you I don't make any more of my own blood. But I still need it. Is there any way to do that without taking it from other people?"

E.V. shook its head.

"Fine." Brittany had a very limited knowledge of blood types. "Do I have to be type specific? Is there anyone's I can't use?"

"*You* don't use their blood." E.V. cocked its head to the side.

"Then what's keeping me alive?"

"Me." The image of Emily gave a proud smile.

FIFTEEN

CONNECTED

"YOU WANT ME to believe you are keeping me alive without blood?"

"Yes." E.V. continued to smile. "Your body is now being powered by my ... for lack of a better explanation ... fluids. My superior blood."

Brittany held her hand in front of her face one more time. She still looked the same. She still felt the same— mostly. But she understood that she was not the same and would never be the same again. She felt her face mouth pull down as she fought her tears.

"I wish you hadn't infected me." Brittany lost the battle; her tears spilled freely from her eyes.

E.V. winced as if in pain. "It's not all bad. There are some good things about having me in you."

"Really?" Brittany wiped her face. "Like what?"

"Haven't you noticed how soft your skin has become? How much better you can see and hear and how clearly you can think? Even your sense of smell. I've improved them all. Because my blood is superior to yours, I've supplied you nourishment on a regenerative level."

Brittany gazed around her room, noticing for the first time that the dark didn't hinder her. Even with the streetlight burned out, she could see everything clearly. She also felt stronger. And her thoughts *were* vaster, but as much as she could think about more, it also meant that more things distracted her.

"It makes sense," Brittany mumbled, not sounding very enthusiastic. "Vampires are known for their strength, speed, and cunning— as well as stealing blood." There were some other things vampires were known for that weren't so neat. "Will I grow fangs?"

E.V. burst out laughing. "No." It changed its tone as it realized that Brittany had been seriously concerned. "No. The myth about fangs came from one of my hosts. He was a prince."

"A prince? A real life prince?" Despite herself, Brittany was excited about this.

"Yes, a real life prince." E.V. seemed to feel the opposite.

"You said that you take a piece of your host with you when they die. Do you still have bits of him with you?"

"Yes, a little." Brittany didn't miss the way E.V. shook as if afraid.

"Tell me about this prince," Brittany asked, hoping for stories about castles, crowns, kings, queens, and princesses.

"His eye-teeth were more prominent. They were like that naturally," E.V. said. "He'd been like that before I came along, and once he died, his teeth didn't change. But the locals who'd come to fear him thought that was a sign of a vampire. People with prominent eye-teeth were hunted and slaughtered for many years following that."

Brittany was disappointed at the response she'd gotten. "Did the prince have a wife?"

"Yes."

"What about her? Tell me about her."

E.V. looked away. "He killed her."

Brittany felt like she'd been slapped in the face with reality. She didn't like it. "He did, or you?"

E.V. didn't answer.

When it was clear E.V. wasn't going to answer, Brittany asked, "How come, in some stories, vampires can become bats?"

"Because I was one, once." The image of Emily shifted nervously.

"You can possess animals?" Brittany wondered what that would feel like.

"Not easily and not for long. It is uncomfortable and equally as disorienting. I only did it because I had no other choice."

"Tell me what happened." Brittany leaned forward.

E.V. seemed to deliberate a moment, then started quietly. "I was inside a man who was crueller than any I have known before or since. He welcomed the changes I brought. He liked how I enhanced his abilities; he used them to become everything he desired. He was a true monster. He was cunning and he trapped me. He understood how I could leave him, so he made sure I never got a chance to jump. The only physical contact he had was with his victims and only after he'd tortured and killed them."

E.V. held its face in its hands as if the memory was too much to bear. "I was partnered with him for more years than I'd like to remember. I finally left him by possessing his pet bat. It's not something I wish to do again— I don't want to and I don't want to have to.

"I was only in the poor thing long enough to fly into town and bite the first person I could find." E.V. shuddered. "But my transfer was very public. Rumors turned into myths and myths became legends."

As Brittany was listening she felt frightened and helpless. When E.V. was done, a general sense of uneasiness had settled over her. Brittany watched E.V., noting the way the image fidgeted as if it were also feeling these things.

"You are just a hallucination— how come you feel so real to me?"

"We are deeply connected, both physically and emotionally. I can sense your thoughts just like you can feel mine. When you detect my anxiety, grief — even my joy — you will impose it upon my image in a way that you can recognize and understand it."

"Does that mean we won't be able to keep secrets from each other?"

E.V. squirmed, or the projected image of Emily squirmed, like it was trying not to answer. "Alright," it finally huffed. "Secrets are tricky. In the beginning a certain amount can be withheld due to our unfamiliarity. As time goes on we will know each other better, so secrets will became harder to keep."

It never said impossible, and while it no doubt hoped Brittany wouldn't notice, it failed to see that she had. Brittany was already thinking of ways to use this to her advantage.

SIXTEEN

CHANGED

"OUT OF ALL the myths, are there any that are true?" Brittany said.

"Most have been misunderstood," E.V. mused.

"Ok" Brittany nodded. "Are there any myths that are closer to the truth?"

E.V. hesitated. It twisted its hands in its lap.

"There's something you're not telling me. I can feel it."

E.V. scowled. "There are a lot of things I haven't told you yet. There's simply too much to tell all at once. All you need to know is that I do not wish to see you harmed in any way. I will do everything I can to keep you safe."

It was Brittany's turn to scowl. She stared out her bedroom window and she could see perfectly, like it was mid-afternoon on a clear day. She scanned the darkness, seeing where the mist was gathering as it settled. Yes, she had changed in many ways but the sooner she understood it the better she'd feel... at least that's what she thought.

She had no intention of letting the subject drop. Brittany was searching E.V.'s thoughts, trying to feel what it was thinking. Suddenly a sharp pain pierced through Brittany's abdomen. She instinctively put her hand over her stomach.

"What?" Brittany's words came out slightly choked. "What's that?" The pain increased and Brittany felt afraid— but it was more than her own fear she was feeling. The hairs along her arms were standing on edge, almost vibrating. "E.V.?"

"It's..." The image of Emily confirmed Brittany's fears— it too looked afraid. "I... I need to..." It also seemed to be panting.

"What!" If possible, the pain was still increasing. Brittany felt squished as if her torso was in a vice. "What's happening?" Then her stomach sank, making her feel as if it was falling out of her.

"Your intestines..." Emily's image faded away.

"Hey!" Brittany snapped, partly from irritation but mostly from the pain. "What's going on?"

"We'll talk later," E.V. replied in Brittany's head.

"Why can't we talk now?" Brittany winced. Her stomach had turned rock hard under her hand. Then the pain stopped like someone had flicked a light switch.

"E.V.?" There was no response. After a few more tries Brittany stopped calling out.

Her mind was racing. In three short weeks she'd gone from being fairly normal to anything but. And she was still changing— still getting stronger, faster, smarter.

As dawn started to break, Brittany used her senses to experience it in a whole new way. She could feel her room warming increment by increment. It caressed her like a soft blanket being pulled slowly across her skin. She watched as the sun lit the sky— sending out red, orange, and yellow hues. She examined the way it refracted not only off the wispy clouds, but also through them. Finally, she watched as the sun slipped up over the houses, its full rays evaporating the overnight condensation and mist from where they had gathered.

Even after all this, it was still early.

She could hear her father sleeping in his room down the hall. She could also sense him; his heartbeat seemed to thud through the air around him. Had Brittany gone blind she still could have followed it right to him. He wasn't the only one— she could feel the neighbors in the house on the right and the family of five in the house on the left. As well as the three across the alley and... Brittany pushed that reality away— it was kinda creepy.

She needed to get up and do something. She made her way to the kitchen. As she cleaned the leftover dishes from the sink, she stared out at her old tree fort. Once the police tape had been removed there were no traces left to give away that it had, only a few weeks earlier, been a tomb for her friend.

Brittany wished she could talk with Emily. Ask her about those final moments. *Had it been hard*? she wanted to ask. *Did it hurt*? She knew that Emily wouldn't be able to answer, not from wherever her friend had ended up. She also knew that E.V. wouldn't tell her, once E.V. returned from wherever it had gone. *Where had E.V. gone? And why*?

"There is nothing worse than questions without answers," Brittany grumbled to herself. Once she had cleaned everything she could she started making breakfast.

"You can't eat that." E.V. appeared as Brittany was finishing up.

Its return startled Brittany— a little. Still, she ignored the return of the creature until she was finished dishing the food onto two plates. "Where have you been?"

"Trust me, you don't want to know." E.V. looked terrible, clothes ruffled, pallid skin, eyes heavy with black circles under them.

One thing Brittany was sure of was that she really did want to know. She wanted to know everything. "Tell me anyway."

"Would you believe me if I told you that not knowing is healthier?" E.V. didn't sound hopeful. "You aren't going to like what you hear."

"I don't care," Brittany said, adding in her head, *and I don't believe you*.

"Ya," E.V. muttered, "I didn't think you would."

Brittany wasn't sure if it was her spoken or unspoken comment that the creature had responded to, and she didn't care. "Just tell me." She crossed her arms over her chest, mildly noticing that her breasts were much more firm than normal. When the creature didn't continue she added for good measure, "Everything."

E.V. slumped into a kitchen chair. "Remember how I told you that you're changing?" It waited until Brittany nodded. "Well, you aren't changing any more. The transformation is done— I am completely integrated now. We are fully *we*."

"What if I don't want to be a 'we'?"

E.V.'s tone changed. "Well, we are a we. There is nothing you can do to change that. I am here to stay. I will be here, in you and with you, until your very last breath."

"And you decide when that will be."

"I could… Sure I could…" it looked at Brittany, "but that's not what I want. I don't want to leave you. And I certainly don't want to end you." E.V. seemed to choke on its words. "I don't want you to end. I mean, I know it will happen… someday… someday." It shook its head. "But that shouldn't be for a long, long time. I know you didn't choose me, but I wanted you."

Brittany felt her eyes widen. "Why?"

It stared at its lap. "Because of Emily. She thought you were something special."

Brittany wasn't sure if she was seeing things or if E.V. was really blushing.

Almost as if the creature had been embarrassed, it changed the subject. "Listen, I had to finish your transformation ahead of schedule." Its voice gained strength as it continued. "If you hadn't eaten that maraschino juice… but it's done now. Just so you understand: up to last night your organs had been slowly shutting down. And it would have been better for both of us if it had continued to do this over the next few weeks." E.V. sighed. "But it's done now."

"What's done?"

"Well, your stomach— actually your whole digestive system, they've stopped working. You wouldn't have been able to digest what you ate yesterday. That's why you expelled most of it. The rest I had to transform before it killed you."

"Would it have killed you too?" Brittany interrupted.

E.V. shook its head.

Brittany turned to stare out the kitchen window at the tree fort again.

SEVENTEEN
IMPROVED

STILL SITTING AT her kitchen table across from the illusion of Emily, Brittany could hear her father's breathing. It was shallowing — becoming lighter — he was waking. She heard him roll over and rub his face. She could even hear his hand scraping over his stubble. It was so loud she felt like she was right next to him.

Brittany flinched when her father mumbled, "Damn." Her head pounded as she listened to him walk across the floor, and the sound of his ensuite door snapping shut was so loud she nearly fell off her chair.

"How do you turn it down?" Brittany said. Her own voice sounded like it was being screamed through a megaphone.

"Don't concentrate so hard." Blissfully, E.V.'s voice was at a normal volume.

The sound of the toilet being flushed was like standing next to a waterfall. And when her father yelped in pain, Brittany instinctively cupped her hands over her ears.

"Focus on something else," E.V. said.

Brittany looked at the freshly cooked eggs giving off heat. She could hear the molecules in the air heating up and turning to steam.

"Not the sound," E.V. said. "Concentrate on another sense."

Brittany focused on smell. The eggs had a stench like heated plastic, with a hint of cream, but even that smelled wrong. "Have the eggs gone bad?" she asked and was thankful that her hearing had gone back to regular volume.

"They aren't bad, you just smell things differently now. Because food is toxic, your sense of smell will reflect that. You will perceive food as inedible and undesirable."

Everything had changed— too fast. She knew that the least of these changes was the fact that she'd never be able to eat again. Yet, she couldn't help wondering: if she had known this, would she have made herself something special for her last meal?

Brittany took a seat at the kitchen table covering her eyes while she waited for her father, who she could hear making his way down to the kitchen.

"You ok?" he asked.

Brittany looked up. Seeing her father through her new eyes she noticed that he was just beginning to develop a hunch on his left side. She could also see all the grey hair in his sideburns. She studied the growing crinkles around his eyes. She saw that his irises had seven different shades of blue in them. Seeing all this, she almost missed how he was looking at her.

"You feeling ok, sweetie?"

"Ya, why?" Brittany tried to sound innocent.

"You were asleep when I got home last night and it wasn't that late, seven, maybe. I tried to wake you up— to see if you had eaten dinner, but nothing I tried worked. You slept like you were in a coma." Brittany felt his panic more than she heard it.

"I wasn't feeling good last night, but I'm..." Brittany looked over at E.V. for a fraction of a second, knowing she couldn't say anything else. "I'm better now."

His eyes narrowed slightly. "Do you think you're well enough to visit your mother's tonight? You remember she's expecting you?"

Brittany winced. She'd forgotten. "Ya, sure. I guess."

Brittany thought about how E.V. had changed her— the greatest of these changes made her wonder if she should visit her mother ever again.

"This looks delicious." Her father had taken a seat across from her.

Brittany stared down at her own plate. She stared at the ridges and valleys that had naturally appeared in her eggs while they cooked. On the surface were tiny groupings of water droplets. The eggs had cooled enough that these were no longer evaporating off and instead were setting like a thin film over everything. Even if she had been able to eat it, this might have put her off. She tried to keep the disgust from her face. Apparently she wasn't very successful.

"Something wrong with yours?" her father said.

"I'm…" she glanced at E.V., "not hungry." But in her head she amended: *for this.*

E.V. snickered at the dark humour and added, "But we are hungry. And we will need to eat."

Brittany sighed. As much as she didn't like it, she knew it was true.

Her father didn't force her to eat. He hadn't noticed how she'd pushed the food around her plate for weeks, and with the steadily growing pile of dirty dishes from Brittany's many failed snacks, he didn't have any reason to think anything had changed.

After breakfast, with both their plates cleared (the contents of Brittany's covertly tossed down the compactor) she headed for the door.

"Where are you going?" her dad asked as she passed him in the living room.

"The mall." She'd stopped to look at him.

He put down what he'd been reading. "It's still really early. Are you meeting up with someone?"

"No, I'm going alone… maybe I'll text Coby to join me." Brittany didn't understand why, but she felt like her father was suspicious of something— *but what?*

"Coby?" Her father sat up. "Coby was here last night. Did you know that? I found him on our front porch. He looked like he had stopped there to nap. I ended up driving him home because he looked sick."

Panic pulled at Brittany. It took all her strength not to race from the house to go straight to Coby's and make sure he was ok.

"Did you know he'd come by? You were already asleep so I thought he was on his way over." Her dad paused, his eyes narrowing while he scrutinized her. "Was he just arriving, or leaving?"

"Leaving." Brittany continued to battle with her desire to see Coby. "We were supposed to go to the movie but," she ran through the events of the previous night and realized that it would be very bad to be near Coby now, "I wasn't feeling well when he got here. I had to cancel. I went straight to bed." She couldn't visit him because she'd hurt him last night when she was hungry. Today it would be too easy to repeat that mistake; she was hungry again.

"Is that all that happened?" Her father's eyes felt like searchlights.

"Yes." Brittany knew that there was no way her dad could really know what had happened, yet he seemed to be suspicious of something. His look made her feel guiltier.

Her dad pushed a button on his phone so that the time was displayed. Brittany noticed he had a fresh bruise on the heel of his hand.

"It's really early." His eyes were on her again, still suspicious. "You're never up this early on a Saturday."

"So?" Brittany crossed her arms. "I couldn't sleep. Now I want to go to the mall to," she hesitated, "shop. Is there something wrong with that? Are you going to tell me I can't go?"

"No." All her father's suspicions seemed to be replaced with concern. "Brit, if you need to talk I'm always here. Or if you need someone who's more qualified I can set up a meeting with my therapist. Or I bet your school has a counsellor you could talk to."

Brittany spun on her heels to leave. "Thanks, Dad," she said. "I've already talked to her."

She stormed from the house, slamming the front door. Then leaned into it. She felt frightened, mad, and guilty.

E.V. seemed to be waiting for her to decide which would be the winning emotion.

"You took from my dad," Brittany said, her voice just a whisper. "Last night, when he checked on me. You took his blood."

E.V. nodded.

"You can do that? When I'm sleeping?"

E.V. continued to nod.

"What else can you do, when I'm unconscious?" Suddenly sleeping felt dangerous.

"That's about it," E.V. said. "When you sleep I can do about as much as I can do when you are awake: I can listen, feel, and extract. Oh, and if you slept with your eyes open, I could watch." It didn't seem happy about this.

Brittany was relieved but she quickly moved on to another emotion: anger. "Why did you take from my dad?"

"The same reason I take from anyone. We needed the blood."

Brittany stood for a few more minutes but couldn't think of anything else to say. Last night they needed blood… today they needed more. Was this how things would be from now on? Was it worth it?

As if E.V. were in her thoughts, it replied, "It will get better."

"When?" She felt the coolness from the door transferring into her hands as she continued to press herself against it. From inside she could hear her father ruffling some papers and could only imagine how that might be hurting his freshly bruised palm.

"Soon, I suspect," E.V. said. "Everything with you has been accelerated. That's why I've needed more than I normally do, even in the beginning."

"You don't normally need so much blood?" Brittany felt like this was the first piece of good news since the creature had stared talking to her.

"No, this is not normal," E.V. said then quickly amended. "I mean, yes, in the beginning I always need a little extra. But once I'm established and things have settled down, I can survive on less than a cup a day."

"Less than a cup a day." The weirdest memory popped into Brittany's head. She remembered the time she had to take her measuring cup over to the neighbor to borrow some sugar. One cup wasn't much. "When?"

"Soon," E.V. smiled. "I'm sure of it."

EIGHTEEN
SCARED

BRITTANY STARTED TO feel conspicuous as she continued to lean against her front door. She could still hear her father turning the pages as he kept reading his paper, unaware that she stood there. But if someone passed by they might think it was odd, and perhaps suspicious. She took a deep breath, pushed off from the door, and walked to the side of her house.

She stopped short. Normally she'd follow the path around the back to leave out the back gate, but she was frozen.

E.V., who had been following, walked right into Brittany and through her. Then it turned back. "What's wrong now?"

Brittany stared at the image of Emily. The sun streamed through it, making it look more ghostly than normal.

Brittany was pretty sure that the sun shouldn't affect her. It hadn't been a problem yesterday. Besides, she'd seen Emily in the sun plenty of times since she'd returned from the farm. Emily never caught on fire and Brittany was sure she'd never seen her friend sparkle. In fact, the last time she'd seen Emily the sun had been glaring down at them from the sky and back up at them from the snow.

Brittany knew it was illogical to be fearful of the sun today. Yet, for all she knew, she couldn't get her feet to move forward. After all, she was a vampire now.

"Oh," E.V. said softly.

"I know the sun won't hurt me," Brittany said as she slowly extended her hand past the shadows and into its rays.

"Well, not the sun per se."

Brittany pulled her hand back so fast she wasn't able to track it even with her new skills. "Per se?"

E.V. sounded apologetic. "Definitely not today." It looked around as if for emphasis. "It's not hot enough. You see, it's not the sun you have to worry about but how hot it makes you."

Brittany looked back at the house and a fleeting thought of going inside and hiding out until the sun set. Shaking off the thought, she slowly extended her hand into the sunlight again. She studied it. She had already noticed how her skin seemed paler. Under the light she could still see her veins. Today they appeared to be less purple-blue and more pink.

"How hot it makes me?" she asked, still watching her hand. It didn't sparkle, for which she was relieved beyond measure. It didn't smoke either, nor ignite or combust. She wondered if she had, would that make things easier? "What happens if I get too hot?"

"Well," E.V. explained, also watching Brittany's hand, "my body's fluid is lighter than yours. It will evaporate quicker. Once a certain amount is evaporated we run the risk of..."

Brittany wasn't watching her hand any more. She had caught the creature's memory — a warm feeling like cuddling up in front of a fireplace, then a screaming sensation and: nothing. She shuddered.

"Ok" Her voice quivered. *No*, she answered her earlier thought, *that would not be an easier death*. "How do I avoid that?"

"Don't get too hot."

Brittany had been moving more of herself into the sun. This statement had her frozen again. "How do I avoid that?"

"I told you, there's nothing to fear today. Just," E.V. stopped and locked eyes with Brittany, "just listen to me."

"Ok," Brittany still didn't move, "I'm listening."

"Not now." E.V. rolled its eyes. "Listen to me— always. I'll tell you if we are heating up too much. Oh, and the better I'm fed the hotter I can get without coming to that end."

Food, blood, Brittany groaned internally. She forced herself to step into the sun and walk normally all the way to the mall.

NINETEEN

HUNGRY

BRITTANY EXPECTED HER time at the mall to be difficult. She hated why she was there — it wasn't like she was shopping for *clothes* — as much as she pretended to be. Picking out her victims was hard. How do you choose who to steal blood from? She'd never been a thief, and now she was the worst kind of thief there ever was. At least a pickpocket only took material things, not things that person couldn't live without.

"How about that security guard?" E.V. asked as Brittany pretended to be admiring a shirt.

Pretend was not the right word. She was pretending to pretend. She was more interested in looking like she was just looking.

"Brittany!"

Her head snapped up and she locked eyes with the guard who'd been watching her.

"That wasn't very inconspicuous," E.V. grumbled.

"It's hard," Brittany said as quietly as she could while she covered her mouth.

"Ya, and you don't want to do it." Now E.V. crossed its arms. "Fine. Be more conspicuous. That way the security guard will come over to talk to you and I can get what I need while he searches you for the items he clearly thinks you've shoplifted."

"Not him," Brittany said through frozen lips as she held up another shirt.

"Why not him?"

Brittany shook her head but took the two items she'd been admiring back to the changing room. Once they were alone she answered in a whisper, hoping it wouldn't carry. "When you take people's... blood... they get tired. I can't do that to a security guard. It's his job to stay alert. Taking from *him* wouldn't be fair."

In the end there were a lot of people Brittany felt it wouldn't be fair to take from. Realizing she'd need to find someone, she decided to focus on anyone who looked healthy and close to her own age. That's when she faced an even bigger challenge: everyone seemed to be really good at keeping their hands, all their body parts, to themselves.

After several failed attempts, Brittany started to feel paranoid that they were on to her— that everyone knew what she was trying to do.

"Don't be so ridiculous," E.V. said.

They were sitting in the food court. Brittany had a tray with a few items from her favorite food stand in front of her. She'd unwrapped them and every once in a while made a show of moving things around. She even went so far as to bring the cup to her mouth and pretend to take a sip from the straw.

"It's just that touching has become so taboo," E.V. said. "Believe me, a hundred years ago it would have been easier to get our fill. Ah, how times have changed." E.V. made a face. "Then again, it could be that you're not trying hard enough."

Brittany blinked and stared over at a group of teens that was just arriving. They were laughing, pushing each other around, and one even picked up a fry and tossed it across the table at another. Just a few weeks earlier that could have been her, Coby, and Emily.

"If we don't get what we need here I'll be forced to take it from someone you really care about."

E.V.'s words immediately brought thoughts of Coby to her mind. "What do you want me to do?" she said around her straw.

"What do you want *me* to do?" E.V. shot back.

Brittany thought on that while her eyes wandered back to the boys. She wanted to go home. Logically she knew she needed blood and it would be better to take from complete strangers. Yet, somehow, illogically she felt that if anyone figured out what she'd become, and what she did... at least with her family she might have a chance at being forgiven.

"Brittany?" E.V. was watching as a boy from the group was approaching. "Now's your chance. What's it going to be?"

She shrugged as the boy stopped in front of her.

He cleared his throat. "Um," his voice cracked.

Back at his table all of his friends were watching, not even bothering to conceal it.

"Um," the boy faltered again, "you using that chair?" He pointed to the one next to Brittany.

She looked down at it.

"Because," the boy looked back at his friends, "we seem to be short..."

Brittany continued to watch the rowdy, immature, stupid boys as they slapped each other on their backs and howled with laughter at their friend.

That's then a thought dawned on her. She glanced around the only half filled food court to confirm her notion: he could have taken a chair from any one of the empty tables. She tilted her head to the side. "Are you asking for this chair?" She patted it. "Or are you looking for an excuse to invite me to sit with you?"

The boy turned beat red. "Um... would... would you like to sit with us?"

"No," Brittany answered a little too quickly, "but I don't mind if you sit with me."

The boy looked back at his friends one last time. "Um... ok." He stiffly sat in the chair he'd been asking for. "My name is Eric." He extended his hand.

Brittany took it and looked towards E.V., giving a quick nod of consent.

By the end of an hour, during which time all five boys eventually came over to sit with Brittany, E.V. was very happy— Brittany wasn't sure how she felt. She left the mall, making only one stop.

"That shirt looks great on you," E.V. complimented, sounding exactly like Emily would have. "You've always had excellent taste."

Brittany glanced down. It was her size, or at least it was the size she used to wear. Brittany could tell that if she continued to shrink, she wouldn't be fitting it much longer.

This made her think about the boys at lunch. They all seemed intent on sharing their food with her— all of which she accepted and was relieved that none of them bothered to notice that she didn't actually eat it. "E.V., what happens if I'm forced to eat?"

"I've already told you: You can't eat."

Brittany made a face. "But what if I do?"

"You can't," E.V. repeated.

"I get that, but say I have to— like someone is watching and I have to *prove* to them that I'm eating?" She thought of when she'd been younger and her father had sat with her, watching her until she'd eaten all her vegetables.

E.V. fidgeted with its sleeve for a moment then opened its mouth to answer, but Brittany cut it off.

"If you say, 'I can't' again, I'm going to scream. Tell me what would happen if I did?"

"It wouldn't be easy. You'd have to fight against your survival instincts just to put it in your mouth. And you have an exceptionally strong will to live, so I'd be surprised if you could. But if you could then you'd have to make sure not to swallow, because your body isn't made for human food anymore."

"So if I swallow the food I'll die?"

"No, not necessarily. There's a small chance you might be able to expel what you ate. If you are able, you should be fine. If not, though, you are very likely to die. It's not a good way to go. I'll spare you the gruesome details."

Brittany hadn't been spared the images. E.V.'s memories painted a horrendous picture of the very long and drawn-out deaths of those who had gone this way.

"So, I guess it's up to me to be creative about making it look like I'm eating."

"I have full confidence in your abilities. I've seen you in action; you have a talent for it."

Brittany wasn't flattered by this statement. "So, why can't I eat?"

"Because I changed you."

"Ya, ya, ya, I get that. But what did you change about me so that what used to be food has now become poison?"

E.V. sighed. "I'm not used to..." It looked directly at Brittany. "Usually people don't want to know the details."

Brittany's responding smile was forced. "Well, I do. I need to understand this."

E.V. nodded. "Alright, let's see; we've already talked about how I've transformed you into a superior being. The areas I allow to function now do so beyond your human potential. For instance, your muscles have improved and they've eliminated your excess fat."

Brittany wanted to argue that she wasn't "fat," but E.V. gave her no space to interrupt.

"Your strength has at least tripled. What I've left out is what happens to those organs that I have starved." E.V. paused. "They've shrivelled up. This is what needed to happen because they are unneeded now. As they starve and shrink, in essence they are mummifying."

"Mummified? Are you serious? Like the Egyptian kings in the tombs?"

E.V. nodded.

Brittany's brow wrinkled. "If I'm mummified, won't someone notice?"

"Certain organs have petrified. But they are surrounded by fat and muscle, so no one will be able to tell unless they give you a physical... or they punch you."

"Who'd want to punch me?"

E.V. shrugged.

Then Brittany thought of something that didn't make sense. "Didn't you say you got rid of all my fat?"

E.V. rolled its eyes. "Excess fat."

"So, I'm not fat any more."

"You were never fat," E.V. said.

Despite herself, Brittany smiled at the compliment. "Wait a minute— if I'm petrified, won't that make me heavier?"

"You have nothing to worry about, your new muscles can handle it. Besides, you won't be that much heavier."

Brittany remembered the night she'd tried to get Emily to weigh herself. Brittany, knowing how much her weight used to bug her, thought if she saw how much she'd lost, Emily might cheer up. Now she wondered if Emily would have been lighter, heavier, or maybe just the same.

"Your petrified organs aren't as heavy as lead or stone," E.V. continued, "and your lungs don't petrify in the same way as your intestines. They have too many air pockets and bubbles in them. As they petrify, they become more like a sea sponge out of water: moveable but dead."

"You've petrified my lungs! Don't I need to breath?"

"You don't. I do."

"So then how do you breath?"

"I get what I need through the pores in your skin." E.V. gave a coy smile. "But you still need to pull air into your lungs and release it, because that is how you smell. And smelling is a sense that is invaluable for survival. You just don't need to smell twelve times a minute. You could probably get away with it once every two to three minutes."

Brittany stared down at herself. It was weird to think that all her insides had shrunk and dried up like a prune. No wonder there was no coming back once E.V. had infected you. But with all these changes Brittany realized that, her insides at least, were far closer to the fabled zombie than what the myths said about vampires.

E.V. watched silently.

"Where did you come from?"

E.V. stopped walking. Brittany stopped and turned towards it.

"E.V.?"

The image of Emily shrugged.

"Surely you can tell me where you began…" Brittany thought she could see shadows of people and places that once were— like ghosts of ancient times.

"My memories don't work the same way as yours." E.V. looked like it was in pain. "I can't remember the same way you do."

"How's that?" Brittany gave up trying to make her vision any clearer. "How do my memories work in comparison to yours?"

"Your memories utilize all five of your senses. When you recall something, it's in full color and surround sound with moving 3D pictures." E.V. shook its head. "My memories are like a very old photo album. The shots are still, and black and white, and each page is in jeopardy of falling apart to be lost— never to be thought of again."

The feelings of sorrow and loss that surged through Brittany didn't entirely feel like they were hers. This felt sad: to exist for so long and have so little to show for it— that was tragic. However, she wasn't sure how she felt about everything E.V. had done; the physical changes as well as taking Emily. She was too undecided to feel this level of anguish.

Brittany continued to see shadowy ghosts. As she watched she became aware that for most, even though they were strangers to her, they felt like they were family. "How come *I* can see them?"

E.V. sounded frustrated. "You see my memories?"

"Ya." Brittany's nod was almost smug. "I've seen quite a few things when you've talked about yourself."

The creature was trying to appear unruffled, but it wasn't fooling Brittany.

Faces continued to appear in Brittany's mind, but the pauses between them were becoming more stretched out. "Were you all these people?"

"Not all of them. Some of them are the people my humans cared about."

E.V. didn't get a chance to answer because someone interrupted them.

TWENTY
DISGUSTED

A WOMAN WAS pushing a stroller, walking at a brisk pace towards Brittany and her hallucination. Brittany turned away from E.V. to watch.

Brittany had always liked to look at babies; the younger, the cuter. As the woman passed, Brittany used all her new abilities to admire the baby. It looked very young, probably under three months, judging by its size. She was bundled up in so much pink, all Brittany could see was her cute button nose, soft rosy lips and long eyelashes that shadowed her flushed cheeks as she slept.

Before Brittany could think *awww,* she heard E.V. say, "Yum."

"Yum?" Brittany gagged on the word. The mother was down the block and around the corner when she found her voice.

E.V. had frozen. "I didn't mean..."

"What?" Brittany said. "You didn't mean 'yum,' or you didn't mean for me to hear that?"

"I didn't say." Its eyes were bulging. "That was *my* thought. You weren't supposed to hear."

The fact that Brittany had made the jump between hearing what the creature said and what it thought wasn't important. She cut it off. "You eat babies?"

"I don't *eat* anyone."

Brittany was shaking. "You know what I mean! Would you take blood from a baby?"

"That's entirely up to you." E.V. looked as if it were a puppy being wrongfully scolded.

"That's not what I asked." Brittany continued to shake, and though she knew her stomach was completely empty and solid as stone, it still felt like she needed to puke. "Have you ever taken from a baby?"

"I," E.V. was backing away, becoming entangled in the shrub they'd stopped next to, "I don't understand why you are so angry."

"Don't you? Hasn't anyone every talked to you about this?"

E.V. shrugged. Only its head and shoulders could be seen above the bush. "Everyone has blood to spare."

Brittany felt her teeth snap together. "Just because they have it doesn't mean you should take it."

"I don't under…"

"Trust me— it's wrong."

"Ok." The image of Emily brought its hands out in a gesture of surrender. "You don't want me taking from babies. I won't."

Brittany wasn't convinced.

They walked the rest of the way back to her father's house in complete silence.

When she got home her father was on the phone having an argument with her mom. "I'm not trying to keep her from you," he said. "She was really sick last night. I was just looking out for you."

Her mom's response wasn't kind.

"Hey, I was only thinking of your new baby. I was trying to protect him," Brittany's dad said.

Brittany wrapped her arms about herself and kept going right up to her room. *To protect your baby* echoed in her head. She lay face up on her bed staring at the ceiling.

Her father wasn't wrong to try and protect her mom's new baby from her. The trouble was that it wasn't the only one who needed protection. He had no clue of the real threat Brittany was now.

Her father's voice cut into her thoughts. "…don't be like that."

Unfortunately, with her improved ears, Brittany could still hear the conversation as clearly as if she'd been listening in on one of the other phones. She tried to distract herself by staring at the ceiling harder, until she magnified it to look like a winter oasis. She didn't need to eavesdrop, even if it was easier to do now.

What they were saying wasn't anything new. In fact, the conversations between her mom and dad hadn't changed much in the four years they'd been apart. It always came back to those unresolved feelings. The same unresolved feelings that were the reason they'd split up in the first place.

Brittany dug the balls of her fist into her eyes to try to block it all out.

TWENTY-ONE
DECIDED

THE VISION OF Emily sat on the edge of Brittany's bed. It was staring at her digital clock; so far it had watched as ninety-three minutes ticked past. The argument between Brittany's mother and father was long since over. They had heard her father promise to bring her over around five.

Five was rapidly approaching.

"Can we please talk?" It was the third time E.V. had asked this.

"What do you want to talk about?" Brittany was certain that she knew.

"How about your feelings?" E.V. said.

This caught Brittany off guard, but she figured it was just another way around to the subject of taking her sibling's blood. She would have none of that. She'd do whatever it took to keep them safe from the creature.

"Ok, my feelings," Brittany said, playing along. "Why do I feel hungry again?"

E.V. smiled as if this was exactly what it wanted her to ask. "You are hungry again because you are expending a lot of energy right now."

"Me?" Brittany rolled to look at E.V. square on. "What am I doing that's taking up your energy?"

"It's your feelings; they are creating adrenaline."

It was true. Brittany was having murderous thoughts. She wanted to end E.V. any way she could, knowing full well that to end the creature would also end her. Yet, for all she'd learnt, it appeared impossible to kill the thing.

Every way Brittany thought of, somehow the creature had already survived it.

"Your adrenaline," E.V. continued, "is using up my energy and that's eating away at our supplies."

"Really?" It wasn't that she didn't believe it, it was that she didn't *want* to believe it. Or, more to the point, Brittany wanted to hurt E.V.

"Really!" E.V. answered.

For the second time in her relationship with the creature, Brittany felt a pain unlike any other. It radiated from her heart and stretched out into every limb. It was like an electrocution. It singed as it surged.

"Ok." Like a sharp slap across the cheek, this was just the jolt Brittany had needed. She had been sulking, having a tantrum really, even though she knew it hadn't been helping anything. "I'll stop," she said and immediately the pain stopped. She sat up and held her hands over her face.

This was it— either she chose death, or she didn't. She wanted to scoff that it wasn't much of a choice. Or if it was, the decision had already been made— because she knew she couldn't kill herself.

"Ok." E.V. had turned to watch her.

"Yes." She would have to be ok because she wasn't ready to die.

"Brittany, please believe me when I tell you that I don't like seeing you in pain."

Brittany was sure that E.V. meant physical pain.

The creature had meant any kind of pain.

"I guess we'll need to find more blood… and soon," Brittany said.

That's when her father called up to her. "Brit? You awake? It's time to go to your mom's. She's expecting you in twenty minutes. I'm driving you. Be ready in five. Ok?"

Brittany cringed. She didn't want to go to her mom's this… hungry. But if she didn't go her mom was going to suspect that her father was keeping her away. Brittany's mom sounded prepared to take her dad to court over it.

"Can we take a little top-up from my father?" Brittany was only thinking of her siblings' safety. She was hungry— really hungry, actually.

E.V. seemed hesitant. "No."

"No? Why not?"

"Because we've already taken more than we should have."

"Really? But he seems fine."

Brittany heard its thoughts. *Fine is a relative thing.* "I extracted more from him than I took from Coby."

"What?" Brittany pulled herself up to stand. "What! How come he isn't passed out right now?"

"It has a lot to do with the speed of extraction," E.V. answered. "A large amount of blood loss over a quick period of time will send a body into shock. A slower extraction will not distress the nervous system as much."

"Why was Coby's extraction done quicker? Is it because you took through his mouth?" Brittany remembered back to the kiss, which felt like a lifetime ago.

"N-no."

"Then what?"

"Because," E.V. gave a self-assured smiled, "Coby likes you."

"What?" Brittany stepped back. She was shocked. *When had this happened*? "How can you tell?" *Coby was just a friend...* but even as she thought about him, and especially the kiss, she realized that she also felt like he was more than just a friend.

"Because of his heart rate. When he's near you it speeds up. Before I was even fully conscious, I could tell when he was around. Of course I am drawn to the blood." It stopped.

"Of course," Brittany retorted quickly as reality set back in.

"You're right," E.V. said, "it was my fault. I should have calculated for the increased blood flow. I didn't. I forgot. In my defence, we really needed the blood. When you kissed him back, his heart rate sped up even more. It was a stupid mistake. I'm really sorry. I never wanted to hurt him."

It was how genuine the creature sounded that softened Brittany towards it. Also, being able to feel its feelings, she could see that E.V. really cared. She didn't yet understand that E.V. cared so much *because* Brittany did.

"Brittany?" This time when her father called, his voice was closer. She heard him on the stairs.

"Ya, I'm coming," she answered.

TWENTY-TWO
OBSERVED

BRITTANY STOOD ON her mother's front porch looking at the illusion of Emily, which leaned against the railing opposite her. Her dad's car idled in the driveway; he wouldn't leave until he saw his daughter safely inside.

"Now you promised you wouldn't take from babies." Brittany's tone was tight, forced through her clenched jaw. "My brother is a baby and my sister isn't much older."

E.V. frowned.

"You promised."

"Yes, I promised, but…"

"But what!" Brittany snapped, causing it to flinch.

"But we need…"

"I know." She thought for a moment then whispered, "I guess you'll have to take from my mom."

Before E.V. could answer the door opened and Brittany's mother greeted her with a warm embrace.

While her mother's arms were around her, Brittany was certain she could feel E.V. working. *Don't take too much,* she thought and was shocked when the creature replied.

"But we need more. I won't take more than we did with your father."

No more than one cup, Brittany demanded— and at that thought she could feel E.V. jerk itself to a stop inside of her.

"That won't be nearly enough," the creature grumbled.

You can take some from my stepdad.

"How?" E.V. knew that Brittany's stepfather made sure not to touch her.

Leave it to me, Brittany said without any plan in mind.

☘   💧   ⁊

For Brittany the night felt terribly long. She saw herself as a villain, searching, waiting, calculating, biding her time. Even with E.V.'s promise, she didn't feel comfortable near her sister, and even more so her infant brother.

She sat in the living room with a tray of untouched cookies on the table. L.J. ran through the room with her arms spread apart like an airplane. Brittany cringed away, afraid that her sister would try and jump into her lap — something that Brittany would have encouraged if she'd been her normal self.

"You really *aren't* feeling well." Brittany's mother's voice held surprise along with a touch of concern. "If I had known... but we couldn't get anyone else to babysit. Not with such short notice... and I've had these plans for over a year." She'd been more musing, like she was talking to herself. She looked into Brittany's face. "You remember my last birthday. I was pregnant — again — and miserable. I was promised that this year would be different. Now that J.J. is here I can go out and have a few drinks."

Brittany turned to look at the infant in her stepfather's arms.

"J.J.," E.V. scoffed, thinking of the inappropriate nickname and not the infant's blood.

Brittany agreed, sensing E.V.'s struggle. *J.J. stands for Jack Junior.*

"But your stepfather's name is Ed."

Ya, at least L.J. almost makes sense. L.J. is for Little Jacqueline. Ed's sister is now B.J. — Big Jacqueline.

Focusing on the names wasn't helping. E.V.'s yearnings were increasing.

Enough! Brittany said.

"But we didn't get enough from your mom, we won't be able to make it through..."

Brittany cut off the creature. *Ok, thing, let's get some from Ed. I'm about to give you your chance so you'd better take it!* Brittany stood. *Just... don't take anything from my brother.*

E.V. promised again.

"Here, I'll take J.J. so you can get ready," Brittany said, reaching out to her half brother and stepdad.

Ed held his son out to Brittany, and she positioned herself so he could pass the baby over, but she also slipped her hand halfway under one of Ed's so that he had to fumble and reposition himself before he let go.

It was so perfect, Brittany was proud of her ingenuity. Even E.V. was impressed. Although the handoff had only lasted twenty seconds, E.V. had taken its fill from the man.

"What you got from Ed felt like more than you took from my mom," Brittany said to E.V. Her siblings were tucked safely into their beds and she was tidying up the house.

E.V. said the first part wonderingly, as though to itself. *Wow, you could tell...* Then it quickly followed that thought up with, "You never said otherwise. I didn't think you'd mind, what with your limited contact with the man."

"You're right, I didn't... and I don't mind." Brittany felt kind of bad that she didn't, but she hadn't ever liked Ed much, so somehow that made her feel better about it.

She thought about how quickly she'd become ok with the idea of stealing people's blood. *It shouldn't feel this easy to be a bloodsucker*, she thought. *It shouldn't feel this easy to take from people I love.*

E.V.'s smile faded as it felt Brittany's mood change. "What is it?"

Brittany's face crumpled, and even though she didn't need air, she felt like she'd lost her breath. "Did you... did we take from J.J.?"

"Believe me, you would have noticed if I did. There's no way I could hide the kind of boost a child's blood would give us. We might have been able to go a full day on just two or three ounces. And besides, you are so observant, I'm sure I couldn't hide even the slightest extraction from you."

"Really?"

She'd been asking about being observant, but E.V. mis-understood. "Oh, ya. The younger the human is, the more pure their blood. Not only is it sweeter, but it lasts much, much longer. It's like eating fresh bread as opposed to day-old. Only it's better than bread, it's like chocolate — really good chocolate — from Europe..."

Just for a moment, curiosity made Brittany waver in her resolve. Her mouth felt like it was watering. *Could it really be as good as E.V. boasted*? "Enough! Stop talking."

Brittany was sure of one thing: she was a danger to her family. She thought of everyone she'd already robbed from: her mother, her father, even her stepfather, and especially Coby, not to mention the five complete strangers at the mall. She was filled with shame.

She had doomed everyone in her life to become her victims. Yet, what was most upsetting was that in only a day she'd become ok with it. She didn't like taking *but she liked getting* the blood. She liked the feel of it in her veins; the sensation of it coursing through her; the strength, the warmth. It was invigorating. So how long before she was willing to take from L.J. or even J.J.?

TWENTY-THREE
DEFINED

"TELL ME SOMETHING," E.V. said. "Why do you think it's worse to take from babies? Don't you know they are better equipped for it?"

Brittany sat in her mother's kitchen. She'd cleaned it until every surface sparkled. With nothing more to do, she'd sat to wait for her mother and stepfather's return.

She thought about what E.V. had said. She couldn't believe it. "It's our responsibility, as the adults, to protect our children. They are so innocent and fragile. They need us to take care of them."

"Is that all?" E.V. seemed confused. "Because it feels like there's more. Your feelings go beyond a sense of duty. You really love them. So much you'd be willing to do things you wouldn't normally do to protect them."

"Well, they are my siblings, even if they are only half siblings."

"But it's not just them. It's all babies. Even that stranger we saw earlier today." E.V. leaned up against the counter. "What is it about babies? Because it's not just you. Even Emily felt this way, and her Gran."

"Kids are..." Brittany couldn't describe it. Instead she thought about the time she used to spend with her brother and sister. She remembered nights, not so long ago: J.J. had fallen asleep in her arms. She hadn't wanted to put him down but to hold him forever. She recalled reading L.J. a book and tucking her in and the way L.J. had looked at her with such trust.

Tears sprang to Brittany's eyes and she cursed the creature for robbing her of these simple pleasures in life.

"I'm sorry." E.V. turned away.

They were both silent, remembering different things.

"You haven't had much experience with babies?" Brittany said as she saw this truth.

"No, the hosts I end up with can't have children once I'm a part of them. They tend to avoid them," E.V. said in a flat voice.

"They don't like this." Brittany saw a flash of people: women. One had been so devastated that she'd killed herself.

"Probably." E.V. hadn't turned back.

Brittany pulled away from the scene with a shudder. "What about you? Don't you, whatever you are, reproduce? Don't you have babies, or offspring?" She resisted adding *or demon spawn*. Brittany tried to imagine what E.V.'s spawn would look like. She couldn't, she couldn't because she couldn't picture E.V. "What do you look like?"

Brittany's wonderings were met with silence.

"E.V., what are you? How do you look?"

The creature seemed to be struggling for words. "I… am… me."

"Yes, but what classification would you fall into? You are an animal, right? So what kind are you? Mammal, reptile, bird, amphibian… insect?"

The longer the silence drew out, the more aware Brittany became of the reality that none of these classifications fit E.V.

The creature itself seemed to be pondering this dilemma. It had scores of memories of existing for centuries. Yet not once, in all that time, had it been asked so pointedly to define itself. It wasn't able to.

Meanwhile, Brittany was coming to a conclusion about a kind of creature already in existence that E.V. resembled. She hesitated sharing. It wasn't a nice comparison, even if it was accurate. Brittany didn't want to hurt E.V.'s feelings, mostly because she was afraid of the creature's anger. If it didn't like being called a monster, how much more upset would it be to be called a parasite?

It wasn't even an hour later when Brittany's mom returned home, supporting her half conscious husband. Brittany leapt off the sofa to help her mother guide him in.

"What happened?" she asked, worried that this had somehow been her fault.

Her mother's frustration was apparent before she opened her mouth. "Tonight was supposed to be my night! I haven't had a drop to drink for over three years! I was the one who was supposed to be tipsy." They were guiding Ed to the bedroom.

"I'm so sorry, Mags," Ed slurred, "I really don't know what happened." He stared through unfocused eyes.

"Really? Ed, you should be the one carrying me in!" Brittany's mother huffed, leaving the room.

"Mom, what happened?" Brittany had followed her mother back down to the kitchen.

"You cleaned." Her mom turned in a circle, looking over the spotless counters and empty sink.

"Mom!"

"When I'm frustrated, I clean." She shook her head, then her eyes fell upon her daughter, and she gave a small smile. "You look like you're feeling better."

Brittany stared, still waiting for her mother to answer her question. Somehow she knew she was responsible, and she waited for her mother to confirm it.

"I don't know." Brittany's mother slid onto a chair at the counter. "He was fine while we waited in the lounge. We were having fun, sort of like old times, then when they moved us to our table, Ed started to act drunk. We'd only had cocktails. When I came back from freshening myself up he was asleep— it was utterly embarrassing! He was snoring. I tell you, I debated leaving him there." She huffed again.

Brittany looked away as guilt twisted through her petrified intestines. Before she could ask, E.V. was ready with an answer.

"Yes, that was us, sort of. With reduced blood, the effects of alcohol are more pronounced. We extracted nearly one pint from him. That's more than the Red Cross takes, so it was bound to have this kind of affect." E.V. added with a note of regret, "I didn't think of that."

That's twice! You'd think that if you've been doing this for so long you'd be better at it, Brittany thought. "Maybe it's just a virus," she offered her mother. "I don't mind coming back next week so you can try again, if Ed's up to it."

Her mother reached across the table to take Brittany's hand in hers. "That's nice of you," she said, fighting a yawn. "Maybe it is a virus. I'm not feeling so great either." Her words were becoming jumbled. "I think I need to put myself to bed before you have to." She fought another yawn, gave her daughter's hand a lame squeeze, and left.

"Yes, your mom too," E.V. lamented. "It took a bit longer to catch up with her because we didn't take as much. I guess it's probably a good thing we didn't."

Brittany wanted to scoff but she could feel the blood as it benefited her system. She could also tell that it wasn't going to last. "How much blood can you take from one person before it's too much?"

E.V. cocked its head to one side, quite bird-like, just as the real Emily would have. "Why do you want to know?"

"Because if you and I are a team, shouldn't I know?"

E.V. looked like it was contemplating whether to answer or not.

Brittany didn't wait for it to deny her the answer. "Exactly how much did you take from my father? And how long will it take for him to get better before we can take again? How much more do you need right now? How often should I expect to feed you? How many people can I take from? And is there anyone you can't take from?"

E.V. was shocked into silence. It knew about being a team— but even when the human accepted that E.V. was there to stay, they normally wanted a modicum of innocence, or more like ignorance. Humans, those that assimilated to the situation, didn't really want to know the technical part. They liked to pretend that nothing was different.

"Come on, E.V., you want me to trust you, so stop keeping things from me."

E.V. deliberated for a few more seconds, but feeling Brittany's mood slipping, it answered, "The average body is made up of ten pints of blood. Up to one pint can be taken, if done slowly and controlled. If it is extracted all at once, it will send a body into shock, which takes close to 60 days to recover from. But if we only take a small portion at a time, say no more than 8 ounces, then the taking is endless."

"And you've already told me that you need more than 8 ounces a day..."

"Quite a bit more, yes— at least for now."

Brittany thought for a moment. "What about animals?"

"They should be considered a very last resort." Whether E.V. meant to or not, it remembered that day, not so long ago, in Brittany's tree fort with the bunny.

Brittany was also remembering that day, only now she saw it from a different angle. "Mittens," she mumbled as memories that weren't hers played themselves out.

ʘ ◆ Ž

Brittany looked down at herself stroking the bunny's fur, but she wasn't herself.

You've been complaining for days! Now's your chance! Brittany heard herself think.

"Emily, it's not that simple." E.V.'s voice was different: frail, sad, and old.

Make it that simple, Gran, or I swear I'll go straight to my dad tonight! He may not believe me, but he'll be concerned enough to have me committed. I'll make sure of it! How would that do for you? Me locked up in a padded cell, no one to snack on!

E.V. stretched and wriggled. It knew this would not end well, but it was so hungry it had to do something. How it wished Brittany would move closer and that it had enough strength to reach out and touch...

Enough! Emily's voice scolded.

Its tentacles weren't as strong as it liked. The process of reaching out felt hard. The animal's fur was confusing, like being under water and not knowing which way was up. Then mercifully, the pulse was detectable; like a beacon E.V.

followed it. Five ounces wasn't nearly enough, but it was more than the animal could spare. A thought formed: *make a jump*. E.V. considered this. Emily would collapse before Brittany's eyes, but would Brittany touch the bunny before she tried to help? If she didn't, there was no guarantee how long it could survive in the animal.

Emily pulled her hand back. She'd seen the creature's thoughts. She saw the desire, the lust E.V. had for Brittany, and she saw how fragile her life really was. It could leave her like that, at any moment, and there would be no way Emily could stop it.

She became a bit more cooperative after that. However, Vampire Gran had a terrible time transferring the bunny's blood into something it could use, so it missed Emily's real plans.

ᘛ ◆ ᘚ

Without meaning to E.V. replayed its last memories in Emily's body.

Brittany gasped and put her hand to her chest. It hurt. "Why does it hurt?"

"Don't worry, it was just a silly memory." E.V.'s voice was soft, regretful.

"I thought you said you didn't remember the same way I do?"

"I don't," It said. "But you remember with all five senses— when my memories become yours, you experience them that way."

"Oh."

TWENTY-FOUR

ENRAGED

"HOW LONG DO we have until we need more blood?" Brittany asked, trying to return to her previous questions.

E.V. didn't have a lot of practice in being fed so well. It was a blessing and a curse. The more it got, the more it used, the more it needed. It would be a never-ending cycle— at least in the beginning, which is exactly where they were. "I'm sorry."

Brittany huffed but held back on repeating the question. E.V. was the master of evasion, or when that didn't work, at speaking in riddles. Instead Brittany wondered aloud, "Em, how did you manage?"

It wasn't a slip— it was deliberate. She was tired of looking at and speaking to her best friend (or a very convincing image of her) and not treating this vision as if it were... Emily.

"Em." Brittany's voice broke as she realized how much she missed her best friend.

"Emily didn't do as well as you," E.V. finally answered.

"No!" Brittany snapped loudly then listened to determine if she had woken her siblings. "No," she hissed, "I don't want to talk to YOU, I want my friend back! I can see her and you sound just like her, and sometimes you act like her too! You just showed me her memory, so let me have her. You said she's a part of you. You've taken everything else from me. Give her back to me."

E.V. kept its eyes downcast, twisting its hands in its lap. "I'm not her."

"Just pretend!" Angry tears pricked at Brittany's eyes. "Pretend like you are and talk to me the way she would have."

Memories flooded out of E.V.: an itchy foot, the sun gleaming over a wheat field, Mr. Daminko standing in front of his silver car, a brick building (it was their school), and finally Brittany's figure formed in her head: she was looking at herself through Emily's eyes. The feelings that accompanied the vision were beyond what Brittany expected; loyalty, respect, delight, relief, and lastly a desire to protect.

"On Gran's farm, all I could think about was you," E.V. said, but its voice was softer. As much as E.V. had Emily's voice, Brittany now heard that it had never sounded like Emily. "Gran didn't make it past the first week. She was sick from the moment we arrived and my mom needed to be by her side almost constantly. Mom was a wreck. She couldn't even remember why she'd left Dad. And then Gran was dead and Mom had to take care of the funeral and the estate and loads of other arrangements. And she was tired all the time, right from the moment we arrived."

Brittany searched E.V.'s face, fighting the shiver that tried to work its way up her spine. As E.V. spoke, Brittany could see it. She heard the sound of something falling to the wooden floor of the hundred-year-old farmhouse. The thud was unique, but there was no way to detect what had fallen until Emily went to investigate.

Gran lay motionless. Her old skin hung loose as if she wore a garment a size too big. Emily had run to her, fallen on her knees before her, screamed— in that order.

When her mom had run in to see what the commotion was, Emily had stood to try and back out of her way. In her haste, Emily's mother pushed her daughter aside, and in the chaos Emily had stepped on her Gran's bare foot.

Of course she'd leapt off it twice as quickly, but from that moment forward Emily couldn't get the feel of her Gran's cold, unyielding foot out of her head. It played and replayed itself for weeks.

"Oh, Em."

"It wasn't supposed to be me," the vision of Emily sobbed. "It was supposed to be my mother. She'd been called to the farm by Gran— it wasn't me the creature wanted." E.V. looked up, deep into Brittany's eyes. "It didn't want me! But it wanted YOU."

Brittany jumped back at the unexpected jealousy, not only in Emily's voice, but that she could feel coursing through her.

"Stop," Brittany commanded.

E.V. obeyed.

"Why did you show me that?" Brittany touched her forehead, trying to forget everything she'd just seen.

E.V. shrugged.

"You know that wasn't very nice. I asked you for my old friend and you gave me this."

"I gave you Emily, the parts of her that remain in me."

"Do you feel like that about me?"

"Like what?"

"Angry, jealous?"

"Yes, I have kept Emily's anger and even her jealousy, but I also have her compassion, respect, adoration, and love."

"Can't you just give me my friend, the way I remember her?"

"No. I can't give you *your* memories of Emily— I don't own those. I can only give you mine."

"Then can you at least give me a nicer one?"

E.V. concentrated.

∞ ◆ ∞

"Don't do this." Emily stood before herself, gazing into a mirror.

"Your time is done," Gran's frail voice replied. "It's too late for you. You have failed. We are finished."

Emily stared wide-eyed, looking as if she wanted to cry.

"Pick my father," Emily begged.

"You know I can't."

∞ ◆ ∞

"Wait," Brittany interrupted.

E.V. tilted its head for Brittany to continue.

"Why couldn't you?"

E.V.'s eyebrows came together in frustration and just when Brittany was sure it wouldn't answer, it did. "Antibodies."

"Antibodies?"

"Yes, when I extract blood from someone, a small percentage of my fluids are released into their body. They develop antibodies against it just like they would for a cold or virus. Once they've developed these antibodies, I am no longer able to convert them. I can't possess someone who I've fed off of."

The ramifications of what E.V. was saying were vast. First, there was the realization that Emily had never allowed the creature to feed off Brittany. It also meant that Brittany's father, and Coby, and her mom, and even her stepfather were all safe from being infected if E.V. left her. But that also meant that her siblings weren't.

TWENTY-FIVE

MOURNED

"WAIT A MINUTE." Brittany felt triumphant as she saw a hole in E.V.'s story. "Emily said you'd never intended to infect her ('infect' was the only way Brittany could describe what E.V. had done, and the creature didn't argue the term), but that can't be true."

"Why not?" E.V. smiled.

The smile reminded Brittany of the way her mother would look at her when she'd brought home a good report card. Brittany could experience E.V.'s feeling— it was as if the creature was proud of her. But it couldn't be more than the way some people thought about their car, Brittany thought. The creature would appreciate each of its human hosts simply for being its hosts.

Brittany couldn't have been more wrong. E.V. liked Brittany a lot more than any previous host.

"In Emily's memories," Brittany continued, "she said that her mother was always tired. Her Gran had convinced Mrs. Daminko to leave her husband and bring her daughter to the farm, right?"

One eyebrow rose on E.V.'s face.

"Ok, perhaps there was some kind of mind control Gran possessed over her daughter?"

E.V. went to scoff but Brittany steamrolled over its response.

"Regardless, Mrs. Daminko was 'tired all the time.' There is only one reason for that." Brittany fixed the illusion of Emily with a hard stare. "You couldn't have infected Mrs.

Daminko— you had already taken from her. She would have had antibodies. You needed someone else."

There was a pause, then E.V. conceded with a solemn nod.

"So you had always intended to infect Emily."

Another nod.

"Then why did Emily think you hadn't? Why did you let her think that?"

If E.V. were being honest, it would have to admit that it had been a poor calculation. In the beginning, Emily had been so fragile, so scared, and so utterly unable to cope. She couldn't function thinking that her loving, protective, adoring Gran had done this to her on purpose. So E.V. had allowed Emily to believe that it had been an accident. As time wore on, it saw the trouble in this: as they started to forge the bond needed, Emily never felt important or special. Then, when E.V. had exposed its lust for Brittany, Emily felt even more worthless.

"That was a big mistake," E.V. admitted.

"Ya," Brittany agreed, watching the creature's memories.

"But in my defence, I wouldn't have felt so attracted to you if Emily hadn't been so infatuated with you herself. She didn't let me touch you. She thought of you almost constantly. She adored you. Idolized you. Before we'd returned she talked about you every day. I felt like we, you and I, were already friends. By the end, I was anxious to meet you."

Brittany shivered. It was creepy to think of her friend acting that way, but she had been no better herself. For every day Emily had been away she thought about, talked about, longed for, and missed her very best friend. Brittany stifled a snicker as she remembered the look she'd caught on Coby's face, more than once, when she was rambling on and on to him about Emily.

"She was a good friend," Brittany sighed. "I miss her."

"Ok." E.V. also sighed... then its voice got softer. It dredged up Emily out of its memories so she could talk to Brittany. "I was terrified. I was sure I was going insane. Less than a week after my Gran died, she started visiting me in my room at night— it was creepy. Then as the days passed, and the start of school was getting closer and closer, she started visiting during the day. In her garden, in her barn, in her living room— I couldn't get away from her. And she started to tell me I needed to… but I couldn't. I couldn't take people's blood— do you know how wrong that would be?"

The tears that had threatened to fall finally broke loose and flowed down Brittany's face. Warm drops pooled on her shirt.

"Is that what you needed?" E.V. asked.

"I don't know," Brittany replied, sounding winded as her tears came faster and fiercer.

E.V. allowed Brittany the time she needed to collect herself. Once she was mostly done, it started to speak. "We…"

Brittany cut it off. "Ya, I feel it. We need more blood." Emily's last words echoed in Brittany's head. *I couldn't take people's blood— do you know how wrong that would be?*

"I can do my best to survive on as little blood as possible," E.V. said. "But I will need your help."

"How?"

"My blood isn't the same as yours. It is stronger and more potent, but it doesn't last outside of your body. When you spit, cry, blow your nose, you are using up my blood. Even some is lost in the act of breathing. In time I'll teach you how to conserve what you can by breathing less often. You won't ever catch a cold again, so you shouldn't sneeze or blow your nose. All that's left is spit and crying— that you'll have to try and manage better."

Brittany felt empty. This thing was going to turn her into a stone— inside and out. Petrified organs and stone-cold emotions.

"Where are we getting our next boost from?" E.V. asked.

Brittany rolled her eyes. *Boost*— like she was an addict looking to score her next hit.

E.V. didn't ask about Brittany's siblings, but the creature's longings were all too clear.

"I'll come up with something," Brittany said.

TWENTY-SIX

HUNTED

OVERLY BRIGHT, UNNATURAL, fluorescent bulbs lit the convenience store. It was quiet. Not many patrons came to this location at one in the morning. The attendant was a dark-skinned younger man. He mildly took note of Brittany walking in then went back to reading his magazine.

Brittany walked up one aisle and down the next. Nothing appealed to her. She had never been one for craving candies (that was more Emily's weakness). Yet, for a minute, Brittany missed the *idea* of eating them. It was a little disheartening to know that no chocolate bar, nor any bag of chips, would ever smell appealing ever again. She longingly remembered the time when they had.

"You know, out of every change, Emily had the worst time with that," E.V. offered. "Food, to Emily, had been so much more than sustenance. She used it almost like a drug to alter her moods. I had a lot of work to do to repair some of her more stubborn thought patterns. We just weren't a right fit in so many ways."

Did Emily ever feed you? How did you keep her alive? Brittany mused.

"Something you have to remember was that my infiltration of Emily wasn't accelerated like it's been with you. And I was able to find a food source sooner.

"While I was Gran, I'd been taking an ounce or two from the mother. When I transferred over to Emily I was able to continue before she was even aware of me. When her father took her home I automatically started to extract from

98

him, upping my intake to three or four ounces as my needs increased. But eventually that wasn't enough. Emily and I had a lot of arguments over this; she refused to feed us, keeping me half-starved and herself in a constant state of weakness and pain."

Brittany could feel the pain of it from the creature's memories— hunger that went unsatisfied for weeks lending itself to the already uncomfortable unfamiliarity of a new host. But Brittany didn't want to experience the sensation of this— she didn't want to have any reason to feel bad for E.V.

Suddenly the hairs at the base of Brittany's neck stood up. She looked around and saw the clerk's eyes on her. She could read the mistrust in them— he was pegging her for a shoplifter. *Twice in one day,* she thought as she grabbed three random chocolate bars. When she got up to the counter she deliberately handed the attendant one bar at a time, being sure to make contact with each pass.

"Will that be all?" the clerk asked, sounding put out for being taken away from his magazine.

Did we get enough? Brittany asked. She'd felt the creature working with each brief contact. Her thumb stung as if she'd received a paper cut.

"Barely," E.V. answered, "but we'd better not push our luck." It was watching the attendant wearily.

He rang the purchases through and Brittany paid him without being able to get direct contact again. The way E.V.'s thoughts were going, Brittany was sure E.V. wouldn't take any more even if she gave it the chance.

"What's wrong?" Brittany asked as she took a short cut down a seemingly deserted alley. She was heading back to her mom's house.

"He tasted... off. His blood tasted sour."

Brittany stopped walking to face E.V. "Has that ever happened to you before?"

"Sometimes..." E.V. had a look upon its face as if it were trying to recall. "Actually, I can't remember if it's happened before."

"So, what was wrong with him?"

E.V. shrugged.

"Could it be," Brittany hated to think it, it felt so prejudiced, "an ethnic thing?"

"No," E.V. was quick to answer. "Blood is blood."

Brittany hesitated, but she had to ask. Her thumb was bugging her too much to leave it be. "Is that why I have this cut on my thumb? Was there something wrong with his blood?"

Now E.V. looked guilty. "No, it wasn't his blood, but it is a problem with blood. I didn't take enough. I need more. Once I get the right amount I'll be able to patch that up."

Brittany thought back to all of Emily's cuts, so similar. It made her shiver.

"Like I told you," E.V.'s voice was soft in Brittany's head, "Emily kept me half-starved."

"So if you are properly fed I shouldn't have these kinds of wounds? What causes them?"

E.V. now looked even guiltier. "That would be me. I have to break through your skin to penetrate into theirs. Your skin is no more resilient than a sheet of paper. When I extract the right amount, I can fix the damage I've caused. If I don't get enough…"

"But you chose not to take enough." *Why should I have to suffer for your choice?*

"Brittany, he tasted wrong! Would you drink milk if it tasted sour?"

"Fine." Brittany crossed her arms. "So why did he taste wrong? Do you think he was sick or something?"

E.V. had already guessed that might be the reason, but it didn't reply as they became aware of the sound of someone approaching.

"Who you talking to, pretty?" This voice was male, but the crunching of footsteps told both Brittany and E.V. that there was more than one of them.

Brittany swung around to face two men. Both appeared to be in their early twenties. Something about them made them look out of place in the upper class neighborhood. One wore an eager, hopeful expression; the other seemed more hesitant.

"Max, tell me you didn't drag me all the way out here for this," the hesitant one almost whimpered.

Max rolled his eyes as he glanced back at his companion. He was quick to return his gaze to Brittany as he replied, "Who am I to argue when fate puts a fox in my path."

"I'm not here to hunt fox. We have bigger game to trap." Max's companion wouldn't even look in Brittany's direction. "Leave her or I'm leaving."

"Tom, check it out— she's clearly high. What's the trouble in a little fun before we get to other things?"

"I'm serious!" Tom tried to sound tough, but Brittany could smell the fear rolling off him. "I'll leave. I will not be a party to trapping fox. It's illegal."

"So are the other plans we had for tonight." Max was slowly making his way over to Brittany, cautiously, like she really was a fox that might spook and run. And she had to wonder why she wasn't running.

When Max had moved within reach of Brittany, a triumphant grin spread across his thin lips. He was sure that he had her. The girl would never be able to outrun him now. As he started to reach out, he almost hoped she would try. He thought of the pleasure he'd take in chasing her, overcoming her, throwing her to the ground, and pinning her there. Then he'd mash his hand over her mouth to stop her screams as he forced himself on her.

TWENTY-SEVEN

CORNERED

BRITTANY WAS CALM— almost serene. The gloom of the alley and the dark of night hadn't impaired her sight in the least. If she were to try to recall these two men, she was sure she could remember every detail, right down to the pattern of acne scars on Max's face. Yet, somehow, she knew she wouldn't have to remember how they looked. She wouldn't be telling anyone about the two men who attacked her.

As Max made his way closer to her, she noted how well-built he was: hard muscles flexed under his thin sweater. Regardless, Brittany knew that everything E.V. had done made the man no match for her, not even both together— not even ten. She could have outrun them, even at this close proximity, but she had a different idea in mind. She moved so that her back was against a tall fence.

E.V., can you cut other people with your tentacles?

E.V. had enough human experience to know that Brittany's calm was rare. But to want to cut? To what end? "I don't understand." E.V. shook while it stood between Brittany and the man, even though it was invisible to Max. *Why wasn't Brittany more terrified? Why was it terrified when it was certain it would survive this?*

When Max grabs me, I want you to take as much blood as you need. *Once you're done, I want you to cut him so he bleeds out.*

Brittany had watched Max approach. When he pushed himself against her, she could feel the heat coming off his body. She watched his neck, sensing his pulse; she felt drawn to it. Soon she was holding herself against the fence, trying not to throw herself onto him.

Brittany wanted to rip, to tear, to cut and to suck, but it was E.V. that did that. So she waited for the creature in her to catch up.

E.V. stood to the side, watching. It was confused.

I'm giving you permission to take from him, but when you're done cut him so he bleeds! Brittany hissed in her head. *That way when he's found by the police, they'll think that he was stabbed*.

"Oh," E.V. said, but it still didn't like it. "But why don't we just suck him dry?"

Because if you do that, we'll have a dead body. A dead body with no blood. Brittany remembered the fuss that was made over Emily's body. Death by stabbing didn't seem to be the issue. It was the lack of blood. *If it looks like he's been stabbed, no one will look for any other explanation for it. We need to be careful to not leave suspicious clues.*

"Oh." E.V. was thrown off-balance by how logical Brittany was being. It didn't want to be logical— it wanted to be highly illogical. It wanted this man far away from Brittany. Better yet, it wanted this man dead, never able to touch Brittany again.

Max felt triumphant as he pushed himself up against the girl. Now he was able to feel how toned and shapely she was. It was so hard to tell what shape people were under all their winter bulk. With her pinned under him, he admired her curves. He'd only been lucky enough to do this once before, and it had been a much more complicated procedure. He couldn't believe how fortunate he was tonight when he hadn't even been looking for it.

"I'm out of here," Tom said without a backwards glance.

Max brought his hand up to Brittany's face. He was able to block her mouth and most of her nose. He applied pressure, perhaps more than he needed. Even if she wasn't going to play the part of an unwilling victim, there wasn't anything that said he had to act any less aggressive.

Brittany could have easily thrown him off. She stayed statue still. *Not yet!* She thought as she felt the creature stretching forward.

"Why not!" The look on E.V.'s face was for murder.

Not the hand. Who ever heard of a lethal cut to the hand? No, give me a moment, I'll reach a much better spot.

E.V. was nervous and couldn't understand why. It didn't like the man's hands on its human and wasn't sure it could wait even a millisecond more. "Hurry up!"

Max was starting to think his victim wasn't just stoned, but really, really stupid. She didn't fight him— she didn't try to squirm free. She wasn't even trying to yell. This didn't stop him. He was going to have his way with her. He was intoxicated by his imminent victory.

That's when the girl seemed to find some fight.

"There you are, sweetheart, I thought you'd gone away." Max felt exhilarated. It was so much more fun when they tried to fight. He pressed himself tighter to her as her hand seemed to be pushing at his waist. It's too late, he thought. Squirm as she might, he had her right where he needed.

Brittany's hand wasn't pushing, it was pulling, un-tucking his shirt and snaking her fingers under his sweater. The moment she made contact with his skin, everything changed.

Max felt it. One moment he was fully in control. Victorious. The next he was struggling against his numb limbs. His ears began to ring, his sight dimmed, and then he was falling. He kept falling; he wasn't sure if he'd ever hit the ground or if he'd just keep falling into some great cosmic abyss.

"Pig!" Brittany spat, looking down at the unconscious face of her attacker. She pulled her right foot back and swung it forward with all her might. She'd forgotten her increased strength, but the snap that signified the breaking of his ribs reminded her.

She watched, satisfied, as the small red stain on his shirt started to grow.

"Such a waste," E.V. sighed.

"Did you get enough?" Brittany noted that there were no new cuts on her hand, and the one from earlier had healed.

"I got close to three pints before he fell." E.V. looked down at Max with longing. Three would last a while, but not as long as four or five.

"Good job on the cut," Brittany said. She watched as the crimson from the fresh blood stained Max's stomach. Then she had to look away as a desire to bend down and take more… to take it all, started to overtake her.

"I think your kick did most of that," E.V. said.

"He was a pig." Brittany squeezed her eyes shut as her desire grew. It was hard to tell if this was all from E.V.'s longings, or if the blood that was oozing out also called to her.

CR ♦ SO

"There could have been a far easier way to extract from that Max," E.V. said as Brittany sat on the swing set in her mother's backyard.

She was swaying mindlessly, her thoughts on the two men as she replayed the events. "Maybe…"

"Absolutely." E.V. thrust its ideas of how the night should have gone into Brittany's mind.

E.V. would have been the attacker, not the victim. It would have lunged forward and grabbed both men. It would have squeezed until their wrists snapped at the same time as it extracted from them— sucking each dry and leaving them in a twisted heap so that whoever found them wouldn't know where one began and the other ended. Or better yet, bury them so deep under the ground that no one would find them again.

Brittany didn't mind most of the images E.V. gave her. The idea of it didn't feel wrong (as she knew it should) and that was what terrified her. "I'm not a killer," Brittany whispered, realizing how easy it would for be her to become one.

She continued to replay the events from the night. She'd heard the siren when she was a block away. She kept her ear trained on them, listening as they discovered Max and started rescue attempts. From where she'd stopped she could hear as they revived Max and loaded him into the ambulance with a weak but stable pulse.

E.V. had been furious. It had wanted the man, both men, dead. Brittany wondered if the creature had been upset because it didn't like to consider itself weak, or if it was feeling defensive because of what Max had tried to do to her.

"That man deserved to die," E.V. said.

Brittany wasn't sure she agreed. She thought of him lying unconscious. Not of the blood, but his face. He was a human being. What gave her the right to take away his life?

"He would have taken yours! He would have violated you and left you for dead. He doesn't deserve any better."

Brittany sighed. "I don't have the right to decide that. Besides, even if I did believe it, what gives me the right to be the one who carries it out?"

E.V. glared. Brittany was far too rational, and her rationality was ebbing its anger away.

Brittany's thoughts had turned to Coby. "Will he ever be able to touch me like that?"

E.V. conjured up the image of Max pressed up against Brittany's body— hard and violent, with the intent to hurt.

"Not like that." Brittany shook her head to dispel the vision. "Coby could never be like that." She thought of Coby. His kind eyes— she'd only just started to notice the way they followed her; his warm hands as he held hers, trying to drive the chill from them; his soft lips, supple and sweet as he leaned forward until they touched her.

E.V. understood.

Brittany rested her head against the chain to the swing. She wouldn't ask again— she was afraid of the answer. Instead she sat listening to the sounds of the early morning suburb.

TWENTY-EIGHT

HATED

AS THE SKIES lightened with the impending return of the sun, Brittany heard all sorts of things: frost thawing; ice settling; a neighbor shovelling his driveway a block away; a couple arguing a few houses down; another couple— not arguing; her sister's breathing as she lay asleep in her bed; her brother's shallow breathing as he lay awake in his crib; Ed's deep snores and her mother's lighter ones.

Even though Brittany wasn't tired, she knew it was time to return to her room to at least pretend she'd slept. She didn't have to wait long. Half an hour later her brother started to fuss. She got up with him, only hesitating a moment as she went to pick him up.

I don't have to tell you to keep your tentacles to yourself, do I?

E.V. didn't respond, but its intentions were clear. It had no plans of ruining things between them. It kept its longings buried and as far from Brittany as possible.

The time was closing in on noon when Brittany's mother finally stumbled downstairs. "Wow, I'm so tired." A yawn punctuated her statement.

"Well, the kids have been fed and gone back down for their naps." Brittany looked at her mother, noticing a dark bruise on the inside of her arm. She wasn't going to say anything, but her mom caught her staring and looked down.

She gasped. "Oh, my, I wonder how I got that."

The answer was forming in Brittany's mind. She remembered back to Coby's bruises, then to her father's palms. As she put it together, she knew that Ed would have a similar mark on the back of his hand.

Brittany didn't say anything about it until she was walking home. It was closing in on dinnertime. She'd stayed to help her mom with the kids all afternoon and even cooked them supper before she left. As the day wore on, her mood slipped. The appearance of Ed and the confirmation of an excessively deep bruise on the back of his hand didn't help.

"Brittany, what's wrong?" E.V. asked.

You leave bruises when you take blood, Brittany answered.

E.V. couldn't see what the issue was. "So?"

So? What are people going to think if everyone I know starts to show up with bruises on them?

"It's never been a problem before," E.V. said.

Never? Somehow Brittany didn't believe it.

"Never," E.V. insisted, but it was lying.

"Umhmmm." Brittany nodded as she saw the truth.

"I still don't understand the problem?"

Don't you think that if everyone I touch gets bruises, someone will get suspicious?

"Suspicious of what?"

Of me!

"How? Why would they?"

"Because I leave bruises." Brittany stopped walking. "No, I don't— you do!"

"Do you know how ridiculous you sound?" E.V. was offended. "Have you ever heard of anything like that? Everyone bumps themselves from time to time— don't tell me you've never gotten a bruise you couldn't place. Trust me, a few bruises will not cause suspicion."

Brittany knew this was true. What she was really furious about was that E.V. was hurting the people she cared about. "I hate you," Brittany said. But she also knew that she was just as guilty— so what if *she* didn't leave the marks with her teeth. There was no difference between a bite mark from her or a hicky from E.V.

E.V. watched intently from the corner of its eye.

Brittany's thoughts were turning to Coby— wondering how he was doing. That was where most of her anger came from. She was worried for him. Worried that he could have died. Worried because she could have killed him.

"His home's not far from here. You could go see him."

Brittany didn't respond. She didn't need to; she'd already turned to walk in that direction.

03 ◆ 80

"Where's your mom?" Brittany asked when Coby answered the door. His face was pasty white and he was sweating from exertion. But looking at him gave Brittany an indescribable sense of relief. She was relieved to see that he was still alive.

"She's ouw gebbing me thome ith -ream," he mumbled like he had something in his mouth.

Coby's smile was wide as he stared at Brittany. The worst part about being sick was that he would miss seeing her, he'd thought. Now that she was here he was jubilant. Even if he wasn't up for the visit, he would never send her away. "You loob bether."

"What's wrong with...?" Brittany came to the answer before she finished the question: *His tongue. You took blood from his tongue and now it's bruised*!

E.V. stayed quiet.

"It'th na ath bad ath ith thounds," Coby mumbled, holding the door wider.

Brittany hesitated before stepping in. She felt as if she was death, and he was so eager to invite her in. She thought about leaving. She didn't like it— in fact, the thought made her want to cry.

"I can make sure he doesn't get hurt again." E.V.'s words were filled with concern. "I promise I will."

Brittany continued to contemplate leaving. Leaving Coby's house, leaving her dad's, leaving her mom's. She thought about taking herself away to somewhere where she couldn't hurt the people she loved. But as she thought this she stared at Coby and realized that she couldn't leave him.

She felt herself gliding through the doorway almost as if she was under his spell.

"Buth enoub abou me." Coby stopped to swallow. "You— you ook bether now!"

"It must have been one of those twenty-four hour bugs." Brittany turned towards Coby to make sure he hadn't fallen over. He stood almost clinging to the door.

He wobbled and Brittany leapt so that she was next to him. Without a thought she put an arm around his waist and helped him over to the couch, where it appeared he'd come from. As she helped him down, Brittany was thankful of one thing— E.V. hadn't tried to take any more of his blood.

"I wouldn't take from him again— not now." E.V. was offended. "How many times do I have to tell you: I am not a monster! In fact, I promise you that I will *never* take Coby's blood again."

Coby shivered and Brittany drew the blankets around him.

"I guess thath goob news," he mumbled then sighed, leaning into the cushions. "Tha means I should tharth to feel bether soon."

Brittany had turned away, willing her tears to freeze before they fell. The last thing she needed was to use up more blood. The quicker she did, the sooner she'd be condemning someone else to this miserable state.

"He'll be fine," E.V. soothed. "Maybe not in twenty-four hours, but soon enough." When Brittany didn't respond, it continued, "I've been doing this for centuries. Trust me, he'll be back to normal in no time."

"I wish," Brittany muttered aloud.

"Wha?" Coby asked as E.V. also inquired the same, only better articulated.

Brittany turned back wearing a sad smile. "I just wish there was something I could do to help."

Coby chuckled. "It'th jus a bug."

Brittany chuckled back darkly.

"Iron," E.V. offered. "He needs iron. He'll need to eat a lot of iron-rich foods."

Brittany thought briefly about ignoring its advice and staying mad. She watched as Coby struggled to keep his eyes open.

"Let me make you something to eat." She left him barely conscious on the sofa.

Having visited many times during the summer, she'd become almost as adept in Coby's kitchen as he was. *What has iron in it*? If she had spoken out loud, her voice would have been so high from panic, it might have squeaked.

"Calm down, he'll be fine soon enough."

Soon enough isn't *soon enough*!

"Ok, I've got just the thing that will help." E.V. directed Brittany in making a rather disgusting drink consisting mostly of orange juice and molasses. Even if it hadn't smelled rancid to her, she couldn't see herself drinking it. It looked like congealed puke.

Brittany brought the concoction out to Coby.

He seemed happy to discover, as he took a cautious sip, that it didn't taste as bad as it looked. Once he was done, his eyes drooped and closed. Brittany let herself out.

"Would you stop obsessing about him!" E.V. snapped as they drew closer to Brittany's home.

Brittany couldn't. He'd looked so pale, so weak, so sick. She'd stopped the tears that continued to want to fall, but the feelings persisted. She'd hurt Coby. In taking what she needed, she'd made him suffer. Brittany's existence had become dependent on other people's sacrifices— and they didn't even get a choice about it.

TWENTY-NINE
CONTINUED

"I DON'T HAVE to take as much," E.V. said. "Like I've told you— if I am fed properly, no one will have to suffer like Coby. I am sorry about Coby," It added quietly, "and your mother... and your stepfather..."

Brittany walked into her father's house feeling miserable and distracted.

"Where have you been?" Her father's voice was filled with concern. "Your mom said you left over an hour ago. And where's your jacket? Really, what were you thinking, Brittany? You've been sick. You shouldn't be walking home on your own like that."

"And your dad," E.V. added

Brittany took note of how heavy his eyelids looked, along with the deep bags under his eyes. She wondered if he'd accept an iron-boosting drink as readily as Coby had. She sighed. "It's ok, Dad. I'm feeling better. Besides, Mom and Ed weren't feeling well enough to give me a ride." She was still too preoccupied to notice the third person in the room.

"O! Britty, babe!" The voice had been high and grating on Brittany's ears even before she could hear better. Now it seemed to resound right through her. "I would have come to pick you up."

The woman who owned the voice didn't give Brittany a chance to deny her a hug as she flung herself at the girl.

Ella Dean had been dating her father for just over a year, and thankfully he'd kept Ella away until he was sure she was the one... Unfortunately, he'd decided that she was. Ella was a tall woman with sharp features and even sharper emotions. "Wearing your heart on your sleeve" wasn't enough of a description for it— she wore her heart on her sleeve, and it bled on everyone she came in contact with.

"Thank you, Miss Dean," Brittany said, trying to free herself from the woman's octopus grasp.

"No, no," Ella said, keeping her arms firmly around Brittany's neck, "you call me Ella."

"No, no, I couldn't." Brittany continued to try and break free without breaking the woman's arms. In her exasperation she thought, *Now from her I don't mind if you take a bit of blood. Take a little extra if you have to.* She had a happy image of Ella being as tired as Coby and not being able to visit.

But Brittany didn't feel E.V. working and eventually was able to break free from the woman's incredibly determined grip without hurting her.

"Isn't she just the best?" Brittany's father had come over. Ella had transferred from clinging to Brittany to supporting her father.

"The best," Brittany muttered, trying not to scowl.

"She made dinner." Brittany's father started to move himself, and his girlfriend, in the direction of the kitchen. It hurt Brittany to witness how much her father was leaning on Ella to make it across the room.

"You know, Dad, maybe I shouldn't have walked home. I think I need to go lie down." Brittany started in the direction of her bedroom.

Ella looked as if she wanted to complain, but Brittany's father stopped her by saying so softly Brittany shouldn't have been able to hear, "We'll talk about it later."

Ella continued to wear a large pout.

"Brittany, come back down when you feel up to it," her father called out.

She nodded and left with no intention of coming back down while Ella was there.

☙ ◆ ❧

"You really don't like her." E.V. was sitting on the edge of Brittany's bed as Brittany paced so softly that even she couldn't hear herself.

I really don't, Brittany fumed.

"What is it?" E.V. was puzzled. This dislike seemed to stem from something irrational, which wasn't like Brittany.

It's... Brittany stopped walking in circles and thought— nothing specific came to mind. She simply ended with, *it's everything.*

E.V. had caught the direction of Brittany's thoughts. "She's too young for your father, and too flighty, emotional, loud, bouncy, clingy— this list is long... Oh, but I guess the biggest strike against her is that she's not your mom."

Brittany just glared out the window.

"You know, she's very much like your mother," E.V. noted.

She's nothing like my mom! Brittany was furious and adamant that the two women weren't anything alike, no matter what evidence E.V. could show her.

Why didn't you take from her! Brittany said, *I told you to, why didn't you?*

"Because..." E.V. twisted its hands in its lap, "because she's pregnant."

"Well, great," Brittany sighed. "Now she'll never leave."

E.V. was confused. "I thought you liked babies?"

"Ya, cute ones. This one will no doubt be an ugly, clingy thing, just like its mom. And I'll have to watch it because Ella is just a baby herself."

"Do you think you'd let me take from it?"

"Sure," Brittany answered quickly, then thinking about it, she amended, "Probably not." She fell into her bed, rolling over onto her stomach to bury her head in her pillow.

Once most of her frustration had ebbed, she sat back up. "Why can't you take if someone is pregnant?"

"Because... because I just can't."

"Is it the hormones?" Brittany spoke softly so her voice wouldn't carry. "Can you taste them?"

"Yes, I can taste them."

"Oh," She was thinking about how much she'd changed. Because of E.V., she was no longer a normal girl. Everything was petrified— frozen. She wouldn't grow. She'd never get to be a normal woman... who knew if she could even have sex?

Brittany didn't feel human. She didn't feel alive. She might be a vampire or a zombie or something in between the two. She couldn't see anything good about this. She lay back down, burying her head in her pillow, willing herself not to cry.

When she woke up E.V. said softly, "Brittany, it will get better..."

"You can't promise that."

E.V. had nothing to say.

Brittany stood up. "We're hungry. We need to eat, again."

THIRTY
STRENGTHENED

BEFORE SHE LEFT the house, Brittany prepared her father a drink. Even though she could hear that all they were doing was sleeping, she wouldn't bother her father while Ella was over. She placed the cup in the fridge with her dad's name on it. Then she snuck out the back door and walked swiftly into the night.

The cold didn't bother her anymore. It didn't affect her as it had only a couple of weeks ago. She was aware that it was somewhere around minus seventeen, yet she'd only donned a hoodie, and that was only because E.V. insisted she wear something.

As they started down the bike path that ran behind the house, Brittany could feel E.V.'s terror.

"What are you afraid of?" Brittany wondered aloud as she continued to feel the building desire to pull the hoodie as far over her exposed head as possible.

When E.V. didn't reply, Brittany stopped walking. From the corner of her eye she noticed the way the nearly full moon was shining off the smooth white snow and reflecting back at her.

"Please, we are too exposed. Cover your head before someone sees… and put on some gloves too."

Brittany swung her hand up before her face and saw immediately what the problem was. It hadn't been the moon shining off the snow— it had been the moon shining off her and being reflected back at her from the snow.

"I'm glowing." Her hand looked like it had been dipped in the dye used for glow sticks. "Why am I glowing?"

"Come, we must cover ourselves and then find sustenance," E.V. urged.

"But why am I glowing?"

"Brittany, we need blood."

"Is that why I'm glowing?"

"No, but we must find food. Please cover up and let's go."

Brittany could feel the hunger— but she could also feel that it wasn't desperate. Not yet.

"Please, we'll talk about this later." E.V. exuded nervousness.

"No." Brittany planted herself down in a snowdrift then fidgeted to make herself comfortable. The snow didn't thaw under her, but it shifted and formed an imprint to her body. "I'm not going anywhere until you explain this to me."

E.V. sighed. "You'll get frostbite if you sit there too long."

"Will I?" Brittany raised an eyebrow in challenge.

"Ok, not so much frostbite, but..."

Brittany cut the creature off. "Out with it— tell me why I glow, and while you are at it, you may as well explain some other things I've been wanting to know about."

E.V. took a seat next to her. "It's the light."

"But I didn't glow last night or the night before."

"The moon has been hidden for the last few nights." E.V. looked up at the large glowing orb. It was fearful of the moon.

"Why are you frightened?"

E.V. didn't like being told that it was frightened. Worse, it didn't like feeling frightened. "I told you, my bodily fluid is different— that it evaporates quicker in the heat. Well, it also responds differently to the cold. If we get too cold we will reflect light like the snow does. This is mostly a problem at night because there is no warmth.

"A luminescent person is not normal," E.V. continued. "That used to be one of the few ways people could tell what we are. Then somehow over the centuries that myth was changed into: we don't come out during the day. Probably because we don't glow during the day. Regardless, when everyone was hell-bent on hunting vampires, I avoided the night."

Brittany could see that it still tried to avoid nighttime. Especially when the moon was full. It appeared that the brighter the moon, the more it affected E.V.'s host's skin.

"Regular light bulbs won't do this because they actually give off a small amount of heat. Also, inside is always warmer, so it is less likely to happen there, but it still can, especially during winter. The summer it is often warm enough, even at night, to avoid this effect. But right now it's the coldest part of the year so your skin is glowing."

Brittany waited for the creature to pause before she asked quietly, "But why?"

E.V. looked surprised. "Because of me. Me in you. You changed. What don't you understand about that?"

"I understand that I've changed," Brittany said. "I get that *you* did this to me, but why? Why? And don't tell me it's because of your blood— or bodily fluid. I get that! I'm asking why— what purpose does this serve?"

"I'm…" E.V. seemed flustered, "I'm not certain why. My hosts have always glowed, they just do."

"You'd think there'd be some reason for this? Like it helps you see better?"

E.V. shrugged. "If there is a reason, I'm not aware of it."

"You don't know? How can you not know? This is you— you should know about you."

"I don't." E.V. raised its voice. "Why should I know everything about me? Do you understand everything about you? Do you know why humans have tonsils? What is the reason for your appendix? You don't know— do you?" It crossed its arms. "Well, I don't know this about me. Some things that I did know have been lost over time. But there's no way of knowing if I ever knew."

Brittany and E.V. regarded each other for a few moments.

"Listen, you are the one who's so worried about appearing normal and fitting in," E.V. said softly. "In the winter everyone bundles up."

Brittany nodded.

"So bundle up."

Brittany didn't like being told what to do, but she listened anyway. "Better?"

E.V. nodded. "Better. Now, what else were you wanting to know about?"

Brittany wondered to herself what else E.V. wouldn't have answers for. Luckily, tonight, the creature had answers for the rest of Brittany's questions.

The story about vampires being powerless to garlic was a cautionary tale. Because he was unable to consume any food, when he had been forced to eat garlic he'd died within days. The creature had done everything in its power to save its human— but once a stomach is petrified all food that goes into it rots. E.V. especially disliked the smell of garlic because of this.

Wooden stakes, holy water, and crucifixes were all harmless.

"Decapitation would kill any host." E.V. rolled its eyes. "No human could survive that. And no matter how talented I am, I can't fix that kind of wound."

Of course, Brittany thought, *that would kill the* host— *but not the parasite. It would leave the creature unimpaired to infest the next person that comes along*. Most times the "next person to come along" was the very person who was hunting the vampire to begin with. Brittany didn't miss the irony.

Finally, the question that Brittany most feared was answered.

"Where did the myth of sleeping in a coffin come from?"

It hesitated for a fraction of a second. Brittany couldn't be sure, but she thought E.V. was suppressing a shudder. "That was brought about by the mean one. I told you he made sure no one would touch him so I'd stay trapped. He figured out that it was the only safe way to sleep. No one bothered him there, so I was deprived of any chance of escape while he was unconscious."

"Why do I still need sleep?"

E.V. appeared relieved at the subject change. "Easy— you are still human. Your brain still needs its REM to keep you sane. Humans don't function well when sleep-deprived. But a two-hour cycle once every two or three days should be enough."

Brittany nodded. "I can't think of anything else," she said. "But I'll let you know when I do," she added, knowing she was bound to think of other things later.

"I'm sure you will," E.V. said.

Sighing, Brittany stood then made her way to the all-night Walmart. Having touched one customer, two night clerks, and a cleaning lady, E.V.'s need for blood was finally quenched.

Brittany wandered home through the sleepy suburbs.

"You're getting very good at that," E.V. said. It was only an hour after they'd set out.

Brittany was about to nod, but instead she looked up to realize she was on Coby's street. She didn't remember deciding to go there, yet now that she was it felt right.

"You never answered my question about Coby," she said. "Will he ever be able to touch me... romantically?"

E.V. only hesitated to try and decide the best way to answer. "Well, as you've seen, you can touch people without me extracting."

But what about kissing? Brittany couldn't bring herself to say the words aloud.

"Yes, you can kiss." E.V. looked pained.

Brittany's emotions pulled the creature in wildly romantic directions. Then they plummeted as Brittany thought about how weak and sickly he'd been on her last visit.

"He will be better in a few weeks," E.V. promised. To Brittany, a few weeks felt like a few weeks too long, but she didn't say so— she didn't need to.

THIRTY-ONE

ADJUSTED

BRITTANY SAT IN a dark alley with her back against a discarded crate. She'd discovered several helpful tips over the past few weeks. Most important, she didn't experience pain the same way she used to— sitting on a hard or cold surface didn't cause her to get stiff, or even uncomfortable. However, if she sat like that for too long, people would notice, so she had to act like it did when they were watching.

She was alone now, so she sat statuesque.

Another thing to be careful of was that she didn't notice when she caught herself on corners, thorns, nails, or any sharp object that could easily tear her skin. When E.V. was well fed, this wasn't a problem— the creature's blood could fix the abrasion with no sign that it had happened in the first place.

When E.V. wasn't fed well enough, that small scrape, scratch, scuff, or graze could become a huge problem. It would gape and even weep, giving off precious liquids until it was fixed. Brittany wasn't aware of these accidents as they happened because there was no noticeable pain, so she had to rely on E.V. to tell her so she could top up her supply.

Brittany had finally been taught how to breathe less frequently. She still had to appear like everything functioned normally. She practiced for days on end to make sure the actions looked natural. She now appeared to be breathing twelve times per minute, when she was really doing it as little as once every few minutes, just to test the air.

Tonight Brittany sat with impeccable posture, waiting, smelling, consorting.

"Aaron isn't on tonight," she said to E.V., whose thoughts were longing for the young freckle-faced boy who worked at the twenty-four hour convenience store. "It's not his night. Tonight it would be Aziz."

E.V. made a disgusted face. There was still no answer to why Aziz tasted so sour and Aaron was so sweet and refreshing. E.V. compared the freckled boy's blood to a child's, or at least as close as it could describe. A child would still be even better. Brittany gave the creature a sharp reprimand any time its thoughts strayed to children.

"Just be glad we found Aaron," Brittany snapped.

E.V. wondered why Brittany still got defensive when it thought of the little people— any of them.

"What we do is already wrong. I won't cross that line."

E.V. saw no line, but it recognized Brittany's stubborn insistence and dropped it.

Brittany sat up a little taller as she focussed on listening. Someone was approaching. The wind was flowing in the right direction to catch their scent before she could make out their features.

The people were at the far end of the alley, coming from a less travelled direction. But the direction didn't matter— Brittany was in the prime position to intercept them.

The couple both walked with a slight stagger, clearly intoxicated. Within moments the smell from their breath confirmed Brittany's suspicions.

"Why are you taking me down here?" The girl giggled nervously.

"I told you," the man said with an edge of excitement, "I've got something I want to show you."

"Why couldn't you show me at the club?" The girl's voice was high— strained.

"Because," the man made an amused sound that came from deep in his throat, "the club was too busy— there was no place to be alone in there."

This being a Friday, the man was being honest. Brittany especially loved the weekend— she could get what she needed quicker with the extra traffic. That way they'd be done sooner. Once this part of her night was over, she could go on to more normal behavior.

E.V. interrupted Brittany's thoughts. "Showing up at Coby's house in the middle of the night is not normal behavior."

Fine, not normal then, but far more enjoyable.

"Speak for yourself."

Brittany was about to say that she'd never try and speak for E.V., but she stopped because she could sense something wasn't right.

The girl had stopped walking.

"What's the problem?" her companion inquired impatiently.

"It's really dark."

"Come on," he said, "are you afraid of a little dark? Don't worry, I'll be here to protect you."

The girl still hesitated. "I don't know. My mom told me not to follow strangers into dark alleys."

"Your mommy," the man taunted. "You still listen to your mommy? Come on, are you a girl or a woman?"

"I'm..." The girl seemed to deliberate.

In that moment Brittany pegged her voice, and she almost gave an audible curse. The girl *was* a girl. And worse, she went to Brittany's school. Brittany could remember hearing her voice in the cafeteria.

"What's the trouble?" E.V. wondered, not understanding Brittany's dilemma. "So we know her? So what?"

Brittany couldn't believe how childlike E.V.'s innocence was at times. *We can't take like we usually do*, she explained in exasperation. *Not in front of the girl.*

Brittany had learned to hang out in this alley because a lot of the bar traffic would pass through on its way to the parking lot. As they would come upon her, she'd pretend to be just as drunk as they were, bumping into them as she crossed paths.

In those brief moments of contact, E.V. could easily extract an ounce or two, which was the limit Brittany had set for the creature. Six or seven encounters were enough to last them to the next night. When it wasn't, Brittany had to do

123

the same while walking through the school halls, which she didn't like doing.

Even though E.V. complained that the high levels of alcohol from the bar traffic made its job harder, and more dangerous for those it took from, the guilt that Brittany felt taking from her classmates made this arrangement far more appealing for both.

There was another upside to this arrangement. Drunks often fall down. This made those mysterious bruises easier to explain. Also no one knew Brittany, so they could never draw the conclusion that the mark came from her— or, even if they did, they wouldn't be able to remember her.

"Ok, so we'll wait for the next person," E.V. said, preparing for Brittany to agree.

Brittany, however, rolled to her knees in a crouch, as if preparing to spring.

"What?" E.V. asked, feeling Brittany's heighten anxiety.

"I've changed my mind," the girl whimpered, "I don't want…"

"No, no." The man's voice had turned hard, cruel, and though it was completely different, to Brittany's ears it sounded exactly the same as her attacker from only a month earlier.

"It's not Max," E.V. said, trying to calm the emotions in Brittany's thoughts.

But Brittany wasn't upset, and she wasn't fearful. She was reliving her attack — the excitement that she felt knowing that she could stop it — more than stop it, she could deliver justice.

E.V., she thought with malice in her tone, *sharpen your tentacles!*

THIRTY-TWO
ATTACKED

BRITTANY STEPPED OUT from behind the bin where she had been waiting. She did it without making a sound, though it wouldn't have mattered. The man and girl were too distracted to notice her— especially so far away.

The girl seemed almost completely overcome with fear as she tried to pry the man's hand off her wrist. He was working to pull the girl further into the confines of the deserted alley where it would be harder for someone to sneak up on him.

I give you my permission to take up to two pints, Brittany said as she snuck forward.

"Two pints won't be enough to hurt him— not permanently," E.V. complained, sensing Brittany's intentions.

I don't want to hurt him permanently, just slow him down for a while. Brittany had gotten close enough that the man and the girl would be able to make her out, if they were looking.

The man was pulling the girl's wrist with such force her hand had turned an odd shade of red. Brittany could tell by the girl's eyes that she was in shock. The pupils were wide, like she wasn't seeing anything. She dragged her feet and whimpered but didn't scream.

"Please, I want to go back to my friends," she begged.

"Tisk, tisk, little girl, you shouldn't be playing grownup if you aren't willing to act the part."

Brittany had been rehearsing scenarios in her head of running up so fast they couldn't tell where she came from. Of shoving the guy so hard his body slammed up against the wall. Of coming up with some great line like, "I'll play your grownup game if you want" But she knew she couldn't do any of that.

Instead, she slowed her pace and made enough noise to catch their attention.

The man reacted instantly. He swung the girl so that she fell into him and caught her more gently than before. "Careful, Simone, I think you drank a little more than you should have."

Brittany saw the relief written clearly on Simone's face. It faded as she saw Brittany. If Simone recognized her, Brittany couldn't tell, but for a moment Simone's lips parted as if she were going to warn her. Instead, she tried one last effort to yank free of the man's hold.

The man wasn't fazed. He had sized Brittany up and had decided that she would be no match for him. He was so bold as to believe he would have his way with both girls.

Simone's body was attractive. A nice full-figured girl. She was wearing a top that clung and even stretched in places. However, Brittany, though not as developed, had a firmness that suggested something far more alluring under her oversized hoodie.

Clouds covered the moon tonight, so Brittany hadn't bothered with covering her face— besides, in the alleyway the buildings cast such perfect shadows that she didn't need to bother. Wearing her hood made her feel too sinister, like a true creature of the night. She might as well be wearing a robe with a cowl.

The man knew he was dealing with another adolescent. Where Simone had looked quite mature sipping her cocktail under the pulsing strobe lights of the hip bar, he wasn't fooled by this new one. She couldn't be much older than Simone, and if he had to wager a bet he'd guess she might even be younger. This assumption made him feel even more confident. He loved how the girls seemed to flock to this bar, and most nights they flocked to him.

Brittany had been approaching with her head tilted down. As she got within arm's length she looked up. She tried to appear startled like this was the first time she had noticed them. "I'm sorry." she took a false step back.

She wanted the man to lunge. It would put him off balance. Of course he'd expect Brittany to run, so he'd be thrown even more when she stood solidly, grabbed him, and used his momentum to make him fall forward. Brittany then expected that Simone would be able to break free of his grasp, and by the look in her eyes, Brittany knew she'd make a run for it. Brittany had been counting on it.

Nothing went according to her plan.

The man didn't fall forward, he fell back. Simone wasn't able to break free of his grasp, so instead of sprinting away, she was yanked down to the ground with him.

The intention Brittany had of resting a knee on the man's chest, pinning him to the ground and perhaps breaking a rib or two, wouldn't work now. Not with Simone watching. There would be no way to explain the clarity of thought that would have gone into making that kind of move. So Brittany improvised and fell onto the man.

With her petrified organs she was heavy enough to wind him as she did a pancake flop across his chest. Brittany slipped both her hands under the man's untucked shirt and immediately felt E.V. starting the extraction. E.V. complained bitterly at not being able to have a full meal, ever, as it obeyed her command to limit itself.

Before E.V. could finish, Brittany thought in a panic, *Don't cut him*!

"No cuts?" Now E.V. was completely confused. It didn't like the idea of cutting and wasting blood, but it was even more put off by the way plans were being changed so erratically.

No cuts, Brittany thought as she felt the man turning limp under her. *How will I explain a cut to Simone? I have nothing I could have cut him with.*

E.V. withdrew, sulking. It had left the man unconscious, ears ringing, head spinning, limbs numb, fighting to remember how to breathe.

Brittany immediately started to feel the effects of being so full. *How much did we take*?

With an innocent shrug E.V. replied, "Just over two pints." As the creature felt Brittany's anger intensifying, it added, "I didn't go over three."

Brittany cursed. Simone let out a choked wail.

"Are you ok?" Brittany asked as she pulled herself onto her hands and knees, draped over the man and Simone.

Simone didn't answer— panic still had its grip on her. She had been pinned by the man's arm as he fell. She now wriggled out from under it, realizing that he wasn't holding her down any more.

"Simone?" Brittany was standing. She reached down to offer the girl a hand. "Are you ok?"

"He was going…" Simone broke off in a choked sound. She had taken Brittany's hand, but suddenly Brittany wondered if it was a good thing that the girl was standing. She looked even less steady on her feet than she'd appeared leaving the bar.

Brittany continued to hold Simone as she bent forward and heaved on the pavement beside the man.

"Are you alright?"

Simone managed a weak shake of her head. Brittany pulled her closer to steady her as she escorted her back towards the bar. Simone fumbled, reaching into her pocket, and withdrew a cell phone. She dialled emergency and explained what had just happened between gasps and sobs.

The rest of the night was long, and though Brittany didn't have a problem with physical exhaustion any more, she felt mentally drained. Not only had Simone's friends and most everyone at the bar dubbed her a hero, but also the bartender was so impressed that he offered Brittany a free drink.

"I'm sorry." She looked up into the friendly face of a young man who appeared to have just reached twenty-one himself. "I'm underage. I don't drink."

He gave a wink. "I won't say a word."

The police had left at this point. They'd taken Simone home with a promise that they'd need to get a statement from Brittany sometime in the next few days.

Brittany shrugged at the bartender. "I still don't drink."

"Bret," he said, "call me Bret. Fine." He poured the glass he'd made for Brittany down the drain. "You don't drink. When you change your mind, you know where to find me. The first drink is on the house. Oh, and I work Mondays, Wednesdays, and the whole weekend." He gave an exaggerated bow.

"Oh, let me take just a taste from him, please?" E.V. said wistfully.

Brittany inclined her head. *How would it look if Bret got mysteriously tired?*

Bret's lips turned up at one corner and he winked again.

THIRTY-THREE

ADMIRED

WHY DID HE WINK? Brittany was pondering as she walked home.

"I think he likes you," E.V. answered. It was clear that the creature within Brittany liked him.

"Bret likes me?" In her surprise Brittany didn't check around her before she spoke aloud. Luckily she was alone. "Why?"

"What's not to like about you," E.V. responded, sounding proud. "My blood has made you your optimum weight, with muscles only where they are needed. Your breasts are firm and perky. Your waist is curvy and flawless. I have improved your skin tone and made your eyes shine. Even your hair and nails are benefiting because of me. We are beautiful!"

Brittany wanted to blush.

"Besides," E.V. added, "you are a hero."

That gave Brittany pause. She thought about that word: hero. Not just the word— the meaning behind it. She remembered back to Max. She hadn't felt guilty after she'd taken his blood, she'd felt justified. Tonight she felt the same way. After all, this guy had tried to take something from Simone, and Brittany was sure if he had gotten away with it, he would have stolen the same from her. He deserved to be taken from. The bruise E.V. gave him would be retribution. Brittany wasn't worried about him feeling tired tomorrow or even feeling tired for a few weeks — even better — a few months.

What if she could find people like this to take from every night? Then she'd never have to feel guilty again, and she wouldn't have to limit E.V. to a few ounces at a time. And what if allowing E.V. to take the blood they needed in turn saved someone else from being hurt by those people? Then she really could be a hero.

"Brittany?" E.V. looked over at Brittany. It was seeing her thoughts just as clearly.

"Think about it," Brittany said in a rush, "we could be doing good. Instead of stealing, we'd be, well, still stealing, but taking from someone who needs to be taken from."

E.V. envisioned a different kind of hero: one that would put a complete end to the bad guys. Its thoughts created a vision where the bad guy would be completely drained— none of this "back on his feet in a few weeks" business. The way E.V. would handle it was that NO ONE would see the bad guy ever again.

Brittany shook her head. "No, not like that. There is a fine line between being a hero and just a bigger bad guy."

There she is talking about lines again, Brittany heard.

"Don't you understand what I mean by a line?"

E.V. shook its head.

"It's like when I tell you to only take two ounces."

"Yes, I understand limits," E.V. snapped. "Where is this line you are referring to? Where does it say you have to be so moral? Where are you getting these ideas of right and wrong from? I've been here, on this earth, far longer than you, and I've never seen any handbook that says how far is too far. Why do you have such high standards about the way you treat other people?"

"That's easy," Brittany lowered her voice, "just treat people the way you'd want to be treated."

"Ya, I've heard people say that before. But you forget, I've seen into more people's heads than you could imagine. Those are just words— no one actually follows them."

Brittany saw E.V.'s perspective but didn't know how to explain it. All she could think of saying was: *the world is what you make it.* Brittany wanted a world that was kind and compassionate, so that's how she tried to act. E.V. still had objections; however, they dropped the subject as they arrived at Coby's house.

In the blink of an eye, Brittany had climbed his drainpipe and slipped through his open window. He slept, his face smooth and worry-free. Brittany tried not to recall that not long ago that would have been her sleeping peacefully. She missed feeling so innocent.

She could tell by the way his eyes rolled around under his lids that he was in REM— he'd be dreaming. Brittany barely slept now. She missed needing to sleep. Now she had so many extra hours, it was enough to make her crazy all by itself.

Coby smiled and Brittany wondered what he was dreaming about.

As the month had gone by, Brittany's dreams had become more and more about Coby: the way he looked, the way he sounded, even the way he smelled. Still looking down at him, she gave an embarrassed smile as she wondered if he was dreaming about her.

After the first few dreams starring Coby, Brittany became fearful that E.V. could see them, just like it was now seeing most of her waking thoughts. Her dreams were so private and intimate— she was worried about what E.V. would make of them.

"I'd make the same assumptions about your dreams as I do your waking thoughts," E.V. said impatiently.

But you still don't see them.

"I already told you, they are formed in a deeper part of your brain. I cannot reach it, my tentacles can't travel there."

Brittany nodded, feeling reassured once again. At least one part of her life was separate from the creature.

Brittany left Coby's room and went downstairs. She pulled an old margarine container from where she'd hidden it at the back of the fridge and took out a portion of liver. Then she quickly assembled her midnight snack for Coby.

She knew she'd find him awake once she returned to his room. She'd been monitoring his breathing and had heard him stir.

Just like every night over the past month, Coby didn't come to investigate, he waited for Brittany to return. And just like every other night, she did. *Like a vision of an angel. Some nights she even glows*, Coby thought.

Brittany heard his heartbeat pick up as she entered his room. Even though her physical heart couldn't do the same, she felt compelled to move more quickly and get closer to him.

Coby didn't hesitate once the tray of food was set before him. He ate until he'd finished everything. She always brought him the oddest combinations of food (like Brussels sprouts with prunes or sardines in tomato juice). No matter what it was or how it looked, it always seemed to help him. Coby wondered if it was the food, or the person who brought it to him.

"How are you doing tonight?" Brittany could appreciate how his color had returned. His eyes were more alert, and he had become far more active when she visited, especially over the past week.

"I told you it wouldn't take more than a few weeks." E.V. rolled its eyes. "He's back to normal, so you can stop fretting now. And you can stop blaming me."

If it weren't for you, we wouldn't have hurt him in the first place, Brittany reprimanded. *We can't do that again! Not him, or anyone.* She briefly thought of her father, her mother, and her stepdad. They had all recovered, of course, but that didn't stop her from still feeling guilty.

"I'm fine. How are you?" Coby said, registering pain in Brittany's eyes.

"I'm ok... but maybe I should stop showing up every night. It's not healthy for me to disrupt your sleep so much." Brittany repeated the words E.V. had just said to her. Almost as if in defiance of the words, Brittany sat down next to Coby.

He had finished everything on the tray. He pushed it off his lap and rolled so that he could wrap himself around Brittany. "Don't stop."

The first time she'd shown up, it was simply to prepare him a drink. Coby had had to miss school for the whole first week. On the second day of his absence, Brittany was so wracked with grief that E.V. suggested they go see him just so she could calm down.

It had taken two weeks of nightly visits for Coby to catch Brittany showing up and cooking him food. He'd noticed that during her visits she was bipolar. Sometimes she was so intimate it made him blush. Other times she seemed hesitant, distant, and distracted. And this jarred even more with her behavior at school. It was almost as if she was someone completely different during the day.

Still, he'd take Brittany this way. He'd take her any way he could. He was tired so he closed his eyes. "I like our visits, don't ever stop."

Brittany took a deep, steadying breath. She felt him emanating heat into her cold-blooded body. "I couldn't stay away even if I tried," she admitted.

E.V. agreed.

Attracted didn't cover it. Infatuated didn't quite sum it up either— she was addicted! She was drawn to him. His smell made her heart soar and her blood boil. Neither of these were a possibility with E.V. in control, but the mind can make up for a lot.

"What is it about him?" E.V. asked as Coby's soft snores filled the room.

Brittany chanced running her hand through his hair. *I'm not sure. It feels like if I didn't have him there would be no reason to exist at all.* This was the truth. All those times she debated putting an end to herself— this seemed to be the one thing that tethered her to stay. She shifted to stand.

Coby stirred. "Don't go. Stay, I'll wake up. We can talk."

"You need to rest," Brittany said, pushing Coby back onto his pillow.

He caught a hold of her arm and tried to pull her down with him. "So do you."

Coby wasn't weak; he had recovered his full strength. But Brittany was stronger. She allowed him to pull her next to him. She liked the idea of dreaming, and it seemed that the only times she slept now was in his arms. She shut her eyes.

"And what am I to do while you slumber?" E.V. was disgruntled. "You know, this makes three nights in a row — that's just plain decadence."

Do some dreaming of your own, Brittany thought as she could feel her dreams pulling at her. *I saw your feelings for that bartender, Bret. Dream a little about him.*

"I don't dream! I don't even sleep," E.V. said in response, but it was too late. Brittany was out. "Humans," it complained.

Coby had stirred at the sound of Brittany's last word. "Humans," she had said — what a strange word to be muttering.

THIRTY-FOUR
RESTED

IT WAS ONE hundred nineteen minutes and fifty-eight seconds later when E.V. finally managed to rouse Brittany. She'd come out of REM, cycling into the lighter, more alert phase of sleep. E.V. could feel it. It poked Brittany. It wanted to stop her before she slipped back into a second REM cycle.

"Really, Brittany," E.V. complained, "you don't need this much sleep!"

I don't want to get up, Brittany said, staring up into E.V.'s impatient face.

"But we will need to leave soon."

Brittany studied the sky. It was inky black, yet she could feel that it wouldn't stay that way for long. She knew it was between three and four in the morning, even without looking at Coby's clock.

We've still got some time, she thought dreamily.

"No we don't!" E.V. snapped. "Not enough for another two hours!" *Which you won't need for at least two more days.*

Brittany shrugged off the impatience and frustration she could feel coming from E.V. then got up and cleaned away all evidence that she'd been there.

ʒ ◆ ⁊

"About being a hero…" E.V. broached the subject after Brittany had returned home and picked up a textbook to read.

Brittany happily abandoned the book. She wasn't reading for pleasure; she had picked it up because she was board. Since being changed, Brittany had read every book in the house cover to cover— twice. Granted, neither she nor her father had been big on reading books. It was Ella's collection and, for an instant, Brittany was almost thankful that the woman had brought them over. Almost— and the instant passed quickly.

Brittany looked to E.V. with a grin of anticipation.

"We'd have to set a few ground rules," E.V. said firmly.

Brittany couldn't stop the chuckle that slipped past her lips. "You want to make rules?"

"Yes. This will not be as easy as you think."

Brittany gave E.V. her full attention.

"You are not invincible— you can still be broken. There are things that even I can't fix." E.V. tried not to let its fears lead into its memories— tried and failed.

It recalled with precise clarity other hosts who had been slashed, maimed, impaled… all died long before they needed to.

Brittany gasped as a vision of Emily falling onto a metal crowbar flashed by.

"What are the rules?" Brittany's voice had a slight wobble.

"Easy." E.V. continued to look at Brittany wide-eyed, as if it were still scared. "You have to let me decide if something is too dangerous for you."

"What do you mean?"

"You have to listen to me. If I say it's too risky— you don't engage. If I tell you to run away— you run."

This wasn't exactly what Brittany had thought of when she envisioned herself being a superhero. But she still wanted to do it.

"And," E.V. furrowed its brow, "absolutely NO knives."

"Why no knives? You can heal cuts— I've seen you, you are quite good at that."

"Little cuts, yes. Not big slashes. When someone strikes with a knife they can open far too much skin in one swipe for me to fix quickly enough."

"How am I going to know if someone has a knife? Remember, I'm not psychic. And neither are you." Brittany could just imagine walking up to some bad guy and saying,

I need to know if you have a knife before I take your blood. Then she wondered if that would work.

"Just stay out of their reach until I say it's ok." E.V. seemed to think for a moment. "It might work better if you had a gun."

"A gun?" Brittany choked. "Couldn't that be more dangerous for me than a knife?" She didn't like this. *Guns are used by the bad guys. I'm supposed to be the good guy— the hero!*

"Real heroes have used guns all through history. Haven't you seen a Western?"

Real heroes, Brittany grumbled to herself. *What's the point of being superhuman if I can't be a superhero?* "Besides," she said, "I read a statistic that said that in an encounter with someone dangerous, I'd be more likely to get shot with my own gun."

"First: *you* will not be getting within reach of anyone, until I am sure they are unarmed. And second: I can easily take care of the kind of wound a bullet makes. Provided I'm well-fed, and you will make sure I am if we are going to do this."

Brittany thought about all the rules for a moment. The truth was she really enjoyed the idea of being the good guy; even if it meant she was the *good* bad guy. "E.V., just where am I supposed to get a gun?"

E.V. gave a sly smile. It was the exact same look Emily gave when she had something exciting to say. "My father keeps a gun up in his closet. He never uses it— he wouldn't even notice it missing, especially if we were to return it every night."

E.V. was oblivious that it was talking like Emily. Brittany wasn't.

For a moment Brittany felt winded at the painful reminder of her old friend, taken from her by the very same creature that now infested her.

E.V. missed Brittany's pain; it was locked in a memory.

ઝ ♦ ଓ

"Are you really going to shoot yourself?" E.V. asked in Gran's frail voice.

"You have to go!" Emily's voice was high and tight with rage.

"I told you: you cannot get rid of me, not like this— not at all." E.V. was trying to sound calm, to not show how much Emily's hate affected it.

"I don't want you!" Emily screamed. Even though it was late, she was home alone. Her father had been called out for a veterinary emergency. She cocked the gun the way she'd been taught to.

"Please," E.V. begged. "This will not end the way you want. You will only hurt yourself more."

"I don't believe you. You've lied to me before." The gun fired.

The memory that followed was of Emily waking up with a healed wound over her heart and a feeling of overwhelming hunger.

CR ♦ ℘

Brittany had seen the memory but kept it to herself. She felt bad for Emily, but she felt worse for E.V. The gun had been intended to hurt the creature, and that made Brittany sad. She pushed the feeling aside— she didn't want to care for the creature.

"Are you sure this is what you want to do, Brit?" E.V. asked, sensing a hesitancy it couldn't understand.

Brittany nodded.

"It could end up being more work than it's worth."

"But we'll be helping people," she said, trying to convince both E.V. and herself. "I don't like that we have to steal people's blood. At least this way I won't feel so bad."

"I really don't understand why you are so upset about that. I take so little now that no one gets hurt. They don't even feel drowsy after."

"We are still stealing. It's wrong. If I have to be a vampire, I need to do something to even the score."

"But it's not like we kill!" E.V. said. "We haven't killed anyone! That includes the two people that I am certain deserved to die!"

"No." Brittany's voice was so loud it caused her father to stir. She heard his snores stop and him turn over. She waited for them to re-start before she continued. "No. I won't become a killer. You may have turned me into a monster, but I am no murderer."

The room felt oppressively loud in the silence that followed.

"Fine." E.V. cocked its head to one side. "We can start tomorrow." And it added to itself, *This should be interesting.*

THIRTY-FIVE

CONTENTED

BRITTANY WALKED TO school with a smile. Things were far from ok, but they felt like they might be getting closer to it. Coby had improved, and though she hated E.V. hearing her admit it, he was back to his former health. Her father, mother, and stepdad were also well.

Apart from having E.V., an uncategorized parasite, living in her and demanding blood through her, she really had little to complain about. Most of her days ran smoothly. She got to hang out with her favorite person on the planet, Coby. And when the day was done, she got to spend most nights with him too.

With improved mental concentration she was far more capable of doing her schoolwork. She soared in gym. She could see and hear better; in fact, all her senses had improved. She was shapelier… and all this took was a little blood sacrifice. But that was the problem.

Blood represents life— if you have it, you are alive. Without it, no human or animal could survive. Yet, there she was, Brittany, an enigma, along with E.V. They were alive without blood… yet without it they couldn't stay alive. For Brittany, taking it was like stealing a person's life force. Even if she was only taking a little— it was stealing something that shouldn't be stolen.

Brittany shuddered.

E.V. rolled its eyes— it was tired of the topic. Brittany really needed to get over this. Yes, blood was life, and because Brittany's body didn't produce it any more, they both needed it. *Really, do lions mourn for the gazelle they eat? And for that matter— before all of this, was Brittany really concerned about all the meat she consumed? What about the liver she now cooked for her boyfriend?*

"But there is a great difference between animals and humans," Brittany hissed after making sure they were alone so no one would overhear her talking to herself.

"Yet you kill the animals to eat them. We aren't doing that. You have me taking less than the Red Cross does! That's like using a sheep's wool to stay warm."

Brittany didn't see it that way. She didn't think she ever would. They were silent, each giving the other space because neither could get the other to see things their way.

"Just don't forget," E.V. added once some of Brittany's fight had ebbed, "if you stop feeding me you'll be the first to die."

Ya, well, I haven't starved you yet, Brittany huffed. *I'm allowed to have my opinion.*

"Ever think that your opinion makes it so we always need more?" E.V. looked sidelong at Brittany. "I've told you that your emotions eat up my reserves."

Brittany didn't respond.

"Brit! Hey, Brit." Coby had been calling for nearly half a block, but she was too distracted to notice.

She stopped and turned, watching him catch up. He went to take her hand. She pulled away from his touch.

"I promised I wouldn't take from him." E.V. said. "Can't you trust me?"

NO! Brittany snapped. But it wasn't the creature she didn't trust, it was herself. She liked Coby a lot, and sometimes because she was so interested in him it was hard not to think of taking from him again. She, Brittany, wanted Coby's blood. This was a scary thought and at times an overwhelming desire. So, when she was even the slightest bit hungry, it was best to avoid contact.

"Everything ok?" Coby tried to sound casual as they started towards school.

"Sure," she said, "just hungry."

Coby noticed again that Brittany was so distracted, it was like a part of her wasn't even there. He kept this observation to himself.

If she wanted to hold Coby's hand today, she'd have to get a top-up from someone else. She chose Liam, the boy whose locker was next to hers.

E.V. didn't point out that Brittany was becoming a bit of a hypocrite. What did it care, the girl was feeding it again.

When Liam showed up, Brittany reached over, giving his arm a rub. "How was your weekend?" she asked. She was careful to avoid any spots that already had a bruise on them and ignored the pang of guilt she felt, because his arm looked like it had freckles that were on steroids.

They can't all be from me, she said to the creature— not a question. E.V. didn't dare answer. The truth was that Liam was picked on quite a bit. It wasn't possible for him to walk through the halls without getting tripped (at least once), but before Brittany had started to say good morning to him, he hadn't had bruises.

"Oh, it was great." Liam looked at Brittany's hand as it lingered on his arm.

He proceeded to list off the events of his weekend, and as the list got longer and longer, Brittany wondered if he was stalling to keep her talking with him.

"Maybe he's so lonely he doesn't mind donating to our cause," E.V. offered.

He doesn't know about our cause, Brittany said.

Even if he knew I'm sure he wouldn't mind.

Brittany frowned and Liam brought his recounting to a close.

He took a breath then asked, "Yours?"

Brittany was about to answer "uneventful" when someone yelled, "There she is! The hero of The Empty Glass."

Brittany released Liam and turned to look at the group of Simone's friends making their way up the hall. They descended upon her, surrounding her and demanding a recap of the events from Friday night.

Coby, whose locker was across the hall, just watched. He'd seen everything: from the way Brittany casually touched Liam to the horror in her eyes as the grade twelve girls swarmed her. He tried to hear what Brittany said but couldn't catch it. It didn't matter— by lunchtime everyone was talking about it.

Brittany had tried to avoid retelling Friday night's events. When that wasn't possible she gave a very modest version of the story. She tried to come off as being just as frightened as Simone. In the end, it didn't matter what Brittany said. Simone and her friends had told and retold the story with so much embellishment that by noon the school might have believed that Brittany had swung into the alley on a telephone line to save the day.

"You are the one that wanted to be a hero," E.V. complained as Brittany continued to sulk. She was making her way towards the cafeteria as quickly as she could through the sea of well-wishers.

"Way to go, Brittany," were the typical awe-inspired words from her fellow ninth graders. "Awesome," was what a few kids from grade ten said. "OMG, that was you!" said someone in grade eleven. But several of the kids in grade twelve, the same grade as Simone, who'd been hearing Simone rant and rave all morning— asked something along the lines of, "How did you do it?"

Brittany tried to avoid them all.

THIRTY-SIX

NOTICED

"STILL WANT TO be a hero?" E.V. asked as Brittany entered the cafeteria and was immediately hailed over to the table where Simone and her friends sat.

Brittany caught sight of Coby sitting in their usual spot. She turned, thinking of ditching Simone and her overly friendly friends. She didn't make it three feet before the group's insistent waves became loud calls. "Brittany! Brittany! Sit with us! We've bought you lunch." A few more steps and Simone had gotten up to personally escort Brittany over to her table.

Coby was watching, disappointment clear on his face.

To Simone and her friends, Brittany had become their mascot. They praised her, patted her on the back, toasted her, and complimented her. They didn't expect anything in return but a shy smile. She might as well have been a cardboard cut-out. They didn't pay any real attention to the girl slumped down on the bench, wedged between Simone and her friend.

Of course, Simone and the rest of her pals didn't notice that Brittany didn't want to be there. They were in grade twelve, so who wouldn't want to sit with them? They also didn't seem to notice that all the food they gave Brittany ended up on the floor. Brittany thought she was being sneaky about it and that no one noticed. But Coby had.

Coby had started to be suspicious weeks back. Today's behavior seemed to tip the scales. He started to compile a list. There was something up with Brittany and he was determined to find out what.

Once lunch was done Brittany dreaded what kind of reception would await her after school, envisioning a group of kids (mostly Simone's friends) camped out around her locker ready to walk her home; or worse, have her hang out with them. Instead, she was called down to the principal's office just minutes into her last class.

She was glad for this as she walked up to the office. The snickers from some of her classmates and the concerned look from others didn't bother her. It was only as she got to the office that Brittany realized facing her "fans" might have been an easier task.

There stood the cop from Friday night.

Officer Brown leaned on the principal's desk, looking down at what appeared to be an average grade nine girl. Never mind that she shouldn't have been out that late, in a dark alley so close to a bar that she professed she wasn't visiting. There was something else that didn't fit. "Tell me again how you found the assailant and Miss Grey?"

E.V. rolled its eyes. This was the third time he'd asked the same question.

I can count for myself, Brittany snapped in her head.

"I was jogging," she told the cop. "When I came around the corner I saw them. I was scared. The way the man was holding Simone didn't look friendly. But I couldn't stop... I think I might have slipped on the gravel. I ended up sliding right into both of them. We all fell and I guess the guy must have hit his head because he didn't get up." After a quick pause she decided to tack on, "Is he ok?"

"Suck-up," E.V. said before adding, "He shouldn't be ok— he shouldn't be breathing."

Officer Brown ignored Brittany's question but maintained eye contact, watching for the typical signs of lying. He didn't find any.

Of course he wouldn't, since Brittany's eyes didn't act the same with E.V. there.

It wasn't like he thought Brittany was lying, per se. She seemed sincere. He wanted to write it up the way the girl said it and be done with the case, yet there were some things that he needed answers for. Officer Brown shifted his weight from one foot to the other while having a mental argument.

He'd been sent to check out a problem. The offender, and this wasn't the man's first offence, had been affected by more than just poor judgment. He seemed to also have an illness that could only be described as sudden onset low blood pressure. But with no cause for this, and him being the third person with the condition in as many months, the authorities were now checking for a source by checking for other, perhaps milder, cases.

This man had had contact with both girls. It was Officer Brown's job to try to find leads or connections. He shifted his weight back while remembering how the doctor had described it. "We have no answers. We've completed a full work-up. There are no explanations as to why his blood count is so low. We've tested for all the known ailments and even some lesser known ones. We've done a full tox-screen and come up with the usual narcotics in his system, but none of them explain this. We need to do more research to determine if this is a virus or a side effect from a new drug. We need answers."

Officer Brown shifted his weight a third time. He had no clue how the two victims factored into the equation. He was certain they didn't. But it wasn't his job to question the order. It was his job to get it done.

Brittany wasn't a fool— something was up.

"Ok," Officer Brown smiled. "We just need one last thing from you." His eyes wandered over to the corner of the room where the school nurse had been standing.

She stepped forward with a needle in her plastic gloved hands.

Brittany jumped. As E.V. retracted every one of its tentacles, Brittany had felt something that could only be described as snakes — millions of tiny snakes — slithering inside her body.

Are they going to inject us? she panicked as E.V. continued to squirm inwards.

"If only… that wouldn't do anything to you or me. No, look at the needle, it's empty." E.V. was more frightened than Brittany had ever felt.

"Don't worry," the nurse soothed, "we just need to take a blood sample.

Is that even possible? Brittany asked. She figured the answer had to be no with the continued withdrawal of E.V.

"Listen carefully." E.V. was popping in and out of Brittany's vision. "You need to do exactly what I say."

Brittany wondered if she was going to die now. She couldn't survive without the creature, and it seemed to be getting ready to leave her.

The nurse had come to stand over Brittany. "Give me your arm."

"Wait," Brittany barely managed to whisper out loud. She wasn't just trying to bargain with the nurse, she was also begging E.V.

THIRTY-SEVEN
CHECKED

"IT'S OK, DEAR," the nurse said, bending closer to stick the needle into Brittany's shaking arm.

"No, no—" Brittany's voice hitched. She could feel E.V. getting into position, "I... I don't..."

"What are you frightened about, dear?" The nurse had ripped open an alcohol swab.

"Needles," Brittany squeaked.

"Come now, it's no different than getting a shot."

"I don't..." Brittany held her breath.

E.V. appeared clearer. "You're doing great. Just a second more... Yes. Now have the nurse hold your hand. And when she does, I want you to squeeze it, not so hard that you break her bones, but hard enough that you appear terrified."

I am terrified, Brittany thought.

"Ya, you can stop that now. I've got this. Just get her hand."

"Please," Brittany felt her lip quiver, "could I hold your hand?"

The nurse looked sympathetic. "I would, but I need both my hands to do this." She leaned in to try and dab the alcohol swipe on Brittany's arm.

"No!" Brittany pulled back.

"Here." Officer Brown held out his hand.

Damn, both Brittany and E.V. thought at the same time. "Give me a sec," E.V. said as Brittany started to feel it changing positions.

You're gonna take from the cop? Brittany could feel her fears intensifying. *But you said we needed to take from the nurse.*

"Well, that was before. She isn't cooperating and we need someone's blood. Now take his hand before he pins you to the table and forces you to let the nurse do it!" This was for Brittany. If the cop did end up holding her down, E.V. could still accomplish what it needed to make the situation work.

Brittany slowly extended her left hand to Officer Brown. He took it and gave what he no doubt hoped was a friendly squeeze.

Once Brittany had Officer Brown's hand, she realized it was too late to do anything different, so she squeezed tightly. *Explain to me again how this is going to work*, she thought.

E.V. caught and held Brittany's gaze. "I will take the cop's blood and feed it directly into the nurse's needle."

Brittany understood where the problem came in. In order to fill the needle, E.V. would have to take more than the 30 cc's needed.

Office Brown winced under Brittany's crushing grip but didn't say anything.

It was almost instantaneous. The moment Officer Brown and Brittany were holding hands, the nurse had dabbed the inside of Brittany's elbow, tied the tourniquet around her arm and poked the needle in.

Brittany not only saw but she also felt the needle being caught and pulled in by E.V. She then felt Officer Brown's blood being transferred from one arm to the other and forced out, filling the vial. She had to look away. More than ever, the sight of the blood made her want it.

"Done." The nurse smiled. She'd removed the needle and disposed of the sharp point. She passed the vial of blood over to Officer Brown.

Officer Brown took it and put it in the container the doctor had given him. He could feel a bruise forming where Brittany had squeezed his hand. He hadn't liked this assignment, but it was his job. Now he was tired and all he wanted was to leave and be done with the whole thing.

ભ ◆ ৯

You took some of the officer's blood, Brittany said as they walked home from school.

"Ya, so?"

Don't you think that was unwise?

"Wise or not, we were running low. It's impossible for blood to go through me like that without me taking what I need."

Brittany didn't say any more, but she continued to worry. She was sure this was going to be a problem for her.

"Something's not right with you," Coby said. He had met Brittany at her locker and walked with her silently to this point. At first he hadn't wanted to bother her, she looked so upset, but she wasn't volunteering anything and his curiosity was finally getting the better of him. "Whatever it is, you know you can tell me."

Brittany stopped and turned to stare at Coby. What could she say?

Coby went on, "I overhead Simone say they had to check her blood on Friday night? Why would they need to check her blood? Brittany, what happened? What's going on? Did they need to check your blood too? Is that why you were called down to the principle's office today? Did they take some of your blood?"

Brittany stayed silent.

He took a breath and reached out to take Brittany's hands, gently holding them up to look at her arms. "Brittany?"

Brittany still didn't answer. Instead she pulled her arms away. All this talk of blood: she was hungry. *What's the equivalent of "stomach growling"?* she asked. *How would I say that now?*

E.V. shrugged.

Coby still waited.

It's like my muscles ache, like when I was forced to run for that whole hour last year in gym. My muscles feel starved.

"Brit, talk to me." Coby stepped closer and put his hands on her shoulders. When she tried to squirm out from under him, he held tighter. "Come on, I'm your friend here. Talk to me!"

She didn't. She couldn't. There was nothing she could say! The truth was completely unbelievable. Brittany now understood exactly how Emily, the real Emily, had felt and why she hadn't told Brittany about it.

"Brit, you are really starting to freak me out! You're acting just like..."

Brittany stared at Coby, her eyes wide. "That's because I am. I am just like her." Brittany turned and fled, leaving Coby oblivious and dumbstruck.

ભ ◆ જ

It was almost three in the morning. Brittany was circling Coby's house, staying in the shadows. It was her way of pacing. She wanted to see him, to be near him, to touch him— and now she could. She was full, or more to the point, E.V. was fully fed.

She had taken the gun from Emily's father's closet as E.V. had insisted. She'd snuck in while the man was sleeping. It was easy with her new senses. He hadn't stirred— even if he had been awake he wouldn't have heard her.

The gun in Brittany's hand made E.V. feel safer. Brittany wondered why. It felt too light, like a toy.

"Believe me, this is not a toy. It can hurt... it can kill." Brittany could feel the creature's excitement in that statement.

"But we won't be killing tonight." Brittany wasn't sure if she was asking or confirming.

E.V. shrugged, and Brittany accepted it.

Brittany had also taken a ratty looking hoodie from Mr. Daminko's closet. It was so big on her that it looked more like a cloak. The most important part was that the hood fell so far over Brittany's face, there would be no way anyone would see her.

She'd then taken a bus downtown to find a "bad guy," someone she wouldn't feel guilty stealing blood from. It didn't take any time to locate one. After all, it was closing in on midnight and Brittany had picked the seediest part of town, so seedy the bus driver had almost refused to let her off.

Brittany caught a pimp in the act of smacking one of his employees around.

"That's no way to treat a lady!" Brittany said, not bothering to disguise her voice.

"What?. This piece of trash?" He threw the girl against the wall. She hit the cement and clung to it. "She's no lady— she's just a piece of meat." He didn't need to see Brittany to know she'd make a fine recruit.

"Keep out of his reach until we're sure he's not armed," E.V. reminded.

Relax, Brittany thought with a sense of irony, *I've got this.*

E.V. didn't respond.

The pimp was slowly approaching, in the same fashion as Max— slowly, as though trying not to spook a wild animal. This made Brittany all the more thrilled about taking the creep down.

The glint of something shiny being slipped out of the man's sleeve brought Brittany's thoughts back to the present.

"Ok, time to use that gun," E.V. said.

THIRTY-EIGHT
SHOT

HE DOESN'T LOOK *so tough*, Brittany thought, not realizing how much pleasure she was taking from the idea of coming to blows with the brute.

The pimp stopped just out of reach. He had a good sense of people and he could tell there was something rebellious about this girl. She was clearly dangerous, but he found that alluring. She'd need to be broken in, and he was having fantasies about doing just that. "What's your name, pretty."

Brittany took one step back at E.V.'s insistence. Its eyes were trained on the knife. He held it so casually, but secure enough that if he lunged, it could cause a great deal of damage.

"You are going to have to shoot him in the arm," E.V. said, "so he'll drop that knife."

You forget. I've never fired a gun before. I wouldn't know how. How can I be sure that I'll hit his arm? Let me take him down myself. I'm sure I can do that.

"You either shoot him or you run away," E.V. answered in a firm tone.

Several things kept Brittany from choosing the latter—she was hungry. Her muscles twinged from it. And the girl, who stood pressed tight to the wall a short distance down from Brittany and her pimp, was watching with terror on her face. She was a victim and Brittany wanted to save her. Besides, Brittany wanted more than anything to take the man down. She *wanted* to see him suffer.

She reached into the pouch of her oversized hoodie. She had to feel around for the gun. She almost wished she couldn't find it so she'd have an excuse to lunge at the knife-wielding man. Surely she could knock his feeble weapon away, and then rip into him. Not actually rip, but close: she could allow E.V. to sink its tentacles in. She craved that so much she could already feel it. She imagined sucking his blood, feeling his strength ebb away under her grip.

"Brit, the gun!" E.V. snapped. It could see the man making plans of his own, slowly inching forward.

He stopped when he saw the shiny pistol being drawn from the girl's pocket. "You…" he cursed and spat. But he was also bewildered. She'd come prepared… *she'd come looking for a fight. Who does that*?

A mean smile spread across the man's tough and scarred face. So she was prepared. So what, so was he. In his left hand he balanced the knife loosely on his palm, as if offering it up. But his right hand had disappeared behind his back.

"Just shoot him," E.V. said.

But he's surrendering. If he drops the knife I won't have to shoot him. Brittany argued. *Besides, I don't know how to aim*.

"Just look where you want the bullet to land and your mind will fill in the rest. It's not any different than throwing a ball."

Brittany didn't think that shooting a gun would be anything like throwing a ball. She also remembered back to the first few times she'd played catch with her dad. She hadn't thrown the ball anywhere near where she was looking. This didn't matter, though. As the man's right hand started to reappear it was wrapped around a gun of his own.

"Point and shoot!" E.V. shouted.

Brittany held the gun up and pulled the trigger. It was easier then she'd thought it would be. She heard a crack like the flick of a whip as the bullet was released. The sound reverberated off the cement walls of the alley. The bullet hit the man in the forearm exactly where Brittany had been looking.

He instantly dropped the knife, but not the gun, which he held tightly in his other hand.

"Again!" E.V. demanded. "Shoot the other arm!"

This time Brittany hesitated, distracted by the patch of bright red seeping into his sleeve, growing from its origin. Some oozed from the hole left in his shirt, trickling down his arm and dripping off his elbow.

It was too late for E.V. to say anything more as the man took his aim. Another crack, louder, deeper, and before it had time to echo, Brittany felt it hit her chest.

His aim wasn't to disarm, it was to kill. He was pissed— no one shot him and got away with it. At this close range he should have succeeded. Brittany should have collapsed before him! The bullet should have ripped clear through her.

Instead, she stood barely flinching from the blow. The feeling she experienced wasn't the same as pain, it was more like hunger. The muscles around the area where the bullet had made contact felt... tingly, like air bubbles were racing through them. Expanding and making her... hungry.

"The blood." Brittany could see nothing but the streams of red that ran down the man's arm, dripping off and forming a small pool at his feet. Now more than ever she knew she needed it.

The man's eyes grew wide as she continued to stand. He'd shot her from less than seven feet away and he hadn't missed. He'd seen the bullet hit, yet there had been no cry of pain. She hadn't even blinked. And now there was no blood. Perhaps she was wearing a vest. He swung his arm up to take a second shot, this time aiming for the girl's head.

"Brittany! Shoot or run!"

She did neither. She lunged forward, closing the distance between her and him in the blink of an eye. She moved like a blur. He didn't get a chance to fire, and then there was no time to aim as she was next to him, on him, crouching over him, pinning him to the hard ground.

She'd tackled him so fast, faster than the bullet he'd lodged into her. Once she had him pinned down, she slowly brought her hands up to either side of his face and gently placed them around his neck.

He instinctively brought his hands up to stop her and pry her off. No amount of struggling worked. Her hands were staying put. They were firmly held in place. Firm but gentle. They weren't squeezing.

Drain him, E.V., Brittany said, her thoughts soft, almost seductive.

"Two pints coming up."

"No," Brittany whispered aloud, "take it all."

The man didn't have time to wonder what this strange girl meant. His thoughts started to race as if he were being strangled. Though he could breathe, he didn't feel like he was getting enough oxygen. His ears started to ring, his eyesight failed, and then he no longer felt Brittany atop him; he no longer felt anything.

For Brittany it was a rush to feel his body deflating under her. She felt his pulse quicken, then slow and finally cut off. She looked down into his glassy gaze. His eyes were empty. He was dead, nothing but a piece of lifeless meat under her crouched body.

She thought of her chest, becoming aware of the area that had received the bullet. Cautiously she lifted the hoodie, taking note of the hole that her finger could fit into. The edges of the material looked singed. Her shirt also bore the same mark. But her skin showed no sign of it. However, under closer examination, she could detect the slightest bump just above her breast.

"The bullet will be there forever." E.V. took a seat next to where Brittany squatted. "I couldn't get it out. It lodged into your lungs. It was easier just to reconstruct around it."

"How come it didn't puncture my lungs or hit my heart?"

"It could never get past your lungs, don't you remember? I petrified them."

"But you said they were like sea-sponges out of water: movable."

"Movable, sure. Still petrified. So, absolutely bulletproof."

"Hmmmm." Brittany thought about that for a moment then asked, "How come I'm still hungry?"

"Because we lost a lot of fluid before I was able to heal the wound."

Just then Brittany heard the sound of gravel being displaced. The girl, the woman the pimp had been beating up, had slid to the ground. Brittany turned to see her legs, which she had tried to pull tight against her chest, slide out in front of her.

Brittany slowly stood up. She was ashamed. The man lay dead on the ground, and she had done that. E.V. was willing to stop, she knew this, but Brittany had wanted to take it all, every last drop.

"The world is better off without him," E.V. soothed.

Brittany didn't respond, even though she agreed— she had always agreed. What she hadn't wanted was to play judge, jury, and executioner. No person deserved that much power. Yet, when she told E.V. to drain him, it wasn't because he deserved it, it was simply that she was furious— and hungry.

"It's ok," Brittany stood over the woman and extended a hand to her. "He's not going to hurt you anymore."

The woman looked at Brittany's hand and scowled. "How am I going to get work now? Who will set up my jobs? Who will get me my pay?"

Brittany was about to drop her hand when the prostitute took it and pulled herself to her unsteady feet.

"Where will I get my drugs?" The woman pulled away from Brittany, wincing. She put a hand on her hip.

She didn't need to remove it and show it to Brittany. Brittany knew that the woman was bleeding, and it wasn't from a scratch. Brittany looked back over her shoulder and realized exactly what had happened. Her bullet had gone clean through the pimp's arm and straight into the prostitute. Looking at the cement wall, Brittany could see the indentation where it had exited the woman and become lodged in the bricks behind her. The area was splattered with the woman's blood.

The woman began to fall over, half from the pain, half too weak to hold herself up. Brittany caught her.

"She won't make it. She's not much longer for this world." E.V. sized up the woman. "And she has just enough to help us get our fill."

Brittany continued to hold the woman, feeling her tremble under her hands. Was she frightened? Was she in pain?

Did she know she was dying? Did she know that Brittany would kill her?

"No one will notice her missing. And if we take from her, we won't have to take from anyone else tonight." E.V. was watching Brittany intently. "Besides, we'd probably be doing some john a favour by keeping her from spreading her diseases."

Brittany wasn't paying attention to E.V. She didn't even notice the woman any more. What had caught and held her attention was the blood. Brittany's senses were filled with it. It was sweeter, laced with some kind of agent that made it look lighter. Brittany was almost sure of the kind of taste it would bring. Where the pimp's blood had been thick and almost heavy, this woman's would flow more freely — Brittany was sure of this.

But if she took some, she knew she'd take it all. This was it, the moment of truth — was she human or a monster?

THIRTY-NINE

TOUCHED

BRITTANY FROZE IN the shadows as she saw Coby return to his window and peer out. That was the third time she'd seen him since she arrived forty minutes ago. She wondered how many times he'd done it before her arrival. She also wished she could know his thoughts as his brow crinkled in what looked like worry.

"Go ask him," E.V. huffed. "We are full for now— *now* would be the best time to do it. Just go."

Brittany stayed planted to the spot. *I can't.*

"What's your problem now?" E.V. asked, but Brittany didn't have to answer. It could see her thoughts. Brittany was comparing herself to monsters. She was debating running away and becoming a recluse, hiding in the shadows and hunting at night. "Brittany, you are not a monster," E.V. said firmly.

"Aren't I?"

E.V. didn't answer because Coby, who had been turning, had stopped and looked out more intently. His eyes narrowed as if he had seen something and was searching for it.

The wind had picked up, tugging at Brittany's hood, threatening to pull it off and expose her face. Remembering her luminescent skin, she held it down.

E.V. had seen the way the moonlight reflected off Brittany's bare hand and lit up the area around her like a lightning flash. "He knows you're here, Brit. Go to him. You'll feel better once you do. You know, if you don't go the blood we have won't last as long."

It was that final incentive that made Brittany move forward out of the shadows and into the low-cut grass of Coby's backyard.

"Brits?" Coby's voice hitched. "Is that you?"

She nodded as she took hold of his drainpipe and started to climb.

Coby was amazed, bewildered, and slightly excited as he watched. When she drew level with him he asked, "How?"

Brittany brought her finger up to silence him, noting the way his heartbeat sped up as she touched his lips. She became oblivious to anything else as she felt her finger warming from his body heat and she homed in on the feeling of his skin under hers. A thought, an all-consuming thought, tempted her. She wanted to kiss him again.

She'd been too frightened in the past, not sure if she could trust E.V.... or herself. Tonight she was certain she could trust the creature. And even more so, she was sure E.V. was more trustworthy than herself. It wasn't the creature's desire that had Brittany craving Coby. *She* craved his touch ... his scent ... and she craved his blood. Thankfully, the furthest thing from Brittany's desires, at that moment, was *more* blood.

Brittany moved her finger over Coby's face, past his chin, down his neck, grazing his Adam's apple and coming to a rest in the hollow of his ribcage, where it lingered, detecting his rapid pulse, his booming heart.

For the briefest of moments Brittany realized that there would be nothing to stop her if she wanted to push her fingers into his chest and capture his wild heart.

"But that's not what you want to do," E.V. reminded firmly.

Brittany's eyes slid for a fraction of a second towards the vision. *Then why do I feel like that's what I want to do? What's happening to me?*

E.V. didn't get a chance to answer.

Coby couldn't believe Brittany was really there, but he wasn't going to waste the opportunity. When Brittany paused, he came to life. He brought both his hands up to her hood, drawing it back to gaze upon her face. Then his hands slid into her shiny hair. His fingers got lost in the strands as he ran them deeper into her curls. With a firm grip he leaned forward.

It was like an explosion, giving Brittany a very similar feeling to when she heard the bullet shot from the gun. As they moved together, she could feel electricity in the air. Every kiss, every stroke of their skin, every breath filled the room with the charge until Brittany felt like her whole frame trembled with the energy.

"Whoa, whoa." Coby had pulled back.

Brittany responded likewise. Time, which had lost all meaning, slowly seeped back into existence. The air lost its charge. Her senses returned to normal. She froze where she'd been leaning over him on the bed.

"Don't you think we're taking things a little too quickly?"

Brittany slowly sat back and started to pull her shirt on.

"Brits," Coby had shifted so he sat next to her, "what's gotten into you?"

E.V. laughed.

What's so funny? Brittany asked with a furrowed brow.

"The answer to his question, 'What's gotten into you?' Don't you see? It's me! I've gotten into you," E.V. said through giggles. "*I* got into you."

Brittany's lips twitched just a fraction; it was sort of funny— and true.

"Brits?" Coby asked more forcefully. "What's going on in there?"

Brittany tried to focus past E.V.'s giggles. She took a moment to admire Coby's lips, his neck, his bare chest, then she noticed his eyes were narrowed in impatience. Not knowing what to say, she shrugged. "Nothing's gotten into me."

He shook his head. "No, there's something more. I've been watching you. Something's going on in there."

E.V. erupted into a hysterical laugh. "Ya, I'm going on in here."

Are you drunk? Brittany scolded. It was not as hilarious as E.V. seemed to think.

"I'm not sure." The creature regained its composure. "We should leave."

Brittany started to get up.

"Stop." Coby had caught Brittany's hand.

She reluctantly allowed him to pull her back to sitting.

He picked up her hoodie and fiddled with it. He appeared to be trying to find the right words. "Do you like me?" His voice cracked and he cleared his throat. "Do you like me like— like ... I mean you come to my room almost every night, and when we kiss ... but just this morning you wouldn't even hold my hand. Why? Why is it sometimes ok to touch you and not other times? Why couldn't I hold your hand?"

"I didn't want to hurt you." Brittany sighed— she hadn't meant to say that.

"Hurt me?" Coby was understandably confused. He was hurt when she wouldn't hold his hand, not when she did.

Brittany dropped her eyes to stare at her hands where they fidgeted in her lap. "Never mind."

"Brittany, what's going on?"

Brittany shook her head, pressing her lips together.

"What could...?" Coby's voice trailed off as he became thoughtful.

Brittany cocked her head to the side at Coby's unfinished inquiry.

Her posture made him do a double-take. He suppressed a shudder, poorly. To cover it up, he said, "You don't seem like yourself anymore. It's almost as if you've become..."

E.V.'s eyes grew larger. "Do you think he knows?"

Brittany kept her head cocked and her eyes locked on Coby. *Knows about you?* That he could figure out what was really happening seemed highly unlikely.

"Well, he's suspicious of something," E.V. huffed. "Like I said, I think it's time to leave."

Brittany wondered if E.V. was talking about leaving his room, or had it meant leaving everything? Running away— as Brittany had been thinking earlier. The idea made her want to cry.

"Now you want to stay," E.V. said, sounding exasperated.

Coby noticed the change in Brittany's expression and mistook it. "Don't worry," he said more gently, deciding to let the topic drop. "I know you're still you. Grief makes people act strange, I've heard. You're still missing Emily, aren't you?"

"Ya," Brittany sighed, wishing that was all that was wrong with her.

"What's this?" Coby's finger had slipped into a hole in Brittany's hoodie.

Brittany looked at him as he held it up with his finger sticking out of the bullet hole.

"Brits?" It looked to Coby like Brittany had taken up smoking and burnt her shirt. He tried to tease. "This looks kinda like a couple of bullet holes."

"One bullet hole," Brittany said. "Just one."

Coby dropped her hoodie. His eyes looked wide enough for them to fall out of their sockets. "Why does your sweater have a bullet hole?"

"I can't tell you."

FORTY

INTERROGATED

"DID... DID YOU shoot yourself? Where were you hit?" Coby started to undress Brittany again with more urgency. His hands shook as he pulled Brittany's shirt over her head. When she got tangled in it, he found a similar hole as he helped untangle her.

Once her chest was exposed, he traced his hand over the approximate spot where the bullet would have hit. Three passes and he found no wound, not even a scar. What he did find was a small bump just above her left breast.

"What's this?" He pressed on it. It felt like there was a marble under her skin.

"You wouldn't believe me even if I told you." Brittany took a deep breath, tasting the air. Sensing Coby's fears, she looked up into his eyes. "Are you afraid of me?"

"Not of you," he shook his head, "for you." Coby's hand stayed motionless above her breast. As the reality of where he was touching sank in, he became embarrassed. He started to remove it, but not before he'd realized a few other things.

First, Brittany, who'd been nice and shapely before, was now toned. Her body was lined with muscles rather than a healthy layer of fat. Secondly, and this he couldn't believe, she didn't seem to have a heartbeat. *No detectable heartbeat*, he corrected himself.

He sat back and continued talking, trying to distract himself. "I'm scared because just before Emily killed herself she came to visit me a couple of times. At night, just like you. She acted really strange. It was like something was going on." Coby tried to hold Brittany's gaze, but her eyes kept slipping sideways to the corner of his room. "Brits, I'm really scared because you are acting just like Emily, and I'm afraid... you'll..."

Brittany wasn't listening to Coby anymore.

E.V. had stepped back until it was almost inside Coby's wall. Inside her, Brittany could feel the creature pulling back too— pulling away. *You visited Coby!*

E.V. flinched. "Emily did."

Why? Why did Emily *do that?*

E.V. wouldn't meet Brittany's gaze.

Did Emily like Coby? Brittany waited for an answer, fuming. When the creature didn't reply, she assumed she'd guessed correctly. *Is that why I'm attracted to him? Is it because Emily was, and because you've kept a part of her, that part still likes him and you tricked me?*

"No!" E.V. cut Brittany off. "No! Listen to yourself. That's not logical. Think about it, you know who I'm attracted to." A vision of Adam from the convenience store and Bret the bartender flashed through Brittany's thoughts. "I'm not attracted to Coby and Emily wasn't either."

This calmed Brittany for only a fraction of a second. Then a new thought caused her even greater distress. "Was Coby attracted to Emily? Is that why he likes me now? Because you are in me, and a part of Emily is in you and so he's only attracted to that?"

"No, no!" E.V. raised its hands in a placatory gesture. "It's not that at all."

Then what! Brittany roared. Coby's room had disappeared; all Brittany was aware of was herself and E.V.

"Calm down, please," E.V. said. "You are supposed to be the rational one."

Well, tonight I'm not!

It was true. E.V. had experienced this before; it was like leaching— the more time it lived in one host, the more their personality traits and characteristics, even their mannerisms, would leach into each other. This time with Brittany, just like every other process, it had started early and taken hold quicker than any other host.

"Please," E.V. tried again, "calm down and I will explain."

Brittany folded her arms over her chest impatiently.

E.V. took a deep breath. "Emily wasn't attracted to Coby. She loved you too much. But she saw the way Coby felt about you— it wasn't hard to miss. He couldn't keep his eyes off you. When Emily realized that *I* lusted after you..."

Brittany's voice was almost non-existent as she interrupted. *Like Adam and Bret?*

"No, not like them. I enjoy looking at them and desire their blood. But with you I wanted all of you. I didn't want to taste you— I wanted to know you like I know you now. And Emily could sense this. She felt the way I longed to jump to you. She wanted to protect you. She wanted to save you from me."

"How?"

E.V. smiled sadly. "She wanted to convince Coby to kill her and dispose of her body— keeping me trapped in her so that I couldn't infect you or anyone else ever again."

Brittany knew the rest of the story— she could see it being played out in the creature's memories.

ᘓ ◆ ᗡ

Emily had gone to Coby not sure of what she'd tell him. She climbed into his room just like Brittany now did. But once she got there she couldn't speak. Her tongue went limp in her mouth. Her lips froze. The creature wouldn't allow her to say anything to him. She slipped to his floor driven to tears with her frustration.

As Coby was approaching her, E.V. threatened to drain the boy dry if she said one word. Emily didn't tell Coby; even once she could she was too frightened of the creature making good on its threat.

It was the same the next night and the one after that. She would go, determined to tell him, and the creature would stop her. The fourth night she lost all feeling in her hands so she couldn't even climb up to his room. Defeated, she sat down in the grass and sobbed.

E.V. had missed Emily's new intentions. That's the night she had gone to Brittany's tree fort. That was the night she rammed the crowbar through her chest.

ભ ♦ ૭

E.V.'s voice was urgent. "Brittany, you need to wake up!"

Brittany had almost seen something. At the very least she was aware that she'd seen more than she was supposed to. If only the creature hadn't distracted her. *What was...?*

"No!" E.V. reached out like it was going to shake Brittany. "You have to open your eyes! Wake up."

"What?" Brittany became aware of more than just E.V. She heard Coby's voice. He sounded far away. As she listened she heard that he was speaking in a high and panicked tone... and he wasn't speaking to her.

"No," he said, "I don't feel a heartbeat. She's got to be dead. She's not breathing." He paused, then said, "Please hurry."

Brittany sat up.

Coby let out quite an unmanly squeal, looking as though he was witnessing the dead being raised back to life.

"What happened? Where was I?" Brittany asked E.V. aloud.

"You, you didn't go anywhere. You've been here the whole time. You fainted," Coby answered in a shaky but relieved voice.

"I... fainted?" Brittany wasn't sure who she had asked. Coby was the one to answer.

"Yes, I watched you go down. One minute you were fine, talking, then you just fell. Your eyes didn't even close. It was awful. I checked to see if you were breathing — but I couldn't find ... Brittany, you weren't breathing!"

Brittany didn't have anything to say. She wasn't breathing — she didn't breath.

"Say something!" E.V. demanded.

"I... I must have been breathing. I'm breathing now." Brittany took a deep breath as if that was all the proof he'd need. But for good measure she added to the lie. "If I hadn't been breathing I would be dead."

"That's what I thought!" Coby jumped at the opportunity to say more. "I," again his voice broke, "I thought you'd been suicidal and you'd taken something before you got here. Like maybe you'd swallowed a bottle of pills."

"Why would I do that?" Brittany asked because E.V. told her to.

"Because clearly you tried to shoot yourself and that didn't work."

"You think I tried to shoot myself."

Hearing it said back to him, he had to laugh. He sounded like a lunatic. "Ok, but still, you were unconscious. I tried CPR but you were cold, and you lay lifeless on my bed. I was sure you'd died. What else was I supposed to do but call the paramedics?"

FORTY-ONE

ABANDONED

"WE HAVE TO leave now." E.V. stood up.

In the distance Brittany could hear the siren from the approaching ambulance. "Oh no."

"Oh no, what?" Coby said, taking Brittany's hand, noting that it was still cold.

"We have to go!" E.V. continued. "You can't be here when they get here. You can't let them anywhere near you."

Brittany stood, easily breaking Coby's hold on her.

"Brits…" Coby's thoughts were racing again. What had felt foolish just moments ago was starting to feel suspicious again. "What's going on?"

Brittany could hear the emergency vehicle turning down Coby's street. Soon they'd be at his front door. "I'm sorry." She turned and bolted out his bedroom window.

Coby tried to see where she had gone but missed it. He couldn't even see a rustling bush as he reached his window. He didn't get a chance to ponder this, however, as EMS had arrived and started pounding on the front door.

From her perch on Coby's roof, Brittany watched the interaction between her friend and the ambulance attendants. When Coby explained that it had been a mistake, the attendants gave him a lecture about wasting their time, the government's money, and taking them away from someone who really needed their help.

"I'm really sorry." Coby held his head low. "You see, I'd dreamt that my friend was dead— only the dream felt so real I didn't realize I'd woken up when I called you."

"I ought to call this in. How'd you like it if someone came to take you down to the police station to give your statement there?" the attendant said. She clearly didn't believe Coby's excuse.

Coby's mom, who'd been woken by the commotion, stood next to her son looking like she wished this was just a dream. She came to her son's defence. "Please, I know my son. He isn't a bad kid. I'm sure he thought it was real or he wouldn't have called. You see, his friend died about four months ago... and he's been really sick. Just a couple of weeks ago he got mono. He was so tired he could barely get out of bed. It was terrifying how sick he..."

The attendant cut her off. "Excuse me, you say your son was sick with mono? Did he experience the normal symptoms: lethargy and tiredness? How long ago exactly?"

Even at where she sat on the roof Brittany didn't miss the meaningful look the female attendant gave her partner.

"Well, he came down with it at the end of January," Mrs. Monroe said. "Why? You think it was something other than mono? Because that's what the doctor said it was, but he also said it didn't follow the typical pattern of the illness."

The attendant was looking at Coby differently now. "Madam, would you mind if we brought your son to the hospital to run a few tests?"

"Tests? What kind of tests?" Brittany watched Mrs. Monroe pull her son closer to her. "You don't think he's still sick? Do you?"

"Well..." The attendants shared an uneasy look as they glanced at each other. "It's probably nothing, but we'd like to be sure your son hasn't contracted something else."

Mrs. Monroe looked like she was turning green. Her arms squeezed a little tighter but at the same time she turned her face away from Coby as though she was afraid he might still be contagious. "I guess," she said, "if you think it would be best."

"We do, ma'am," the older, male attendant said.

Brittany watched as Coby was given fifteen minutes to collect some belongings before being loaded into the back of the ambulance. She knew she should be worried about what they might discover, but instead she was afraid of how long Coby could be kept away.

"You worry too much about the wrong things," E.V. complained. "He'll be back by the morning, I'm sure of it." It felt certain that the doctors wouldn't find anything and was now glad that it had promised not to take from him.

E.V.'s words didn't console Brittany, nor did its thoughts. She climbed down from his roof and wandered, not paying attention to where she was going, until she found herself in the least likely place she could imagine.

She hadn't visited her old tree fort since the day she'd discovered Emily's body. The place was empty now. Even the bunny's cage had been cleaned away.

Brittany sat with her back against the wall. The moon shone bright through the single window. With no one around, and no one able to see, she exposed her hand and stretched it into the moonbeams. The light caught it and reflected off the walls.

E.V. stood watching cautiously.

"The disease they're looking for is me," Brittany said quietly, then amended, "well, actually, it's you."

E.V. nodded. Brittany's accusation wasn't threatening, just factual.

"Tell me, has this happened before?"

"Plenty of times," the creature answered quietly.

Brittany was somewhat distracted by her hand in the moonlight. Under it, her skin seemed translucent. She could see her veins — the creature's tentacles — so clearly. To her, they looked no different than they always had. She looked up. "How does it end?"

"Depends." E.V. was trying to be elusive, but Brittany was viewing the creature's memories as if they were her own. Hunting parties with pitchforks and other crude weapons sprang into her mind. There were also several scenes of lynch mobs cornering, capturing, and stoning the creature's hosts.

"Have there been any more recent?" Though the memories were gruesome and terrifying to Brittany, she wondered how things would go in the twenty-first century.

E.V. had nothing to offer. It slid down the wall to sit quietly. It was thinking of the past century. Pretty much from the beginning of the Industrial Revolution, with the explosion of scientific discoveries, the belief in demons and monsters had declined. All of this made it easier for E.V. to hide in plain sight. However, it had noticed a rise in fascination with the supernatural in the world again.

"I... I'm not sure what would happen if we were discovered now."

This time it was Brittany who supplied the images. They weren't from her experiences, but from various science fiction movies she'd seen. They would no doubt strap Brittany to an examination table in some overly white room and then slice her open, categorize and disassemble her, and E.V. along with her.

E.V. seemed to be choking on its words. "We... we can't let that happen."

After a moment in which both girl and creature tried not to dwell any longer on the gruesome topic, Brittany asked, "How have you managed not to be discovered over the last century? Especially with all the medical advances?" She waited for the creature's memories to kick in.

"My answer has many parts," E.V. explained. "First off, Gran: I lived with her for fifteen years and her husband for nearly twenty years before that."

Despite its best efforts, the memories came. They flowed out of the creature in reverse. Brittany watched as Gran passed away. Then she was frail and so close to death that she convinced her daughter she needed to visit— that was made easier because her daughter's husband started to act differently. Gran had taken to visiting the Daminko household at night and taking just enough blood to make Mr. Daminko tired and constantly irritable. In these visits she would stand over her granddaughter, wishing the girl a long life with the creature.

Brittany shivered but kept watching as the scene continued to play out backwards. Now Gran was old, yet fit and healthy. She lived alone on her farm, but she wasn't unhappy. She tended to her chickens and grew a garden of beautiful flowers. Mostly Gran survived off the chickens and the occasional nighttime visit to a stranger's house in a neighboring community. She also never resisted if someone came calling. It was exceptionally ironic to the older woman when those overly friendly Jehovah Witnesses solicited at her door. She'd invite them in for tea so they could explain things better to her, then she'd allow the creature to take a few ounces. For her it was like if the blood bank making home deliveries.

Moving back through time Gran had, at one point, been far more active in the community... but two problems were occurring. First, most of her acquaintances were starting to notice how overly tired they were becoming. The local family doctor was diagnosing chronic fatigue syndrome so much, he wanted to call in someone who could test for toxins in the area. The second problem Gran faced was that a little wasn't enough. After a while she found that she wanted more— she eventually wanted it all.

Going backwards even further still, Brittany witnessed Gran being infected with the creature. Gran's husband had died and given his wife the gift of the creature.

"Wait a minute." Brittany had to cut the creature off. "A gift? He gave you to his wife as a gift?"

FORTY-TWO
HUMAN

"YES." E.V. SEEMED offended. "I was a gift. Henry saw me as a blessing. I'd kept him alive beyond his expected lifespan. With me in his wife, he'd be giving the same to her. He'd also be giving a bit of himself so that he wouldn't be leaving her, at least not in her eyes."

"How did you extend his life?"

E.V. smiled. "He had cancer. I got rid of that. If I hadn't come along, he would have died within six months."

"Cancer," Brittany said softly. "You can cure cancer?"

"Yes, for my host." E.V. was nodding. "But not just that. Henry was in the army fighting overseas. As you have discovered, I am a great asset when it comes to being shot."

"Where did Henry catch you?" Brittany remembered a flash from a lot earlier in their relationship, where E.V. had jumped from one host to the next, not having the ability to speak the same language.

"Very good," the creature said. "The very first war Henry saw was Vietnam. In it, he came across an enemy soldier and caught him. His name was Soo Sung.

"Soo Sung was weak and foolish and hadn't kept me well fed," E.V. continued. "Henry overpowered him and tried to take him as a prisoner of war." It scoffed. "Soo Sung thought himself a brave warrior who would willingly give up his life to keep his secrets. I helped him achieve this faster than he could have on his own, but because I survived, Soo Sung's secrets lived on in me. I have never been the type to feel any great attachment to the plight of you humans. I was not loyal to Soo Sung's cause. I jumped to Henry and brought all Soo Sung's information with me.

"Once we got over the initial shock of getting acquainted, I was able to reveal more information than Henry could have ever imagined. With it I helped Henry climb through the ranks of his unit and become the most valuable member of his division. I not only saved his life more times than I can remember, I helped him live a very successful one."

Brittany stayed quiet. E.V. also didn't speak but continued to remember. It allowed Soo Sung's short life to unwind and moved backwards through at least four other hosts of the same origin that lasted varying lifespans. Soo Sung to Henry wasn't the only jump from one culture to another. As Brittany silently watched she witnessed several other crossovers, often during a battle. As the memories grew older still, they were becoming faded, harder to see, and several had holes, large gaps that spanned an unknown amount of years and perhaps even through more than one host.

Brittany was surprised to see something more clearly. The landscape reminded her of movies from medieval times with royalty and peasants. The castle she stared at was magnificent, but what caught her attention were the things that were planted in the fields as far as her exceptionally good eyes could see. At first glance they looked like man-sized Q-tips.

The image cut off abruptly. Brittany was wrenched back to reality, staring at E.V., who looked back with guarded eyes.

"What was that?" The tree fort was dark now that the moon had shifted in the sky. It was setting. Brittany could feel the sun, or more to the point, the heat from the sun as it slowly crept over the horizon.

"Nothing," E.V. lied.

"Don't tell me nothing. I saw it! I saw something." The image was imprinted on the inside of Brittany's eyelids. As she tried to discern what she was looking at, she gasped— the Q-tips were heads. Rows and rows of human heads mounted on poles stretching out away from the castle.

"E.V.?" Brittany's voice was high and it squeaked— but not from the actual image. It was at the realization of how easy it would be to become that kind of monster, the kind who would do such a thing and not have a problem with it.

"This is what happens when you lose your humanity."

"What does that mean?"

"Your humanity, the thing that keeps you connected to your species. You are human, you always will be. I didn't change that. However, I am not human, and I never have been. So it is up to you how human you choose to stay."

Brittany thought back among the many hosts E.V. had inhabited. They each brought their own sense of humanity into the mix, some more and others less. She thought about Gran and remembered seeing her in the garden day after day; that was something she held on to from her old self. Gran also had been a part of the community for years, joining in on many of their events. Even her visits with the Jehovah's Witnesses were a way of connecting with "her" kind.

For Henry the thing that kept him human was Gran, his wife. He could never abandon his life, because it would separate him from her.

Brittany looked at her own life and understood that there was only one thing stopping her from becoming everything her worst nightmares could conjure up. Only one person kept her from becoming the creature that could mount her victims' heads on poles and not be bothered by it.

Coby.

She needed Coby. He kept her human. This realization made the next three days without him very hard.

ɔ꧁ ◆ ꧂

As the sun's first rays fell across her yard, Brittany crept to her house and then sat in her room, waiting for her daytime life to begin. All the extra time she had only made that last hour of night seem to go slower. As her father woke and slipped into the shower, Brittany went down to the kitchen and, just to give herself something to do, made breakfast.

It had been over a month since she'd prepared her father a meal, but today she was feeling the need to be charitable. She even made enough for Ella. But she didn't stay to see how they enjoyed it; she left before either could make it down to the kitchen.

Her pace quickened as she neared the schoolyard with the anticipation of seeing Coby. Now that she understood how much she needed him, she felt anxious. She was curious about his visit to the hospital, the questions asked and the tests performed. But that wasn't why she was anxious. Her anxieties stemmed from the realization of how much she needed him. She felt less human without him. She wanted to feel normal. Coby never showed up.

After a painfully long seven hours, Brittany headed to his house and waited for him there. She stayed from 3:15 all the way to 6:15, when Mrs. Monroe usually arrived home from work. All this waiting made Brittany feel extra irritable. When Mrs. Monroe didn't show up, she nearly tore the shingles off the roof.

"Calm down," E.V. said as the sun was setting. With the authorities looking for a cause of this mysterious outbreak of fatigue, Brittany hadn't allowed E.V. to snack throughout the day, not even from Liam, such a willing victim. Now with her outburst of excessive emotions, E.V. was feeling peckish.

"We don't have much left now." It had its hands on its hips.

Brittany just scowled.

"Brit?" E.V.'s tone changed from displeasure to worry. It couldn't see her thoughts and that made it nervous. "Do you plan on waiting here all night?"

Brittany wasn't thinking clearly. She wanted to see Coby. Without him, she feared what she might do. But she conceded that E.V. was right— she needed to feed it.

"No, we'll be hunting tonight." She could feel the creature relaxing.

Brittany was more interested in the blood than she wanted to let on. She feared that without a reason to stop, she might stay out all night gorging herself. How many people could she devour before the sun started to rise? She shivered at the thought.

FORTY-THREE
MISSED

THIS EVENING AS she snuck out, Brittany didn't need to take Mr. Daminko's gun. She now had her own after having disposed of its previous owner.

This gun felt more like a lethal weapon; it had weight, and as Brittany fired it, the sound was more impressive.

Why do they always have knives? Brittany thought as she crouched over her second victim of the night. It seemed for the next while she might have to survive on a diet of felons, though she hoped not. They all seemed to have thick blood.

"Why?" she asked E.V. as she uncovered the grave she'd dug for the pimp and his prostitute the night before.

"It's got to be something to do with their profession. Maybe some kind of narcotic?" E.V. stood over Brittany as she dug deeper still.

"Does it affect you?"

"Not so much. I guess I use up a tiny bit more to filter it." It seemed to think for a moment. "No. Not enough to make a difference. Tell me," E.V. changed the subject, "why don't you feel as bad about taking these lives as you do when you think of someone like the boy at the supermarket?"

Brittany had reached the bodies. She looked down at their lifeless, pale faces and shrugged. "I guess it's their potential. These two, well especially the pimp, have a really big possibility of being harmful to people around them. The boy from the supermarket, well, he's more likely to do some good in the world."

"What does anyone know about potential?" E.V. said. "The boy from the supermarket has just as many chances to cause destruction; one wrong turn in his car and he could be harmful to many. The pimp could just as easily do something redeeming. No one can know these things." E.V. stopped, regretting its words.

Brittany felt guilty as she looked down at her four corpses, then another thought distracted her. "Do they rot without blood?"

The answer came with the vision of heads on poles. "Yes, they rot. And they smell."

Brittany nodded to herself. "I'll have to find a better spot then." She was returning to a far more practical way of thinking now that she was better fed. The solution was so simple, it made Brittany laugh.

Having gone to the dump with her father to get rid of an old sofa, Brittany knew that there were hills of garbage that went down for miles. Old dump piles were covered with dirt. Grass now grew atop the junk.

She brought her two victims from the previous night and the two from this evening to the city dump located on the outskirts of town. Then she quickly excavated an older-looking hill. Once her victims were buried, she covered them over, returning the grass perfectly where it had been so that no one would suspect anything.

The task done, Brittany didn't know what to do with herself. It was far too early to return home to her boring room. She wasn't paying attention to where her feet were taking her until she found herself staring up at Coby's window. The house was dark and quiet. Brittany could hear his mother sleeping soundly in her room.

Coby's room was empty. He still hadn't come home.

"What are you doing?" E.V. questioned as Brittany took hold of the drainpipe.

"What does it look like?"

Brittany was halfway up, staring down the vision of Emily. Once Brittany made it to Coby's bedroom, she quickly slid his window open. E.V. now stood on the inside barring her way.

"I just want..." Brittany whispered but stopped as her senses were filled with the scent of Coby.

"Let's eat again," E.V. suggested, still standing in Brittany's way. "I think I've got room for one more, at least most of one."

Brittany climbed through the window, moving right through the image of Emily. Once in she stopped and turned back. "You get full?"

E.V. nodded.

"What happens if you do?"

"What happened when you used to get full?"

"I'd stop eating. But what if you're in the middle of someone?"

"Hmmmmm," E.V. said, "it's been too long since that's happened."

"Hmm," Brittany said in return then fell silent. Being in Coby's room, surrounded by his aroma, made her remember more human things. It made her connect with her feelings. She sighed as remorse washed over her: remorse and regret for the night's activities.

"I guess more hunting is out." E.V. slumped down atop Coby's bed.

"Do you think Coby's ok?" Brittany asked, taking a seat on his bed too and burying her nose in his pillow.

"I wouldn't be concerned about him," E.V. answered. "Remember, it's not him they're looking for. They are testing him to try and discover..."

"Us," Brittany said, feeling even gloomier. She wondered if they'd figure it out and what they would do if they did.

"You forget, you won't let them find anyone else. That's why I'm not to feed during the day, and we now kill at night."

Brittany rubbed her face. The plan had felt simple and even good when she'd thought it up, but with four dead bodies she wasn't so sure anymore.

"How many pimps do you think there are?" she wondered. *How long until they run out?*

"Don't worry, downtown is larger than you realize. Besides, once we've removed a few, more are bound to turn up."

Brittany had stopped listening. There wasn't much she could do about it. It was either kill pimps or steal from innocent people, and most days it felt like she needed to do a little of both. The only alternative was to die. As much as she disliked what she was becoming, she liked the thought of dying even less. Besides, her dying wouldn't stop the creature. It would move on to someone else. Someone else who might not care as much as Brittany.

Brittany listened to Mrs. Monroe as she rolled over in bed. She struggled with a growing desire to wake the woman and demand to know what was happening to her son. She fought it for the rest of the night, winning only marginally. As morning crept closer, Brittany returned home and put on the ruse that she was the same girl she had always been.

The next day was the same as the first and the following day was a repeat. As the time passed Brittany was feeling worse and worse. The third night she'd only managed to find one person she deemed detestable enough to kill, so E.V. was also out of sorts.

By lunchtime on Friday, Brittany could barely concentrate. She was so preoccupied that she bumped right into Liam and almost fell over.

"Whoa." Liam caught her. "Are you alright?"

NO, E.V.! Brittany scolded, but she was too late to stop it.

"Trust me," the creature said, "you need it."

But the bruises! Brittany shook her head.

"What's wrong with you today?" Liam asked, still holding Brittany.

"I was just…" E.V. was right, she had needed it. With two ounces of Liam's blood in her she felt better. "…hungry. I *am* hungry." She was barely able to meet Liam's eyes as she mumbled, "Thanks." She pulled away from him as a desire to take more — to take it all — started to grow within her.

I hate you! Brittany cursed as she walked away.

E.V. kept pace. "You're welcome."

Brittany's vision was swimming in her rage. *You've turned me into a monster*!

"I have not turned you into anything you were not capable of being before," E.V. argued.

Brittany turned and ducked into the girls' washroom, trying to avoid the crowded halls. *I never craved blood before you infected me!*

E.V. crossed its arms and stared at Brittany through the smudged mirror. "We need to eat."

I don't care! Brittany smacked the side of the sink, feeling the porcelain give under her palm and the whole thing groan in protest.

"Are you angry that you need blood to survive now? Or are you upset that you want more?"

I don't just want to "eat" — I crave more... so much more.

"I've already told you," E.V. said casually, "the kind of person you are is up to you."

Brittany sagged and moaned softly. "I need Coby."

"He shouldn't be away much longer." E.V. didn't get a chance to say any more as Simone walked in.

"There she is," Simone said in an exasperated tone, like she'd been looking for a while. She had entered the bathroom with a group of her friends in tow. "Come on, Brittany, we saved you a seat at our table."

Brittany allowed the girls to escort her to the lunchroom, where the rest waited. She felt E.V. take one or two ounces off of at least three girls who touched her. Now that she felt better, she was able to truly feel worse.

FORTY-FOUR
EXHAUSTED

BRITTANY HAD PLANNED to go to Coby's house again after school, but before she made it out of the building, she saw Mrs. Monroe walking towards one of his classrooms. Brittany quickly met up with her.

"Mrs. Monroe, how is Coby?"

Coby's mom looked at Brittany. For a moment she looked upset, like she somehow knew it was Brittany's fault that her son was in the hospital. Then the look changed to pity. "Oh, he's fine, dear." She patted Brittany's shoulder.

Not a drop! Brittany commanded, feeling E.V.'s longing within her.

"Why? Why can't I. You know if I do she'll sleep better tonight."

If you do and she feels more tired, who do you think she'll talk to about this. Her son is already in the hospital. If she goes in for tests then the doctors will have a connection. How long till that connection leads them to me— to us?

E.V. didn't answer, but it also didn't take any blood from the woman.

Mrs Monroe had been answering Brittany's question. Brittany missed part of it, but not the most important part, "...ming him home tonight. You can come over tomorrow to see him if you'd like."

With this news Brittany went home to play out her night-time routine. She did the human things that she now found mundane and time-consuming, the biggest being dinner with her dad— and Ella, since she was there more often now. Brittany cooked the meal and even sat with the two.

As she pushed the food around her plate, Brittany was trying to decide which she liked better: when she was alone with her dad or when Ella was there. She decided Ella being there made it easier, because the two were usually so distracted by each other that neither noticed Brittany wasn't eating.

"Oh," Brittany's dad spoke up as she was starting to clear the table, "I spoke with your mom today. She feels it's long past time that you go for another visit."

Brittany thought back to her last visit. "I guess it has been a while."

"Yes, I figured as much. I told her you'd be coming over in the morning. Be prepared— I think she wants you to babysit."

Brittany nodded.

She left when her dad and Ella started to get snuggly. She had hoped that the woman's growing belly would put a halt to their nuzzling, but for now it seemed to be making it worse.

She hadn't planned to end up at Coby's— at least not so early. Yet somehow that was exactly where she found herself. She knew that he wasn't home yet, but as much as E.V. insisted, and Brittany even agreed, she couldn't get her feet to move her away. It was as if neither the creature nor Brittany was in control of them. Once inside, she slumped onto his bed.

E.V. stood with its arms crossed, towering over Brittany. "We can't stay— we need to go and eat first. Surely you must see the danger of being here when we're so hungry. I know I promised I wouldn't take from him again, but you coming here now will make it harder for me to keep that promise. Come on, Brittany, this isn't fair to me... Brit?"

Brittany was straining her ears, hoping, waiting to hear Mrs. Monroe's car returning with her son.

"Brit!" E.V. stepped forward to try to shake the girl. Of course a hallucination couldn't do that, but the creature inside was a different story.

Brittany felt E.V. vibrating, which made her whole frame tremble.

"Brittany!" E.V.'s tone changed.

Brittany wasn't responding.

The creature now recognized the problem. "Brittany, you need to lie down and shut your eyes." It had been over three days since Brittany last slept.

"Brittany, come on, listen to me." Even though E.V. had stopped shaking her from within, Brittany continued to shudder. It could feel its reserves depleting— every minute they used up far more than they could afford. "Please, lie down."

Between shudders, Brittany managed to lie back and slowly roll to her side. "Why-am- I-shaking?" she asked, her voice coming out staccato.

"Because you are mentally exhausted." E.V. was more worried than it wanted to let on. "Just close your eyes, dear." It used Gran's voice.

Brittany felt like she was falling into a great chasm that she might never be able to get out of. Her eyes flew open. "I can't."

"What's the problem, hon?" Gran's tone was soft and full of compassion.

"I can't," Brittany repeated. "He's not here."

It was then that both E.V. and Brittany realized just how much she had come to depend on Coby. Brittany didn't feel safe enough to fall asleep without him. Even being in his room wasn't good enough. She needed Coby.

E.V. was worried that Brittany was going into shock. It had happened before. If they refused to sleep they either went insane or their minds would simply shut down. But E.V. didn't have to worry long.

Both creature and host tracked Mrs. Monroe's engine from several blocks away. They listened as the car was shifted into park on the street in front. First one, then two doors were opened and closed.

"Yes, Ma." Coby's voice reached Brittany's ears and she perked up enough to sit up.

"I'm just saying…" Mrs. Monroe chastised.

Brittany could hear their feet crunching the snow on the way to the front door. She could tell that Coby was in front.

"Where are you going?" his mom called after him.

"To do my homework," he replied with a false note in his voice. Brittany could feel him on the stairs, but as much as she wanted to go to him and greet him, she couldn't move.

"You haven't been home in days, don't I get to see you?"

"It's only been three days. And you spent all of them at the hospital with me!" Coby called back to his mom from outside his bedroom door.

Brittany heard the turning of the door handle, then his voice came to her in a whisper. "I hoped you'd be here."

Brittany felt Coby at her back, drawing her next to him and wrapping his arms around her.

"Are you tired?" Coby pulled a few loose strands of hair away from her pale face. Her eyes were so heavy that she couldn't keep them from closing. As the spinning began, she could feel Coby's warmth; it kept her from feeling like she was tumbling into oblivion.

"When did you sleep last?" he asked, nuzzling his nose into the back of Brittany's cold neck.

"Three…" Brittany fought to stay conscious as the sleep washed over her, "…daysss…" her efforts were in vain.

"That's right, dear," E.V. soothed in Gran's voice, "you sleep."

Coby was saying the same thing, but both Brittany and the creature missed it.

FORTY-FIVE
RESEARCHED

WHILE SHE SLEPT, Coby started to put together the last few pieces of the puzzle Brittany had left him with before he'd been carted off for testing. His time away had been far more productive than anyone could have imagined.

Coby had been able to compile a conclusive list of all the oddities he'd witnessed in Brittany since Emily's death. Granted, he had wondered how wise it was to research this on the hospital's WiFi, but he hadn't been patient enough to wait until he was home.

His questions hadn't taken him where he thought they would.

When he'd entered "vampire" in the search engine he'd gotten so many sites it would have taken forever to sift through them. So he ruled that out. Instead, he tried to research what he'd noticed. First she had become fit and at the same time stopped eating. She seemed to be sleeping less, and she was more distracted. She also moved quicker. She left bruises on people when she touched them. She was colder than normal and he was almost certain she didn't have a pulse. Then there was the bullet hole.

The combination of all these only came up with one answer— pregnancy... Coby was certain that wasn't the answer. He decided to go to one of the "ask the experts" sites. He posted the same question on all seven sites he found. It said: "My girlfriend..." Coby didn't know what else to call Brittany "...has been acting strange..." then he listed off all her ailments from the almost normal to the completely bizarre.

The first response wasn't encouraging. *Dude, she's pregnant.* *You still need to have sex to get pregnant, right?* Coby replied. *Yup.*

Then she's not pregnant.

Just because she's not having sex with you doesn't mean she's not having sex.

Coby decided not to return to that site. Instead, he switched screens to check out the others.

Between the six sites left he'd gotten several replies on each. Eight of them told him to buy her a pregnancy test. Three suggested getting her tested for a rare virus, each naming a different one. One asked if her symptoms went away when she was around kryptonite.

And then there was one answer that he was sure was what he was looking for. It was a simple five-word reply: *same thing happened to me.*

He responded with *I need to talk to you,* and he posted his email. The moment he hit enter he regretted it. While he debated taking it down, he heard the wind-chime alert his email made.

The reply was simple, just as the posting had been: *What would you like to know?* Coby noted that the return address was *lookingforsomethingmore18@...*

Coby typed, *What was it?* Then he went about taking his email address down from the "ask the expert" site. By the time he had done that lookingforsomethingmore18 had answered. Coby thought quickly that this person must be a quick typist, then he began to read the five paragraphs he'd received.

It all started with a camping trip and a corpse. After the first night the girls had gone to the lake early to swim. On their way back they got lost. We found them— it was easy once they'd started screaming.

When me and my friends got to them we saw why they were in hysterics; a half rotted corpse lay against a tree. I took charge and got the girls out of there, then we found a tarp and I covered the body. With the corpse contained, we headed to where we could get cellular service.

The authorities took a while to locate us and even longer to question us. I was the last to be released. Once I was done my buddies had already torn down our camp and taken the girls home. I stayed and I caught the discussion the cops had about how odd it was that the dead man hadn't been consumed by wild animals. From the rate of decay he'd been there for a while before the girls discovered him. Yet he hadn't been touched. He'd sat, as if waiting, propped up against a tree with no obvious cause of death.

I don't care what my therapist called it— it was freaky how clearly I could recall the corpse. I was haunted by a memory of his face. It was so vivid, it kept me up at night, well, that and my itchy fingers.

I was told that I had been infected by poisonous oak but I never got the rash that would have gone with it. Anyway, once the itchiness was gone I'd started to notice other things like: I was incredibly strong, had faster reflexes, and I didn't need sleep for days.

After reading this, Coby couldn't get the chillingly eerie story out of his thoughts. He missed the part where LFSM18 didn't answer his question. He replied immediately. *This is creepy, that's kinda what happened to my friend. Only the body she found was our friend's. And sometimes she acts like she's seeing things I can't.*

That was when lookingforsomethingmore18 responded with a phone number. Coby called it almost immediately.

"Have you contacted me to mock and condemn?" The voice on the other end of the line was hard and angry.

"N... no," Coby stuttered, feeling very much as if his life could be in danger for upsetting the guy.

"Then what do you want!" The guy's voice sounded more animal-like than human.

"You told me to call you. I'm CMonroe. I have a friend who I'm worried about. She found the dead body and now she's ch... changed." Coby started to wonder about his sanity. Why was he talking to a complete stranger, especially one who sounded so dangerous? What had made him go to such extreme measures?

"Oh?" The voice turned softer.

This sent a chill up Coby's spine. He almost hung up. But he didn't.

"This friend of yours, what's her name?"

"I'm sorry." Coby hesitated, still debating if ending the conversation might be smarter. "I can't tell you." It was his fear of offending LFSM18 that kept him from hanging up. That, and curiosity. Coby was sure that the person on the other end of the phone had the answers he was looking for.

LFSM18 answered in a too-casual voice, "You won't trust me and yet you expect me to believe what you're saying?"

"Why would I lie about this?"

"Well," LFSM18's voice was filled with judgment, "it's not me who's calling from a hospital pay phone."

Coby kicked himself for not realizing that the caller ID would pick that up.

"Let me guess," LFSM18's voice had turned mocking, "you're calling from the psych ward."

"No." Coby was offended, but if he were being honest, over the past twenty-four hours there were times when he felt that that's where he should be.

"Ok, strange boy, why are you calling me from the hospital? Do you think it's a good place to pick up chicks?"

What a weird thing to say, Coby thought. Again he felt like he should just hang up. He ignored his instinct. "I'm here because I called 9-1-1 after my best friend had passed out and I couldn't find a pulse or a heartbeat."

When Coby didn't go on, LFSM18 said, "And?"

"And she woke up and ran away before the ambulance came. When they showed up they wanted to arrest me for wasting their time. To cover, I'd told them that I'd dreamed Brit had died and called them before I realized it was a dream."

"So they arrested you and you confessed the truth and they sent you for psychiatric evaluation?" LFSM18 coaxed.

"No." Coby was losing his patience. "No. They wanted to arrest me but my mom begged them not to. She told them that I had been very sick and wasn't fully recovered."

"Did she lie or were you really sick?" The interest in LFSM18's tone was unmistakable.

"Well, I had been sick. My doctor said it was mono. When my mom told the paramedics that, they insisted I to come to the hospital for tests."

LFSM18 was silent for so long, Coby started to wonder if he'd been hung up on. Finally, the man spoke in a soft and soothing voice. "This illness, you were tired?"

"Yes, that's what happens with mono."

"How tired?"

Coby thought a moment. "I was so tired I couldn't stay awake for nearly a week. And I might have been delusional."

"Anything else?" LFSM18's voice had become its softest yet. Like listening to silk slipping over the palm of your hand. "Anything else odd? Any bruises? Any strange swelling?"

"Ya," Coby stuttered, feeling like he'd made a mistake that he'd regret later, but unsure what the actual mistake was. "Ya, my tongue had swollen so I couldn't talk."

The pause this time wasn't as long. "Interesting. This Brit, Brittany I assume, is she your girlfriend or just a friend?"

"Sort of girlfriend... I guess. We've kissed and we've held hands." Coby thought about it for a moment then added, "She likes to visit in the night and snuggle with me. But then there are times when she doesn't want me to touch her." Coby tried not to sound put out. Then he remembered something. "Funny you should ask about bruises. There is this kid at school, kind of a nerd. He has a locker next to..." It was at this moment that Coby realized that he'd already given LFSM18 Brittany's name. "His locker is next to Brittany's. She never used to talk to him before. Now she says good morning almost every day. He's covered in bruises. What do you make of that?"

"I think this is a conversation that would be better face-to-face."

They made arrangements to meet in the afternoon of the following day.

FORTY-SIX

INFORMED

THE HOSPITAL CAFETERIA wasn't too crowded when Coby arrived at three that afternoon. He was easily able to spot LFSM18 sitting at a table with a stuffed bunny in front of him— like he'd promised.

The dude was attractive, not that Coby was into that, but it was plain to see. Every woman in the room, from the teen girls to those much older, was craning her neck to check him out— even the little old ladies in house coats and hospital slippers were doing double takes.

He had a medium build, but it was clear that he would be able to hold his own in a fight. He was clean-shaven, like he had finished only minutes before getting there. His complexion was flawless. Clearly he was old enough to have grown out of the acne phase. His hair was dirty blond, shiny, and styled back so it was off his face. His hazel eyes seemed normal enough, yet they looked as if they were years older then their owner.

He seemed to recognize Coby instantly, though Coby couldn't figure out how.

LFSM18 waved him over. "I got us drinks," he said as Coby sat down across from him. "I figured Coke was the way to go."

Coby watched as LFSM18 brought his drink up to take a gulp. Then he looked down at the unopened can in front of the stuffed toy. He was feeling hesitant again. The guy didn't look much older than eighteen, and there was nothing about him that appeared threatening— it was just a feeling.

Coby had to clear his throat before he spoke. "I don't even know your name."

The fizzing from the freshly opened can in Coby's hands seemed to distract LFSM18 for a moment. "I don't really know yours either."

"Oh." Coby felt unnerved once more. He tried to recall if he'd forgotten to give his name— but decided it didn't matter. "Coby."

"Well, Mr. Coby Monroe, you can call me Mr. Michaels. Or Mike for short."

"Mike." Coby tried to smile and swallow down the lump in this throat.

Mike's eyes were trained on Coby as if he were trying to see more than the boy that sat in front of him. "So, Coby, you say that Brittany is giving someone bruises."

"I didn't say that!" Coby said louder than he'd intended. He took a moment to scan the room, noticing many pairs of eyes on Mike. Coby continued more quietly. "You think Brit had something to do with the bruises?"

Mike seemed to shrug without commitment. "You're the one who brought it up."

Coby narrowed his eyes. "What do you think's going on? You're the one who wanted to meet. So? What do you think it is?"

Mike stretched out so that he was leaning against his chair. Coby swore he heard the girl at the table behind him sigh. Mike's lip twitched so that it looked as if he were repressing a smirk.

Coby continued to stare through narrowed eyes as he waited.

"Fine," Mike half sighed, half chuckled. "I think your girlfriend may be possessed."

"Possessed?" Now Coby's eyebrows rose.

Mike nodded and continued. "If she is, there will be a few ways you can check."

"Possessed, like, by a demon?" Coby couldn't believe it. "Isn't that a little bit... insane?"

Mike didn't seem to take offence to Coby's doubts. It was like he expected this reaction. "It's biblical. Though most people don't believe in it anymore. But just because you don't believe something doesn't make it any less real." His voice became heavy like someone recounting a bad experience. "I've seen it for myself... several times now."

"Is that what happened to you?" Coby asked.

"Yes," Mike answered without a moment's hesitation.

The only thing that kept Coby from thinking that Mike might be a resident of the floor above his was that he made it sound so believable. Besides, something strange was up with Brittany.

"Now, pay attention," Mike said, "First off, don't mess with the demon or the human if they are tired. You said she visits you at night to nap?" He shifted in his seat and continued after a nod from Coby. "When you get home have her lie down with you. Wait for her to fall asleep. Most of the things you need to check for will be easier if she is sleeping..."

"But I shouldn't mess with her when she's tired."

"Tired and awake." Mike's tone was bordering on irritation. "Haven't you noticed that when she sleeps, she doesn't stir for two hours? Surely you've noticed that when she's sleeping she doesn't breath."

Coby hadn't noticed that. He stayed quiet as Mike went on to give him a comprehensive list of things to do.

ભ ♦ ૪૦

With Brittany wrapped securely in his arms, he was able to run through the list.

She certainly wasn't breathing. Coby felt his heart skip a beat. He already knew that he wouldn't find a pulse or the heartbeat that ought to go with it. But it felt more real with Mike's list to back it up. Coby shifted so that he could press one hand firmly down on Brittany's stomach. Just as he'd been told, her skin felt normal and soft, but under that it felt like she had rocks for intestines.

The next item on the list was glowing. He remembered noticing this before but still had to double check. He held Brittany in his arms under his window. She didn't stir, just as Mike promised she wouldn't. He exposed her cold skin to the moon's rays and had to stifle a gasp.

This was it. There was only one more test to perform, but Coby couldn't bring himself to do it.

ભ્ર ◆ ฒ

"I won't cut her." Coby crossed his arms, keeping his voice low with some effort. The women who continued to stare at Mike weren't trying to eavesdrop— they just wanted to check the guy out, repeatedly.

"I assure you, if she is possessed it won't hurt her."

"And what if you are wrong?"

"What's a small scratch compared to demonic possession?"

"I can't do it."

Mike shifted forward. "You'll want to be certain. We don't want to try and exorcise her if she isn't really possessed."

"Why do we even have to exorcise her in the first place?"

"Because if she has a demon in her, she is suffering. She is a prisoner in her own mind. Trust me, that's no way to live."

"But how can you be sure that's what she's feeling?"

Mike fixed his gaze on Coby, his eyes cold. "I've been there. Death would be better."

"Ok, say a demon is in her... and she's trapped. Say she's stuck watching herself do all these horrible things. She'd be able to see it all. So how would it feel to her if she saw me cut her? I can't." Coby's voice hitched. "I won't."

"Fine." Mike sat back with a fire blazing in his eyes. As the anger seemed to subside, he said, "That would have been the easy test. If you're not man enough to cut her, then there is another way. But trust me, this will be much harder."

ભ્ર ◆ ฒ

As Coby continued to hold Brittany, who was a corpse next to him, he wondered how many people were like this. Surely not many. Or maybe there were tons? What if there were so many that humans were the minority? Coby shook his head to dispel these useless thoughts.

He took a steadying breath and reminded himself of what had to be done once Brittany woke. He hoped she'd sleep on forever, which would contradict one of the items on Mike's list. Coby didn't expect her to.

At exactly 9:07, two hours to the minute after Brittany had lost consciousness, she started to stir.

FORTY-SEVEN

OFFENDED

E.V. HAD FELT Coby poking and prodding, even moving Brittany; it was anxious to have the girl wake up.

Brittany pulled in a deep breath of air and tested it. She didn't understand where E.V.'s worries were coming from. She couldn't taste any danger. She did, however, taste Coby's aroma; it was thicker with his presence. It made her smile.

"Morning, Sleeping Beauty," Coby whispered into Brittany's hair.

"It's not morning." Brittany rolled onto her back and opened her eyes.

"Ok, good evening." Coby smiled. "Feeling better now?"

Brittany "hmhummed" her response. She felt much better, especially as she experienced the warmth of Coby heating her. She couldn't deny, however, that she also felt worse. E.V. would need to be fed— and soon!

Coby shifted to sitting, reached into his back pocket and pulled out a knife. Before Brittany could react, he'd run the blade across the palm of his hand.

Brittany gasped, sucking in the scent of Coby's blood. She brought her hand over her mouth while she asked, "What are you doing?" But she didn't wait for his response. Instead she scrambled to the foot of the bed, trying to put as much space between her and Coby as possible. The desire to lunge towards him almost overpowered her.

Why is he doing this! she screamed at E.V. in her head.

E.V. was watching Coby intently. "Because he knows what you are."

Shouldn't he be terrified? Doesn't he know how dangerous I am? Brittany continued to move backwards until she fell to the floor with a loud thump.

"Your generation has idolized the vampire, turning them into teddy bears and heroes. He probably doesn't understand the danger he's put himself in." E.V. was having a hard time concentrating past Brittany's desire. "You'd better leave now."

Brittany didn't. She didn't want to— only she wasn't sure why she didn't want to. Her head was spinning. She was already hungry and Coby's blood was already far more enticing than anyone else's. As she continued to suck in Coby's scent, she wondered if she stayed because she didn't want to leave Coby, or was staying to finish him off. Without an answer, all she could do was stay rooted to the spot.

"Why are you doing this?" she said once she could manage the words.

Coby's head appeared over the foot of his bed. He wasn't about to tell her that someone else suggested he do this. "I thought you might be thirsty now that you've had a good rest."

Brittany's eyes darted between his window and Coby's hand.

E.V. stayed quiet, waiting to see how this would end.

"Come now." Coby pushed his hand, now in a fist to contain the blood flow, at Brittany's face. "You must be hungry."

"Don't do that!" She kicked his hand away and scrambled to the opposite side of the room, where she shut her eyes and pressed her head to the wall.

"Don't you want my blood?" Coby's voice had changed to barely contained hurt.

Brittany opened her eyes and watched as he climbed off the bed, moving slowly and deliberately. She saw in his eyes what she'd suspected in this voice— her refusing to drink his blood made him feel rejected.

Brittany moaned.

"I know that you need it." He stopped at arm's reach from her.

"You don't understand."

"What do I need to understand?" Coby crouched down so that their eyes were level. "You need blood. I've got extra. I Googled it, that's how people can donate." He started to open his palm.

"Stop!" Brittany's head was swimming. The scent of Coby's blood filled the air so that she choked on it. Of course she wanted it! Even before she understood what she was doing, she had wanted it— *his*... and she wanted it all.

"Come on Brits, I'm giving it to you." Coby held his hand out further. "I want you to have it."

E.V. was staring at Coby's half opened hand. "Brittany, I know I promised, but he's right; a few ounces won't hurt." It turned away as if not looking could lessen its desire.

Brittany sat wide-eyed, not knowing what to do. How could she take from Coby again? She'd come too close to killing him the first time.

"I won't make the same mistake this time. I can be good," E.V. said. "Besides, he's giving it to you. It's not stealing if he offers."

E.V., right now it's not you I'm worried about. Brittany felt a longing that was more demanding than she'd ever experienced before. *I can't take just a little. I won't be satisfied with just a few ounces!*

"I'll stop you," E.V. said.

Brittany chuckled darkly— she was sure that in her state E.V. wouldn't be able to stop her.

"It's either you take some or we've got to get out of here!" E.V. snapped. All this stress was depleting what little reserves the creature had.

"Why are you doing this to me?" Brittany looked Coby in the eye. She too was avoiding looking at the blood, which was turning a deeper shade of red as it congealed in the palm of his hand.

"Because," Coby's voice hitched and faltered and Brittany heard his heartbeat speed up, "I'm... I'm in love with you." He continued to hold his hand out, allowing the pooled blood to dry and crack in his cupped palm.

Brittany pushed her head against the wall so hard, she felt the drywall giving way under it.

"Such a waste," E.V. sighed. "We should at least take the blood that he's already bled out."

How can we do that? Brittany wondered.

"You will have to drink it," E.V. said with a twist of humour.

Brittany shut her eyes. *What?*

"You need to put it in your mouth— but don't swallow. I can't collect it from outside the body but I can extract it from inside your mouth."

Fine. It was disturbing how fine she felt about it. "Alright," she whispered to Coby, "alright." She leaned forward slightly and watched as he brought his hand to her mouth. She shut her eyes when she felt the warmth of his palm touch her lips. Her tongue tingled as she lapped up the blood.

She was shocked at how cold the blood had gotten in such a short time. As it coated her tongue, she could taste that it was thick, like homemade gravy. Its bouquet was light, on the sweet side. As she pulled more of it into her mouth, she noticed a few lumps. No doubt they were clots. They carried a heavier, more concentrated taste.

Still with her eyes shut, Brittany gently closed her lips over Coby's cut and gave one great suck. Coby winced but Brittany missed it. She was far too distracted by the taste of his fresh blood, warmer, deeper, richer.

Before she could take another pull, she felt his cut close under her tongue. E.V.'s tentacles had been lapping at the blood that Brittany had collected in her mouth. In the process they had healed Coby's hand. Brittany released his hand and turned away.

Coby wasn't sure what he'd expected. This, however, was a complete shock. This had felt kind, Mike had told him to expect a monster. Brittany wasn't acting like a monster.

He examined his hand and saw that it was healed as if he'd never cut it in the first place.

"That was… hmmm, I don't know what to say."

Brittany hadn't turned back.

"Did you get enough?"

"No." She didn't want to answer but the word had slipped out.

"Why? What happened?"

Brittany sighed, refusing to answer this time. She turned to look at him, feeling sorry that she'd taken as much as she had.

Coby misunderstood. "No worries, I can get you more." He rolled onto his knees to stand.

"Don't," Brittany reached out and grabbed his arm to stop him.

He turned towards her. "But if you need..."

"Please," she pleaded, "please don't."

Coby bent closer. "Brittany, you need more."

She gave a forced laugh. Here he was explaining the truth that she knew. But he didn't understand. "That's not even how I take it." Her voice had turned hard.

"Oh?" Coby felt a chill go up his spine at the first hint that Mike had lied to him. "It isn't?"

"Nope." She locked eyes with Coby. With the few ounces she'd managed to suck out, before E.V. stopped her, Brittany now felt stronger... and weaker.

The taste of him tickled the back of her throat, causing her to feel like she needed a drink, yet she knew there was only one thing that would soothe that tickle.

"How then?"

The desire for more of his blood was growing, taking on a personality of its own. Brittany had let go of Coby's arm and was forcing herself not to move.

"Brits, will you show me?" Coby reached out to brush her cheek.

That was the tipping point.

Without thinking Brittany caught Coby's arm again and used it to spin him so that she trapped him with his hand behind his back, but the momentum didn't stop there. Once facing away, she pushed him down onto his stomach and crouched over him, pinning him under her knee. She knew that if she applied enough pressure, she could have snapped his spine.

Somehow she resisted. Instead, she brought her hand up to place it on the side of Coby's neck. *Show him, E.V.,* she thought, realizing that she was behaving more like a monster than E.V. had ever done.

"No," E.V. said.

Brittany scowled.

"Think about what you are doing. You are completely out of control. If you get me to take from him now, there's no telling if I'll be able to stop in time. Give yourself a minute to calm down."

Brittany tried to calm herself. She took a deep breath, but the air was laced with blood and fear. That, along with the taste of Coby's blood clinging to the back of her throat, made calm nearly impossible.

"Why don't you let him go?" E.V. asked soothingly.

Why don't you do what I told you to! Brittany said, still angry but feeling closer to controlling it now.

E.V. rolled its eyes. "Ok, but we've already taken two ounces, so unless we want to hurt him, I shouldn't take much more. No more than four." Even as E.V. spoke, it could feel that Brittany didn't know herself whether she meant to hurt him or not. "To be safe I'll only take three," it added, making the decision for both of them.

Coby lay under Brittany without moving. It was sort of a necessity. He knew he was completely pinned. But that wasn't all of it. He knew Brittany was upset, that he'd upset her. So he lay waiting to see what she would do next.

He didn't feel the extraction, but he felt the effects of it. He wanted to chuckle as he realized that he'd felt this before. As a general tired feeling seeped over him, he remembered back to a day not so long ago, in the school cafeteria— the first day he'd noticed Brittany's cold hands.

That wasn't enough, Brittany complained when E.V. told her it was done.

"Then find someone else. I'm not ending Coby this way. You need him, you love him, you could never forgive yourself — or me — if you ended him. Brittany, believe me, you don't want to kill him."

Maybe not, Brittany responded, *maybe I do want to kill him*. She told herself as well as E.V., but she released Coby and stood up.

"Trust me, you don't."

Brittany didn't argue. Instead she focussed on watching Coby slowly roll over.

"Done?" he asked.

How can he act so casual? Brittany wondered. It was a rhetorical question— she didn't expect E.V. to answer.

Coby tried and failed to stifle his yawn.

"I've got to go," Brittany said and bolted out the window before Coby could reply.

ଓ ◆ ଚଠ

Brittany had left. Disappeared right out of Coby's second storey window to do whatever it was she did in the night. He'd waited until he was sure she was really gone, and then waited a bit more, fighting the exhaustion he felt. The exhaustion pulled at him to shut his eyes, if only for a few seconds. He knew a few seconds would be all he'd need to pass out.

This was what had happened the night he kissed Brittany and became sick. This was why everyone was getting sick. This was what the police were looking for. It was Brittany.

With the assurance that Brittany was gone and wasn't returning soon, Coby made his way over to his computer to check for mail. Sure enough, Mike had sent him something. *Coby, you still alive?*

He wrote a quick reply: *Yup, I'm still here.* But he hesitated because he was having new feelings of mistrust. Why would Mike write a question like that? It almost implied that he hadn't expected Coby to survive the test. Had it been less of a test for Brittany and more of one for him? Why had Mike said he needed to cut himself to offer blood when, if Mike had been possessed himself, he should have known that that wasn't how the demon took the blood?

Coby rubbed his neck, feeling a bruise starting to form where Brittany had held him. Instead of sending his response, he got up and checked what his neck looked like in the mirror. It was chilling how similar it looked to the nerd's arms. Yet in this location it could easily be mistaken for a hickie.

Coby went back to his computer and changed his response. *It must have been my imagination. Maybe I was going stir-crazy after being dragged off to the hospital. After all, I was only one floor away from the psych ward. I checked Brittany again — she's missing half the signs, and when I cut myself she barfed and freaked out. Now I've got a massive cut on my palm and if my mom finds it, I'm sure to be sent back to the hospital. Thanks for your help. Apart from my wounded hand, I'm glad you were wrong about Brit. Good luck in your demon hunts.*

He signed and sent it, hoping that would be the last he'd hear from Mike.

FORTY-EIGHT
TOLD

BRITTANY STOOD WITH her back against the cement wall in the deserted alley. "He's mad! He's gone completely insane!" Brittany kicked at the corpse that had been her first meal for the night. The dead pimp had been discarded face up, eyes open, staring with a lifeless, glassy look toward the heavens. His body was flipped and rolled to the middle of the alley by the force of her kick.

"Tell me, E.V., has this ever happened to you before?"

E.V. trembled at the sheer, unadulterated rage it felt circulating through Brittany. Before it had time to collect its thoughts, Brittany seemed to be in its memories searching for her answer.

She found two reference points.

The first was old— before the Industrial Revolution, before electricity, cars, and even running water. The date was uncertain but the images were clear.

E.V. had possessed a young boy, though in that era he was considered a man. He had proposed to the prettiest girl in the area, and she'd accepted... but he had been conscripted and sent off to the war before they could wed. It had been his job to dispose of the dead. That was where he was infected with E.V. He was only at the front for a week when the battle was won — by the other side — and he was sent home.

He underwent the worst of his transformation completely oblivious to what was happening. It all took place as the wedding preparations were finalized. With the wedding date in five days the young man realized that he had become something otherworldly. His gentleman's party almost turned into a massacre. At any rate, all who attended suffered a month-long hangover.

The man...

"Charles," E.V. supplied as a later memory of him surfaced out of sequence.

Charles disappeared that night. But he'd taken his love for...

"Petunia," E.V. said.

...his love for Petunia into his new form. He loved her deeply, and as Brittany saw it she felt his remorse. He stayed away from Petunia, to protect her from the creature he'd become. But he didn't really leave her, or when he did he was never gone long. He watched her from the shadows, waiting for her to pick up and continue on with her life.

He was anxious for her to court and fall in love again, though he knew he'd die inside when she did. He wanted to see it to know she'd found the happiness he'd robbed her of when he left.

"But she never did," E.V. said sadly, remembering how *they* had felt.

Petunia never remarried. Eventually she moved to a new community and started a new life— but not really. She was a schoolteacher living alone in a room at the back of her little red schoolhouse.

Eventually Charles visited her while she slept. First just once— after years of fighting with himself, then again, and again, staying longer and longer each time. And finally staying until she woke in the morning.

Charles explained to Petunia what had happened to him, mostly. She was so happy to see him again that she accepted it and told him she loved him no matter what type of man he was. They married. Charles took a job and fit into the community like any gentleman of that age, and Petunia lived as his wife.

She let Charles feed off of her regularly, becoming so good at donating that after only six months of their union, he was sustained off her alone.

"They lived happily for more than twenty years," E.V. said to finish the story.

"Weird." Brittany breathed out. She could not imagine Coby becoming her blood sponsor.

"Well, of course you can't. Not now! I'm too young in you. But he can donate some, and I will be sure you don't kill him. Remember, we are a team."

Brittany shook her head. Charles and Petunia felt more like a fairy tale than what could be reality.

"Ok," E.V. said, "what about the other couple?"

But they didn't get a chance to discuss it, since Brittany smelled someone approaching.

Even without the scent of alcohol, she would have known the man was smashed by the way he staggered along. She also guessed he was homeless because he was layered in at least two pairs of track pants and five shirts of vastly clashing colors.

She would have left him to stumble off to wherever he was going, but two things sealed his fate. First, he noticed the dead pimp, and then he noticed Brittany standing in the shadows.

He opened his mouth to shout, whether in shock or alarm Brittany didn't wait to find out. She lunged and tackled in one swift move. She hit the poor man with such force that he fell. His head slammed to the asphalt with a crack. It knocked him unconscious. Or killed him. Either way, he was dead within the minute.

E.V. worked quickly, stretching out of both of Brittany's palms where they'd landed, one on the man's neck, the other on the top of his head. Still, Brittany was impatient. She craved to be doing something more.

Coby's blood still painted her mouth and tickled her throat. It laced every breath she took. She wanted to wash it out, to scrub it away. She knew that there was only one thing she could do to be rid of it. She also knew that no one's blood would be as delicious, as inviting, as satisfying as his. Yet she had to get rid of his taste somehow. She was contemplating biting into the homeless man and sucking his neck or wrist. Even his stomach would do.

"Too late." E.V. wiped its mouth. "I'm done. Maybe next time, if you warn me first." It was only joking.

"Ok, E.V., the next guy, preferably a pimp this time, I want the first crack at him."

The creature stood motionless, staring down at Brittany, who sat on her latest victim like a princess on her throne. Her fingers were bunched in the dead man's greasy hair. Her other hand squeezed his neck until there was the distinct sound of a bone breaking, or several at once.

"That's two," E.V. said softly. "Don't you think we should call it a night? Two is plenty, and that's not counting what we got from…" It stopped talking, but its thoughts had already said Coby's name. "Brittany, I think I'm full…"

"For the next guy, I get the first bite," Brittany said through her teeth.

"Brit, we don't need any more. We've got plenty to last until tomorrow." E.V. was frightened by Brittany's thoughts. "Don't you want to see Coby again before it gets too late?"

She did. But she didn't. She swallowed. The action felt stiff after months of not doing it. Whatever particles of Coby's blood that stuck in her throat didn't budge. "I need to wash this taste away. I can't be around him smelling his blood in me."

E.V. sighed. "Fine, let's bury these and go to another part of town. It shouldn't be hard to find one more person."

FORTY-NINE
TASTED

Brittany thought of the pimps she'd been feeding off, how their blood made her feel thick — like when she used to eat pasta. She thought of the prostitute. Hers had given Brittany a bubbly kind of sensation — the kind you'd get from drinking pop too quickly. Brittany also thought of Aaron's blood, the sweet feeling — like ice cream used to do to her.

For her it wasn't the taste— it was how it made her feel.

She continued to contemplate. She thought of Aziz's blood— strange how the stuff didn't touch her lips, didn't pass through her mouth, it didn't travel down *her* throat, yet his blood made the back of her tongue tingle like she'd eaten something rancid. And then there was Liam's: it made Brittany's mouth water when E.V. extracted it.

That's when she allowed herself to remember Coby's blood— just the scent of his gave her excited shivers that started in her scalp and raced down her spine, radiating through her until even her toes tingled.

Why do I want his more than anyone else's?

"Because you like him. Humans are attracted to their mates with all of their senses. It only makes sense that in your changed state you'd find his blood the most appealing."

She stopped for a moment to consider this.

Several blocks away a siren went off. Brittany could detect E.V.'s panic. She jogged across an empty street and darted into the back alley, where she crept along keeping to the shadows. *We're not going to get caught*, Brittany assured E.V.

This wasn't the root of E.V.'s fears.

Brittany stopped to stare at the image of Emily. "Why are you so afraid?"

E.V. couldn't tell Brittany that she was reminding it more and more of the one human it did not want her to become. The man had turned savage, he had enjoyed the blood too much, and he had enjoyed the kill. E.V. hadn't enjoyed being a part of him. It didn't want that again— and it didn't want that for Brittany. All it could give in answer was, "I don't like the night."

Brittany laughed. "Are you afraid of the night? Aren't vampires supposed to own it?"

"I am not a vampire."

Brittany was using her senses to check all around her as she talked. "Yes, you are no vampire— but I am one."

"Right, but not everything they say about vampires is true."

"Yes, yes." Brittany rolled her eyes. E.V. didn't have to tell her that she was far more active than most of its other hosts. "Don't worry, E.V., you don't have to fear the night."

"It's not the night I'm fearing. It's the creatures that come out during it."

"Is there anything more scary than a real life vampire?"

"Yes." E.V. said. "Murderers."

Brittany turned to stare at E.V. "Vampire, murderer, what's the difference."

"Murderers kill for the sheer joy in watching their victims die. Some even take pleasure in making sure the victim's death is painful. I am not a murderer. This is not a sport for me. I do not thrill in the death of others."

Brittany stayed quiet, wondering if she should call herself a vampire or a murderer now.

She didn't get a chance to think about this for long. She'd come upon someone who was a good candidate to be her next victim. He stood with his back to the alley, one hand holding the building while he peed against the brick wall.

She watched the man finish and straitened up, zipping his jeans, while turning.

"Brittany, you can still…" But E.V. was too late.

Brittany had already made up her plan of attack. She'd shifted into a tackle stance and said, *Remember, I get the first bite.* In her anticipation she forgot E.V.'s rules.

Before the creature had the chance to remind her, Brittany had sprung from the shadows, flying through the vision of E.V. as she did so.

The man, however, had not been as unaware of Brittany as she had presumed. He was ready for a fight. He slipped his hand inside his coat and when he removed it he was brandishing a knife.

The blade struck Brittany mid-chest and sliced cleanly in a diagonal path all the way down to her hip. The man was pulling his arm back for a second strike.

Pain would not be the right word to describe what Brittany felt. She didn't experience pain any more— but she did feel cold. Cold and wet— and alone. From the moment the blade struck, E.V. withdrew itself, sending every tentacle to the area that needed its attention most. Numb would also be a good word to describe what she felt.

However, none of this halted Brittany in her quest for blood.

The man had managed to make a second stab. The blade was lodged in Brittany's shoulder— that's when things turned against him. The surprise of his first strike had kept Brittany from slamming his body against the cement wall. The force would have flattened him, crushing several bones.

No longer disoriented, Brittany took his second blow with a plan in her head. As the blade sank through her skin, she pushed herself against him so that the hand that was holding the knife was pinned under her shoulder.

The man let out a roar and punched at Brittany with his free fist. She took his punch squarely in the chest and smiled as she heard the distinct sound of several knuckles breaking. The man's second roar was far closer to a yelp.

Recognizing that things were not going his way, the man tried to tug his pinned hand free so he could bolt. But he couldn't— Brittany had him trapped.

He let out a scream of frustration along with all the words he'd use to describe his employees.

Brittany snickered at the names. Keeping his right hand pinned, she brought her knee up and pressed it into the man's chest.

The feeling of her heavy leg lodged firmly against him was something close to what one feels as they are experiencing a heart attack. The man brought his broken hand up to try to push Brittany's leg away.

She punched his shoulder, causing more bones to shatter. His arm fell lamely to his side.

Once he'd stopped cursing, the man roared at Brittany. "Well, get on with it, girl. What are you waiting for?"

Brittany was waiting for E.V. She needed the creature to make the first cut. But E.V. was busy knitting Brittany's muscles back together. The first gash had been fatal. Had she been one hundred percent human, Brittany wouldn't have survived more than a minute. She also might have experienced her guts spilling out. But Brittany wasn't a normal human any longer, and E.V. managed to keep Brittany's petrified intestines in place.

The creature appeared at Brittany's side, its eyes trained on the knife that was lodged deep in her shoulder. It felt a mixture of resèntment and relief. "You could have been killed!" The tone reminded Brittany of a mother's reproach after stopping their toddler from running onto a busy street.

But I wasn't.

"No, but you very nearly were. Don't *ever* be so rash again." E.V.'s eyes stayed locked on the knife. "I can't fix that until it's removed."

You can fix it after. Brittany said, not wanting to wait any longer to taste blood. She felt the man's heart thumping in his chest— hard, loud, as if it were calling out to her. *Bri-ta-ny Bri-ta-ny.*

"It needs to be fixed now. You're losing fluid."

We have lots to spare, and we are about to extract the blood you'll need to make more.

E.V. continued to send resources to Brittany's shoulder, causing her to start to heal around the blade. "Brit, it needs to be fixed now."

"No, I want blood," Brittany snapped.

The man was confused. He was waiting, watching— unsure if she meant to kill him or play with him. Her words clarified that. As he started to squirm, Brittany leaned into him harder and harder. His ribs threatened to crack and his lungs were depressed as if a python was coiled around him.

"Who are you?" he asked, allowing precious oxygen to escape.

"I'm the last girl you will ever see."

It would have been a good line, witty and honest, had Brittany snuffed him out the moment she'd delivered it. She didn't.

She had brought her mouth to his neck. *Cut him so I can suck him dry.*

"Not with that knife still in you." E.V. folded it arms over its chest.

If you won't cut him then I'll bite!

"Fine. Good luck with that." It knew that Brittany wouldn't be very successful. A human bite is only capable of creating a flesh wound. She wouldn't get much blood from that. "Brit, just remove the knife, and I will gladly slash him open," E.V. tried to reason.

NO! Brittany roared in her head while her teeth tried to work their way through the man's rubbery flesh.

"Ok then." E.V. watched Brittany's unsuccessful attempts. "You know, you could use the knife to cut him yourself." Either way the knife would be out and they'd both get what they wanted.

Brittany was determined to prove E.V. wrong. She was desperately trying to gnaw her way to his artery— without any success.

That's how his employee, a prostitute, found them.

FIFTY

JUDGED

THE WOMAN HAD been hurrying back to her pimp, her fists filled with wads of cash, her eyes on her feet like an obedient slave. "Here, John," she said as she approached. Until she looked she hadn't known that John had company. "Sorry." Her eyes fell once more to the ground. It wasn't the first time she'd walked in on John being paid in this fashion. In fact, she'd tried to work off a bit of her own debt that way.

John, who was on the edge of unconsciousness, tried one final attempt. "Mees... hlp."

The girl hadn't heard. Brittany had. She pushed on his chest so that several ribs cracked. One punctured his lung, but he was already unconscious from asphyxiation. Brittany let him drop, not done with him but aware she'd now have to deal with the girl.

Brittany wrenched the knife from her shoulder. "Is that better?" she grumbled toward E.V.

"Much." E.V. ignored Brittany's sarcastic tone and went to work on the wound.

The prostitute had clearly misunderstood what was going on. She offered her advice. "He likes it when you..." Sneaking a peek, she gasped at the sight of her employer lying on the ground. "What... what did you do to John?" The money fluttered out of her hands. She fell onto her knees and crawled over to the pimp's unconscious body. "He's dead!" The girl's voice rang out in hysterics.

"Not yet." Brittany crouched down, taking the knife she still held and placing the cold blade against the girl's jugular.

"Why are you doing this?" the girl managed to ask over her tears.

"Because you have something I need," Brittany growled, piercing the girl's skin. She lapped at the crimson stream that flowed out.

Brittany took her fill then had E.V. finish the rest off. She buried the bodies in the dump then wandered the downtown streets aimlessly.

Her thoughts were a swirling mess. When she thought of the blood, she felt elated and energized. She couldn't wait to do it again. When she thought of the prostitute's question and the look on her face, she felt crushed. Where was her humanity? How could she allow herself to become such a monster?

"You're not a monster." E.V. said. "However, I do think you make a very fine vampire."

"But I am not a very good human."

As much as E.V. hated Brittany feeling this way, it liked that the girl's thoughts were returning to something more rational.

"I've lost it. I'm not a human any more. I've become like *him*— the one you feared."

"You are nowhere close to being like him... not yet. You haven't lost all touch with your humanity."

"I don't feel very human." Brittany gave a choked chuckle. "I feel like a beast. I feel like you; like a blood-sucking parasite who steals lives. You are right, I am a very good vampire."

"Well, Brit, you are a vampire— but that doesn't make you less human. Vampire is the name humans gave to those humans that were changed by me. All of them were still human, and so are you."

"Do humans crave blood? Do humans enjoy killing!"

"Some do. Some enjoy it very much, even without me in them. Brittany, it was just new to you tonight— your first time tasting blood. It will get easier, you will get better at it."

Brittany didn't respond.

"You know what you need?" E.V. didn't wait for Brittany to ask what. "You need to be around other people. You need to remind yourself what being human feels like."

"Great, it's nearly one in the morning. You got any ideas of where I could find some humans to be around at this hour?"

"Coby."

"No. I can't. I can't go back to him like this. Not now. Not after what I've done."

"First you tell me you have to taste the blood so you can go back to him. Now you can't because you did!"

E.V. was worried. It worried that Brittany might never return to Coby. If Brittany never saw him again things weren't going to end well. "Come on," it said, "just go to Coby. I promise you will feel better."

"Why?" Brittany growled, feeling her rage flare. As it subsided, she changed her tone. "Can't you see that I want to? I will… just not tonight. I can still feel the monster inside me." For once she wasn't referring to E.V.

She'd sucked the prostitute dry, and though the girl's blood had coated Coby's, washing away his flavour, it was a far cry from the taste she wanted. Brittany had even taken some of the pimp's. He was dead by the time she got around to him, so sucking on his vein felt like trying to drink a thick shake up a tiny straw. The pimp's blood had been more appealing than the girl's, but it still wasn't what she really craved.

"Ok," E.V. said as an image formed in Brittany's head. "I know where to go."

ca   ◆   so

The bar was full and loud. The doorman waved Brittany in without hesitation or ID. Brittany saw that she was the only one who got this treatment.

Bret was serving people at the bar. Brittany noticed the way the blond streaks in his hair caught in the strobe light that was flashing to the music. For a moment she found herself drawn to it. She darted around the people bouncing in rhythm to the beat. When she found an empty stool she sat.

Bret came over almost immediately. "Well, if it isn't the little hero. Long time no see. What can I get you?" His voice barely made it over the noise.

"Nothing," Brittany replied. Sitting there among all the humans made her feel better and worse. She wasn't having thoughts of killing, but she didn't feel like she belonged. She didn't have a single connection to any of them.

"You have a connection with Coby," E.V. said as its eyes stayed trained on Bret. It was very interested in connecting with him.

Bret gave a smile. "No charge, it's on the house. Anything for our little hero."

Brittany wished he'd stop calling her that. She was no hero. "I'm not thirsty."

"Then why are you here?"

"To be with people," Brittany blurted out.

"You're lonely?"

Brittany wanted to answer that she wasn't lonely— not with E.V. there. But she played along, nodding. Bret let her stay.

As two drew closer, the crowd thinned until only a few were left. Finally the bouncer made his rounds to expel the last of the stragglers.

"Leave her, Jordan," Bret called out as he was starting to clean. "She'll keep me company while I lock up."

Jordan was used to Bret having pretty young guests. He shrugged and shuffled off, leaving only once Bret and Brittany were there.

Brittany watched Bret clean while resting her chin in her hands. After he was finished he came to stand next to her, examining her with his head cocked to the side. When she looked back he asked, "Ready to go home?" His eyes were intent upon her.

E.V. enjoyed the feel of Bret's eyes as they continued to admire its host, so much that its tentacles started to vibrate. This made Brittany shiver and feel itchy.

"You want to run away with me?" Bret asked almost too quickly for her to hear— but she did hear it and she was sure she heard it right.

If E.V. were in control it would have answered yes. But the creature was not in control. Instead Brittany replied, "I'm sorry?" because as sincere as he sounded, she was sure he had to be joking.

Bret cracked a grin. "Time to go home, little hero."

Brittany scowled. Not only did she not like to be called that name, she didn't like the way Bret said it, like he knew it wasn't true. Still, she followed his advice and headed home.

FIFTY-ONE

TEMPTED

ONCE SHE MADE it home, Brittany still had a few hours to wait before her dad was up. "You're up early again," he said as he walked past her into the kitchen.

"Couldn't sleep," Brittany said, getting up to follow.

"Wanna help me make a fancy brunch? Ella's coming over."

Brittany agreed. It was strange. She had been looking for the things that made her feel human and at the same time avoiding the things that were human to do. A few hours with her father had her feeling almost normal. Even having lunch with Ella made Brittany feel better in a way.

"He's kicking," Ella squealed, dropping her fork and turning so Brittany could reach. "Have a feel."

"He?" Brittany stalled, not sure she really wanted to touch her soon-to-be stepmom's swelling belly.

"Yes, we had the ultrasound yesterday. He, our little Frank Jr."

"What is it with naming your kid after you?" E.V. started to complain.

Shush, Brittany reprimanded. She had extended her arm and gently put her hand on Ella's growing abdomen. Upon contact Ella's belly rippled and shook as if the baby inside were responding to Brittany's cool touch.

"Oooooh," Ella crooned, "I think he likes you! I've never felt him this active."

More likely he senses danger, Brittany thought.

"Just imagine the taste." E.V. was having thoughts of its own.

Brittany pulled her hand away. *You will not.* The creature was instantly compliant. It took Brittany a moment or two longer to get her own thoughts to cooperate. Now that E.V. had mentioned it, Brittany couldn't deny she was a little curious.

Ella didn't notice Brittany's look of horror. She was too busy turning so Frank could get a feel. "Wow, he really is kicking!"

While they were distracted by each other, Brittany cleared her untouched plate. Later she headed off to her mom's.

This evening it wasn't E.V.'s desires that pulled at Brittany. Though the creature wasn't making it easier.

"You know just a little won't hurt. Maybe they'll be a little more tired and go to sleep sooner. Where's the downside?"

J.J.'s cries were grating on Brittany. All he wanted was to be held, rocked and reassured, as infants often do. But Brittany tried to touch him as little as possible. With each passing moment she could feel her resolve slipping.

We'll visit Aaron after Mom's home, Brittany promised. Though she wasn't sure any longer who she said it for.

"Go hold him," E.V. said. It was, annoyingly, in perfect control of itself, "feed him, tuck him in— you have my word I will not take from J.J. He will be safe from me. I promise— and I keep my promises."

"And what about me? Who will protect him from me?" Brittany's unshed tears could be heard in her voice.

"You can't take anything without me... unless you intend to cut him open."

That was the sobering thought Brittany needed.

છ ◆ જ

They walked along a deserted street out of the suburb. It had been torture waiting for her mom and stepdad to return home that night and then having to wait some more until both parents had fallen asleep. Brittany was sure that was what going crazy felt like.

"Are *you* going to be drinking tonight?" E.V. asked.

No, no more blood for me.

"Ok. Are you gonna visit Coby?"

Not tonight.

"Why not?"

Just the mention of his name had Brittany recalling with perfect clarity how good he'd tasted: sweet, warm, inviting... She licked her lips. She was craving him with an unquenchable desire. "I can't. Not yet. I can still remember him. I need to forget how he tasted."

E.V. made a face. "But you need..." Brittany shook her head.

Brittany was well aware of her needs. Though Coby was at the top, his blood was tied for first place. How bad would it be if the need for his blood won out? How much worse would she feel if she killed the one thing that mattered to her? It was a perfect catch-22 and until she was sure he'd be safe, she wasn't willing to risk it.

ఇ ♦ ఙ

After hunting Saturday night and "playing" human all Sunday with her dad and an increasingly annoying Ella, Brittany was in a far fouler mood while she hunted on Sunday. Being truly addicted to the blood, she hadn't managed to stop herself from drinking the night before, and this night was no different.

She brought down her fourth victim. Bringing her lips next to the girl's neck, she waited till she felt E.V. make a cut so she could taste the blood. Brittany had been hoping that this one would be good enough to take away the memory of Coby's. It wasn't. They never were.

It was almost midnight; Monday was quickly approaching. Brittany wasn't sure how she would make it through a full day of being at school with Coby. Part of her didn't want to find out.

"Well," E.V. stood with its hands on its hips, "what other option is there?" There were two: stay or run away.

FIFTY-TWO
ATTRACTED

"OR WE COULD find Aaron. I bet we could track him down. Let's see if his blood is better." Brittany had a feeling with the way E.V. was attracted to it, that it might be. But he hadn't showed up for work all weekend. She talked to Aziz. Aaron had missed two of his shifts now.

E.V. was shaking its head. "I couldn't. I'm really, really full. I probably shouldn't have let you talk me into this last one."

Brittany stared down at the dead girl. "But she was so small."

"Their outsides have nothing to do with how much blood flows through them. Ten pints is ten pints."

Oh. Brittany didn't know what to do now. There were a few hours before she'd need to be home. Without paying attention to where she was going she wound up in the back alley where she'd "saved" Simone. She was about to turn and leave when she noticed she wasn't alone. She watched as the person at the far end of the alley hoisted garbage bags into a compactor. She could see him clearly, but he showed no signs of knowing he had an audience.

"Hey." E.V. had been distracted by its full stomach. It finally turned its attention towards the guy. "That's Bret!"

Brittany knew that E.V. didn't have a heart— not an actual one. But it sure felt like the creature's heart was fluttering; or it was making Brittany's heart flutter. It could have been what caused her to take a few steps towards him. She stopped once she realized what she was doing.

It was too late. Her movement had caught Bret's attention. "Who's there?" he said as he peered towards her.

Brittany debated making a run for it while E.V.'s thoughts were consumed with moving itself closer.

What is it about him? Brittany asked, realizing that she'd missed her opportunity to bolt. Not that she was sure she would have been able to. Feeling E.V.'s determination, Brittany wondered if she'd be able to make her legs operate if they were trying to take her away.

E.V. wasn't sure what exactly it liked about Bret. "He's really good looking, don't you think? His eyes are so passionate. His chest, with all those muscles… His hands…"

I hadn't realized how much you were into looks, Brittany said, a little too cutting.

"Fine then!" E.V. snapped with venom in its tone. "What is it about Coby that gets you all mushy?"

Coby?… Coby is… Just thinking about him stirred up her desire for him. She still wasn't sure whether it was for him or more of his blood. This made her sad, and she knew until she straightened it out she shouldn't see him again. *I think I'll be skipping school tomorrow*.

She hadn't noticed Bret cautiously walking closer. "Hello?" He stopped, his eyes showing something Brittany couldn't make out. "Well, if it isn't the little hero." A sly smile played at the corner of his lips. "What are you doing here? Are you waiting for someone else to save?"

Brittany could feel E.V.'s emotions within her. They were swelling. It was solely because of that that Brittany's lips twitched into a grin.

"Or did you come back so we can run away together?" He had moved closer still, his eyes focused on Brittany's oversized hoodie that looked more like a short cloak.

"N… no," Brittany stuttered, unsure she meant it. She pulled her hood back to get a better look at Bret. *What about him? Bet he'd tastes good enough to take away the memory of Coby's…*

For all the humans E.V. didn't take notice of when they talked about taking their blood, it was different with Bret. The creature objected so much, it cut off Brittany's musings. She felt it writhing inside her— rebelling at the thought.

"Did you come back to get a drink from me?" he asked.

To this Brittany smiled.

E.V. screamed, "NO!"

Relax— I know that he didn't actually mean from him.

Bret took her smile as assent. He turned and headed toward the back entrance of the bar. She didn't hesitate to follow him and, as if he knew she would, he never turned back to check.

Just like déjà vu, Brittany sat on a stool and watched Bret clean. He washed down the counters, tidied up the bottles and mopped the floors. He performed his nightly routine, paying very little attention to Brittany.

"I gotta go downstairs to get some stock," he said, leaving without a backwards glance.

When he returned he brought with him a chillingly familiar smell.

"That's blood!" E.V. said in alarm.

You think he cut himself?

"That's not just blood— that blood smells good."

Bret stepped behind the counter and placed a glass in front of Brittany. The contents were thick and unidentifiable by sight. The smell, however, was a different case. There was no mistake to Brittany's expert nose. It was sweet blood. Attractive blood. Not Coby's blood, but something very close. The smell pulled at her.

She pushed her stool back, causing it to scrape against the floor, producing an annoying noise that would have hurt even without her heightened hearing. Both Brittany and Bret flinched.

"Don't you like it?" Bret asked with an innocent look.

"Is it yours?" were the first coherent words she could manage. E.V. was further gone— all that emanated from it was panic.

"Heavens no. I know how dangerous that could be."

"How does he know?" E.V.'s thoughts were still hard to discern through its fear.

Brittany's voice was stronger. "How do you know?"

He chuckled. "Come on, I work in a bar. I've seen all types."

"There are more..." E.V. had said "of us" but Brittany asked, "...like me?"

FIFTY-THREE

TAUGHT

"YES." BRET CRACKED a wide grin, sounding like he was trying not to laugh. "Goodness, you didn't think you were the only one, did you?"

Brittany nodded.

This time Bret didn't restrain his laughter. "No, my dear, you are not the only one. I've met a few others. Though none quite as pretty." For the first time he reached out as if he meant to touch Brittany. His hand snapped back before he did.

"I won't take from you," Brittany promised, having pulled herself back to the bar. E.V. was longing so much for Bret's touch that Brittany's chest hurt.

Bret chuckled darkly. "Just the same, we'll keep this relationship strictly hands-off for now. I know all about you and your kind."

"Really." It was a challenge. Brittany found his claim far-fetched. How could he know about E.V.? It hardly knew about itself.

"Like I said, I've met a few. I once met one that had memories going all the way back to creation and the great mutation."

Brittany didn't say anything. She was wondering, once again, how many creatures like E.V. could exist. How many could be living, walking, talking, hunting as she was. *How many more could there really be?*

"I can tell that you are a new host," Bret's voice drew her back, "though you have been quite smart in handling your transformation."

"How? How can you tell?"

"Because you've kept your secret hidden for so long. Your need for blood would have gone completely unnoticed, even by me, had you not decided to play the hero. What happened? You must have known that getting involved like that would leave a trail. Why'd you do it? Why did you save her? You didn't seem to care for her. So why?"

Brittany was miserable. She recognized that was the moment everything had changed. She'd doomed herself with that one single act of kindness. Not wanting to be a monster, she had tried to use her transformation for good, and ended up exposing herself. And why hadn't she listened to E.V.? Why didn't she turn a blind eye and leave?

E.V. was having its own thoughts. As much as it was still attracted to Bret, it feared him.

What are you afraid of now?

"He knows too much." E.V. said, but the better thing to say would have been: he knows more than me.

"She just talked to you, didn't she?" Bret's grin widened with his confidence.

Brittany felt defensive. E.V. wasn't a girl. "It!" she corrected.

Bret snickered and for some reason that annoyed Brittany. *Like he knows so much more than us*! But it was clear that he did, which annoyed her even more.

"Calm down." Bret raised his hands in a gesture of surrender. "Don't be upset."

Brittany glared.

"Now, don't take this poorly, but trust me, you are infected with a she."

"And how can you tell?"

"Simple: only a true girl can infect girls."

"Oh?" Brittany's next statement was triumphant. "But it has infected males before! Loads of them— most of its memories are filled with male experiences."

Bret rolled his eyes. "I never said she *couldn't* infect men. I said that only a *female* can infect another female."

Brittany stayed quiet. So did E.V. Bret watched, almost as if he was waiting for something.

Finally E.V. said in a frightened voice, "Brit, ask what he's going to do now that he knows about us." Memories of its last discovery filled E.V.'s thoughts (and Brittany's head); It— *she* had barely escaped. (*what a weird concept*) She... her... not an *It*.

"What does she want to know?" Bret asked more kindly.

"It is afraid." Brittany didn't want to accept that E.V. was a "she." That made it feel too personal. Brittany had quite liked thinking of E.V. as an *it* or *the parasite*. Now she couldn't and it disturbed her. "It thinks you are a *hunter*. And you are going to try and put an end to it."

Bret was shaking his head before Brittany had finished talking. "No. I am not a hunter," he said with contempt. "Those were vile men who didn't behave any better than monsters. Your friend is right to fear them. I am not a hunter."

His words helped calm E.V. a little. However, Brittany didn't feel any more relaxed. "So, how many of these... creatures exist?"

"Hunters?" Bret scratched his chin. "I'd wager not many. Since the Industrial Revolution they've become a dying breed."

"Not hunters," Brittany made a face, "this thing inside me."

"Doesn't yours have a name?"

Brittany hesitated. "Well, it/she didn't come with a name... but we've made one up."

"What name have the two of you decided to call her?" Bret said mockingly.

"E.V." Brittany answered after another pause. Saying it aloud made her feel foolish.

"E.V.?" Bret rolled it around in his mouth. "Where did that come from?"

"Well, she was in Emily before me. And she appeared to me as Emily. So once I'd figured out some things I nicknamed her Emily the Vampire. E.V. came from that."

Bret gave one curt nod. "Who was she before Emily?"

Brittany answered, though she wondered why Bret seemed so interested. She also answered who E.V. had been before

Gran and, once he knew that, who the creature had been before Gran's husband.

"Why do you want to know?" Brittany asked after Bret had asked who E.V. had been before Soo Sung.

"No reason." Bret shrugged, but he looked like he was trying to appear less interested then he was.

"You never told me how many of these creatures exist," Brittany reminded him.

He sighed and took a deep breath.

While waiting for his answer, she rested her elbows on the counter and noticed the cup under her nose as the smell wafted up to fill her senses.

"You gonna drink that? It would be a waste if you didn't. Blood doesn't last long once there isn't a body keeping it warm, unless it's been properly stored."

"I know." Brittany was about to ask her question again, but Bret cut her off.

"You know, do you?" He nodded approvingly. "So you've already started drinking? Impressive."

Brittany shrugged. She pushed the glass away and again before she could re-ask her question, Bret cut her off.

"You don't like it?"

"I like the blood a little too much."

Bret slid the glass back.

Brittany pushed it away.

"Is it not your type?" He slid it back.

She pushed it away. "Type makes a difference?"

"Sometimes." The glass was repositioned under Brittany's nose. "Smell it, does it smell sour?"

Brittany breathed in, though she didn't need to. "It's not sour." She felt her craving growing.

E.V. groaned. "I am too full."

Brittany slid the glass away.

Bret picked it up and held it out to her. "Is it too cold?"

"No." With it closer to her nose, her desire for it made her eyes water.

"Then what's the problem?" He moved it closer still. All Brittany would have to do was tilt her head back and Bret could have poured it into her mouth.

"E.V. is full."

"So? Are *you* full?"

Brittany looked past the glass into Bret's face, surprised that he didn't know the most basic rule. "I can't eat. I've been changed. My stomach has been petrified. I would die.

"Aw, my sweet, I've got many things to teach you," Bret said.

FIFTY-FOUR

MISTRUSTED

BRET PUT THE cup back down but didn't continue.

"What?" Brittany asked as E.V. said the same in her head.

Bret leaned across the bar so that he could whisper in Brittany's ear. "You can drink blood. Blood will not rot in you."

"What? How?" Brittany had pulled back from Bret to look him in the eye.

"You breathe it in."

"I'd drown!"

"You won't. You don't need air. Your lungs have become the perfect storage place. You only need to hold it for a few hours until your E.V. is ready, then she'll be able to extract it right from them. When she does, you'll be able to refill them. Full lungs should be able to last you a good long while." Bret stepped back, crossing his arms. "I can't believe you didn't know this. Neither of you!" He looked deep into Brittany's eyes as if he were speaking solely to E.V. "How have you survived this long?"

"She says she guesses she's been lucky," Brittany repeated with less conviction than E.V.

"Yes, she has." Bret had turned away with the glass. He placed it in a bowl and filled hot water around it. "She really has," he repeated to himself.

Brittany missed him turning back— her attention was on the blood-filled cup. "What are you doing?"

"Reheating it."

Brittany's eyes looked up at the microwave.

Before she could ask, Bret supplied the answer. "Uh-uh, to reheat blood it has to be done slowly. Naturally. The microwave would cook it— that would turn it into something poisonous to you. We don't want to poison you."

Brittany closed her eyes. The smell of the blood as it was warming in the water was almost too good to resist. Her eyes shot open as the smell intensified.

"Here." Bret was holding the cup under Brittany's nose again. "It's ready."

"How do you know?"

"Because you don't look like you can wait any longer."

Brittany pressed her lips together, shaking her head.

"What's the problem now?"

"I don't want to be a monster."

"You know," Bret took a casual stance but kept the cup under Brittany's nose, "if you satisfy your bloodlust you won't have to be so out of control. Fill yourself with this and I guarantee you won't crave it as much."

Brittany took the cup. Bret was careful not to let her touch him. She'd pressed the lukewarm glass to her lips.

"Once you're full, then you can see your boyfriend without having to worry about hurting him again."

His words, coupled with the triumphant look that flitted through Bret's eyes, had Brittany putting the cup down so hard it almost cracked. "How'd you know I have a boyfriend?"

Bret gave a casual shrug as if he didn't think his statement warranted the reaction it got. "Easy, a pretty young thing like you, surely boys would be flocking to you. And out of all of them, I'm sure there is at least one that you have feelings for."

"How'd you know that I'd hurt him?"

Bret raised his eyebrows. "Didn't you?"

Brittany started to nod then shook her head. "But how did you know?"

Bret's smile was to disarm. "It's a very easy mistake, very common. Isn't that why you're so hesitant?"

This time Brittany just nodded. But E.V. narrowed its eyes as if... she — right, *she*... didn't believe him.

Brittany told Bret E.V.'s request— or more like demand.

"You want me to drink the blood first?" He looked down into the contents of the cup.

"E.V. doesn't trust you."

"Ok." Bret picked up the glass and brought it to his lips.

Brittany couldn't watch. She couldn't imagine trying to drink blood before E.V. had changed her. She wouldn't have been able to. "Stop." She looked back.

Bret held the cup next to his lip. A thin red line stood out. As he lowered the cup to the counter, he used his free arm to wipe the blood off on his sleeve.

"I'll trust you."

E.V. still didn't feel as confident.

Brittany raised the cup to her mouth but held it there, unsure what to do.

"Um, right, I need to teach you. Keep in mind that this is nothing like eating or drinking. The first time it's not going to feel right. Just try and relax and don't give in to the panic."

Bret instructed Brittany to take a mouthful and hold it. Brittany hesitated as E.V. gave an extensive list of objections. Finally Brittany said, *You were the one who liked him — besides, if he kills me then you'll be able to be as close to him as you want — I'll make sure you can infect him.*

E.V. stayed silent as Brittany took a deep breath and poured as much of the blood as she could into her mouth.

"Good. You're doing good," Bret said. "That was the hardest part. Now I want you to try and expel all the air from your lungs through your nose."

Brittany felt like a chipmunk as her cheeks puffed out from the contents she continued to hold there.

"Ok, now relax, this is it. When you're ready, breath in through your mouth pulling the blood down your throat and into your lungs."

Brittany stared. *Breath in*, she wanted to scoff. Like it was just that simple.

The minutes dragged on. She could go forever without breathing— but how long could she stay like this? The longer she did, the more the blood's taste settled on the back of her tongue.

As Brittany continued to try to convince herself to do something that felt completely unnatural and failed, E.V. got curious. She was full, so she couldn't take much, but she found enough room for a taste.

It was as E.V.'s tentacles permeated the thick blood and recognized who it had come from, that Brittany gasped. She managed to pull half the contents in her mouth down her throat, but the other half spilled out of both corners of her lips. She choked and sputtered as she felt the blood sliding into her lungs.

FIFTY-FIVE

APPRECIATED

BRET HAD WATCHED with a mildly amused expression. When she looked up, he was holding a cloth out to her.

As she cleaned her face she felt the blood in her lungs. It was a heavy feeling, yet somehow satisfying. She tried to hand the cloth back to Bret. He didn't take it. Instead he pointed at Brittany's hoodie. She followed his fingers, seeing that she was covered in various sized splatter marks. The red was obvious over the tight weave of the grey material.

"I can run that under the water for you. See if we can't get the stains out before they set." Bret kept his arm outstretched, opening his palm.

Brittany didn't move. She stared Bret square in the eyes. "Where did you get the blood from?"

"A donor." He shrugged as if having a bit of spare blood lying around was normal.

"A donor?"

"Yes, an anonymous donor. Haven't you heard of the blood bank?"

Brittany didn't like Bret's patronizing tone. E.V.'s feelings, however, ran deeper. "I know blood," the creature stated. "Like I said, that was Aaron's blood." Brittany nodded.

"What's the problem?" Bret had taken a step back, putting more than an arm's length between them.

"We know the blood. We've tasted it before. We know the person it belonged to."

"That's…" Bret cleared this throat. He had wanted to say amazing, but he amended it to "…interesting. And weird, don't you think? Of all the bags I could have taken, I got someone you know. Really weird, right?" What he wasn't saying was that he had never known a creature with such a defined palate as to discern who the donor was. Normally their experience didn't go beyond typing, A, B or O and the Rh factor. He'd have to be careful with this one.

Brittany dipped her finger in the glass, which was still half full. The blood was getting cold but in comparison to her temperature, it still felt right. After a few swirls she brought her bloody finger to her lips, breathing deeply to give it a good sniff. When she closed her eyes, she thought she could smell Aaron.

Brittany opened her mouth and extended her tongue so that it touched her finger. The taste was sweet, like gummie bears and slurpees and cheap chocolate bars. She moved her finger deeper into her mouth and brought her lips around it as the taste pulled at her.

Bret made an odd sound, something between a cough and clearing his throat. "Definitely more attractive than any of the others I've met."

Brittany had opened her eyes to stare at him. He'd moved himself as far back as he could, pressing himself against the opposite counter behind the bar. His hands were turned so that they held onto the counter edge— like he was trying to hold himself in place.

"Is he afraid?" E.V. asked. "Does he want to run away?"

Why should he be afraid of us? Brittany looked down at herself again. The smaller blood spots were turning into a darker rust color, but the larger ones were still a vibrant red.

Bret continued to stare.

Brittany picked up the cup. In one swift move, she'd poured the rest of the contents into her mouth. Knowing what to do now, and what to expect, she braced herself and inhaled. This time the liquid flowed more smoothly down her throat. She assessed herself and figured her lungs were about two thirds full.

She wiped her lips on the sleeve of her hoodie then slipped her arms inside it and pulled it over her head. Wadding it into a ball, she held it out to Bret.

He continued to stare, his mouth gaping.

"You said you'd wash it?"

"Yes." But he stayed planted on the spot.

Brittany gave her hoodie a small shake and, when he still didn't move, she let it drop and stood up.

Bret's eyes raked over her body.

Being tired of shirts that were constantly threatening to fall off her, Brittany had gone through some boxes of her old clothes that her mom was saving for her siblings to grow into. She'd found a shirt that fit her in grade three. It was covered in friendly-looking skulls— the popular pattern of the time. It had fit nicely, only stretching a little over her chest. She had also dispensed with wearing bras now that her breasts had been petrified. They were so perfectly shaped that even a Barbie doll would be jealous.

That's where Bret's gaze had come to rest. He couldn't stop himself from admiring every line of the girl that was now so easy to see under her child-sized shirt.

E.V. couldn't deny that she was enjoying every moment of attention Brittany was receiving from Bret. Her longings for him to reach out and touch them created an aching feeling in Brittany's chest.

For Brittany these feelings reminded her of her own feelings for Coby. "I'm ready to go now," she said to both Bret and E.V.

These words seemed to break the spell Bret had fallen into. He made that strange noise again, clearing his throat. "You want to run away with me?"

This time there was so much hope in Bret's question that Brittany knew he wasn't joking. "No, I'm ready to leave here and go... home." She only paused briefly as she thought of her father's house, and her mother's, then she thought of Coby's— that was where she felt like she was home.

"Ok. I'll get this cleaned." Bret picked up the sweater and moved towards the stairs that led down to the storage room and the industrial sink.

"While you're down there, you don't happen to have any more of that blood, do you?"

Brittany couldn't see the triumphant smile that spread across Bret's face. "As a matter of fact, I have just enough for one more glass."

FIFTY-SIX
STOPPED

HER LUNGS FULL, Brittany set the empty glass next to where her hoodie was draped over the counter.

"There are a few more things you need to know about drinking blood. First," Bret said, handing Brittany a glass of water, "you need to rinse out your mouth."

"Why?"

"Because you'll want to wash away the leftover particles."

"Why can't E.V. extract them?" Brittany could feel the thin layer of blood coating everything: her tongue, the roof of her mouth, under her tongue, and even her teeth.

"Three reasons. There is too much. E.V. is full, and you need to get rid of the pigment. But you need to be sure not to swallow. Just swish and spit. Sort of like a wine tasting."

"Do I need to gargle?"

"No, it's just from your uvula forward."

"Uvula?" Brittany interrupted. It sounded like too dirty a word for something in her mouth.

Bret smirked. "You're uvula is the bulb that hangs down at the back of your throat." He stopped to enjoy Brittany's embarrassed face, then he continued. "It's your mouth that gets the most air. When particles of blood are left there, they will dry out and start to smell. You don't want to have breath that stinks like a rotting corpse."

Brittany made a face while nodding. *Did you ever do this with Gran? Or that count?* Brittany asked.

"No." E.V.'s memories of the count's rotten breath made Brittany's nose wrinkle more. Gran's was only slightly better, but that was because she worked with E.V. to get as many of the blood particles as possible and she never ate when E.V. was full.

Brittany swished and spat three times. After Bret handed her a dry cloth to mop up any leftover moisture, she then held her mouth open to let the remaining water evaporate. Once done E.V. was instructed to use her talented tentacles to make sure that nothing was left.

෪ ◆ ஒ

Bret had driven Brittany to the convenience store near her mother's house. They were both silent. Bret tried not to get caught as he snuck sidelong glances at the girl. It was now overcast enough that he suggested Brittany keep her damp hoodie off. The bloodstains had been successfully removed, but it hadn't dried.

She had agreed, though the dampness wouldn't have bothered her she didn't want it to ruin Bret's car seat. He drove a little beater that he seemed to love. As they'd entered the car, he made a comment about how his car didn't look like much, but he'd been through a lot with it: graduation, where him and seven friends squished into the barely five-seater; a year of touring across the country, and a few trips over the border; helping his buddies move; camping; even living out of it one summer.

Brittany mhummed, not paying close attention. Her thoughts were on Coby. She felt secure because his taste had finally been washed away, mostly by the rinsing and drying. Even better, her lungs were filled to the brim with good blood. She wouldn't be "hungry" for hours, maybe a whole day. As the car bumped along, it lulled her so that she became aware of how tired she was. She knew that she needed to get to Coby so that she could sleep.

She left Bret's car with a hurried goodbye. He drove away with a casual "Don't be a stranger."

Brittany's breathing quickened as she saw Coby's house in the distance. Drawing closer she searched for the sound of him sleeping— it wasn't until she was halfway up the drainpipe that she realized she couldn't hear him sleeping because he was awake.

Coby sprang out of his bed and rushed over to Brittany the moment she appeared in his window. His relief was tangible, flavouring the air around him. "I'm so glad you came back. I was so worried that I'd scared you away." His arms wrapped tightly around her as he lay his head down on her cool shoulder. "I'm sorry. I'm so, so, so sorry."

Brittany brought her hand up to his neck, tangling her fingers in his hair. She had her back to the wall. Feeling his heat, hearing his heart pound, smelling his scent. She had thought she would be safe, but she was wrong.

She slid to the floor, Coby still clinging to her.

"Brittany, you are exhausted. You need to sleep. Tell him that you need to sleep!" E.V. commanded as murderous thoughts swirled around Brittany's head.

She wanted to squeeze Coby till he popped like a grape. She wanted to pull his head back until it separated from his neck. She wanted to punch a hole in his chest and watch his heart as it beat down to its last painful thud then remove it and save it in a jar like a trophy.

"Brittany, you're just tired. You need to rest. You need to sleep!" E.V. said.

"Brittany?" Coby pulled back to look at her after her hand had dropped from his hair.

E.V. had withdrawn herself from Brittany's arms, causing them to go numb. Brittany knew that if she wanted she could still perform every one of her desires even without the creature's tentacles in their right places. But she would have to really want to. The lack of E.V. would make everything ten times harder, like driving a car without power steering.

"I'm..." Brittany looked up at Coby, from his cropped brown hair to his hazel eyes, with more green than brown and a few flecks of gold. His face still held vestiges of baby fat, but that was quickly disappearing as he moved into puberty.

I won't hurt him, she told E.V. *I don't want to hurt him.* Not only because she loved him but also because he was too nice-looking to be destroyed by draining his blood.

"I know." E.V. stood with hands folded in front of her chest. She believed Brittany but wasn't ready to move back into the girl's limbs so quickly. There was a world of difference between what Brittany wanted and what she would do.

"Brittany?" Coby's voice was softer.

"I'm..."

Coby placed his hand at the side of her face. "You're what?"

But Brittany was lost again. Coby's hand was so soft and warm— and it smelled so good. She turned towards it so that his wrist was next to her lips. She brushed them back and forth, feeling the veins under his skin as they carried his blood into his hand and back up his arms. They sped up as Coby's pulse quickened.

Coby felt his skin tingle and heat up under where Brittany's cool lips brushed him. He started to have desires of his own. He was far less successful in controlling his.

Coby brought his face next to Brittany's so that as she turned back to face him, their noses touched. Their reactions were identical, like an electrical shock had gone through them. They gasped in unison and leaned closer until their lips met. Coby was the first to open his mouth. Brittany responded only a moment later, once she was sure she wasn't going to follow that action by biting down on his lip with such force she'd remove it from his face.

Coby's hands roved over Brittany's body, finding the bottom of her hoodie and dragging it up and over her head. It was tossed aside with no thought about the bullet hole or why the hoodie was so damp.

Sitting back on his knees, Coby looked down, appreciating all of Brittany's curves that were so well defined under her t-shirt.

E.V. wasn't as impressed with the way Coby looked at Brittany. She still preferred Bret. Brittany's feelings, however, were large enough for her and the creature inside.

Brittany rolled up onto her knees, bringing her hands up into Coby's hair, pulling him towards her so their noses touched. Next their mouths met and her hands began to glide over the rest of his body. She noted the way he felt under her. Everywhere she touched heated up, causing her hands to burn.

It was a struggle finding the balance between passion, desire, and lust. As their passion grew so did her desire. As her desire mounted so did the lust: blood lust. As if the three were connected. She felt his soft skin under her fingertips, so easy to tear open if she just angled her nails and pressed down. She could sense his blood rushing just inches away. It would flow out of him so freely and warmly. She tasted his tongue as it slid past her lips— Coby tasted less sweet but far more attractive, like a well-prepared steak.

"Ouch." Coby had pulled away, bringing his hand up to the back of his head.

FIFTY-SEVEN
HURT

BRITTANY HAD LET go the moment Coby yelped. She dropped her hands to her lap, watching a clump of his hair fall to the floor. Blood glistened as it dripped from several strands.

Coby continued to hold his head, not daring to remove his hand. He knew it was bleeding. He could feel it— warm and sticky, wet and oozing into his fingers. He watched Brittany as she stared back. How had it gone wrong?

They had been kissing— and while they kissed her hands had travelled over his chest, down his thigh, around his waist and up his back to tangle in his hair again. As one hand traced his spine, he'd shivered, and he remembered hearing himself moan. That's when he'd pulled her tighter so that their bodies pressed so close, it was as if they were one.

…and he'd bitten down on her lower lip. Coby brought his free hand to his lips. They tingled, feeling cool as the fluid on them evaporated.

Brittany continued to stare.

E.V. had fixed the tiny cut on Brittany's lip, then she had extracted the blood she needed from Brittany's lungs. Brittany still had plenty of blood in her, and E.V. didn't need any more either, so the blood that was drying on the clump of Coby's hair next to Brittany's knees and the blood that oozed at the base of his skull wasn't needed— wanted was a different story.

Coby ran his tongue along his lips. They tasted bitter, like what he'd expect cactus nectar to taste like. But he also noticed that they were smoother. They had been affected the same way as his palm had been healed during Brittany's last visit.

"Brits?" Coby held out his clean hand. The other stayed pressed tight to his skull to try and stop the bleeding.

"No." She pushed herself back against the wall, her head finding the crevice it had made only two nights earlier. She rested it there, making the indentation slightly bigger.

"Bri…"

"Stay back!" Brittany brought her hands up, holding them stretched out, palms forward.

Coby stopped. He saw red smudges on three of Brittany's fingers. His blood. He wondered if she'd noticed.

Of course she had. So had E.V. It was a testimonial to how full the creature was that she wasn't extracting it.

It was an even greater show of willpower for Brittany to keep her arms extended. All she wanted to do was bring those fingers to her tongue and lick off every molecule. She knew once she started there would be no stopping. From there she'd lick off every strand of hair she'd pulled out, like licking chocolate mousse off the tines of a fork. When she was done that, she'd move on to Coby's neck last, and that would be the last of Coby.

All Brittany could do was hold herself back from starting as Coby continued to bleed and poison the air.

E.V. applauded her.

Don't congratulate me just yet, Brittany thought, watching Coby slowly get to his feet and back out of his room.

At that moment he realized Brittany was dangerous.

As he cleaned himself in the bathroom, he tried to figure out what had really happened to Brittany. He had been reading up on everything paranormal: vampires, demonic possession, even a little on the occult. He decided that vampire was the closest possibility. There might not be fangs, and she might not bite— but it was still all about the blood.

He used rubbing alcohol to clean himself up, watching himself in the mirror, wincing from the pain. Eventually, as he continued to dab the base of his neck with fresh cotton balls, his bleeding slowed then finally stopped. Positioning himself to look at the back of his head, he could see the good-sized flesh wound. It took eight band-aids, overlapping, to cover it. Coby cringed as he tried to imagine how he'd get them off later.

He thought about the way Brittany behaved and tried to decide if she was still Brittany. He played with the idea that Mike might have been telling the truth. Even though he felt like that was Brittany, there was something more.

Coby returned to his room and to Brittany. She had stayed where he'd left her, only having moved her hands to her knees. She looked like she might be meditating.

He went to work on cleaning the floor first, picking up his hairs, stopping only long enough to see that Brittany had pulled them out, roots, follicles, skin, and all. It looked like what the Natives used to call scalping, only not so big. His had been the size of a quarter. He wrapped that up in rubbing alcohol-dowsed toilet paper then poured copious amounts from the bottle onto the laminate floor until all the red had dissipated and his room stank with the noxious fumes.

Finally, Coby looked into Brittany's eyes. "I'm going to clean your hands now."

Brittany cocked her head. "Aren't you frightened of me?"

Coby had gone to work on her fingers, dabbing them softly, rubbing them gently, moving slowly and deliberately. "Yes."

Brittany's hand twitched and Coby froze, watching her.

Nothing was involuntary for Brittany. Every action, every movement, was a result of either Brittany's choice, or E.V.'s. "Then ask me to leave and I will— I will go and I will never come back again."

Coby was watching Brittany's hand: one finger was left. "I don't want you to leave," he said, then added in a choked whisper, "And I certainly don't want you never to return."

"But you're scared of me."

"Uh-huh." Coby wiped her final finger clean and put the cleaning stuff off to the side. Again he moved with great caution. He leaned closer and put one arm around Brittany's back, the other under her legs. He stood cradling her in his arms. "But I still love you."

FIFTY-EIGHT

POSSESSED

COBY TOOK BRITTANY over to his bed and laid her gently down. "Now sleep, my sweet," he said, lying next to her and closing his own eyes.

In her dreams Brittany saw Gran and Henry, their unique relationship along with their deep love for each other. As her dreams progressed she saw herself and Coby replacing them. They dated. They married. They lived happily ever after with endless possibilities.

Somewhere in Brittany's mind she realized that E.V. hadn't taken her future away, E.V. had just altered it. Like becoming a vet instead of a doctor. Slightly different but a lot the same. And with E.V. Brittany would be stronger, smarter, and able to do so much more.

There was no reason Brittany couldn't be with Coby and do everything a couple could do. Brittany rolled onto her side. Her dreaming had taken her in a whole other direction now.

"Hmmmm," Brittany sighed as she started to become conscious. Two hours of dreaming didn't feel long enough.

"Are you better now?"

Brittany could feel Coby at her back, his steady heartbeat emanating from his chest into and through her. "Yes." She could think more clearly and felt more in control. She breathed in and she could tell that her lungs were still half full.

"Good." Coby pulled himself to sitting. "We need to talk."

Brittany rolled so she could look up at him. "What do you want to talk about?"

"You."

"What about me?" Brittany felt hopeful for the first time since she had been infected with E.V. She didn't understand why E.V. seemed so fearful.

"Do you know what's happened to you?" Coby stared deep into Brittany's crystal blue eyes. "Do you know how this happened?"

Brittany nodded.

"Good." As he watched, Coby tried to decide what he believed: his theory or Mike's.

Coby had begun to believe that Mike was half, if not all, crazy. The dude had taken to sending emails on an increasingly insistent basis. Mike kept trying to warn him about demons and begged him not to get tricked by the spirit inside.

Now, with Brittany next to him, and everything that had happened, Coby found himself highly undecided.

"Can you explain it to me?" Coby asked softly.

"No!" E.V. snapped, feeling the direction of Brittany's thoughts. "How can you even think of telling him!" She was outraged. "Don't you dare utter a word about me! Just tell him you are a vampire. He'll understand that. He won't understand the rest."

But I want to tell him everything.

"Please," E.V.'s voice turned to begging, "please. He won't understand. He'll freak out!"

No, he won't.

"Yes, he will! If you tell him that I'm here too, he won't understand. He'll want to try and take me out of you."

Then I'll tell him you can't be taken out of me— that you're here to stay.

"He won't believe you. No one ever does."

Some have, haven't they? Brittany wanted to be more certain. *What about Henry and Gran? Or Charles and Petunia?*

"Even Henry didn't tell Gran about me for years. And Charles never told Petunia. Please... just say you are a vampire." As the creature fumbled with its words, Brittany could see it. It wasn't just one memory but several jumbled together. A few ended with hangings and in one, the most recent, E.V. and her host ended up in a mental ward. "… they never believe us."

Coby's not like that, you'll see.

"Please don't," E.V. said, her voice closer to a whimper. "Please. Please don't."

This time, when Brittany froze, Coby didn't panic as much. Yes, she was stone cold, her eyes frozen open, having glassed over to stare lifelessly in his direction. It was hard not to panic, but this wasn't that different from how she slept. *The eyes were open though, that was creepy.*

Brittany breathed in, causing Coby to breathe out. That's when she clued in that she had frozen again. She blinked and looked up into Coby's relieved face.

"Where did you go?" His eyes narrowed as he studied her reaction.

"It's hard to explain."

He gave a nod like he wasn't done but changed the subject. "I've been doing some research on the occult… on demonic possession."

"Oh ya?" Brittany had to swallow down E.V.'s panic. "Demonic possession?"

"Ya, I've been trying to figure out what's going on inside of you."

"And what do you think it is?"

Coby answered hesitantly. "Um… well, mostly I want to say you've become a vampire." He chuckled at the absurdity of saying it aloud. "Or something close to one."

"Vampire?" E.V.'s relief flooded through Brittany, allowing her muscles to relax. "That's your opinion?"

"Well…" The truth was that Coby would have believed demonic possession more easily if it hadn't been Mike who suggested it. He really didn't want to trust the guy.

The image of Emily started shaking so hard, its teeth were chattering.

Calm down, will you. You got your wish. He just said he thinks I'm a vampire— isn't that what you wanted?

E.V.'s fears were growing as she watched Coby's face. "He said demonic possession. That means he's been thinking about it. Even if he doesn't believe it for now he could easily change his mind. Once they think demons— exorcism isn't far behind!" E.V. could recall all too easily how unpleasant those were and how much it broke her hosts before it killed them.

Brittany saw just a glimpse of the horrors. *Coby would never be able to do that to me.*

"I wish I could share your faith in h…"

"What's going on when you do that?" Coby interrupted.

"Do what?"

"Your eyes, they get glassy and you seem… distracted. But distracted isn't quite right. You're spacey … no, absent … No," his brow furrowed as he thought, "It's like you freeze up … like … like you're talking to someone in your head."

"Oh, do I?" Brittany tried not to respond to E.V., who was screaming at her to run. *Shut it. Every time I have to address you, he sees it!*

"There," Coby had moved closer, "right there. What were you thinking? What's going on?" Suddenly he believed that there was a demon inside her, or something else.

"It's…" Brittany didn't know how to respond. "Why would you think of demonic possession?"

"Is that what's going on?" Coby was staring intently into Brittany's eyes, looking for some way to see the truth.

As E.V. continued to tremble, Brittany felt herself shaking. "I can assure you I'm not possessed." She'd tried to sound confident, but the creature's shakes had ruined the effect.

"Then what would you call it?" Coby worried as he felt Brittany trembling. It shook the bed.

"Well…" E.V.'s emotions were seeping into Brittany. *Would you please calm down, he won't hurt us!*

"Brittany, what's wrong?" Coby's hands pressed down onto her chest. Something was happening under her skin. He wondered if she was in pain. He worried that the evil spirit had fooled him. What if Brittany was trapped and feeling like death would be better?

Brittany saw E.V.'s intentions just moments before the creature could execute them. It planned on taking Coby's blood. Not just taking a few pints. E.V. intended to drain him.

FIFTY-NINE

MISUNDERSTOOD

BRITTANY ROLLED OUT from under Coby's hands so quickly, he would have missed it even if he hadn't blinked. When she hit the floor she didn't stop. She positioned herself under Coby's bed, ready to roll and run if she needed.

"Brittany?" Coby's head appeared at the right of his bed.

Brittany shifted to the left, keeping out of reach but still firmly under the bed frame. "Stay there."

"What's going on?"

"I'm ok." Brittany felt her emotions being pulled in conflicting directions as E.V. continued swing between fear and rage. "Just don't touch me."

"Are you hurt? Tell me what's going on?"

Brittany took a deep breath, feeling her reserves being depleted. She looked over to see the vision of Emily trying to strangle Coby. Being a figment of her own imagination, E.V.'s attempts were futile and had the creature not been so furious, it would have been funny. Brittany closed her eyes and responded. "E.V. calls it infiltration. I call it sort of like an infection."

"E.V.?"

"E.V.," Brittany sighed. She could feel all of the creature's emotions eating through the rest of their blood stored in her lungs. "Emily the Vampire."

"Vampire? Emily's a vampire? But... but Emily died. She's dead. Isn't she?"

Brittany opened her eyes and turned to stare at Coby. "Yes, Emily is dead, but it started with her. She was infected with a parasite." Brittany watched Coby's face, hoping she'd see acceptance. "Didn't you notice that she wasn't herself when she came back from the farm? That's because she'd been infected with this thing, and it changed her. She hadn't been trying to commit suicide when she drove the crowbar through her heart. She was trying to kill the infection. But she didn't know that killing herself would only release the parasite, and because I was the first person to touch her, I was infected."

Coby tried to freeze his expression before it showed the shock he felt. Though nothing he'd read, or even Mike had told him, had prepared him for this— it sounded chillingly like demonic possession to him. He continued to stare as Brittany explained how she'd been infected by something that had never been discovered, never properly classified. How it had consumed her blood and replaced it with its own bodily fluids. That's why she didn't need to eat human food. That's why she needed blood. Brittany continued to explain that this thing communicated with her, taking the form of its last host: Emily.

"You see Emily?"

"Clear as day," Brittany said.

Coby was torn; he wasn't sure what to do. But his choice would be decided by the answer to this simple question. "Brits, does it hurt?"

"Hurt?"

"Are you in pain?" Coby shifted to try and get closer and Brittany cowered back from him. "Is it hurting you?"

"No." She could see the concern in his eyes and she wished there was some way she could reassure him. She was painfully aware that there was nothing more she could do or say to try to convince him. He either believed her or he didn't.

Coby took a long time deliberating over it. "Ok," he said. "How does this work? It's an infection..."

"Parasite," Brittany corrected softly.

"Right, a parasite." Coby said. "How does it... how does it function?"

Brittany slid closer— she trusted him. E.V. wasn't as certain, so Brittany still stayed out of his reach. "As far as I've put together it's an amazing creature— ageless and beautiful, like a phoenix. She starts out as a single-celled organism— microscopic. She enters her host through direct contact from her last host."

"Who has to be dead."

"Ya." Brittany's reverence faltered slightly. "So, she's absorbed through her new host's skin and then carried in their bloodstream until she reaches the heart. That's where she lodges herself and starts to set up. Within a few days she's transformed from just a few cells in the heart, to making it her body, or like her head. Sort of a cross between the two, really.

"Next she moves into the person's veins, taking them over inch by inch until they are completely transformed into her tentacles. From there she starts to feed your organs her bodily fluid and she decides which to keep and which to starve and ultimately petrify. It's during this process that I stopped being able to eat food."

"When did it start to communicate with you?" Coby felt horrible. Even if it wasn't demonic possession, it was still something very wrong. But the worst had to be the way Brittany talked about it, like she admired it.

"About a week into it I started to have visions of Emily. At first I didn't understand, so I ignored them. As time went on they got clearer. I thought that I was going crazy, so I continued to ignore her until I passed out the night you found me."

Brittany had been inching closer and closer until she was within reaching distance. Coby stretched out his hand. He wanted to do something, say something. He wanted to ask her if she was really herself, but he knew if she wasn't, this thing would just lie. Mostly he wanted to touch her, as if somehow being able to feel her under his fingers would help him to know the truth.

She batted his hand away. "I said don't touch me. If you touch me, E.V. will take your blood."

Coby froze. If anything, this statement was proof that Brittany was still herself, that the two were separate, but he still had to ask, "You said the creature now controls your heart and your veins. Does it control your mind?"

"No. I am in control of my thoughts, but she can hear most of mine and I can hear almost all of hers. It's also still me that controls my actions. She can't make me move. All she controls is my veins— that's how she feeds me. It's also how she takes the blood we need, so if you touch me right now, she'll take as much as she can from you and you will get sick... or worse." Brittany shook her head. "You see, she's not very happy with me right now. She didn't want you to know any of this."

"I would suspect not," Coby said. "Why do you keep calling it she?"

Brittany didn't want to tell Coby about Bret. She wasn't sure why, but she didn't want him to know that someone else knew more than she or the creature about her and her kind. "Only girl parasites can infect girl hosts."

"Oh." Coby didn't know what to make of it. He wanted to believe Brittany, every word, though it seemed so far-fetched. It also made sense. How her blood had changed— whatever had come out when he bit her wasn't blood. It also explained how Emily's body, once discovered, had no blood; the creature would have used it up. Perhaps the cuts had been the creature's way of expelling its bodily fluid before it was discovered. When its fluid had hit his lip, it reminded Coby of rubbing alcohol in the way it evaporated so quickly.

It all fit, yet how could he be sure that this was really what was going on? "Brittany, tell me the truth, is it torture?" Mike's words echoed in Coby's head.

"Not most of the time." Brittany gave a weak smile.

Coby shifted so that his face was mere inches from hers. He looked deep into her blue eyes, willing them to show him the truth. "Is that really what's happened to you? Honestly?"

Brittany didn't falter, nor did she blink. "Yes."

"Ok" And in that moment he decided to believe her— completely. He cracked a smile. "So, my best friend is a vampire."

Brittany shrugged. "I guess that's as good a description of this as any.

"Sure." Coby's breath fell across her face and she felt herself drawn to it. "What's the best part about this?"

"Being with you." Brittany closed the gap so that their noses almost touched.

He smiled in response. "And what's the worst?"

"When I am with you."

SIXTY
LOVED

BRITTANY CLOSED HER eyes and pulled back as Coby's scent started to overwhelm her.

Coby didn't know what to say— *what was there to say*? He got up and climbed back into his bed. It was a lot to process. He needed to think and Brittany seemed to need to be alone. Though alone wasn't the right description. According to this new information, she was never alone anymore. She needed some time alone with her parasite.

See, Brittany said once she felt calmer, *he's not going to do anything bad.*

E.V. wasn't convinced. "The day is still young."

Will you let him touch me now?

"For now."

Brittany slowly slid herself out from under Coby's bed and stood up.

Coby had watched her emerge— it had been nice to watch, but once she was upright he couldn't stop himself from laughing. A silly thought had occurred, or maybe he just needed a reason to laugh.

"What?"

He tried to control his snickers. "My mom once said she forbade monsters in her house. She promised me that there would never, ever be any under my bed. You just proved her wrong."

Brittany gave a forced smile, then she shook her head, making clumps of dust fly off and fall about her.

Coby dropped his hands and stared into Brittany's face. "But if I could wish for anything: it would be to have you, my sweet monster, visit my room every night. If I had it my way I'd make you take up residence under my bed permanently."

Brittany was watching Coby closely, trying to figure out if he was being serious or still teasing.

"You never used to do that." Coby gestured to her stance. "Tilt your head like that. That's an Emily pose. It's eerie how similar you act to her sometimes."

Brittany nodded. "Ya, it's an E.V. thing. With each host, she takes a bit of them with her when she leaves them. In a weird way Emily is still alive in me."

"Does that mean that a piece of you will always exist in the creature now too?"

"I guess."

"So, it's sort of like a part of you will never die." Coby moved a bit closer.

Brittany crinkled her nose. She didn't feel great about this— it wasn't her that would live on, it would be the bits of her that the creature took along with it, almost like it was stealing them.

Coby moved even closer still. "Can I... can I touch you now?"

She nodded. "E.V. promised to behave, for now." Brittany wondered how long "now" would last.

"Good." He brought his arms around her and squeezed tight.

His intensity shocked Brittany. She gasped. As the air hit her lungs, she realized they were empty, and because of the high emotions, E.V. was nearly empty too. "Um, Coby."

He groaned. "What now?"

"I'm hungry."

"What does that mean?" But as if he knew, he let his hands drop.

Brittany cocked her head, staring out the window a moment. Dawn was approaching, and soon she'd have to return home so she could pretend to get up and go off to school like all normal fifteen-year-olds do. "It means I'll have to be careful and wait until I can..." She stopped, not wanting to say the rest aloud.

"Get some blood," Coby said for her. "Is there anyone you can't take from?"

"Some people. And there are a few I shouldn't take from."

Coby raised an eyebrow, waiting for her to explain.

"I can't take from anyone who's pregnant."

Coby nodded. "Sure," he said like this made sense, even though it didn't. "And who shouldn't you take from?"

"Well, I shouldn't take from you…"

"Why not, I've got plenty to spare." He held out his arm wrist up then pulled it back with his eyes narrowed. "Just a few ounces, E.V."

The shock of him speaking directly to her caused the creature to be speechless.

Brittany wasn't as surprised, but for some reason she didn't like him talking to the parasite. "*I* shouldn't, Coby. It's me, not E.V., that likes your taste too much. When I start I don't want to stop."

"Hmmm." Coby took a deep breath. "Can you wait till we get to school? I've seen that Liam is a willing victim." A look of jealousy passed over his face. He took a moment to re-arrange his features. "Or Simone and her band of followers. They haven't complained."

Brittany sat down next to Coby, staring at her hands in her lap. "You've noticed."

Coby brought his finger under Brittany's chin and pulled her head up so he could look into her eyes. "I've been watching you for weeks. I'm happy now that I understand what's going on."

"Please," Brittany moaned, feeling not only her desires mount, but also E.V.'s fears grow. She wasn't sure she could trust either of them in this state. "Please don't touch me."

Coby dropped his hand. "If I want to touch you, you need to be fed first." It wasn't a question.

Brittany nodded. "It's ok, I can wait till we get to school." She figured that would give both her and E.V. time to calm down. Plus, they were less apt to do something harmful in front of so many witnesses.

"But what if I want to kiss you now?"

"You… want to kiss me… now?" Brittany said.

"You'll need some blood first."

If she could she would have blushed, since it was she couldn't seem to make eye contact. She nodded her answer.

"Ok, I've got the perfect solution," Coby said in a rush. "Take some from my mom."

"What?"

"She's right across the hall. It's perfect."

"But..."

"No, listen, here's how I figure it— she's got several ounces to spare. There was this one website for blood drinkers that said two to eight ounces is safe for a regular donation. The worst side effect is feeling tired. So I'm thinking that if my mom was slightly more tired today, all she'd do is go to bed earlier and then I could spend more time with you." Coby had gone to wrap his arm around Brittany but stopped himself.

Brittany couldn't believe she'd let Coby talk her into it. She hadn't agreed with the first argument, but after his fifth time reassuring her that he wanted this, she caved. Mostly because she wanted to be able to kiss Coby.

E.V. was much happier. Somehow she equated his behavior as his acceptance of the situation.

Sneaking into Mrs. Monroe's room was easy, so was taking her blood and sneaking back out. What made it harder was the added feeling of violating the woman. Brittany wasn't just stealing her blood, she was taking it while the woman slept, unsuspecting, unable to say or do anything about it.

How did Gran not feel bad about this? she wondered to E.V.

"Years of practice." Gran had felt bad, but after years she learned to ignore those feelings.

Brittany tried to ignore those feelings as she snuck back into Coby's room. Once there he distracted her.

He'd been waiting for her return and caught her in his arms as she shut the door. He guided her to his bed, then made sure to keep his hands on either side of Brittany's face and was careful not to bite her again.

Brittany wasn't as behaved in the hands department, but she was far more controlled when it came to biting. As her bloodlust subsided, it made room for other desires to surface.

Coby released Brittany, panting. He lowered his head to her shoulder and rested it there until he could catch his breath. "Wow…"

"Wow," Brittany agreed. The memory of their *wow* got her through the rest of the morning, where she played normal while allowing E.V. to take from anyone who touched her, including a few teachers. By the end of the day she was confident she had enough to be with Coby for the afternoon, but there was no doubt she'd need to feed again to get through the night.

"What do you do in the evenings," Coby swung Brittany's hand as they walked home from school, "when you aren't visiting me?"

Brittany had been enjoying the sensation of Coby's hand wrapped gently around hers. She wore a soft smile— if this was to be her life now, she knew she would be content with it. She answered without putting too much thought into her words. "Play human mostly."

"Play human? But aren't you still human?"

"Sort of… I guess. That's what E.V. keeps telling me. But none of it feels as important anymore."

"I guess not." Coby had brought Brittany to his front door. He didn't open it. Instead, he turned and embraced her. Their lips met and their bodies collided as if that was the way they were meant to be; like keeping them apart was the unnatural state.

Neither was sure how they managed to make it in and onto his sofa.

The more Brittany practised being in control of her monster side, the better she got. Coby followed her lead; as she explored new areas of his body, he'd respond in kind. They were still entwined, hours later, when Coby's mom returned home from work. Coby reluctantly untangled himself from Brittany before his mom could walk in on them.

"I guess it's time for me to go home too." Brittany had been slower at releasing him. She left, ignoring Mrs. Monroe's look of disapproval.

SIXTY-ONE
ENDED

AFTER THEIR THIRD victim, E.V. was satisfied. "Ok, one more so I can fill my lungs."

"Why not go to Bret for that?"

"Because the night is still early, and his bar will be full. How would it look, him feeding me blood with all the other people there?"

Drinking, or breathing in the blood directly from her victim, wasn't like taking it from a glass. By the end Brittany looked like she had a starring role in a massacre. She went home to rinse, clean, and change.

As she stood in her bathroom letting the last bit of water evaporate out of her mouth, E.V. chuckled. "You know, if you filled your lungs first, before I'm full, I could help you with this part."

"I don't know why I didn't think of that."

As she finished speaking, there was a knock at the door. "Brittany? Is that you?" Ella's voice was concerned. "You ok? It's kinda late to be up. Is something wrong?"

It was too late to do anything with the wet, half wrung-out clothes in the tub— at least she'd gotten the blood out. "Everything's fine." She unlocked and pulled the door open.

Ella squinted into the dark room. She had turned on the hall light. In contrast the bathroom appeared pitch black to her. "Why are you in there with the lights off?"

"Um, I was too tired." Brittany tried to walk past Ella.

"Wait a sec." Ella caught Brittany by the wrist. "What's going on with you? You've been very quiet lately. Out so

259

much... are you upset about something? Do you have a problem that I've moved in?"

Brittany tried to keep the surprise off her face.

E.V.'s shock was less concealed. "She lives here now? Since when? When did she move in?"

"Brittany," Ella's grip tightened, "you're so cold!"

"I'm fine." Brittany pulled her arm away and quickly walked up the hall to her room.

It didn't take long before she heard Ella crying to her dad, "I don't know why she doesn't like me."

Brittany thought about that statement as she headed to Coby's: she no longer "didn't like" Ella— it was more like indifference to it... all of it. Her transformation had changed a lot of things she used to think were so important.

ଔ   ◆   ଚ

Climbing into Coby's room, she could tell he wasn't asleep, even though he lay still under his covers. She took this as an invitation and slipped between the sheets, sliding next to him. He shivered but drew his hands around her then gasped.

"Where are your clothes?"

"Over there on the floor."

She went to sit up and point, but he held her down. He hadn't seen her naked yet. He'd been working himself up to it. If she had sat up he would have gotten the full show, and somehow he felt that that would have cheapened the experience.

"Relax." He started to pull up his blanket to cover more of her chest but stopped. "Brits, what's this?"

He was referring to the place where the knife had struck her in the shoulder. E.V. had healed most of Brittany around it so that there was a quarter inch where the skin could be pulled open.

"Oh." She watched as he put his finger into it. "I got stabbed."

"What? Why were you stabbed?"

"Sometimes they fight back." She ground her teeth at the memory.

"Who? Who's fighting back?"

"The victims."

"Victims? Whose victims? Your victims?" Coby had unconsciously put more space between himself and Brittany.

"Ya, some of them aren't so willing to die."

"Die!" Coby sat up so fast, he brought most of the sheets with him. He looked down at Brittany— shocked. Shocked at what she said and what that meant, and only mildly aware that she was completely naked. Before he could give that any thought he was distracted by another scar. It ran from her hip up to just under her breast. "Brittany."

She leaned up to look at it too. "Oh, ya, that was his first strike. Took me by surprise, the…" She grumbled out a word that Coby had never heard her use before. It wasn't pretty.

"Brittany!"

"What?" She sat up, crossing her arms over her bare breasts. "What? I told you what I am."

"No." Coby shook his head. "No, you never told me about this."

"Well, what did you expect? I need blood… lots of blood. More than one person's worth."

Coby brought his hands up to cover his face. It made sense. He didn't like it.

"We should go now." E.V. stood next to the bed, panic returning.

I don't want to go.

Coby uncovered his face. "*It's* talking to you, isn't it? What's it saying? What is it telling you to do now!"

"He doesn't understand, Brittany." E.V. was standing at the open window. "We need to leave now."

No, he's just a little upset. He'll calm down. We'll work this out. But even as Brittany said this, she saw a look on Coby's face that told her she might be wrong.

"Stop talking to it! Talk to me!" He'd grabbed Brittany's face to force her to turn towards him.

It was instinct. Brittany wasn't even sure what she was doing. And it certainly wasn't E.V., who would have had Brittany out the window and down the street.

261

One moment Coby was squeezing Brittany's chin hard enough to cause a bruise (if she were able to bruise), the next she was tackling him so that he fell out of the bed and landed like a pancake on the floor. In an instant she had one knee on either side of him, pinning his arms to the floor. His legs were free to flop and flail about futilely, but all he managed to do was kick out at his bed. Brittany heard the sound of his shin bang against the unyielding wood.

"Brittany?" His eyes watered with the pain, but his voice wavered from fear.

"Let's get one thing straight. I am in control of me. I choose who we take from. I decide how much. I pick who dies."

"Ok, ok." Coby brought his hands up to Brittany's thigh, trying to displace her. All he managed to do was scratch her once before she caught and held his arms.

"Stop hurting me," she growled. E.V. had fixed the small wound, but it was costing her. Brittany felt it as the creature extracted from her lungs. She was impressed, however, that E.V. didn't take from Coby.

As she continued to hold on to his wrists, she knew how easy it would be to snap them, and she was also aware that E.V. wouldn't try to stop her if she decided she wanted to.

"Brittany, get off me."

She stayed immobile, trapping him.

"If you are so in control, then get off of me!"

"Do I need to leave?"

"Maybe." Coby arched his back, trying to get her to shift, knowing it wouldn't work. He still had to try.

"If I go I won't come back."

Coby shut his eyes. "I don't think I can be ok with this. I wanted to be…" He opened his eyes because Brittany was gone. As he sat up he saw that her clothes were gone too.

He sat up so fast his head spun. "Brittany!" he called out, trying to get up and run to his window. His leg buckled under him. Dragging himself up, he hopped over to the window and called out. "Brittany! Brittany. Brittany?"

He sagged against the window frame. His muscles twitched in protest. His leg ached and he could feel the bruises on his arms setting in. Bruises from her squeezing or her taking? He couldn't know for sure and suddenly it didn't matter.

"Brittany, come back," he whispered. "I don't want you to go."

She hadn't gone. She stayed on his roof, listening. She'd heard everything he'd yelled. She also heard him wake his mom and she listened as he came up with a lie for how he hurt his leg. She then watched as Mrs. Monroe helped her son to the car and took him to the hospital.

SIXTY-TWO
BEGINNING

WHEN COBY GOT back up to his room, he contemplated checking under his bed, but he talked himself out of it. Brittany was gone. He sat down heavily. He was sad, yet he wasn't sure that her leaving was a bad thing. He swung his leg in its air-cast into bed and rolled until he was comfortable. His eyes shut easily and he was asleep in moments.

As his snores filled the room, they lulled Brittany to sleep where she lay hidden under his bed. When she woke from her two hours of REM, she stood to look at Coby— her love. She felt hurt that he had reacted so badly. The dream of them being together, growing old together, was gone. She felt the tears coming and willed them to stop. As they did the feelings shifted from sorrow to anger, but Brittany couldn't tell if she was angrier with Coby or E.V.

The creature stayed silent, waiting for Brittany to decide.

Over the next forty-eight hours, Brittany stayed home. She'd convinced her father she was ill— it hadn't been that hard to do. Sitting in her room, she considered her options.

"Let's run away with Bret," E.V. said. "He knows us. He understands us."

That's just your crush talking.

E.V. didn't argue.

She could try to reconcile with Coby.

"He hates us. He hates you," E.V. said, still feeling fearful of him. "Didn't you see the look on his face when he realized what you do?"

Brittany didn't argue.

She could run away by herself, becoming the creature of the night that she now believed she was.

"We are no creatures of the night," E.V. said quietly.

Aren't we?

"No."

No matter how long they talked, they couldn't find a solution. In the end, Brittany left a note for her father saying she had run away. Then she stayed, hiding out where no one would expect to find her.

In the beginning it was mostly in the old tree fort, or sometimes even in her own room. She also spent a lot of time in Coby's room (when he was at school). Even if people were in the house, Brittany was so quiet she was never detected.

During this time E.V. was the only company Brittany had. She didn't speak to Coby. She didn't visit Bret. She didn't even see her father or mother.

As the months passed, Brittany became as acquainted with the creature's past hosts as it was. Sometimes even more so, because as the creature shared, its memories became easier to recall.

Its existence had started somewhere in the dark ages. Of course, time back then was not measured as accurately as it was now, so it was hard to discern when exactly the creature's life started. There was also no answer or explanation as to how she had come into being, she just was, quite suddenly, which was a shock to her too. And though she had a vague idea of how she functioned, she was not sure how she knew.

"Tell me about your first host," Brittany murmured, barely audible.

E.V. deliberated for a moment. "Well, she was very young. Not much older than L.J."

E.V. didn't need to speak any longer. Brittany could see it.

She saw the house. It reminded her a little of the gingerbread house from a nursery rhyme her father used to tell her. But house might not have been the best description — cottage better suited it. It was nestled on a hillside and was surrounded by lush and tall green grass. The grass spread out like an ocean in every direction. It was only interrupted here and there by large grey-blue rocks. There were no other houses, or cottages, as far as the eye could see.

The girl, Abelena, had three older brothers, and their mother was swollen with another child on the way. The oldest, Jax, was ten.

A sense of innocence and immaturity emanated from the girl— but there was the same feeling about E.V., as if she too were a young child who didn't know what she was. Brittany watched in fascination as Abelena's life played out— her discovering that she needed to touch people to feel better and watching her siblings becoming weaker every time she did.

All except Jax. He never allowed Abelena to touch him — he always made sure there was something between them — a blanket, the sleeve of her shirt or his.

E.V.'s memories were flavoured with fondness as she recalled Jax. His round cheeks. His green-blue eyes. His fair skin. His high, boyish voice. His mop of light brown hair. An old memory formed, one E.V. had lost until this moment.

"Come." Jax held a gloved hand out to Abelena.

She took it at once and was led away from the grave of their middle brother. "Euell is sleeping?" Abelena asked. "When will he wake?"

Jax shook his head. "Not sleeping, Lena." He used the nickname only he called the girl. "He died. He will never wake again."

"Oh." Abelena considered that for a while. "Will I be dead one day? Will I never wake up like Euell?"

Jax stopped to look down at his sister. "Not you, my sweet. No, little Lena, you will not die, not like Euell."

Abelena's cheeks lifted into a full smile. Jax smiled widely back.

He led her over a hill and a far walk to the neighbor's. Crouching low he took her to their sheep pen. The fluffy white animals shuffled nervously at their approach.

"Careful," he cautioned, "quiet. Be still. They won't spook if you are very still..."

SIXTY-THREE
EXISTING

BRITTANY WATCHED AS Jax taught Abelena how to hunt and kill animals. He taught her to cut them open and inhale their blood into her lungs. He explained that she should not take too many of the neighbors' chickens and sheep, but she was never limited to the wild hares she could catch nor the billy goats that sometimes wandered down the hills.

"One day you will be old enough to move away. I'll take you far away from here. We will live together in the city. You are not meant for the country like this, my sweet." His voice had been casual and light. Only the weight of his hand holding hers could give away how much he cared.

As she drank from the animals she grew stronger, but her body was not growing. Her mother had the doctor come to their house to check her. Her mother was worried— after losing Euell, and then her new baby, she feared that she all her children would be taken from her.

After examining Abelena, the doctor also seemed concerned. He left in a hurry promising to return. He never did.

Two days later Jax disappeared. When he was found in the woods it wasn't clear what had killed him— but he was dead.

Once he was buried, E.V. remembered sneaking out of her house in the middle of the night to lie atop his fresh grave. She didn't know what to do without him.

One morning as she returned, she was approached by Braxton. He was the only other sibling left alive. He was barely seven now, and Abelena was nearing four. He'd offered her his gloved hand and she'd taken it.

E.V. wanted to turn away from her memory, as Abelena followed. She already knew this part, but she let the memory continue so Brittany could watch.

Braxton took Abelena to a tall rock formation far away from their little cottage. He dropped her hand and started to climb. She followed. Once at the top Braxton stood facing away, looking out at the rolling hills. Abelena came over to join him. Her eyes stared down the cliff— this side of the rock was further from the ground, and at the bottom lay a field of smaller rocks, their sides were jagged and sharp as blades.

Braxton slowly turned to face Abelena with a look of loathing twisting his childish face. "You are not my sister."

"Yes I am," she said softly.

"You are not Abelena," Braxton accused.

She didn't know how to respond.

"You are a monster!" Braxton yelled. "You killed Euell, and Momma's new baby." Braxton's fists shook. "You killed the doctor. I found him in the woods, and now you are killing our momma." Before she could figure out what to say, he pushed her.

Abelena was falling, racing towards the rocks that would cut and tear into her.

Brittany tried to pull out of the memory but was unable to. She felt each and every sharp edge that sliced and ripped into Abelena. Still trying to pull away from the heavy sensation of dying, Brittany was stopped at E.V.'s insistence.

"Wait."

Brittany took deep breaths while forcing herself to maintain the vision. Abelena's body fluid drained from her until she was empty. All her moisture evaporated quickly, even with the lack of a strong sun.

"What am I waiting for?" Brittany asked through gritted teeth. The vision was dark now, but she could still feel things taking place. A strange sinking sensation, like she was a balloon losing air.

"That's her veins collapsing," E.V. said. "With no fluid in them they fall flat and disintegrate." Her feelings of remorse and loss over Abelena were easy to detect.

Brittany continued to wait. It felt quiet, dark and a little as if she were trapped. "E.V., where are you?"

"Where I always end up. I'm in the heart."

"But how? Isn't Abelena dead?"

"Yes, Abelena is very dead. She is long gone. I cannot hear her, I cannot speak with her. She is gone." Her voice was filled with grief. She grieved Abelena. The girl had been her friend. E.V. mourned her dying, even now years and years later.

"So how do you still exist?"

"I'm not sure, but I do. Remember how I told you once that it would be easy to kill you— but not me?" Brittany nodded. "Well, here it is. My first death. The first memory of my first human's death. But I survived because I am not flesh and bone."

As a new sensation started. E.V. asked, "Do you feel that?"

Brittany did— a sense of pulling while being pushed at the same time, then it was as if she was adrift on a sea. No, it was as if she had *become* the sea.

"What's happening now?" Brittany felt panicked, though in the memory there was nothing but calm.

"I'm the least vulnerable I can ever be," E.V. sighed.

"But what's happening?"

"I am being reduced down to the cells that I am composed of."

Brittany was confused but didn't speak. The liquid feeling became still, like a pond that sat untouched. Its surface was unmoving, glassy, smooth— harmless-looking and beautiful. Then, as if the water had been dammed up and the dam had broken, there was a great rushing.

"What's that!"

"I have been found. I am becoming someone new." This was explained in an excited tone. But E.V. was worried.

"What's wrong?"

"This is when I am most vulnerable."

Brittany pulled away from the sightless memory. She blinked, worried that something was wrong with her eyes, but it was only from nightfall that her vision was tinted with darkness. "Explain."

"When my human dies, I die a little with them. As I lose them I become me— just me. My cells separate, each containing all the information I need to rebuild once I'm found."

"When you die, can you infect more than one person?" It made sense if each of her cells had everything they needed to start a new life. Much like a sperm— each sperm could create a new life if it were given the eggs to do that with.

"No," E.V. snickered, "I need to be touched by a human and absorbed."

"Yes, but if more than one human touches you, couldn't you become more than one vampire?"

E.V.'s eyebrows came together as she thought. "No," she said after a while. "No, as I'm absorbed, I mix with the human's DNA and there is a signal sent out to the rest of my cells. Those that aren't bonded with the proper DNA will perish. Once I've coded to one person's DNA, my cells cannot survive unless the right person absorbs them. Of course, the longer the contact, the more of me gets absorbed."

"How many of your cells does a human need to get infected?"

"One."

Now Brittany made a face. "How many cells are you made of?"

E.V. shrugged.

Brittany lay silent, feeling the moon making its way across the sky.

"Will you visit Coby tonight?" E.V. interrupted the silence as the hours dragged on.

Brittany wanted to shake her head.

E.V. stopped her. "It's been forty-eight hours. You'll need to sleep soon."

"I can't." Brittany stifled a moan.

E.V. knew Brittany's dilemma. She couldn't because she longed to do more. That first night she'd been angry, but now that had ebbed away. Brittany missed Coby's touch, his voice, the way his eyes felt on her. If she returned to his room, she wasn't sure she'd be able to resist her desires for more.

"Besides, I'm not sure I'm welcome there anymore." Brittany thought of the vampire myths and the need to be invited into someone's house— though completely false, she still didn't want to go there feeling unwelcome.

"He did invite you."

"When?" She was still remembering the way Coby had looked at her.

E.V. smiled. "Coby said, if I could wish for anything, it would be to have you, my sweet monster, visit my room every night. If I had it my way I'd make you take up residence under my bed permanently."

"I'm sure he didn't mean like this."

E.V. shrugged, not discerning the difference. "Well, you are going to need sleep. If it's not him, then how will you get your REM?"

Brittany could see E.V.'s thoughts reaching towards Bret, but the creature stopped when she felt Brittany watching.

"Alright, we'll hunt, then we'll go sleep under Coby's bed." She didn't promise not to do more, because she wasn't sure about that herself.

E.V. shrugged. She still wished Brittany would agree to Bret instead.

SIXTY-FOUR

HIDING

BRITTANY'S DAYS WERE filled with the company of E.V. and her former lives. Her nights were filled with creating corpses and breaking into Coby's room to sleep. Now as she dreamed, Brittany seemed to have an instant replay of the stories E.V. shared during her waking hours. Some nights she woke knowing more about the creature than it did.

E.V. had the average occupancy of about five years in any given host, young and old, girls and boys alike. Most hosts' lives ended in violent sword fights; bar brawls; wars; bandit attacks— general violence. She lived in her hosts and moved between them mostly undetected by anyone.

Though she was mostly undetected by humans, animals were a different story. Some horses would spook around her like they could sense her. She was thrown once or twice because of that. Most dogs didn't take kindly to her either, and all cats seemed to distrust her.

In the beginning the awareness of vampires, or of the supernatural, was more common, so E.V. had to be more careful. As the years passed, the belief in true vampires died out and gave way to less suspicion and more concrete, scientific theories. But E.V.'s memories of the witch hunts and trials remained sharp.

It shared the many experiences of being set on fire, decapitated, hung, drowned, and quartered. Fire was the worst way to go because it very nearly took E.V. with it on more than one occasion. Yet somehow, miraculously, the creature had awakened anew, usually in the ones who had accused her of being a witch in the first place. After the first two burnings, E.V. learned to jump while her current human was being tied to the stake.

Beheading was no more or less uncomfortable than other ways, though it was vastly disorienting for the humans. When faced with a beheading, E.V. would offer her host the option of her ending his or her life before the guillotine took them. No one needed to watch as their head fell away from their body. Besides, if they wanted to experience that, she always had the memory of the first one.

Hanging and drowning weren't harmful. E.V. was thankful to whoever got the signs of witches wrong. Or got it wrong that she, inside a human, would make them float. Due to the petrified organs, they would sink. Yes, E.V. had memories of her hosts surviving both of these methods, but after they did, the hosts wouldn't be alive for that much longer.

No matter how far they ran, news of their survival would travel and soon she would be captured again. The second attempt at execution was always far more efficient. Quartering, where the humans would be strung up and pulled apart, was a popular way after that. As if surviving the first attempt had offended the humans and they now wanted to inflict the most pain possible. Again, this was an instance where E.V. would offer suicide as a way to avoid the experience.

"You really have cared for every human you've infected, haven't you."

E.V. could only think of one exception to Brittany's statement.

Even though it had been through the prince that E.V. gained most of her knowledge about her abilities and their limits, she despised him.

Brittany found it ironic that his was the longest-standing partnership. But partnership wasn't the right word. E.V. might have infested the prince, but the prince was a wicked and evil man. Her time with him was torture for her. She was his prisoner and, as a prisoner fears their captor, she feared the prince even to this day.

During these memories she had been predominantly in Romania. As time went on, she found herself travelling all around Europe and some of Russia. She could remember being in France, Spain, and England. She had even travelled to China. It wasn't clear, but she may have also ended up in India for a while.

She'd somehow made it back to England, before being carried to North America during the settling of the continent. She wasn't discovered there until after Charles. She then tried to get back to Europe, but her ship went down and she ended up in Asia.

Eventually, she'd infected Soo Sung, who fought in the Vietnam War. That's where Henry found her.

The rest was well known to Brittany. After twenty-two good years, Henry's time was done. He never met his son-in-law, nor did he get to see his granddaughter. E.V. appreciated them as much as she could for Henry, and Gran still felt like she had her husband, which gave her the strength to go on for over fifteen years.

From Emily to Brittany was one of the creature's shortest turnarounds.

"Who was your favorite?" Brittany wondered.

"You are."

Despite herself, it made Brittany smile. "Other than me?"

"Petunia."

"But you never possessed her." She'd died from pneumonia thirteen years into her marriage to Charles, who had taken his own life within a year.

"No, I never possessed her. Charles felt guilty about that. We talked about whether she would have been able to survive the illness that took her if he hadn't been allowing me to feed off her. This is something I still can't answer. I felt bad about it too. I loved her just as much as Charles— perhaps in some ways more so. I wish I had never fed off her, then I could have possessed her and she could have had a longer life."

"Who was your favorite to be in?"

"Still you."

Brittany shook her head. "I get it, but after me, who?"

E.V. wasn't sure Brittany really understood. She shrugged. "I like them all enough. Each had something interesting to share... but not one of them stands out above the rest. Apart from you."

"Fine," Brittany chuckled. She realized that was a huge compliment— perhaps the best she could get from the creature. "Thanks."

E.V. nodded.

SIXTY-FIVE
BONDING

STILL LIVING IN the shadows, Brittany fed E.V. well and drank deeply, keeping her lungs full. Her hunting had become so effective that she no longer needed to worry about whether the victims had knives or carried guns— she was too quick. It got to the point that they didn't even see her coming and they were dead before they could figure out what had hit them. And though it didn't matter to her now, she was the hero she had wanted to be. All her efforts were paying off. The streets had become safer due to the lack of pimps, prostitutes, drug dealers, and thieves.

From the shadows Brittany watched as Ella's stomach got bigger and bigger. She watched as J.J. grew into a toddler and L.J. became a preschooler. She watched Coby get so good at using his crutches that they became an extension of himself, until they were no longer needed.

What Brittany didn't know was that as she watched, she was being watched.

⁂ ⬥ ⁃

It was fall. The days were getting shorter and the nights longer. Brittany was relieved. She'd found it hard to wait out so many daylight hours, constantly having to find new places to hide.

Coby's room had been lost to her as school let out for the summer. Though he'd taken a job at the convenience store near Brittany's mother's house, she never was sure about his shifts. She didn't mind hiding under the bed for a few hours, but hours and hours on end was more than she could handle.

The old tree fort had been torn down to make way for a much more child-safe structure. And with the baby finally here, Ella was on maternity leave, so now not even her room was safe any more.

Ella had taken to going into Brittany's room to cry for hours on end. Brittany was surprised how much her stepmom could cry. Whenever the child slept, Ella would slip into Brittany's room, curl up on her bed and sob. Sometimes she'd complain, yelling even.

"Brittany," Ella had called out one time while Brittany was trapped in her closet. Brittany was sure she had been discovered until Ella followed with, "Where are you?"

Still, she couldn't leave, and she ended up listening in on the woman's rants. "You know it wasn't fair you taking off like that! With you gone your father does nothing but grieve you. Now they are telling us to consider you dead. Dead! How is your father supposed to feel now? You've broken his heart.

"And your mother— she's so sad. She calls all the time to tell me how sad she is." Ella's tone had turned angry. "You know, I never would have thought you such a brat. But you taking off like this— it was a very selfish thing to do. I hope you never come back. I hate you.

"I can't believe I had wanted us to be friends," Ella added before she dissolved into wails. If Ella was still talking, Brittany wasn't able to make out the words. Brittany had taken up permanent residence in her mom's attic after that. But even that had its problems.

"We didn't get enough last night," E.V. complained as she felt herself getting hungry.

I know. You'll have to wait.

"I'm not sure we'll be able to."

What do you want me to do? The answer formed in Brittany's head. She saw herself sneaking down to L.J.'s room and taking a few ounces while the girl napped.

"You are a monster," Brittany whispered towards the vision of Emily. It wasn't a reproach, it was said more like a fact. That would be a monstrous thing to do, yet Brittany didn't expect anything less from the creature.

"Look who's calling the kettle black," E.V. rebutted, her tone playful.

Brittany didn't argue; she too was a monster, just not *that* kind. For her there was still that line.

E.V. got up, stretching. "I'm so bored. There's nothing to do!"

"Read the latest vampire book," Brittany offered.

E.V. kicked out at the glossy-covered novel. They both watched as her foot sailed through the thick book. "I can't believe what passes for vampire tales these days."

Brittany smiled and lay back, staring up at the rafters. She'd stared at the same spot for so long, she knew every bump and line. She magnified her sight as she noticed a spider on the ceiling. That little corner of the roof would feel like an entire world to the tiny creature.

"Do you know who you want to move on to when you're done with me?"

E.V. stopped pacing. "Wha…"

"It's ok. I don't mind. It's not like I'm doing very much living here." Brittany continued to watch the spider as it set up a web, spinning and dancing like it was in some eight-legged ballet.

"No, I haven't thought much about that." E.V.'s voice was strained. "Brittany, I don't want to leave you. I don't want to lose you."

"You're kidding me, right?" Brittany sat up to watch E.V., trying to catch her lie. "After everyone else you've lived in. All the things they've done. All those experiences. What have you got going for yourself with me?"

Cocking her head to one side, the image of Emily answered. "Love. I love you." With all her others hosts E.V. had never felt this way. "I don't need anything more than you, Brit. And I don't… I don't want to lose you."

Brittany lay back down, staring up at the spider again.

"What can I do, hon?" E.V. asked in Gran's kind tone. "You know I don't like to see you in pain."

Brittany continued to stare at the spider, giving a half-hearted shrug.

E.V. nodded once and changed the subject. "Are we visiting Coby tonight?"

"I guess I should, I need the sleep." She didn't have to add that she missed him, even if it was only to inhale his scent and hear his heartbeat.

છ ♦ ᔆᖇ

Coby's face was smooth and relaxed. His eyes were closed but they moved about as if he were seeing something in his dreams. He had thinned out over the summer as he'd lost the last of his baby fat. Now his jawline was strong and defined. He slept on his back, head facing up, a position he'd gotten used to while wearing his air-cast. It now felt familiar to him. His breathing was deep and even, unaware of the monster that stood so near.

As she always did on the nights she returned to him, Brittany contemplated slipping into the bed next to him instead of climbing under it. *What's the worst he would do?* she wondered, but she resisted, as she had for nearly five months now. Once positioned directly beneath him, she rolled onto her side and shut her eyes.

When she reached consciousness, she lay still. Her routine was to sneak out before Coby woke, but somehow he'd stirred before she was done sleeping. She didn't need a clock to know it was five in the morning. Coby was still in bed, but there was no mistaking that he was awake. A moment later the noise that had stirred him repeated itself.

He rolled and picked up his cell phone from off his night table. "Mike! It's too early for a chat." He grumbled to himself while he typed out a response.

"I worked the late shift last night..." he continued to complain until he was cut off by the sound of a new text.

"Fine." Coby had shifted to sit with his feet dangling over the side of his bed for a moment.

He got another text and grumbled, "Impatient much... I'm doing it now." Brittany heard him punch his reply while he got up and walked over to his computer.

He turned it on and Brittany could hear him tapping on the keys. "What could be so important at five thirty in the morning?" More tapping. "There's the local news." There was a moment's pause then Coby said, "Holy crap." He sat down heavily on the chair at his computer desk.

Brittany had shifted and braved bringing her face to the edge of the bed, where she could stay hidden behind Coby's sheets, which had fallen halfway off. She moved them aside a little to get a clear view of the computer screen. What she saw made her want to gasp. She stopped herself but blinked and looked harder.

The scene was self-explanatory, which was good because there was no sound. A chopper was circling a large crew of workers who were excavating an older part of the city dump. They were mostly dredging up debris. Next to it, however, was something unmistakable: three body bags.

Coby hit the volume.

"...it's not clear how many bodies are down there, but it is clear someone has been using the old dump as a burial ground. The first was found on a routine check of the area. Workers are sent to the older sites to test toxicity levels. As our waste settles and starts to decay, it can sometimes give off harmful gases." This explanation was accompanied by a crude animation. "When that happens, special pipelines are sent down to the pockets of gas and lit, so it can burn off. At one such location the digging crew uncovered a limb. The limb belonged to known felon Eddie Sharp, who was on probation and went missing over four months ago.

"Eddie was only the first of many to be discovered. In the last hour they have uncovered three more. Most have been identified, but the authorities aren't releasing any more names now. They are, however, asking that if anyone knows about this they contact their local police station. They are taking anonymous calls." The camera was back on the reporter. "What makes this worse is that there are rumors that they don't think this is the only spot the killer's been using. Plans to dig up several other locations are underway.

"We will continue to bring you updates as this story unfolds. This is channel..."

Coby had hit the volume. He leaned back in his chair and sighed, "Brittany, was that you?"

SIXTY-SIX

FOUND

BRITTANY HAD SHRUNK back under Coby's bed. When he said her name aloud, she waited to see if she'd been caught. However, Coby's tone suggested he was simply speaking to himself. At least he didn't follow it up by crawling under the bed after her, so she figured she was safe.

Coby worked at his computer for a few hours more. Tapping away. Eventually he'd turned it off and gone about his morning routine. When he left for school, Brittany crawled out and went over to his computer to check for updates. In the three hours, they had uncovered two more of her hiding places for the bodies.

Brittany turned up the volume to listen. It was a different reporter. This one had a deep voice. "It is reported that a security camera caught someone leaving the site at about one this morning. The person was unidentifiable under the large hoodie." A clip of Brittany hopping the fence was played. "Authorities are telling everyone to watch out for someone five foot five, weighing approximately one hundred and fifteen pounds." The clip was replayed. "It's clear this person has been doing this for some time. See how they aren't even slowed down by the barbed wire. The authorities are saying that with the number of bodies they've uncovered now, this must have been a fairly regular routine. Of course, no one knows how the person got the bodies in, if they had help or why they were killing these people in the first place.

"Some names are finally being released." He reeled off a few dozen as the screen displayed the workers continuing to excavate a hole. The camera focused back on the reporter outside the fence next to the dump. "There is a hotline for anyone to call if they think they have information about this serial killer." The announcer gave a ten-digit number as it and a corresponding website scrolled across the bottom of the screen.

"We'll return to this breaking event as it unfolds..."

The news was updated every thirty minutes throughout the day. Brittany couldn't help staying to watch. As more bodies were uncovered and more names were released, they started showing photos of the faces that went with the names. Over ninety percent were mug shots.

The reporter from the three o'clock news wondered, "Should we really be trying to find this person to arrest them or hand them a medal? After all, he has made our city safer. I don't know about you, Marc," she turned to face her co-anchor, "but I feel much better living here knowing these people are off the streets."

Marc gave an uncomfortable smile. A new name had been released, and this one hadn't been a pimp, drug dealer, or even a hooker. It was a young boy.

Brittany remembered him, his fine, almost female features, his high prepubescent voice, his clean blood that had flowed smoother without the inhibitions of all the toxins she tried to ignore with the rest. She'd enjoyed his taste so much that it had caused her to debate giving up her ideals of only taking from those she felt deserved death...

Brittany's attention snapped back to reality as she heard a car door slam shut.

"Thanks for the ride." She heard Coby's voice clear as day.

The person he was with seemed to clear his throat with his response. "N... plm."

Brittany listened to two sets of feet making their way into the backyard. The fence gate banged shut.

"Wait here, I'll get you that thing from my room."

Both E.V. and Brittany knew there would be no sneaking out the window now— not if she wanted to remain unseen, not with someone waiting in the backyard. She dove under the bed.

Coby entered his room confidently. His eyes flickered to the computer and he couldn't help but grin. This morning he'd only suspected Brittany was there when he thought he'd seen her face reflected in the computer monitor, peeking out from under his bed. Now he was sure even without seeing her.

He moved a few things around on his desk— just a part of the show. Mike arrived at his bedroom door within minutes, giving a swift knock and coming in.

"Sorry, man." Coby continued the ruse. "I can't find it. I'm sure it's around here somewhere. Just give me a sec."

Brittany couldn't see more than his feet as Mike walked over to Coby's window to stand facing out. She stared at his work boots, thinking she didn't like Mike— but it could be because she didn't know him.

"You don't have to watch your car," Coby said. "This neighborhood is a safe one. It'll be fine. Now where did I put..."

Mike didn't reply but stayed by the window.

"Just hang on a sec, I might have left it in my mom's office." Coby left, shutting the door with a deafening snap as he did.

Brittany had never felt so trapped. She wanted to run, but with this Mike person still standing at the window, there was no way of leaving without being seen, and she wasn't ready to reveal herself like that.

I'm just being silly, they'll be done in a few minutes and then I'll get out of here.

E.V. wanted to agree, but she was having a harder time— something about this situation felt like a trap.

Coby returned to his room after an excruciatingly long seven minutes. Brittany had counted the seconds. He crossed the room to give something to Mike, who grunted his response.

"No problem. Oh, hey, I wanted to check the updates." Coby was at the computer. He turned the volume up so that it overrode all other sounds.

Brittany couldn't hear the birds nesting in the tree outside, nor Mike's car still running in the alley, and she couldn't hear if Coby and Mike were moving around the room. She fought the desire to make her way to the edge of the bed and peek out.

"What do you think they're doing?" E.V. asked.

Beats me, Brittany said, feeling extra irritable.

"That brings the total body count to 97," the news reporter was saying, "and there are rumors of at least five more burial locations yet to be excavated."

Brittany did the math in her head— if they intended to find everyone, they weren't even halfway done. She shivered. How did it get to be so many?

"Wow, that was a lot," E.V. said. "I guess when you look at it altogether, two or three a night for 187 nights... yikes, they have a long way to go. I wonder how deep they're digging. They can't have gotten everybody if..."

Enough. Brittany held in her moan. Until now she had never looked at it all together. It was too much. Brittany couldn't keep from sighing, and she was glad because if she couldn't hear Coby and his friend, they were sure not to hear her.

"I guess we should slow down now. I don't need so much anymore." E.V. stretched her tentacles out to their fullest. "We will be fine on less."

Brittany might have wanted to say something, but ever since she'd inhaled, she had started to feel funny.

"Oh no!" E.V.'s face turned white beside hers.

Oh no, what? Brittany could feel there was something wrong, but she didn't understand. She'd never felt this way; it was as if her skin was shrinking around her.

E.V. had kept Brittany from getting too hot over the summer by insisting they hide out in her mom's basement on the hottest days. The days when they needed to were few. Summer heat was a concern, but most days would only be a discomfort. With their blood intake up and Brittany's lungs always full, it had never become any kind of threat.

"How did it get so hot?" E.V. panicked.

With the breath of air, Brittany had realized her lungs were empty, and all that was in them now was the hot air. The same hot air that settled all around her, lapping at her, burning her skin and pulling at E.V.'s precious fluids, causing them to ooze out of her pores and evaporate off.

E.V.'s reserves were depleting quickly. They had to get out. *Door or window?* was the only thought the creature had. But Mike was still standing at the window and the door was where the heat seemed to be coming from.

I vote window, Brittany panted.

Good choice, and if anyone gets in the way we'll have an immediate food source, E.V. said.

Brittany wanted to argue with that. What if it was Coby who got in the way? But her thought was lost in the sweltering heat. It took all her concentration to roll and drag herself out from under the bed.

What happened next was a blur.

Coby had seen Brittany's hands appear on the opposite side of the bed from where he stood. Mike had told him to stand by the door by the heater he'd set on high. Mike was leaning against the closed window in what could only be described as a hazmat suit, something one would wear when cleaning up chemical spills.

Brittany glanced over, realizing that there would be no extracting from Mike in that. The light glinted off the faceguard and Brittany looked away, intending to push her way past this human in a Martian suit and break out of the window.

As she collided with him, he was more solid and much more ready for the shove than she'd expected. His arms came around her, holding her easily, despite her best efforts.

The computer had been muted. "I can help," Coby yelled.

Brittany was stuck watching as Coby ran towards her where she was pinned by the super-strong spaceman. She saw E.V.'s plans and as her thoughts swirled, she couldn't think up any reason to stop the creature.

"Coby, stay back!" were the first clear words Mike said.

I know that voice was the last thought Brittany had before all went black.

SIXTY-SEVEN
CAUGHT

COBY HAD FROZEN at Mike's command.

Mike slowly lowered Brittany to the floor. "Shut that thing off."

Coby sprinted over to the heater and unplugged it. He also opened the door, feeling instant relief as cooler air was drawn into his room. He then made his way over to his bed and climbed onto it so he could watch Mike attending to the unconscious Brittany.

Mike had one of Brittany's eyelids cracked. The pupil followed Mike as he peered in. "Hello, little creature," he cooed softly, "I know you're in there."

"Freaky," Coby said as a chill raced up his spine.

Brittany's iris shot over to stare at him until Mike released her eyelid and it fell shut.

"The demon is conscious, even if Brittany isn't?"

"The demon is always conscious," Mike said, picking up Brittany and slinging her over his shoulder.

"Does that mean it can do things while Brittany sleeps?"

"It can do the same kind of stuff it could do while Brittany is awake."

"And that is?" Coby was following Mike out his back door. He glanced around to see if anyone was there.

"Extract blood and take care of its house," Mike answered.

"It's house? You mean Brittany's body?"

"That's its house."

Coby stayed quiet. The way Mike held Brittany was not how he'd expected. Every touch, every move, was as if Mike were being careful— not of accidental touch but of something more. Coby was glad for Brittany, but Mike's movements were… it was as if Mike loved her. Not the girl but the creature inside.

Mike laid Brittany across the back seat. When he straightened to find Coby in his way, he made a face.

"I thought you told me she was possessed. That the demon is in her controlling her."

Mike rubbed his chin. "Yes, I did."

"Did you lie to me?"

"Yes, I did."

Coby narrowed his eyes and planted his feet firmly in place, ready for a fight. He didn't stand a chance. Mike had snatched Coby's arm and twisted it around his back so quickly, he didn't see the move coming. And then Mike had his hand on Brittany's bare arm.

Mike crooned, "That's right, my sweet, drink up."

Coby yawned, fighting his exhaustion, realizing that if the creature took too much, this could kill him. But he couldn't do anything about it before he passed out.

☙ ◆ ❧

Brittany woke up to E.V.'s urgent nudging. "Wake up, wake up, wake uuuuuup! Wake up now— WAKE UP…" As she became conscious, she was aware that she was propped up in a chair, her arms and feet bound to it so that she was trapped. Before she opened her eyes, Brittany listened.

She could hear soft snores— and she'd know them anywhere. *Coby,* she thought miserably.

"Yes," E.V. said. She'd been listening to him snore for over four hours.

What happened?

"How should I know? You're the one with the eyes!"

What did you hear?

"Coby and that Mike guy had an argument."

Why not call Mike by his real name. Brittany ground her teeth. *Bret the betrayer.*

Brittany could see that E.V. agreed with the title she'd given him, yet there was something more that Brittany couldn't see.

How did this happen? Why are Coby and Bret friends? Why did they capture me? She wanted the answer to the last question the most. She was upset. If they had just talked to her, she probably would have come willingly.

As Brittany continued to brood, she realized she felt stronger— the creature was full. *How?*

"Bret fed us." In her mind Brittany could see E.V., and she looked as if she were trying to hide her face.

How?

"Just exactly how you'd think— he brought me people, then he had them touch you so I could drink. And I had to. I just had to… I was so thirsty."

Brittany understood. *I just wish you had taken from Bret.*

"I tried…"

Brittany could feel the creature's hesitancy. She could sense it holding something back. *What?*

E.V. shook her head.

What? What is it? There was something— just out of reach.

"No. I'm not supposed to tell you."

Brittany fumed, and in her frustration she pushed, wiggled, and searched for what E.V. was hiding.

"Stop!" E.V. said. "Stop, I'll tell you, but you aren't going to like it."

Brittany wanted to snort. *I already don't like it.*

"Well, you'll like this even less."

SIXTY-EIGHT
TRUTH

"BRET ISN'T HUMAN," E.V. said. "At least he's not human like Coby. He's human like you, Brit. He's got his own parasite, or Bret is the parasite and who knows who the human is? That's how he knows things about us— about me. He's been educating me, kind of. Telling me about me and the others like me. And he's been explaining my purpose to me."

What is your purpose? Brittany asked. She didn't like the way E.V. spoke about Bret like he had impressed her.

E.V. shook her head.

What is it?

Another shake.

Come on, why won't you tell me?

"I don't want to." The image of Emily was busily picking lint off its sweater.

E.V.? Brittany felt panicked at how easy it seemed for the creature to keep its thoughts from her. *E.V.?*

"Oh, relax. I will tell you, just not yet. Soon, later..." E.V.'s nervousness seeped through. "Please, open your eyes. I need to see where we are."

For a moment Brittany felt as she had in those first few days— she felt like she couldn't trust E.V. She pushed that thought aside and tried to figure out where she was without looking. She could sense that she was somewhere dark and cool. It reminded her of her mother's basement.

Bracing herself, unsure why, she took a quick, shallow breath. It was a relief to exhale the stale air that was left over from the last time she'd breathed in.

E.V. appreciated Brittany's relief, but she felt too much hesitation to truly enjoy it. She didn't like keeping secrets from Brittany. The severing of their bond was nothing short of cutting off a limb, but she was trying to find a way out of the mess. Of course, first she'd have to figure out exactly what kind of mess they were in.

What do you expect to see when I open my eyes?

"I don't expect anything," E.V. answered, but a flash of a room slipped through her thoughts.

You already know where we are. You've already seen it. Brittany watched E.V.'s memories as Bret held her eyelid up and stared into them to talk. *What did he say to us?*

E.V.'s voice was small. "He wasn't talking to us…"

Fine! What did he say to you?

The creature just shook its head.

Brittany huffed aloud while studying the memory. It was useless. All she could see clearly was Bret's face and his lips that seemed to be constantly moving. With a second huff, Brittany opened her eyes.

The room was clean and well-organized. Against the walls were evenly stacked boxes all with their labels facing out: whisky, rum, scotch. "Are we in the basement under the bar?" Brittany was bound to a chair. On the floor to her left lay two bodies, and she didn't have to look twice to know they were dead. On the right was Coby. His back was to her. She stared at him, seeing his frame rise with a breath.

"Coby." Her voice cracked.

Hearing her, Coby stirred. "Brit? Are you ok?" He moaned and twitched against the binding that wound around his wrists and ankles.

She shook her head, which she knew he couldn't see. "Ya, I'm fine."

Coby fought to roll over. With his hands tied behind him, it took a moment to get it done. "He tied you up too," he said, clearly shocked.

Brittany tugged against her bindings with no success. *You couldn't cut through these with your handy tentacles, could you?*

E.V. shook her head.

Brittany felt tempted to ask if the creature couldn't or wouldn't.

Without the girl knowing it, E.V. had tried, several times. The attempts had left her depleted and just a tad testy. "Bret knows all about what I can and can't do. He bound us in something we wouldn't be able to escape from. He doesn't want to free me... at least not yet."

Coby had wiggled closer. "Brittany, I am so sorry," he choked. "This is all my fault." He continued to try and move closer.

"Don't touch me."

He didn't listen. He brought his head to her bare foot and pressed his cheek to it. "I am so, so sorry I didn't trust you." Brittany could feel Coby's tears. "What I've done, what I allowed to happen to you, it's unforgivable. Kill me now— I deserve to die. Please finish me off, E.V." He pushed his cheek against Brittany's cool skin.

Brittany hadn't warned Coby not to touch her because of what E.V. might do. She'd warned him because she was furious at him. Her anger melted.

Don't hurt him, she told E.V.

E.V. had no intention of doing so.

"What's going on? Where are we? What happened?" Brittany asked.

"Oh, Brittany, it horrible," Coby said, still leaning against her foot.

"What? What's horrible? What's going on?"

Brittany could feel E.V. pulling away. Coby didn't say anything either.

"E.V.? Coby? What is it?"

There was no time for either to reply before they heard someone approaching.

"It's almost time." Bret's voice was tight with barely containable excitement.

"Quick, pretend you're asleep," E.V. said.

Coby didn't need to be told. He squeezed his eyes shut and pulled his head to his chest, not daring to breath.

"Hmmm," Bret grumbled as he reached the bottom of the stairs and turned to face Brittany. "Well, it's not like I wasn't expecting this."

His eyes roved over the duct tape that was wound around Brittany's limbs. Not just in a single loop but spiralling to span the whole length of each of her arms and legs, making her look as if she had shiny, silver skin.

"My sweet, are you in control? Or do you continue to let the human call the shots?"

"What's that supposed..."

Bret moved so he stood in front of Brittany. As she'd opened her mouth to speak, he'd pulled his hand back and slapped her so hard the chair wobbled.

"Ouch."

"You, Brittany, will remain quiet if you wish to stay conscious."

Brittany bit her tongue to keep from asking her question aloud. *E.V., what's going on?*

E.V. was preoccupied watching Bret. She was fearful of him and yet she was also in awe.

Bret walked around Brittany three times. She resisted the urge to turn her head each time he circled behind her. Instead she only followed him with her eyes.

"I think you are ready," he said softly, "and after tonight I will be ready too."

SIXTY-NINE
CHOSEN

ON HIS THIRD turn around, Brittany felt Bret's hand on her. As much as she wanted to pull away, she managed to keep still.

His fingers slid down her neck and over her shoulder. They stopped at the inside of her elbow, hovering there for a brief moment, then he produced a pin and poked her. As he removed it, he squeezed her arm. The fluid that now circulated through Brittany's system, E.V.'s bodily fluid, was forced out of the small puncture wound.

Only three drops escaped before E.V. fixed it. For E.V. this was instinctive and involuntary.

Bret seemed to be amused. He watched for a second, and before the drops could evaporate, he swept his fingers over the area and brought them up to his nose. He sniffed then licked at it slowly with a growing smile. "Sweet. Sweet, ripe, and ready."

"What?" Brittany couldn't stop herself from asking, though it came out more like an appalled gasp.

"Silence!" Bret brought his hand back and slapped her across the face again.

The force of the blow stung worse than anything Brittany had felt in ages. Worse even than the knife that had sliced her open many months back.

"Ouch!" Again Brittany couldn't stop herself from saying it.

Bret's hand pulled back once more. "I'm warning you, my sweet, get a better hold on your human." He dropped his hand without hitting her and stared into Brittany's wide eyes.

What does he mean?

"I don't know," E.V. answered. She was lying.

"What do you mea...?"

Bret brought his fingers up to Brittany's lips and pinched them shut, none too gently. "Yes... yes, I can see you've let your human run amuck. All your humans, I'd wager. It's like I was telling you earlier, you have never learned to control them and because of that they have controlled you. Turning you weak, making you settle for far less than you deserve. Less than the creatures we were meant to be."

Brittany tried to shake her head to free her lips. Bret's grip doubled and for a moment she feared he might be able to rip them clean off her mouth. She stopped with a whimper.

"Don't worry, soon I will be able to show you everything you need to know." He studied her eyes a moment longer and his voice changed. "Soon, just one more night."

Bret left shortly after he'd removed the dead bodies. He had a bounce in his walk and a smile on his face.

ત્ર ♦ ಐ

"Coby? Coby?" Brittany had been terrified to speak for almost an hour. Then she feared that Bret might return and was anxious to act quickly. "Coby?"

At first Coby had feigned sleep, but at some point he was no longer faking.

"Coby?" Brittany's voice rose with her panic. She had already tried to get E.V. to talk to her, but the creature had refused. Nothing she said would get it to explain. Just like earlier, Brittany could feel the connection between them was broken. The creature was able to keep its secrets. "Please, Coby, I need you. Wake up."

He shifted his head and his eyes fluttered open. "Where...?" he asked but didn't finish as he remembered exactly where he was.

"Coby, what's going on?"

He groaned then pulled his head up, looking all about the room. "Is he gone?"

"Yes. Coby, what's going on?"

He turned to look at Brittany. "Are you still you?"

"Ye... yes." Now Brittany felt hesitant— when had she not been herself?

As she thought this E.V., pulled back even further.

"Coby?"

"Brittany," Coby shifted, trying to circulate his blood flow, "it's crazy. It's all crazy. Mike's been talking about... about killing hundreds of people."

"Killing them how?"

"That's the craziest part. He wants to mate with you... but not you, with the thing in you."

"H-how?" Brittany shivered at the thought.

Coby shut his eyes.

"Coby? How? What did he say?"

Coby opened his eyes and his face crumpled. But he answered. "He said that first... first he'll infect you, the same way E.V. did."

"Can he do that? E.V. is already here. Where will she go?"

"She won't go." Coby swallowed hard. "She'll be in you too."

"They'll both be in me? Is that even possible?" She knew Coby wouldn't have the answer but she hoped E.V. would— and would tell her.

Only Coby answered. "I don't know. He never explained that part."

"I didn't expect *you* to know." Brittany shook her head. She tried to find E.V.'s thoughts, but the parasite was so far withdrawn that it almost felt like she wasn't there. "What happens after?" Brittany asked.

"Once he's done what he needs to E.V., he'll leave you." Coby stopped but there was more.

"Where will he go?" Brittany searched the spacious room with her eyes. "Who will he infect?" Bret had cleared away the two corpses. There was no one there but her and Coby. "Coby?"

"Isn't it obvious?"

SEVENTY

CONTROL

"AFTER DOING WHAT he needs with me he's going to infect you? Why?"

Coby didn't want to answer.

"Coby? Why you?"

"Because once he's done with E.V., and he's in me, he'll have one more thing to do. And he said it will be easier to do because you already like me."

"What will be easier because I like you? What does he need to do?"

Coby was shaking his head. "Once I'm infected— you and I have to…"

This time when Coby didn't continue, Brittany understood why. "Us, you and me… we?"

It was cruel. All those times Brittany had wanted this. Every night as she'd hid under his bed she'd fantasized about it. She'd imagine his body pressed against hers. She could remember how he'd felt— she hadn't forgotten the last time she'd felt him next to her. She'd craved feeling that again, and only barely fought the urge to re-enact it on several occasions.

Now it loomed before her and she knew it would end her. "So, what happens once we…?"

"You will create millions of little parasites to infect the world with."

"How?"

"I don't know, I never heard him talk about that part."

"E.V.?" As they'd talked, Brittany felt E.V. getting closer. Like a growing pressure. "You know, don't you?"

The image of Emily shimmered into Brittany's sight. It gave a slow nod.

Brittany saw how fragile the connection between them was. She knew how quickly the creature could take it back.

"Does E.V. know?" Coby asked.

"Ya, but she's not telling me."

"Why not?"

"E.V.?" Brittany's voice was soft. She could feel the creature's distress. It was leaking into Brittany's consciousness—flooding it, more like.

"I... I can't save you. I wanted to save you."

"E.V.?"

"If I leave you— you'll die. If I don't then Bret will have his way with you and you will be far worse off. The only way I could save you is to leave you. But I can't do that. I can't leave you. I can't kill you."

"What?" *What are you saying*?

"I wanted to hate you," E.V. explained. "I tried to hate you so I could leave you. I wanted not to care about what would happen to you, because it's going to happen. I wanted not to care but I couldn't. I do care. I don't want Bret to... to... But I can't stop it. He's going to... and it will destroy you, then kill you."

Brittany shut her eyes against the pain in her chest as E.V. shook.

"Brittany?" Coby tried harder to pull free from his ropes. "What's going on?"

"E.V....." Brittany gasped. "E.V.'s crying."

"Why?"

"Because... because I'm going to die."

No matter how hard Coby pulled against his bindings, he wasn't able to break free. All he managed to do was chafe his wrists raw. When Bret returned, Coby was passed out from exhaustion.

"Ready, my sweet Lena?"

Brittany wanted to shake her head, but E.V. was in control now.

୬ ◆ ୭

As Coby had jerked, strained, and cursed trying to free himself, E.V. had finally explained things to Brittany.

"Bret was there at the very beginning. Remember it? I was in Abelena and he was Jax. When Braxton killed Jax, Jax infected Braxton. But Braxton killed Abelena before Jax was fully acclimatized. He's been searching for me ever since— for centuries."

"That makes sense," Brittany said.

"Jax was frantic when he lost me. He's been searching for me. He's been miserable without me. He loves me," E.V. sighed. "He really loves me."

"But not me."

"It's nothing personal. It's not you specifically, it's all humans."

"The man animal is a plague upon the planet." E.V. recalled what Bret had told her while Brittany was unconscious. "We are here to fix the problem. Lena, can't you see that humans are in danger of overrunning the world? We are the answer to this problem. We are the failsafe that puts overpopulation into balance. When humans grow too numerous, we are triggered to mate. If we don't, humans will become so numerous they will overtax the planet. It is our responsibility to keep the population down— to keep humankind in check.

"Together we will make an antidote," Bret said, his voice tight with passion. "You and I will create the solution. We will multiply, and you— you, my sweet Lena, you will become saviour to all. With every touch you will rid the excess of this generation. Our creation will save our world.

"It is a pain, my love," he continued in a growl. "You used to know this. You used to know who you are and the greatness you were meant for. So listen, my sweet Lena, this is important. You must use this body as you were meant to— and when it is done you must leave it. And this time you must remember yourself so we can find each other quicker and the world won't have to suffer as it has for the last three centuries.

"You are the female queen. It is your job to find me. You are designed to know these things." This time Bret growled, no words, just a vicious rolling noise. "You can't know how I've been searching for you! How panicked I've felt, especially in this last century. I've seen the human plague grow and multiply unchecked for far too long. It is a sickness that has spread vastly, and continued to do so more rapidly the longer we were kept apart.

"It will be such a relief once you and I come together to fulfil the roles we were created for." Bret's voice grew wistful. "Lena, my sweet one, it has been far, far too long."

SEVENTY-ONE
BETRAYAL

"HE'S INSANE!" were the first words Brittany could find.

"No," E.V. replied. "He knows his purpose— and mine."

"You're not seriously thinking he's right... are you?"

"I agree in principle." E.V. hesitated. "But not in practice. Not now."

"Oh, really? If you really believe Jax, then what's your great objection?"

"You, Brittany. I object because of you." E.V. blinked, shifting the tears in her eyes. "I love you."

Brittany felt winded, like she needed to breathe, even though she knew she didn't.

"For every other host Bret was right— I should not have allowed them to control me. But for you, Brittany Watts, I have delighted in you. I am glad you are in control."

Brittany still didn't know what to say.

"Brittany?"

"You love me, so you say, yet you'd destroy all those people without feeling any regrets? Wouldn't it make you even a little sad to think of all those lives lost?" Brittany couldn't add up the number of people this would affect.

E.V.'s face was confused. "When have I ever worried about a human's life?"

Brittany quickly answered. "Petunia, Gran, Coby, ME!"

"They were all personally connected to me. Since when have I cared for someone who wasn't of importance to my human?"

"So... so, you won't care about Coby once I'm gone?"

"Coby won't be Coby once you're gone. Coby will only be Coby for a few more days."

"What about Little Jacqueline? And Jack Junior?"

"I've made you my promise."

"What's your promise going to do to save them? Will you keep it once I'm gone?"

"I will— for you."

"But what about your antidotes? Will they be safe from that? You can't promise me that, can you? And what kind of world will it be once you've rid it of so many humans? I don't want L.J and J.J. to have to live in a world overrun with monsters and death."

E.V. didn't respond.

"Do you really believe that that is what you were created for?"

"Yes, I do," E.V. answered, though she was reluctant.

"You think your purpose is to destroy thousands upon thousands of people?"

"Can you not see the state humanity has gotten itself into? Do you not see the trouble of your overpopulation? Thousands— no, millions, die from it, and even more will die as man continues to prosper. How much worse will things get if we do not do as we were created to do? Yes, I believe Jax. It is our job."

The creature fell silent and so did the girl.

"Brittany," E.V. began again, slowly. "Man was created to go forth and multiply. That was his mandate right from the start, and he has done it well. I, Jax and I, we were created to keep harmony in the world. Too much of anything is unhealthy."

"Stop talking," Brittany commanded through clenched teeth. "Just stop." All through their relationship, Brittany had called E.V. a monster for one reason or another. Now she didn't say it, but the creature had become the worst kind of monster to her. E.V. was talking about killing— and not just to stay fed. Killing people like they were pests to be exterminated. The worst part was how unaffected E.V. was by it.

"You don't understand," E.V. said sympathetically. "I understand. But you are not meant to. It is my purpose— or

301

at least it *was* my purpose. It is not mine anymore. Not now. Not with you. This is not the right time."

"Huh?" Brittany's head was spinning. E.V. wasn't making any sense.

"I will not allow Bret to succeed."

"You won't? I don't underst..."

"What don't you understand? This should be simple. I love you. I love you as I have never loved any other human. I consider you special above all the rest. It is my deepest desire to protect you. It causes me pain to see you upset. I cannot comply with anything that will hurt you. It is because of this that I will not allow you to be the person to bring Jax's antidote into this world. Even if I agree they need to be brought. I will not allow you to be the one who changes the world." She continued, "You will not be used to create this bad future you fear. I know how that would break your heart, and I can't bear the thought of that. I will do whatever it takes to make sure you are not the mother of our destruction. I will protect you from that— even if it means I must kill you."

Brittany stayed silent.

"But that will only be my last option," E.V. said. "I have another plan first."

"You have a plan?" Brittany's voice was dazed. "What?"

"Simple. I will find a way to free you. Then we will run, and we will keep running until there is no place left to run."

"How will you free me?" Brittany pulled against her silver bindings for emphasis.

"I will find a way," E.V. said. "Do you trust me?"

"I," Brittany thought for a moment to be certain, "I do."

"Good. I need you to do everything I tell you to."

ʘ ♦ Ž

E.V. was in control and she'd gained it through submission, not domination, as Bret would have had it. The girl and the creature acted as one. A team. Bret couldn't tell, not even as he passed out of the body he'd possessed and into Brittany's.

Brittany heard the body hit the cement floor. She squeezed her eyes shut and waited for the new invader. She wasn't sure what to expect, but she figured he'd appear to her in the same way E.V. had. She wasn't that far off.

In her head she could see Bret's memories playing out like they were hers. Bret was the name of the human who belonged to the body that now lay dead at Brittany's feet. Jax was the creature's name. He'd kept it from when E.V. had been Lena.

Jax spoke to her now. "Your memories are filled with holes. My sweet, you are far more lucky than I could have guessed." He was talking about the many near misses E.V. had endured. He pulled her memories up as easily as using Google to search the Internet. A vision of a wall of fire made him, E.V., and even Brittany flinch. "Fire even, very fortunate."

As Jax started to conjure up E.V.'s memories of Brittany, E.V. asked, "You spoke of more like us, are there many females?"

It did the trick— he was distracted. "No, my sweet, you are the only one. In fact, you and I are the only ones left from the originals. Only we are capable of creating more like us. Our creation will have the ability to take on both male and female roles. However, all that are passed into females will be limited to one lifespan. Once their host is done, so will they be."

"They will get only one life?" This made E.V. sad.

"Why do you fret, my sweet?" Jax said. "Is that not the same as any human?"

It made sense, but it still made E.V. sad— even she couldn't understand why she felt that way.

"Tell me of the others? The originals? How many were there? Where did they come from? What were they like?"

"They were what they were," Jax answered elusively. "We did not get along."

"We? You and them?"

"You and me— and them." There was a hard edge to Jax's tone.

"Were there many?"

"Not so many," Jax said in a growl. "Let's not talk of this. All you need to know is that you, my sweet, were the best of them."

"What makes me the best?"

SEVENTY-TWO
REVEALING

"YOU ARE THE best, my sweet, because you are the queen. The first and the best of any of us. You were the one who was formed from our mother queen. You are no feeble offspring, you are the reincarnate of the very one who created you.

"Why don't I remember this?"

"Because," Jax seemed to falter, "there was a mistake. Your process was interrupted last time. You had not finished your task. You had to abandon it before it was time. I had to force you out and transfer you. I brought you to that child so you could be safe and grow up within her. But that human stole you from me."

Brittany, who continued to keep her presence a secret, could see it. She saw Jax, trapped in his brother— not yet in control. He saw his Lena fall, saw her being crushed, and then was forced away by Braxton's feet as they carried him back home. It was days before he could get back to where Lena had been pushed. By the time he did, she was gone.

Once fully in control of Braxton, Jax killed his mother and left to seek out whoever the girl had become. He learned that Abelena had been taken by an unknown man and left at the town's morgue. The man had continued on his journey across the country. Braxton never caught up with him but followed rumors of him boarding a ship. His ship never turned up where it should have.

Jax abandoned Braxton for the captain of a ship. Being a captain, he was able to travel from port to port, keeping an ear out for stories of vampires, never giving up on finding his Lena.

Now that he could really see her, Jax realized that she was not the same after so many centuries apart. As much as he loved her, he despised what she'd become. She felt too close to a human, a fact that he wasn't able to keep hidden from either Brittany or E.V.

"I disappoint you," E.V. said.

"It is not your fault. You could not avoid it. Once we are done with this we will be able to restore you."

"But I am who I am now."

"*Who!*" Jax said in a growl. "What heresy! You, my sweet, are no who! You are a being, a creature, far vaster than a who! You are much closer to a god than the misguided humans you've so willingly adapted yourself to."

Jax sighed. "Ah, but I know you cannot see that now. You will. You wait— I'll show you. Once our task is done I will give you back what has been missing for too many centuries. You will remember what you are. You will regain all that you've lost, and you *will* understand."

"Can't you teach me it now?"

"I cannot teach it. It is a part of your DNA that was taken from you."

E.V. didn't like that Jax was telling her she was incomplete. That a piece of her was missing... had been taken. "Taken by who?"

For the first time ever Jax was flustered. He deliberated while E.V. pushed. "By me," he finally confessed.

"You!" Rage flooded through E.V., Brittany, and Jax. "Why would you do such a thing?"

"I had to," Jax said. "I didn't want to— it was a necessity."

"Why?"

"Because... because it was the only way to save you."

"Save me from what? From who?"

"From them. The others." Jax's voice gained in strength. "They were going to destroy you. I couldn't let them. But they would have been relentless. So I gave them what they wanted. I gave them you— but only a part of you, while I kept the rest of you safe and hidden. And when it was finally time I found that girl and her brother. You were meant to be safe there. You were supposed to get better. I meant for you to be strong enough to return to yourself. To reclaim the whole you."

Jax took a breath and spoke more calmly. "Ah, you cannot understand the years I've grieved over this mistake."

E.V. was speechless, but Brittany wanted to ask what it would take to return the part that was missing. E.V. spoke up for her.

"Simple." Jax took the question to mean that Lena was agreeing. "We must return you to your old self."

Simple nonsense, Brittany thought quietly. *What does that mean?*

Jax mistook Brittany's voice for E.V.'s.

"All will be explained and revealed in its time. For now we have a task to complete. Then I will take you back to yourself and you will know and be all that you were created to be."

Something about this gave E.V. a chill, whether it was what Jax was saying or the way he said it, she wasn't sure. She wondered, though, what would happen if she didn't like who she had been? What if she didn't want to return to being that?

Jax could not detect her thought; he was too busy concentrating.

"Is this supposed to take so long?" E.V. asked impatiently. She hoped that once he was done he'd untie Brittany and that would be their chance to escape.

"No." Jax sounded as if he were in the middle of a wrestling match. "If you'd just stop fighting the process, we could be done already."

It wasn't her— it was Brittany. And it was useless to think that Brittany would stop.

"What are you doing?" E.V. asked as another distraction, this time for Brittany, who had started to feel as if her veins were on fire.

"I can re-write your DNA. Once I've created a new code, you'll continue to reproduce it. After I've become Coby, I'll deposit the last ingredient needed. For each sperm I give you, you will be able to create an entirely new and unique one of us. You will need to pair each offspring with a human— one per person, as I instructed before."

"How will I be able to control that?"

"Oh," Jax chuckled, "it will be easy for you. Trust me, you'll get the hang of it quickly enough."

"So what happens if I give more than one offspring in one human?"

Jax's chuckle became a rolling laugh. "Then that person will be very confused. If more than one offspring is released, they will both infect the human and they will fight for control. It would be like someone who has two personalities. But don't worry about that now. For now, your job is to relax and allow me to do as I was created to do."

E.V. couldn't relax, because Brittany wouldn't, and it felt like hours before Jax was done.

His voice filled Brittany's head. "I am ready to be released. Call the boy over."

Brittany didn't co-operate and E.V. didn't try to make her.

"Lena?" Jax asked. "My sweet?"

What happens if I don't? Brittany asked. *What if you stay trapped here— in me? Will you die?*

"I suppose I would." This time Jax recognized Brittany's voice. He took on a forced casual tone. "However, I promise, you will die before me if that happens."

Brittany didn't doubt his sincerity. *I've made my peace— I'm ready to die.*

"Those are some very big words." He sounded as if he were taunting her. "But what do you really know of dying?"

Had she not been tied down, Brittany would have crossed her arms over her chest. She was ready to die. She was ready for E.V. to kill her.

"Do you really think Coby will allow that to happen to you?" Jax asked.

He knows I'm going to die either way. What can he do to change it?

"All I need is one touch."

But if I tell him to— he won't touch me.

"Wouldn't he?" Jax said smugly. "There is a vast difference between knowing something that is unavoidable and watching it happen. I don't think the boy is as ready to watch you to die as you are willing to die. I bet my life that he will not sit around without attempting to stop it."

I don't care!

"Sure you don't," Jax chuckled, "but poor Coby does. He will not lie there once you start howling in pain. And I assure you that I will make your end as painful as I can."

I won't howl— I won't even whimper. Brittany bit her lip as if to brace herself.

Jax didn't bother to tell her how wrong she was.

"Don't hurt her," E.V. said.

SEVENTY-THREE

DESTINE

"WHY SHOULDN'T I hurt her?" Jax asked.

E.V. didn't have an answer— not one that he would consider listening to.

"I wonder if your feelings are mutual? Lena, have you ever stopped to consider if this girl would be as compassionate if the tables were turned? Would she be so willing to sacrifice herself for you?"

E.V. did not have a response, even though she heard Brittany's unspoken answer. Brittany did not think she would feel the same.

Their silence was enough. "That's what I thought..."

"But it doesn't matter," E.V. interrupted. "I don't expect Brittany to return the sentiment. I didn't extend it just so it would be returned. I gave it because I wanted to, because I love..."

"You disgust me."

Jax's voice ripped through Brittany's head. It was so loud, she instinctively tried to flinch away from it. A pain that went beyond description followed his outburst. It was so sharp it made her eyes feel like they were about to explode.

"What?" she panted aloud.

"What's that?" His voice took on a mocking tone. "That is me squeezing the life out of your E.V. We can't both occupy the same body. You won't let me out, so I will snuff her out. If only one of us is going to survive this, then I will be sure that the one remaining will be me."

"E.V.?" Brittany squeaked. Her thoughts shook from the pain.

"She's a little busy right now, what with the dying."

You can't kill her! You wouldn't.

"What's to stop me?"

You love her. Brittany scrambled for more reasons. *Besides, you need her. How are you going to work out your population control without her?*

"You hear that, Lena? Now, suddenly, this human cares about our cause." The pain in Brittany's chest increased. "But it is not the truth. I'm sure you can feel the lie. That is how humans act. They will lie and cheat and manipulate to get their way. They only say what you want them to. They will not be honest. They lie right to their very death. And you want to be like them!"

"Stop!" Brittany screamed. "You're killing her!"

Coby stirred at the noise. It had been two days now since he'd had anything to eat or drink, and he was feeling weak. If something didn't change, he'd be dead in the next thirty hours.

Seeing that the boy was stirring, Jax let up, just for a fraction of a second.

His waver caught Brittany's attention. "Stay where you are!" she commanded Coby as she saw him trying to move closer to her.

"Brits?"

"Stay there. Bret is dead, and Jax is going to infect you if you touch me."

"Brittany." He moved as close to her as he could without touching.

"I will kill Lena!" Jax demanded. "Once she is dead you will not survive for long. Coby will have to touch you— he won't be able to stop himself. He'll want to try and help you. Then I will be sure to jump to him."

But your plans to destroy mankind will die with E.V. I don't believe you can do that.

"You're right." The pain stopped. "I cannot kill her. But I don't have to." The pain returned at double strength. "This will not kill my sweet Lena, it will only force her to jump.

Once I am safely established in Coby, I will find a good candidate for Lena, and I will be sure that she is safely transported. Then, when she's ready, we will do this again with far better results."

Brittany gasped. That's all it took. She gasped and Coby pressed his face into her foot. "Brittany?" he said.

"Coby," Brittany moaned, but it was too late. She could feel Jax leaving.

She felt the rushing and suddenly it felt like there was extra room under her skin, like being in an oversized sweater.

It was done. Coby was infected. There was nothing more she could do.

"Brittany? Are you ok?" Coby asked, keeping his cheek to her foot.

"It doesn't matter," she sighed. "It's too late. It's done now."

"What's done?" Coby was clueless.

"It's all done." Brittany said. "Bret's dead, Jax infected me, he changed E.V. and now he's in you."

"Me?" Coby pulled back. "He's in me now? But... but I don't feel any different." He turned to look at the lifeless body lying on the floor behind Brittany as if that might help confirm things for him.

"You wouldn't. It'll take a few days before he's changed you."

"When will he be able to control me?"

Brittany shrugged— the movement pulled against her bindings. "I don't know."

"When did E.V. start to control you?"

Brittany slowly shook her head back and forth. Even after all this time Coby didn't understand how things worked between E.V. and her. And he never would, because Jax was a very different creature than E.V., even if they were the same species.

"Two days," Brittany answered flatly. She and E.V. had seen how Jax infected people while he was sharing their body. His way was very different than E.V.'s.

"That's not long. Can I kill myself before he has a chance to take over?"

Brittany gave another shrug. E.V. didn't offer anything.

Coby closed his eyes. "I guess it's useless. It's not like I can do anything all tied up."

☞ ◆ ☜

Brittany could feel the moon, even if she couldn't see it. It was high in the sky before Coby stirred again.

"How do you feel?" she asked.

He licked his lips and swallowed hard. "Thirsty."

"Do you feel Jax there?"

Coby closed his eyes, breathing deeply. For a moment it looked like he might have fallen back to sleep. "Maybe... what does it feel like?"

"Like you're not alone."

Coby's lips curled up into a smile. For a second it didn't look right to Brittany. The smile disappeared almost as quickly as it had formed.

"Coby?"

"I... I don't have any extra voices in my head— that's what E.V. is to you, right?"

"Sort of." E.V. was a whole lot more than just an extra voice in her head, but she wasn't about to try and explain that, not now. "How do your ropes feel?"

"Tight."

"Can you break free?"

"No."

"Try," Brittany said, because Coby hadn't even tried.

"I've already tried," Coby said, exasperation clear in his voice.

"Try again."

"What's the use? I can't get free of them. I've been trying for days now. And my muscles feel odd, like they are going numb. I'm so cold." He shivered.

"Just give it one more try," Brittany said, feeling hopeful.

SEVENTY-FOUR
FINISHING

COBY STRUGGLED ONCE again, and he was surprised that the ropes seemed to loosen. At first he didn't believe it— he thought he was imagining it. Then one wrist broke free. "Would you look at that…" He pulled his arm out and the second one seemed to come out without him trying. "Hey, Brits, exactly how strong are you?"

"Strong enough to be free if I'd been tied up with ropes."

"Oh ya?" Coby sat up and raised his arms triumphantly over his head. "Now," he said while he rolled to his knees and didn't bother with untying his legs, "let's see about getting you out of this duct tape."

Brittany suppressed her frustration that it had only been duct tape keeping her bound all that time. E.V. didn't suppress herself. "Of all the common…" Once Brittany was completely freed, she jumped to her feet.

Coby mirrored her action. "What now?"

"How do you feel?"

"Exhilarated." Coby caught and held Brittany's hand. "Why?"

"We don't have much time."

"How much do you think we have?" He kicked the ropes that had bound his legs across the room.

"Another day— or slightly less," E.V. answered and Brittany relayed it.

"There's a lot we can do in a day," Coby said, bringing Brittany's hand up to his face and kissing it.

Brittany shook her head. "I need to put as much distance between you and me as I can."

"Brits," Coby pulled her closer, "at least give me an hour. I don't want you to leave."

"I don't want to go! But I have to." She pulled her hand out of his. "You heard Bret talk about what would happen if we... I can't let that happen."

"I know. I know." Coby turned away. "I don't want it to come to that. I just," he turned back, "I just wanted one last meal. Don't I deserve that? After all, it's not only you I'll be losing."

Brittany felt her heart breaking. Even E.V. couldn't deny that Coby had a point. "Fine, but just one meal."

"I know a great restaurant just a few blocks away. Let's go."

"No." Brittany's word stopped Coby, who was halfway to the stairs.

"No?"

"We can't leave yet. We have to wait for the sun to rise."

"Why?" Coby looked from Brittany to Bret's dead body to the boxes stacked up against the wall. He was tired, hungry, and restless. His muscles ached in a strange way and he wanted to be doing something — going somewhere — making some kind of plan.

"Because I glow in the dark."

Brittany's answer pulled Coby's attention back to her. "Right," he said. "Wow, soon I will too." This reality cut to the bottom of the problem. "Let's wait upstairs," Coby suggested.

They both were confused by how clean the main part of the bar was. There was a sense of disuse about it. Then as they were leaving they saw the note on the door: *Closed for fumigation, sorry for any inconvenience.*

Breakfast was quiet. Coby didn't eat much, though he'd ordered a plate of everything on the menu. After a few bites off one plate, he'd discard it and move on to the next. Three plates in, the waitress asked for money up front. Coby produced a wad of cash he'd taken from the bar's cash register.

He sat across from Brittany, a plate of "the hearty man's breakfast" before him. He raised his fork piled high with scrambled eggs. "To friendship."

Brittany bowed her head and mused to herself. If she'd known when E.V. was changing her, would she have behaved the same? Cherishing her last meal.

"To new beginnings," Coby toasted on a piece of bacon.

"To horrible endings," Brittany added.

Coby shook his head as if to dispel the thought. "To our life together, no matter how short."

"Brittany," E.V. interrupted, "we need to go."

She nodded but didn't comply. Instead, she continued to sit and stare at Coby, her long-time friend, her first love, her comrade in arms. As she stared she realized that she was more attracted to him than she had ever been. She couldn't bear the idea of leaving him. When the time came she wasn't sure she'd be able to go.

E.V. felt this too. It was the mixture of Brittany's love for Coby and her own attraction to Jax. Yet E.V. was determined to keep the girl safe. "Brittany…"

I know.

With his last plate cleared away and a healthy tip left on the table, Coby locked eyes with Brittany. "That was weird. Nothing tasted right, and even though I'm full, I still feel… hungry. You know what I mean?"

Brittany nodded, remembering her own transformation. She marvelled that it had been almost a year ago.

"Walk me home?" Coby said.

"You're going home?" Brittany felt panicked. She knew she had to leave, but she was still unable to.

"Well, not to my home. I'm Bret now— so I was going to go to his home." Coby made a frustrated face. "I can't go back to my home, can I? I mean, I've been missing for about a week. What would I tell my mom?" He made the same frustrated face. "Besides, soon I'll be a danger to her— I shouldn't ever go home, should I?"

Brittany looked into Coby's eyes, seeing the sorrow there and feeling it echoed in her mind. Coby was going to lose everything. But so was she. Soon, in mere moments, she'd be running away, never to see her own family again. Neither of them had been able to say good-bye to anyone.

Coby reached out and put his arms around her, perhaps seeing her own pain.

Far too soon, he was letting her go. He gripped her shoulders and pushed her away to stare in her face.

She expected to see more remorse, but instead he looked excited. "Brittany, at Bret's there are supplies for travelling. A car and clean clothes. These can help you escape."

Brittany agreed and followed Coby toward the restaurant exit.

"Hold on," he said turning back around, "I need..." He smiled awkwardly. "...nature's calling."

Brittany nodded. That was something about being human that she didn't miss.

"You must be starved," Coby said as they walked down a deserted street. He held Brittany's hand, and she could feel his warmth seeping into her. She could also feel that he wasn't as warm as he used to be; another reminder of how little time they had left.

"We are hungry," E.V. confirmed in Brittany's head. She nodded, answering them both.

"There's a homeless shelter on the way to my apartment. We could swing past it, find you a good meal."

Brittany flinched. It was involuntary.

"You have a problem with that?" Coby didn't hide his shock.

"Yes."

"Why? You killed all those people before, why do you have a problem with it now?"

"It was only a couple hundred," Brittany said, shame coloring her tone, "and they were not innocent people. I don't like taking from people who are innocent."

"Believe me, my..." Coby stuttered, "my deluded friend, most people are far less innocent than you think."

Brittany didn't respond.

"Come on, you need to eat."

She couldn't deny that.

"You don't have to kill anyone today," Coby said. "This place is usually quite busy. You could take a little from several different people."

She allowed Coby to lead her to a street where there were lots of people milling about, forming a haphazard line. At the front was a sign that read *Soup Kitchen*. Coby pulled into the back of the line and struck up a conversation with the person he stood behind.

"Can you remind me, sir, what are the shelter's hours..."

SEVENTY-FIVE
LEAVING

BRITTANY WASN'T PAYING very close attention. She felt E.V.'s mouth watering— the feeling was close to what it felt like when her stomach growled.

"It's been far too long." Now that food was so close, E.V. was having trouble being patient.

But don't take too much, Brittany said.

"It's going to be hard."

Please E.V., try!

"Ok, Brittany, I won't take too much."

"Can you believe that?" Coby had turned around to Brittany. He had his hand on the other man's shoulder. "This guy lost his shirt on a bet last night." Coby laughed a little too forcefully. "His actual shirt."

Brittany eyed the bare-chested man.

"That takes talent, he deserves a handshake." Coby took the man's elbow and extended his hand to Brittany.

Brittany took his hand and let E.V. do what she did best. Too soon the man started to swoon.

Enough!

"No, it wasn't nearly enough," E.V. complained as she stopped.

Coby continued to hold the man by the elbow, keeping him from falling over. "Take it easy, my friend," he said, gently lowering him to the ground.

The sight of the homeless man resting against the building wasn't that out of place. Several people were doing the same all along the wall. With the man propped up, Coby stood and struck up a conversation with the next person in line. He continued this until E.V. was full.

Brittany felt far worse, even though she felt much better. She walked behind Coby in silence, not daring to look back as they left the street. She didn't need to see the dozen people she'd knocked unconscious. She could remember how they looked and the memory was more than enough to haunt her.

Bret lived in a building that looked condemned, but once inside it was rather well kept up. The walls were a bright cream color, even appearing to be freshly painted. The halls were nicely lit. The doors in the stairwell looked secure.

Coby led the way to the top floor, six storeys up. When he opened the door from the stairway, Brittany gave a low gasp. They hadn't entered into a hall, but into a luxurious loft apartment. The ceilings looked to be doubly high, and the only things that blocked her view of the entire apartment were pillars.

The apartment was sparsely furnished with expensive looking items. Tall stools stood next to the huge kitchen bar. Two sofas and a few armchairs were placed around the glass coffee table. A polished piano was in one corner next to a bookshelf lined with pristine-looking books. Most of the titles were classics.

"What do you think?" Coby turned back to the door and slid the bolt to lock it.

"This is not what I expected."

Coby smiled, nodding.

"I can't stay." Brittany stood glued to the spot, looking at the door with the simple bolt. So simple it wouldn't have stopped her from getting out. Yet it seemed to be doing just that. "I have to go."

"You have to go." Coby's tone was resigned. He walked towards one of the sofas. "You have to go." He sat and looked up at her, as if expecting her to leave.

She willed her feet to turn — to walk out the front door — to take her away. They weren't listening.

Her eyes felt as if they were being disobedient too. They focussed on Coby's lips: soft, inviting, sweet. She remembered vividly how they'd felt on her own, even if it had been too many months since she'd felt it. Too many months. She needed to feel it again, just one last time.

She didn't see him get up and move to her side. She felt like she'd blinked and he was next to her. Almost as if she'd willed it into being.

Coby leaned closer and placed his lips on hers. It made her sigh. Her mouth opened and his mirrored the action. His sweetness painted the inside of her cheeks. She brought her hands up to trap his head against hers. His hands wrapped around her waist and pulled her tight against his chest.

Her desire to taste Coby's blood was just as prevalent as it had always been. Knowing that it wouldn't be blood for much longer only increased the desire. It built like an explosive pressure. Brittany felt Coby's tongue against her lips— before she could do what she really wanted, she pulled away.

Coby stood watching Brittany through guarded eyes, but his arms stayed wrapped around her like a vice. "What?"

"I can't seem to get away from feeling like I want to bite you."

Coby smiled. "I was just thinking the same thing."

Brittany felt a jolt of shock run through her. She'd almost forgotten— she'd wanted to forget. *Just how close is Coby from being changed?* she wondered.

E.V. stayed silent— her longings were also more intense knowing Jax was close.

"You have to go," Coby said, dropping his arms.

Brittany started to shiver. Coby brought his arms back around her and she could feel that he was getting colder, but he was still warmer than she was.

"You're shivering, are you cold?"

"A little."

"Do you normally get cold?"

"Sometimes."

"When?"

Brittany had to think. "When I'm hurt." She recalled the knife slicing through her chest. "And..." she thought harder, "and a little when I'm tired."

"Do you think you're tired now? When was the last time you slept?"

She thought back to when she'd been knocked unconscious and wondered if that counted.

"I don't think so," E.V. said. "There was no dreaming— no REM. Whoa, Brittany, it's been days!"

"I am tired." Her voice shook slightly.

"Come have a nap." Coby started towing her to the sofa.

Her feet followed willingly. "I'm not sure this is a good idea."

"Why not?" Coby guided her to sit down.

"Because you will not be you soon, and I will not be safe anywhere near you once you aren't."

Coby nodded. "Ya, you're right. I know you're right." He started to stand with the intention of moving away from her.

"No." She caught his hand and squeezed. "Don't go away. Stay. I don't like sleeping without you." Her eyes were so heavy, they were closing before she'd finished talking.

Coby positioned himself so that Brittany's head was cradled in his lap. "Ok." She couldn't see the content smile he wore, but it was clear in his voice. "I'm not sure what to expect once Jax is in control. But I know the worst part for me will be never seeing you again. Never having you close enough to touch. I know I'll miss that the most."

"I know the feeling." Brittany pulled herself tight against his chest. She could hear his heart beating, like she had all those nights when she'd slept so close to him before. It lulled her to sleep.

"Brittany," E.V. said as Brittany felt herself slipping into unconsciousness, "don't..."

It was too late. Brittany had breathed in Coby's perfect scent and felt the rise and fall of his chest. She was asleep.

SEVENTY-SIX

LOSING

"BRITTANY! BRITTANY!" Coby's voice was filled with urgency. "Please wake up! Wake up! You need to go. You need to leave now! He's... Jax, he's almost..." His voice broke off into a choked growl.

E.V.? Brittany was finding it hard to pull out of unconsciousness. She couldn't feel E.V.— she couldn't feel Coby. She wasn't even sure she could feel herself. She wondered if she was even awake; if this was just a dream.

"Brittany," Coby begged.

"I can't ... I'm still ... I'm too tired," Brittany mumbled. She could feel herself being pulled upwards onto her feet. Was she walking? Or was she dreaming that she was walking?

"Please, Brits, I don't want to hurt you."

E.V., help me.

Again, E.V. didn't reply and Brittany couldn't feel her. E.V.? E.V.?

"I'm going to take you to my car... I mean Bret's car. I'll leave you there with the keys in your pocket. I'll try to keep away. But it would be much better if you could wake up and take yourself where I can't find you. As soon as you can, drive as far as you can and don't come back— ever."

When Brittany was finally able to open her eyes, it was dark outside.

"What happened?" She was alone, but she could feel E.V. with her.

E.V. was quiet. Something wasn't right.

"Where's Coby?"

"Gone," E.V. answered. "We need to leave."

Brittany nodded and searched around for the car keys, which she found in her pocket. It only took her two tries to start the car up. The first time the engine choked because she gave it too much gas. It took a few blocks to get the hang of how to keep the car going in the direction she wanted without veering off course.

E.V. stayed quiet the whole time.

With several miles and two cities between her and Coby, Brittany pulled the vehicle over to the side of the road and cut the engine. The moon was casting its rays and causing her skin to have a faint glow even inside the heated car.

"E.V.?"

The creature was heavy in Brittany's chest.

"What? What's going on?"

"I've failed."

"How? When?"

E.V. didn't tell her, but she let Brittany feel its memories.

E.V.'s memory of Coby trying to wake Brittany was clearer, and E.V. could even feel Brittany trying to pull out of unconsciousness.

Coby had taken Brittany to the car and left her there. But he'd returned. Then he'd left. Then he'd returned. Then he'd left... This pattern was repeated too many times to count.

Sometimes all E.V. could hear was him outside circling the car. Other times she heard Coby begging Brittany to wake up and to leave. "I don't know how much longer I can stop him," was the last time E.V. heard his voice.

The next time he returned, no words of warning were uttered. The only sound was the car door being opened, then closed...

"Ok!" Brittany pulled away from E.V.'s memory. "Ok." Her skin crawled.

Brittany stared out at the dark sky. Stars littered the expanse, some winking, others in vaguely familiar patterns. She felt tears sliding down her cheeks.

E.V. didn't appear to her, but she was present. "I'm sorry."

Brittany only managed a weak nod. She kept her eyes on the stars. This was it. This was the end. "When will I start to infect people?"

"Immediately." E.V.'s voice was soft.

Brittany leaned back in her seat and stared out the windshield. After a long time she asked, "Why did you want me to run away? It's too late. Coby succeeded, so why did I have to leave him?"

"Because Coby isn't Coby." E.V. sounded upset. "All that's left is Jax."

"Coby. Jax. What's the difference? He's won. I'm infected. Everyone I touch from here on in will be infected with his offspring— his antidote for the world."

E.V.'s sorrow seeped into Brittany. More tears started to fall and again, she didn't try to stop them. "E.V., why did you still want me to leave?"

"Why would you want to stay?"

Brittany shrugged, but she knew the answer. Even though she couldn't say it, E.V. saw it.

"You wanted to stay with Coby— even if he wasn't Coby any more."

Both stayed quiet, continuing to stare at the sky.

E.V. appeared in the passenger seat. She turned to stare at Brittany. "Why aren't you angry?"

For the first time ever Brittany was the one to play with her hands in her lap. "What's getting angry going to do? It's too late— it's done."

"That's it. That's all you have to say?" It didn't matter that Brittany wasn't angry. E.V. was enraged enough for both of them.

"What more is there?" Brittany said.

Before either of them could say any more, there was a soft chirping sound. Brittany recognized it as the ring of a cell phone. She followed the noise and picked it up from under her seat. "Hello?"

"This is not how I wanted things to go, my sweet. But it will suffice." Coby's kind voice was marred by Jax's presence in the boy, but it was still Coby's voice.

Brittany wanted to run to him, wherever he was.

"Don't," E.V. said through her clenched jaw.

"Brits?" This time Coby's voice sounded like Coby. This only made Brittany hurt more when it changed into Jax's hard tone. "Your time is quickly coming to a nasty end. I will be happy once it is done. But right now I have one last lesson for you, girl: as I'm sure you've discovered... my antidote is ready. Even as we speak my offspring are poised for release. How the world will change now. It will be cleansed." Jax paused then continued. "There is something you may not know, and I wanted to be the one to tell you— even if you were heroic enough to kill yourself, it won't make a difference. My offspring, my glorious antidotes, will still flow out of you with each and every touch."

He paused then addressed E.V. "Now, Lena, my sweet, I beg that you return to me. Take control of that wretched human and come back. I can help. I can advise you. It doesn't need to be so painful. Come to me. I will help you. I can show you who you really are."

"Fat chance," E.V. said. "Brittany, hang up. I don't need to hear any more."

Brittany took the phone away from her ear and slowly closed it. Then she turned to E.V. "Is that true? Even if I'm dead these things will still be released into the world?" She bit her lip to stop it from quivering.

"No..." E.V. answered.

"Bret... Coby... I mean Jax... He lied?"

"No..." Again E.V. was interrupted.

"So, he was telling the truth. Even if I die your offspring will be released to infect everyone who touches me— perhaps even infecting some more than once so that not only will the become vampires, but they will be vampires with multiple personalities?" Brittany's voice rose as she thought of this— it was hard enough to contend with one parasite, but to have more... She didn't want to think about it any more.

"Calm down," E.V. said firmly. "I can still fix this."

"Calm down?" Brittany's voice broke. "How can I be calm? Whoever I touch is doomed to become like me. Doomed to

hunt down and kill like I have, perhaps more than I have."
She closed her eyes. "I will infect the world, because I will
touch people— dead or alive, I will be touched. There is no
avoiding it. That's that."

"That is not that," E.V. said softly.

Brittany turned to stare at the image.

E.V. took a deep breath. "We both knew that we were on
a path leading to your death, and I decided I would go out
with you. There is a way to end me without touching another
person. We don't have to infect the world — we don't have
to infect anyone — not one person. We can end it all now."

"How?"

SEVENTY-SEVEN

DYING

E.V. TURNED TO stare out the front window into the inky night. She was about to reveal how to kill herself, and it wasn't easy to do. "Drive until we reach the ocean, then drive yourself in."

"How does that fix things? Jax said I'll still infect people once my body is found because you can't die."

"That is not true," E.V. sighed. "I assure you that if I drown I will die."

"You can't drown."

"Actually, I can. It just takes hours, almost a full day, but if I'm forced underwater for long enough, I will not be able to endure. Remember, I still need oxygen, and without it I will die." E.V. turned to stare at Brittany, waiting to see if the girl still had an argument.

"What about your offspring? Can they survive without air?"

"Right now they can't survive without me. I will see to it that they come to their end before me and even before you are done."

Brittany could feel E.V.'s conviction. She could also sense that it would be a sacrifice. As they'd been talking Brittany had become aware of millions of minuscule tickles moving about just under her skin, waiting for their chance at life. "There are so many of them."

"Yes, there are, but they are not resilient, like me— they are fragile, like you," E.V. said. "Jax doesn't know this— how could he, he's never been a part of this process. I can be sure that they perish, but in order to do that I will have to be in peril myself." She turned and said, "Brittany, it's time to die."

With a resigned nod, Brittany turned the key until the engine started. She shifted the car into drive and pulled back onto the highway. The girl, with her parasite, drove into the night, through the next town, and kept driving until they reached the ocean.

Then she drove them off a cliff.

Brittany was conscious of the distinct noise the front bumper made as it broke through the wooden barricade. What surprised her was that the vehicle didn't plummet immediately down the sharp embankment. Instead, the wheels seemed to find a ledge of dirt and loose grass, which it skidded over, as if giving the girl one last chance to change her mind.

But her mind was made up, and within a second her last chance had passed. The next sensation was weightlessness. Brittany surprised even herself as she stretched her arms out as far as they would go, pushing off the seat as she shut her eyes.

I'm flying, she thought. *At least I could experience flying before...*

Her thoughts were cut off by the impact of the car hitting the water. The force of it caused her body to crumple into the dashboard.

She had expected that to be the end.

She was wrong.

෬ ◆ ෨

When Brittany became conscious again, the first thing she realized was that she felt cold. Cold like she had those first few weeks when E.V. had been transforming her.

"Are you here?" she asked aloud, keeping her eyes closed.

"I'm here," came E.V.'s calm voice. "I won't leave you now."

Somehow this comforted Brittany. She sighed and opened her eyes— then gasped. "We're under the sea."

E.V. smiled. "Yes, we are. But not as far under as I'd hoped we'd get."

Brittany shivered. "Why am I so cold?"

"You lost a lot of fluids. Your arm broke, almost clean off, when we hit the water. I fixed it, but I'm spent, and I'm afraid I wasn't very good at fixing it."

Brittany held her broken arm up and saw that it now stuck out at a strange angle. "Why?"

"I couldn't set it without your help."

"No, not why is my arm bent. Why did you save me?"

E.V. chuckled. "It's an involuntary habit. I wouldn't have been able to stop myself even if I wanted to. But truth be told, I didn't really want to. I wanted your company... at least for a little while longer."

"We aren't doing very well, are we?"

"Not well at all." E.V. sighed again.

"How long, do you figure?"

"Every second I die a little more. We don't have long now."

Brittany stopped, trying to feel what E.V. was talking about. "It's not you that's dying, it's them." She could feel something like tiny pops of carbonated bubbles inside her chest. "I had no idea they were all so individual. I'd thought they'd be just little copies of you." But as she thought on it, she wasn't sure if feeling bits of E.V. passing away would be any easier to experience.

"Yes," E.V. paused. "They are each unique. That surprised me too."

"Does it hurt for you?"

"A little. It hurts me to think that they were created to die. I don't know them. I can't feel what they'd be like if they had had a chance to live. It's sad for me to think that they will never get that chance." E.V. had never experienced this kind of pain personally, but it reminded her of how Brittany felt when she thought of L.J. and J.J..

"I'm sorry," Brittany said softly.

"I'm sorry too," E.V. replied, and though she felt sorry, she wasn't angry.

Both the girl and the creature were quiet. The only noise was the subtle sound of the water lapping against the metal frame of the car as it slowly seeped in.

Only after all the pops were done did Brittany speak. "It's going to take hours for me to drown like this."

"Days," E.V. half-heartedly teased. Looking down and watching the car filling, she made a quick calculation. Really, they only had seventy-seven minutes before the car filled.

"I don't think I can be patient for that long." Brittany thought back to what Jax had said about being willing to die and watching it happen. Her resolve was set, but the suspense might undo her. "Is there something I can do to hurry this along?"

E.V. knew the girl wasn't trying to hasten their last moments together, so she offered, "Break the window."

"I can't." Brittany looked out at the empty black sea.

"I understand. It's hard for me too, now that we are so close to the end. I don't want to lose you either. We will still be together once the air is gone. We will have some time for proper goodbyes."

Brittany turned to stare at the image of E.V. one last time. "I can't break the window, because of the water pressure. I could kick it all I want, and it wouldn't crack. But I can open it."

Brittany reached down and started to turn the crank of the driver's side window. As it slipped open, water immediately started to rush into the car. Brittany gasped as it sprayed into her face, but she continued to turn the handle until the window was fully open. The cold of the water almost felt warm on her skin. As her feet, legs, torso, and eventually her chest became submerged, panic finally took hold.

"Relax," E.V. soothed, "I've got you."

Brittany closed her eyes, feeling the water rising on her neck. She started hyperventilating, knowing that she soon wouldn't be able to breathe. Even though she knew she didn't need the air, she still panicked at the reality of it— it was a symbol of her eminent end.

"Relax," E.V. repeated softly. "This isn't the end yet, I've still got you."

Brittany continued to pull in air at an alarming rate. She felt the water tickle her chin and very quickly lap at her bottom lip.

"Brittany, relax."

Brittany couldn't.

"Please, please trust me," E.V. said.

Brittany's fear made her deaf to the creature's pleas. Her mouth closed as she tasted the salty ocean on her tongue, but her nose continued to pull in the little air that remained.

"Brittany, it's going to be ok."

This time she heard and responded by holding her breath.

The water slipped up past her nose and over her hairline. Brittany could feel the hairs on her legs and arms being caressed by the soft currents that tried to establish themselves in the confines of the car. It tickled and stroked her, causing a calm to fall over her as she accepted how close she was to the end.

She brought her hand up to her face to rearrange her hair, which swam across her vision like seaweed waving farewell.

"I'm glowing," Brittany said, causing the air in her lungs to bubble out of her mouth and float away.

"Yes, you are." E.V. snickered at the girl's obvious delight. "Why does this amuse you?"

Because... because it means you are with me. Brittany smiled warmly. *Why do I glow? It's day now, the sun is up.*

"But it's cold here twenty feet under the surface. By the time the light makes its way to us, it's lost its effect."

Brittany sighed. *You know, I've grown to love you.*

"I know." E.V.'s voice was a whisper.

I would sacrifice myself for you — I think.

"Brittany, you already have."

When Brittany passed into nothingness, E.V. gathered as much of the girl's self as she could. She wasn't sure why, perhaps to keep her company for the few more hours she would survive. She remembered Brittany's intelligence. She thought fondly about Brittany's compassion. She embraced Brittany's wisdom.

E.V. wished she had more time to remember everything Brittany had been, but it was done. She finally felt what she'd been waiting for, the sinking, the separating, the moment when she would become one. One and alone— the way all things ended. With that final thought E.V. welcomed her final death.

☙ ◆ ❧